TEN REALMS: BOOK 7

The Sixth Realm

Part 2

MICHAEL CHATFIELD

Cover Art by Jan Becerikli Garrido
Jacket Design by Caitlin Greer
Interior Design by Caitlin Greer

Paperback ISBN: 978-1-989377-83-3

King's Hill Evolution

Aditya looked around the room. Most of the outpost leaders were there. They had all become closer since gaining complete control of the Beast Mountain Range Outposts.

Aditya sat at the top of the U-shaped table, with several ex-outpost leaders sat on either side. Now trade leaders, military commanders, mercenary liaisons, crafter liaisons, ambassadors, and more. They created the core power within not only King's Hill but the outposts connected to it.

Most of the outpost leaders took the position because they needed to, but their skills lent them to other activities they would be better utilized in. Now that they had the opportunity, he was sure they could use their talents for the best of Beast Mountain Range.

"In conclusion," Caius Sidonius said to the murmurs of the crowd, "we will soon finish the first set of roads to connect the outposts to King's Hill—the Ring Road that circles the Beast Mountain Range and the Compass Trade Route. There are several other trade routes that could be upgraded to roads to increase trade from different neighbors. We are working with the military and mercenary liaisons to see which of these paths we can cover, talking to the trader liaisons to evaluate the profit that will be brought into the Beast Mountain Range, and keeping an eye on our neighbors to see who will play nice and who are eyeing us. I would prefer to not give the enemy a path right into our heart." He bowed to Aditya and sat.

One of the outpost leaders raised their hand.

Aditya nodded for them to continue. He rarely talked in these meetings, acting like a neutral party.

"I'm sure your own doves have been hearing information from the forces outside of Beast Mountain Range. So far, they have left us alone. Will they continue to do so in the future, and can we deal with it? We are a group of traders and mercenaries with a massive forest filled with powerful beasts that are getting stronger. What if one of those beasts weakens an outpost and someone takes advantage?" The outpost leader's words gained nods from others.

Looking for promises and reassurances. They had taken control over the Beast Mountain Range, but changes always brought vultures.

Aditya glanced over to Pan Kun, the leader of the military, and the mercenary liaison past him.

Pan Kun stood. He was a quiet and simple man, but his power made the outpost leaders wary of him.

"The King's Hill army will support the outposts if fights break out. We are proposing training for the outpost guards to increase their fighting ability so the army can reinforce them easily and work together without issues."

The mercenary liaison spoke next. "We have started to register the different mercenary groups operating in the Beast Mountain Range. If there is a beast outbreak and they are inside the outpost, then, according to the contracts we have with them, for better treatment and preferential prices, they will assist us in defending our outpost, doubling the effective fighters we can call upon."

There was grumbling and muttering but, it seemed to mollify most of the people.

"What about profits? We have not seen any profit come out of King's Hill. All of it is spent as soon as it comes in!" another outpost lord said.

The treasury leader, Lass, stood. Being of the older generation, everyone quieted as he spoke. "King's Hill is in a period of rapid expansion. We have linked everyone together. We are training a large army that's growing to support our needs. We are repairing the damage done to the outposts, moving people between outposts, and offering loans to increase the number of traders and mercenaries coming to the area. We might not earn any profits for several years, but have we not all benefited? Better equipment is being sold every day. We have crafters who can make gear for us instead of having to rely on buying from passing traders. We have several trading groups who have set up their bases in our outposts. It is possible to even buy mana stones and weak true alchemical concoctions."

His words fell on everyone's ears, to remind them of their recent gains that came with uniting the Beast Mountain Range. He rolled on.

"Yes, the beasts are stronger, but their materials are more valuable. Our population is swelling. We are able to produce food in some outposts, and we're amassing a great amount of food in case someone does attack our small nation. Although we might not have yet received any returns from the King's Hill Outpost personally, the benefits are clear. Advancing our own cultivations and levels. Who here in this room is not above level fifteen?"

Lass had weathered the good times and the bad. The older outpost leaders could see the hope and possibilities of King's Hill. They looked to the future instead of the current state of affairs.

The healing they had received from the Alva Healing House hadn't changed their appearances, but the aches and hidden wounds upon their bodies had been healed.

Aditya adjusted his position in his seat, staring at the people along the tables. It hadn't been immediate, but more were coming over to his side.

Putting down the mantle of outpost leader, what they could gain actually increased.

There were very few who wanted to remain as outpost leaders. They liked the benefits, but managing it all, they had achieved their positions through strength, not managerial prowess. Still, Aditya had plans for them, making them regional governors, if they had the ability.

The outpost leader who had raised the question lowered his head slightly under the gaze of the others.

Aditya cleared his throat before the atmosphere turned. "We should talk about the auction and events that are happening in the coming days."

Emmanuel Fayad stood. He led the trader faction. Half of his family worked to push the trade of the King's Hill as fast as possible; the other half were part of the army, serving and protecting King's Hill Outpost. His own Shadowridge Outpost lay under the command of King's Hill, creating a precedent that allowed others to annex their outposts, bringing them into the fold for personal gains. Aditya had also followed. In his mind, King's Hill, Vermire, and everything in the Beast Mountain Range were owned by Alva.

"In two months, we will be hosting the largest auction that the Beast Mountain Range and the surrounding area has seen. High-level Novice items, mid-level Apprentice gear will be on sale. The auction will bring in people from across the realm. My contacts have informed me that people from the Blue Lotus are assessing King's Hill to possibly place a branch inside the city." Emmanuel's voice dipped as everyone sat up straighter.

"If we can get them to put a branch here, we must prove that we have people willing to buy and sell in the area, that we have adequate defenses, and that our city has a high enough standard. For the next few weeks, people will arrive from across the realm, and people might even descend from higher realms. This is an opportunity to show the ability and wealth of our Beast Mountain Range. Gather more Experts and elites to join the mercenary bands, our own administration, and military. Create new trade routes, and bring more of the nations and groups outside the range onto our side."

Emmanuel waited a moment for people to calm down.

"We will not allow the different outpost leaders or administrators to participate in the main auction, but there will be a second auction, an exchange where people will be able to bring out items in secret and put them up for others to bid on."

They grumbled but they'd already claimed the best gear. All of them had treasures and resources they couldn't use and couldn't find the right person to sell them to. The second auction would solve that problem.

Emmanuel took a seat, and Aditya rose.

The room fell quiet. Aditya had never imagined the outpost leaders would look to him, waiting for his every word. He hid his mirth as he pulled out a box. Inside were several medallions.

"Beast Mountain Range trial—I thought it stopped?" someone asked.

"That's what the high realmers think," Aditya said. "These medallions were found inside some of the beasts. Through thorough examination, we found hidden doorways. There is a counter above the door that decreases each day that passes, and there is a recess for these medallions to be placed."

"The trial always took place on a platform before," an outpost leader said.

"It seems that has changed. The trial will open in two months' time. I have enough medallions for each outpost to elect seven people to undertake the trial. with a dozen extras. Each outpost will elect their own fighters. For the remaining medallions, anyone can compete for them."

"You want to tell outsiders?" someone hissed.

"If people want to be part of the trial, they will have to fight within the Beast Mountain Range. If they are to attack us, they will lose access to the trial. Who knows—if pushed to the brink, we could destroy the doors to the trial that only we know about," Aditya said.

A chill ran through the room with the narrowing of eyes and upturned corners of mouths.

On the outside, it looked like a gift, but in truth, it bound other nations' leaders. It was a gift they couldn't turn down. What if they stopped their people from competing? Power was the only rule of the ten realms. Cutting off ones path would only cause strife.

"At the very least, the competition will inspire people from around the Beast Mountain Range to visit."

"I have heard that people can go missing after the trial," one leader said.

"Yes, people can die. It is not without its risks. Also, it is said that there is a higher level to the trial and that people can get guidance and go into seclusion, greatly increasing their ability, only to reappear later, unable to speak of the secrets they have learned. Even if these people are unwilling to tell us, they are still our people and can add a few elites to our forcs," Aditya said.

The meeting came to an end, and Aditya headed to the next one.

He barely sat in his officewhen there was a knock at the door.

"You want to get that?" Evernight sat at a secondary desk, writing out a message. Holding a report in another hand.

The tension between them when she had first appeared was nearly gone. The two of them were closer now, more like co-workers—just that she was working on a project she couldn't tell him all the details about.

"You want to hide?" Aditya said.

"It's Lord Quan, and if we want him to come to our side, he's going to learn some secrets," Evernight said.

"Are you a guard, maid, or secretary?" Aditya muttered as he stood, stretching.

"A secretary for now, but an agent first and foremost," Evernight said absently as she kept working. The report on her desk and in her hand disappeared into her storage ring, taking out another report.

Aditya opened the door and found Lord Quan standing there. The old mercenary still had his scars, but his eyes were brighter, as if he had returned to the time of his youth.

"Lord Quan," Aditya said respectfully as he waved for him to enter.

"There is no need to call me Lord Quan anymore. Don't I work for you now? Call me Old Quan." His eyes landed on Evernight turning to Aditya in question.

"Don't worry. She's reliable." Aditya closed the door. *She's got more secrets than you or I combined.*

They took their seats. Aditya opened his mouth, and Old Quan raised a hand.

"I am an old man and not so good at these games, unlike you young ones," Lord Quan said. "It's easier if you speak plainly with me."

Aditya nodded. "I am thinking of creating a consortium, with you at the head of it. Training people with good fighting potential and turning them into warriors who can create mercenary bands, join the army, and increase our military might. And a crafting arm to promote more crafters coming to the area and to create weapons and equipment we can use instead of relying on outside sources. We have some crafters here, but we aren't able to raise any ourselves."

Old Quan sat forward, his relaxed air falling away. "I don't know anything about crafting. Consortium? You sure you don't mean a sect?"

Aditya forced himself to not look at Evernight.

"Trust me. Beast Mountain Range Consortium sounds better. First and foremost, it will be an academy—a place where people can go and learn. If we call it a sect, the other nations will think we're being ambitious. Also, sects have a lot of contracts and oaths. I want to make this open to the people in our outposts and the outside kingdoms."

Old Quan breathed in through his nose-thinking.

"Lord Aditya, your plans don't cease to amaze me. Still, you didn't answer the question about craft teachers."

"I can find people who know crafting, and I can find someone who will run it all. I need someone who can inspire faith. Your outpost was more of a base of operations for your mercenaries, many of whom have elected to join the military. You have a lot of energy and not much to do with it. With the position of consortium head, you would have access to training resources, cultivation manuals, and more.You would be free to train yourself and others as you see fit," Aditya said.

"Who could join the consortium? Would they have to be from the Range?"

"No, they could be from other places, as long as they show ability and loyalty."

"What about slots for the Beast Mountain Range trial?"

"If it continues, then the consortium would get a certain number of spots that the students could compete for. I want you to bring out the fighting spirit of our people," Aditya said.

"It will also conveniently take people's eyes off you. Unite the people. Get them to look past their own outposts and at the Beast Mountain Range as a whole. Have people from outside sending their young to train. Impressive way to divert attention and tie others to our ship," Old Quan said.

Aditya laughed and rubbed the back of his head awkwardly. "Your eyes have grown sharper with age, Old Quan."

Old Quan smiled. He rubbed his chin with a rough hand, and his smile grew larger as the brightness in his eyes increased. "A consortium leader…I always cursed those old, stuck-in-their-way bastards who care more about the profits and numbers. I cannot say that the consortium will make you any money, but I will give you the finest crafters and fighters I can." He pursed fis lips. Aditya pulled out a contract, placing it between them.

Old Quan reviewed the contract and raised an eyebrow. "Seems that you have some secrets you want to keep." He cut his finger and pressed blood to the paper.

The contract shone; the words seemed to lift from the page and wrap together, forming a black chain before it floated over Old Quan's wrist and sunk into his flesh.

It disappeared as if it had never existed.

Old Quan's smile was a little nervous as he held up his arm to Aditya.

"Well, it looks like you have me for another fifteen years." He laughed.

Aditya smiled and nodded.

"Yes, I guess we do, Mister Quan. It is good to officially meet," Evernight said as she stood from her desk and grinned.

Quan stared at her in surprise.

"Vermire, King's Hill—I'm merely the manager," Aditya said. "The power and force behind it are more powerful than any nation in the First Realm. Evernight is my confidant and the passage through which my orders come."

"So, uniting the outposts?" Old Quan asked.

"That was his idea. Most of this is his idea. We have been supporting him from the shadows. Pretty impressive, really," Evernight said.

"What do you want with the Beast Mountain Range?" Old Quan's casual attitude was gone.

"Not much, really. We need a way to operate in the First Realm without being seen, and for a long time now, we have been. We recruited people from the First Realm, from Vermire, and throughout the Beast Mountain Range and beyond. We want good people who are loyal. Think of us like a big mercenary group. We want to entice people to join us."

"And what do you do with them?"

"We give them a place to expand their horizons and provide opportunities they never even thought about." Evernight released a seal. Aditya could feel her power swelling, reaching higher and higher.

Old Quan seemed shaken. "You're more than four times stronger than me, at least."

"I swear on the Ten Realms with my life that the power I work for only wants to give the people who we recruit an opportunity to join us and increase their power and abilities," Evernight said. The power of the Ten Realms descended upon her. Nothing happened as it faded away.

"Bit extreme," Aditya said, as he started to calm down.

Evernight rolled her eyes, and Aditya snorted.

Old Quan stared at them both, at a loss.

"I have to borrow Old Quan for a few days. Will that be okay?" Evernight said.

"What for?"

"Well, if he's going to run the consortium, he should know what he is teaching people and see some proof, no?" Evernight said.

"I haven't seen these schools or people, other than the fighters and healers from the power behind you, but he gets to see it by just signing a contract?" Aditya complained.

"Don't worry. When the rulers come back from their adventure, they will want to meet with you." Evernight smiled and then glanced over to Old Quan.

He seemed to have recovered a little bit.

"No wonder you were able to raise yourself up so quickly. While you had greater resources, you're still the man I have come to know, and I can see how much trust you're putting in me. All right, let's take a look at this power of yours, miss."

"I like him—up for an adventure." Evernight smiled and moved to a bookcase. A formation activated and the bookcase opened, revealing a ladder below.

"See you soon," Aditya said.

They disappeared and the bookcase closed.

Aditya opened his door. "Have Pan Kun come and see me, please," he told his guards.

"Yes, my lord." They bowed, and one ran off.

Pan Kun arrived shortly afterward, taking a seat opposite Aditya. After his training, he was less rowdy and seemed to have channeled his energy, creating a hyper-focused fighter.

"I saw your report on banditry and the beasts in the area. What is happening with that?" Aditya asked.

"The bandits come from various groups. Some are people who had ran from the outposts. Others are groups with plots on Vermire. More are just criminals who came to the Beast Mountain Range to hide in the mountains and forests."

"I heard that you personally led an attack yesterday?" Aditya asked.

"We have been following a group of bandits who have been attacking different caravans. Using trackers, we were able to find their base. We took down the camp. Those who survived were pulled back in chains to be workers or put to death, depending upon their crimes."

"What about the victims?"

"None of the groups under our protection were attacked, but ten percent of the value of materials recovered will be passed to the victims of the group and paid to people who were able to give us information about the bandits," Pan Kun said.

"Kill those who have to be killed, and bind the ones who become our laborers with oaths. I do not want to give them any chance to escape. They will be an example to others: Bandits are seeking their own downfall in the Beast Mountain Range, though we will not question one's background if they want to join a group of mercenaries. Clearing the Beast Mountain Range is good, honest work," Aditya said.

"I have made sure that the message is passed along. I am sure our masters have pushed out the information themselves."

"What do you think of these new beasts appearing?" Aditya asked.

"They're tougher. Not hard for the army to deal with, but they'll challenge the mercenaries. The materials and resources one can get from them are impressive. New danger zones have been created as there are different animals moving around. Was it on the part of our masters?"

"Evernight had said that they put out some items that would increase the growth rate of the beasts. With the low population over the last few years and with so much space, the beasts are making a comeback. I think their new average power will be higher than previously." Aditya shrugged.

"What if we were to tame some of them?"

"Tame some of them?" Aditya said.

"If we have some beasts to move through the forests, we can deploy the army faster, have better supply lines, and they can even assist us in battle," Pan Kun said.

"Not even the powerful armies surrounding us are able to field their own legions with beasts," Aditya said.

"Their biggest issue is supplies. There are elite troops that have beasts under their command, but housing and feeding them costs a lot. They are in cities and towns; we are in the Beast Mountain Range. We can buy supplies for beasts a lot cheaper or gather them easily enough. Finding and raising the beasts and *then* taming them is the hardest part."

"When is your next handoff?" Aditya said.

"We are sending the next batch of advanced trainees in a week." Pan Kun smiled.

"Don't look so damn eager."

Pan Kun's scowl turned into a grin, his serious air dissipating somewhat. "We're all in the same boat. You know, I think you've offended the right people."

Aditya rolled his eyes and groaned, and Pan Kun chuckled.

"Well, Evernight should be back before then. I'll ask her about it. Giving me more work to do!"

"You always seem to survive."

"I heard you're seeing a lady?" Aditya asked.

"News travels fast around here. I had her looked into."

"Come on—and you didn't tell me?" Aditya hit the man's shoulder.

"Well, you know, it's early days," Pan Kun said.

"If you went and got her checked out, you're hoping it goes longer," Aditya said.

Pan Kun coughed. He didn't look like the stern commander who had walked into Aditya's office.

"I was right! Come on, tell me about her."

"Well, she's a healer. She was one of the people who had helped me with my eye."

"A healer? From way back? You *are* playing the long game there, my friend!"

"Well, she was busy, and I was busy. Then one night, I saw her, and I asked her if she would like to get a meal. She agreed, and we went out. We talked for hours, and then, well, we kept seeing each other." Pan Kun shrugged.

Aditya laughed and pushed his friend's shoulder again.

"Well, I hope it all goes well. Don't mess up!" Aditya said.

"Thanks, man," Pan Kun said dryly as Aditya gave him a wide smile.

"Fuck this place, fuck these *realms,* fuck these *people,* and fuck this goddamn swamp!" Campbell waved his hands to get the stinking swamp mud off him.

"Come on, Doc. We need to keep moving," Kanoa, a heavyset, dark man said, his eyes moving across the forest.

A bird whistle came from behind the group. Kanoa felt a spike of adrenaline and left the others to assist Campbell out of the swamp. He checked his crossbow and knelt, looking to the other vets and half-trained fighters he'd gathered.

They spread out, moving into the tree line. Kanoa kneeled in a ditch, ignoring the water freezing his knees. *The Ten Realms might suck balls, but at least I was able to heal my knees.*

He let out a series of musical whistles once they were set.

It wasn't long until he heard pounding feet on the ground.

Sung, a tired-looking man, rode down the road on a horse. He looked like a bag of shit and his horse looked drained, but there was determination in his eyes.

He brought his horse to a halt, and Kanoa got out of the ditch to greet him.

"Looks like the mercenaries are coming. We need to get moving."

"How long do we have?" Kanoa checked behind them.

"A day or two, maybe?"

"If we can get to the outposts at the Beast Mountain Range, we can use the traders there to move around, confuse them. There are people coming in from all across the First Realm—be hard to track us in that," Badowska said.

Kanoa stared at his group, fifty-four people in total. They had wandered the First Realm, finding other people from Earth. They'd banded together, common allies.

Queen Ikku had found out about their group, strange clothes, and spells, and she had sent her people to capture them. She wanted to own them, get them to tell her everything, so she could use what they knew to grow her power. They were nothing but tools here, too low level to do anything but run.

He had sixteen veterans from various branches and militaries; some of them had been currently serving. The civvies were all skilled in one area or another—they had teachers, doctors, and construction workers. Thirty-eight more of them. If they joined another empire or group, they would be used by them, little more than slaves. Kanoa and the others wanted to get away from the system, make something akin to what they had back on Earth. Kanoa had started running two years ago, and he hadn't stopped. He had reached level eleven using a crossbow and his sword, killing people and beasts, but it wasn't enough to push him any higher.

2 Sixth Realm Position

Delilah arrived in the Third Realm. The special team guided her through the press of people.

They diverged like a river meeting a rock around Captain Khasar, and people looked over in awe, seeing the carriage bearing the seal of the division leader.

Delilah's group headed over. All of them wore hoods and had different techniques and spells that altered their appearances. Delilah thought that Gong Jin was being paranoid, but she gave in to the man. He had been the second-in-command of Special Team Two, but with the influx of trained special team members, he now controlled his own special team. He had matured quickly. Even though he was the same age as her, she felt that he was like a deep ocean: calm on the outside but with hidden deadly currents just below the surface. It was hard for anyone to become a special team member and stay there.

"Isn't that Captain Khasar? Isn't he in charge of protecting the division head? Just who is the VIP to get him to come down to the totem?" people whispered.

Delilah's group reached Captain Khasar. He bowed deeply to her and opened a carriage door. The group got into the carriage. He followed Gong Jin and Delilah into the second carriage.

"Who are they to get this kind of treatment?" someone asked as the door closed behind Captain Khasar.

"Good to see you again, Captain." Delilah pulled down her hood and smiled.

"And you, too, Miss Ryan," Khasar said. He smiled and glanced over to Gong Jin.

"Gong Jin, leader of her protection detail," he said bluntly.

"You have very capable protectors." Khasar looked over Gong Jin. "I am Captain Khasar, in charge of Master Alchemist Hei Zen. I know I speak for him and myself when I ask you to keep Miss Ryan safe."

"Don't worry, nothing will happen to her while I am alive." Gong Jin gave him a thin smile that wasn't really a smile, grasping Khasar's hand and shaking it.

"Old Hei is finally heading to the higher realms?" Delilah asked.

"Yes, he got the news not long ago. You know how he is. He doesn't want to make a big thing of it. He will quietly leave and let his replacement take his position."

"Another Expert-level alchemist has appeared in the Third Realm?"

"They are sending someone down from higher. They want them to get more experience, and Old Hei's contributions and ability means that he'll be welcomed with open arms into the Sixth Realm academies," Khasar said.

"You will go with him?"

"That is my job. I'll have to increase my Strength if I want to keep protecting him past that. We are taking on new guards who are much stronger than my people. Honestly, we all are going to get an immense amount of resources and help from the Alchemist Association, though we will need to pass their test to make sure that we can remain his guards."

"You ready for it?"

"Yes. Old Hei said that he will support us and has been making all kinds of pills to help us increase our Mana and Body Cultivation. If we can't make it to the standard the Alchemist Association requires with the help of a Master Alchemist, well, then, it is not meant to be," Khasar said.

They made idle chit-chat before they reached the headquarters. Khasar and his people led the way, and the special team scanned the area. They wore masks, and their black cloaks hid their identity.

Delilah left them at the door to Old Hei's personal quarters.

She walked in, seeing Old Hei working with Feng Fen, his assistant. They were going over papers and talking in low tones.

Feng Fen looked up and quickly dismissed himself, closing the door behind him.

"You think that you can get away without saying goodbye?" Delilah pouted.

"It is the Sixth Realm. I am sure that I will see you there if you decide to go," Old Hei said.

Looks like he saw through my levels a long time ago, Delilah thought.

Old Hei continued, "I will need to stop in the Fifth Realm for some resources, increase my cultivation, and confirm my personnel before I head to the Sixth Realm. Once there, I will become a professor, teaching micro-Alchemy and focusing on the small things that an alchemist should take into account when they are refining their concoctions." Old Hei's face nearly split in two with his smile and the fire in his eyes.

"Congratulations." Delilah clasped her hands and bowed deeply.

"Is there a need to do that anymore between us?" Old Hei stood and came around the table to lift her back up.

"You are my grand teacher, and you've helped raise me to the level of Expert. You have cared for me and spared no cost. I owe you so much. This is the least I can do. You won't accept any gifts from me!" she half-complained.

Old Hei closed his mouth, the corners still pulled up in a smile as the creases of his eyes pinched together in joy.

"Teaching you and Erik has been one of my greatest pleasures. I only hope that I can teach more people and see how far they will reach."

He took out two pill bottles and passed them to Delilah. "Take these. The first pills are Mana Condensing. They will allow you to increase your Mana Cultivation rapidly. The second are the Soul Revival pills. The power will seep into your bones. If you are attacked and gravely wounded, they will allow you to reach a new peak in power to escape and hold your wounds together. You will still need to heal, but it will give you time to get away—about four days—though your wounds will be worse at the end of that period. One for you, one for Erik."

Delilah looked at the Master-level pills with apprehension. She didn't want to take advantage of Old Hei but there was no way he would let her refuse these.

"Thank you, Old Hei," Delilah said, moved by his generosity.

"Here is the information of where you can find me in the Sixth Realm."

She smiled and took the slip of paper and pill bottles.

"Good! Now, do you have some of that food?" Old Hei grinned.

She laughed and pulled out a small plate of food. She had personally requested all of Old Hei's favorites from Kanesh Academy's Expert-level cooks.

Old Hei took a deep breath of the piping-hot buns. "Truly, the cooks have us alchemists beat!" He laughed, and they moved to his favorite spot on the balcony.

Delilah pulled out more plates of food before serving tea and sitting down.

"I wish Erik were here. He's been gone for, what, seven months now?"

"Nearly that long. I hope he's back soon," Delilah said. *If something happened…*

"Erik and Rugrat are tough rocks. Be hard for them to crack and fall," Old Hei said. It seemed he had seen right through her anxieties.

"I do wonder what they're up to." Old Hei sipped his tea and looked out over the Division Headquarters, as if his eyes could pierce through the stars and reach the Sixth Realm.

Across Dungeon Lands

Storbon and his people stopped off to the side of the road that led into the outpost.

"Up ahead is Knugrith. It is one of the smallest outposts. There is not much of value here other than the green-gold tree, a type of tree that can be harvested to make paper that's great material to create mana scrolls with. We have brought you this far; where you go from here is your decision. You have looted items from the tower. It should be enough to start you off."

Their faces were filled with thanks. Most of them looked as if they were ready to collapse right there.

"Thank you, thank you for everything," a man, Arthur, said as he held onto his boy. The pair bowed their heads.

"I don't know if the people who captured you will be looking for you now that the orcs have disappeared. I would suggest that you start a new life, one away from where you were kidnapped. With your loot, you can get up to the academies, take a totem down to the lower realms, and establish yourselves," Storbon said.

"Can we come with you?" Aidan, Arthur's boy, asked.

"We can't help you any more than this."

Storbon could see Aidan's desire to follow them.

"Everyone has their own secrets," Arthur said, consoling his boy before he checked behind at Storbon. "Thank you."

"Maybe our paths will cross in the future. You've got one hell of a dad there, Aidan," Storbon said.

The others talked over one another, thanking them, crying, and bowing their heads. Most of them offered the loot they had as a token of thanks.

"Our job is done. Your life is your own," Storbon said.

Storbon and the others pulled out their mounts and got on top.

"Live well and help others," Erik said.

The special team rode away.

"That is the last of them inside Knugrith," Rugrat said.

They stood on a berm, watching the gates as the last of the people they had saved entered the outpost.

Knugrith was a town made of wood, except for their simple wall. Several guards patrolled with their bound beasts.

"How far is the next place?" Yao Meng asked.

"Three days' ride," Erik said to a collective of sighs and groans.

"Use your illusion spell scrolls on your faces and remove any magical traces. Then we'll get moving," Rugrat said.

They altered their appearances and made sure there were no magical tracking spells on them.

"Come on, mount up!" Storbon said. His panther appeared, and he jumped on it. The others mounted, with Melika being hauled up by Tian Cui. Storbon and Rugrat led the way; Lucinda sent out her flying beasts to scout the road ahead.

They had been working together so closely for so long they had come to anticipate one another's orders, proactively acting.

"Wandering Hero," Yao Meng hummed across the private communication channel as he accessed his notifications.

"What does it say?" Storbon asked.

Yao Meng read it out.

Title: Wandering Hero

When those in need have cried out for help, you have aided them without care of your own safety. As you wander the realms, you leave it a better place.

Rewards: +10% EXP

One Star Hero Emblem

"What the hell is a star hero emblem?" Yao Meng asked.

No one had any answers.

Melika stared at them all talking to one another before she focused on riding.

"Another Ten Realms mystery," Erik said.

They talked for a little before the conversation died down and kept riding toward Ivaris.

Erik checked his quest rewards as well.

Quest Completed: From Orc Jaws

Adventurers, lost souls, and villagers have been captured from the lands surrounding the orc territory and sent deeper into orc territory. Find these prisoners, free them, and escape the orc territory.

You have rescued all prisoners, and they have escaped safely.

Requirements:

Free the Prisoners

Lead them out of Orc territory

Rewards:

Wandering Hero Title

+12,500,000 EXP

35,321,860/108,500,000 EXP till you reach Level 61

Lee Perrin thanked the street sweeper with a smile and turned away. His expression turned dark as he walked.

Where are you, Melika?

He had left her at the inn to make sure that everything was ready for her admission into the Faded Scroll Academy.

When he came back, Melika was gone. She had been kidnapped.

The street sweeper had said that the people he was tracking went into the sewers. Not the ones that led to the treatment facility—the ones that lead to the dungeon. Once people were in the dungeon, it was easier for them to disappear.

They're smart. They must have planned this out. Who knows how far behind them I am? Looking for Melika, he had learned of other low-level people who had disappeared. With no position or friends in high places, the guards took the report and pushed it to the side.

Lee felt bitter as he walked back to the run-down inn they had been lodging in. People talked in hushed tones, slowing down and creating a crowd around the inn.

Lee moved around the crowd toward the inn entrance. He would pay his tab then head into the dungeon. He wasn't the strongest fighter, but he could never leave a student beh—

His thoughts were interrupted when he saw the two people in front of the inn: a woman wearing heavy-plate armor and a man with a bow on his back and daggers on his hips. The waves of pressure they released made it feel as if there were two raging beasts waiting for prey to enter their sights.

Lee Perrin's heart lightened.

"He's going up to the tiger and tigress. Does he not fear for his life?" someone said when they saw Lee Perrin in his simple pants and shirt that had been repaired time and time again. His black hair was pulled back in a ponytail, and his beard reached his chest. Staring at him, one might take him for a beggar or someone down on their luck.

The woman looked over. Her eyes widened, and she stomped toward Lee.

"Would they kill him in broad daylight?"

"What did he do to offend such people?"

The man's eyes slid over.

While the woman forged her way through the crowd, he flowed past onlookers. His movements made it look like he glided past people.

"Teacher!" the man and woman yelled, arriving at the same time, bowing from the hip.

People around them gasped.

"T-teacher? Just how strong is he to have such students?"

"Teacher, not teacher? Why do you think they say that?"

"There are all kinds of address for Masters. Who knows why they pick their names?"

Lee smiled awkwardly, hearing bystanders call him Master. He sighed. "Wei Shi, weren't you supposed to be off with the Blood Steel sect developing a new area of your dungeons?" he admonished the armored woman before his sharp gaze turned to the archer. "Rafael, aren't you doing selections for the Fighter's Association? Your teacher says he has high hopes for you to use this to enter the elite ranks of the association."

Lee's eyes were bright and clear while the powerful duo bit their lips, scared to be turned away.

They paused, holding back their lies.

"Teacher, when we heard that someone dared to attack our junior sister, we had to come," Wei Shi said into the ground.

"Teacher, you do not accept anything else from us and have guided us to our teachers and onto the right path. You are the force that pushed us forward. Without you, how could we have reached this stage? Our junior sister has disappeared, and you have been slighted. How could we not come?"

"Too well said." A man entered the courtyard. On his chest, he wore the symbol of an Expert wood crafter. Behind him, there were others with fierce temperaments and powerful gear. There were men and women in their teenage years, those who had reached middle age, and others who looked older, like Lee's father.

Seeing them all, Lee's heart swelled.

"Little Tullus, you became an Expert carpenter? By your temperament, it will not be long until you reach the point to challenge Master? Rob, you tamed your fiery temper and became a true mage. Your Mana Cultivation has greatly increased. You are still working on your exercises, right?

"Mo Chi-Hye, don't hide in the back, you little troublemaker. I heard what happened at the School of the Floating Pen! Focus your mind on your studies instead of your pranks, Little Miss!"

He rattled off names as each person walked over. They had grown so powerful in their time apart; they were like tigers that had been given their wings, soaring high into the sky.

They stepped forward, cupping their fists, and bowed.

"Teacher!" they yelled to him.

He looked over them all and then sighed. "Lift your heads," he said in a soft voice. How could he be angry with them when they rose with grins and smiles? Glancing to those around them, few of them had met one another, but they were all proud students of Teacher Perrin.

The softness in his eyes faded and turned hard as he thought about Melika.

"I found a good seedling. I brought her here to meet a teacher I thought might suit her. She went out to see the sights and never came back. I have looked for signs of her and have only just found out she was kidnapped."

The thirty or so people's eyes focused, and the air stilled, threatening violence and destruction.

"Come, this is no place for us to carry out this conversation," Lee Perrin said.

"There is a place from the Fighter's Association nearby that we can use," Rafael said.

"You are in the Fighter's Association as well?" one of his other students asked.

"Don't start using one another to climb the ladder. Rely on your own strength. You can spar with him later, Sam," Lee said.

The man with a saber scratched his head.

Lee sighed and indicated for him to show the way.

The crowd cleared a path as the group made it to the Fighter's Association. Upon showing his badge, the flustered attendant quickly readied a room for them all.

Lee looked over them. From all walks of life and with various abilities, they were the children he'd never had.

If anyone could find Melika, it was this group.

"Looks beefier," Rugrat said as they rode up toward the gates. The walls here were made from a black stone, and formations were carved into it. Five kilometers of land around the small city had been cleared away. Buildings reached dozens of floors up. Elevators could be seen charging up into the rock above and out of the dungeon while others entered the depths. Guards wearing academy sigils manned the walls.

A dangerous air surrounded them, causing the guards' eyes to sharpen.

"Trade really picks up. Traders come from the smaller supply stations and outposts and use the elevators to sell their supplies in the academies above. This dungeon is massive," Yuli said.

"Three times the size of the city above," Erik said.

"A nice hat on a whole bunch of fucked up," Yao Meng muttered.

"If the academies were to fall, the population inside the dungeons would expand until they could flood out and create a beast tide. Like the one we dealt with at Alva Village," Storbon said.

"Feels like it was years ago," Tian Cui said in a small voice.

"Everything changes with time. Come on, I need a shower and a forge!" Rugrat said.

"You think you'll break through?" Yao Meng perked up as they followed the line to enter Ivaris.

"I don't know, but I'll give it my best shot!" Rugrat laughed.

"I could do with just sleeping for four or six days. I know my scouts could eat through a stable's worth of food," Lucinda said.

"Without them, we would've had a much harder time," Storbon said.

"Maybe I should start learning to be a beast tamer?" Yao Meng asked.

"You a beast tamer? Well, I guess with how you smell, they would think you're one of them," Tian Cui said.

"Hey, that's offensive to my beasts," Lucinda said.

They laughed as Yao Meng opened his mouth and then closed it with a frown.

"Just stay with the explosives and your rifle," Erik consoled Yao Meng and grinned.

"Five Earth mana stones a person," the guard said as they reached the front of the line.

Rugrat passed over the funds and canceled the communication channel. "Do you have smithies here?"

"Eastern side. There are some workshops there and more in the city above. Ten stones to take the elevator," the guard said in a bored tone.

"Thanks." Rugrat nodded.

The group passed through the large, black walls. They looked up at the holes in the ceiling and formations that had been carved into the stone to drop attacks on anyone who made it into the gate.

The tunnel rang with noise. Melika moved in her seat to look ahead. They exited into a large open area where all kinds of beasts were pulling carts. Merchants hawked their wares; inns advertised their unoccupied rooms; others were selling Stamina potions. The group pushed on. After a quick glance, these merchants and sellers could tell that they weren't interested in their items and tried their tricks on others.

They found an inn away from the main hustle of the city.

"All right, Melika, always go with someone else or stay here. Everyone else, two days of R&R. Do as you want. Only need one person back here at a time. Drinking allowed, but have a detox with you and ready to use," Storbon said to his team. Storbon broke down tasks for everyone and left it to Yao Meng to figure out watch shifts.

Rugrat and Erik stripped off their gear at their own beds.

Rugrat shook out the cloak, used his Clean spell on it, and put it in his storage ring. He scratched his head. It had pushed down on his hair the entire time, leaving his head and beard almost painfully itchy.

The Ten Realms's Alvan rip-tape straps on the side of his carrier opened, and he slid out of it. With the feeling of air against his clothes and losing the weight across his upper body, he felt naked.

"Damn, these plates get heavier each time," Rugrat said.

"They weigh about thirty kilos now." Erik tapped on the vest and lay it out as he checked the different pouches, refilling them.

"Thirty kilos...damn, doesn't feel like it," Rugrat said as he checked his vest too.

"You're the smith," Erik said.

"Yeah, but I don't make most of these items. What a single person does doesn't change much. Crafters in Alva are just the people who make a blueprint, teach others, and quality test the products that are made in the factory lines. Right now, we can't make Expert-level gear on an assembly line, but with time, I think we'll be able to do it. The factories for the military work day and night to make weapons, armor, clothes, rations, and more for the Alvan army. Most armies in the Ten Realms take years to grow. They can only hire so many people because the older generations have died out and can give them their weapons and gear. It's like the Russians in the Second World War. They have people, but they don't have the gear and weapons." Rugrat finished restocking his vest.

"We don't have people dying all the time, but we have the mass-producing industry of Alva to support the army's rapid expansion," Erik said.

"Yes, and our blueprints are shared, so this carrier, the actual carrier, doesn't change much, but the plates are altered all the time. The plates are simple enough to make. The standard plates are made on an assembly line and cut to size; then, formations are stamped in and filled. We can produce ten carrier plates an hour at that speed. Say someone comes up with a better combination of iron and enhancers, well, we can alter the production line and run off ten prototypes in an hour. A new formation, do it once, prove it works, modify the stamp, and bingo—you have a newly enhanced carrier." Rugrat sat on his bed and pulled off his blouse. "Heck, you can use the blanks from the carrier to make new formations. Get them from the line instead of bugging a smith. Leads to people innovating instead of making the same old thing. Constantly improving at a rapid rate."

"So, with the formation sockets?"

"We have a formation tester. They use the old armor plates, put it in, and test it out. Something works, then they can study it more or start producing it on scale in the factories. Leads to more research to make the formation smaller, stronger, and more power efficient, same as technology back on Earth.

"Instead of taking years to create a new formation, it can take months. Testing can take minutes instead of weeks, and implementation, well, it could take months to create the factory line to make the formation. Once it is up and running, it can produce them until the end of time. If it is made by traditional formation masters, they would increase their skill level and then never touch it again. This leaves our formation masters to innovate, and we get shiny, new, badass gear.

"Bonus, we're recycling-conscious. If a formation fails or when we replace the old ones, we take all of that, refine them back down, and use them for something new. Bingo-bango, technology wonder of the Ten Realms."

Rugrat frowned.

"Something wrong?" Erik asked.

"Just, well, my theory, the one that I was thinking of using to break through to Expert. I was thinking of how a weapon should work together with a person completely. That it should be an extension of themselves, seamless." Something nagged at Rugrat, but he couldn't place his finger on it.

"What are you thinking of doing?" Erik asked.

Rugrat pulled off his boots, releasing his feet from their prison. He grunted as he dropped the shoes to the floor and moved his toes freely.

"A new type of weapon, one that is linked to the user. A kind of amplifier for whoever is shooting. I have been working with Earth rifles, but with a mana rifle, it amplifies the spell you place on the round and uses formations to shoot it out. The more power you have, the greater the power of the rifle." Rugrat started to get excited. "A mana railgun!"

"A railgun?" Erik said. "But most of those are mounted on tanks."

"The issues are power supply and heat. Here, the power supply is mana stones, and the heat can be dissipated by the enhanced heating and cooling runes!"

"Sounds feasible," Erik said.

"What are you going to do?"

"Cultivate my mana. I'm falling behind. I can build up the Metal mana within my mind, then I can passively temper it over time."

"Well, if you come to the smithy, there is plenty of Metal mana, more than just in any normal place," Rugrat said.

"Sounds good, though tonight is on me!" Erik raised his voice so everyone could hear him.

There were grins and smiles among the others.

Melika was still quiet, but after being with them for a few days, she wasn't afraid, though she was still apprehensive.

First Annual Crafter's Competition

Delilah and Fehim entered the large hall that had been created as part of the crafter's competition.

There were several different areas that people could wander through. Crafters from various ability levels, realms, and disciplines filled the area. They'd brought their friends and families with them. All of Alva seemed to have shown up. People were talking with their friends, meeting with their heroes, and having discussions with peers.

All while food and drink were supplied.

Delilah and Fehim were trailed by four members of the close protection details as they met up with Tan Xue, Julilah, and Qin.

"It looks like things are going well," Delilah said in greeting.

"Just wait until tomorrow. The real fight will start in those arenas." Tan Xue grinned.

"It's not fair that we don't get to compete," Qin complained.

"You just want to beat more people with your formations. Did you not have enough fun in the academy?" Julilah asked, looking innocent as she drank from her cup while Qin glared at her.

Fehim coughed to hide his smile, and Tan Xue elbowed Qin, who lowered her head grumpily.

Delilah smiled openly.

"It's unfair. Why can't we have the Experts fighting it out?" Qin complained.

"If we have all the Experts competing, then who will tally up the scores? This is for Alva as well. When we have the competition in Vuzgal, then we will naturally need to show off our ability and position," Tan Xue said.

"We can take this time to teach others and share our knowledge. Isn't that better than fighting it out?" Delilah said.

"I guess. Just—competing is more fun! I can remember the looks on the faces of those guys still," Qin said.

"Next year, you'll have all the competitors you could want. Think of how the people of Alva will have grown by then and all the people who will come from across the realms to challenge us," Julilah said.

"And we have the arena now. We can set up monthly competitions as well as testing our different ideas," Tan Xue said.

"It will be an exciting series of matches tomorrow. I am looking forward to them all," Delilah said.

"It's certainly ignited the fighting spirit of the crafters. They want nothing more than to show off their skills. They spend all their time hidden away, and they don't get the kind of praise or support that fighters or people in the military might get," Fehim said.

"All Alvans are the quiet show-offs." Qin grinned.

"Quiet show-offs?" Delilah chuckled. "I think that other crafters might die of shock if they heard you!"

Tan Xue, Julilah, and Qin were all together as they entered the stadium. The interior arena had several towers that one could sit in and look at the other arenas through the glass or formations broadcasting the other crafting competitions. Bars and taverns across the city were showing livestreams of the competitions. They were being shown in the other floors and in the Dungeon Core Headquarters.

"I don't think I have seen so many people in Alva," Qin said as they got drinks and sat, watching over people's heads.

"I'm just thankful we are in the teacher's lounge. There are so many crafters here. If we were in the general seats, we would be getting mobbed with questions," Julilah said.

Tan Xue laughed and sipped her drink. "All the students who were learning away from Alva have returned. Some wanted to show off their skills, others wanted a reason to come home, and others just want to see their fellow crafters show off their power. The traders came back, as well, because the crafters who rise in these competitions will get a lot of resources behind them. They could really increase their overall abilities rapidly."

"And it is always best to support a crafter when they are younger to build up a greater feeling of familiarity. That way, if they require anything in the future, they will look to you. Also, they'd be happier to sell their goods to you or help you create special items if you ask," Qin said.

Julilah played with her glass, frowning.

"Something on your mind?" Tan Xue asked.

"I was just thinking about how everyone is coming here. I didn't realize there were so many Alvans. I never felt that I was connected to the people in Kaeju, but in Alva, I feel like all the people around us are our people. Feels like belonging or something a bit more distant than family, but only barely so."

Tan Xue hugged her from the side, and Julilah smiled.

Julilah had a hard life in Hersht. Her mother had four children from different fathers. Her manager took control of them and had them working in different seedy jobs; anything they earned, he kept. Some of her brothers and sisters were pickpockets; others worked hard jobs at all hours, aiming to get resources to cultivate or increase their level. Born at level zero, they had to fight for every level in a realm where the majority were over level ten. A casual slap could leave them bruised and battered or with broken bones.

Tan Xue thought back to the day she had been walking back to her smithy with a supply of iron ore and had seen a young girl. Her little body shook as she squatted on a stoop. It looked like she was sleeping, except for the occasional jerkiness as she cried silently into her clothes.

Tan Xue checked around, making sure it wasn't a scheme. She mulled it over in her head, debating whether to talk to the girl or walk on by.

She cleared her throat and the girl flinched, observing with wide eyes and ready to run in a moment. Her clothes were haggard, and she looked malnourished.

"Are you okay?" Tan Xue asked, not sure how to talk to her.

"I, uh-uh, I didn't steal anything!" the girl said. That fear in her eyes, that flightiness and tension in her body, made Tan Xue feel vulnerable herself.

"I didn't say that. This is my shop." Tan Xue pointed at the door behind the girl.

The girl got up and skittered to the side, watching her the entire time as if she might rush out and grab her.

"I didn't mean you any harm." Tan Xue tried to be as non-threatening as possible. "My name is Tan Xue. I'm a smith."

The girl seemed to have an internal debate. "I'm Julilah."

"It's nice to meet you, Julilah." Tan Xue moved to the door, opening it and revealing the smithy beyond.

"Ah—"

Tan Xue turned at the sudden noise from Julilah and waited patiently.

"I like your door. It's warm and the designs are pretty."

Tan Xue glanced at her door and the formations carved into them. "Well, feel free to look at the formations whenever you want."

"Can I really? Most businesses chase me away." Julilah looked down, her eyes growing heavy.

"Ah, I'm just a smith. Not many people come here to find me. Just no talking when I'm working. And I better not catch you skipping work to come and find me!"

"I don't have a job," Julilah said.

"Go talk to Miss Warren on Ling Street. She's always in need of young helpers to take messages across Hersht." Tan Xue turned and smiled to herself as she walked into the smithy.

Too bad it hadn't lasted. Julilah had gotten a job and some security, but she continued to come around, growing bolder and wanting to become her student. Tan Xue tried to protect her and push her away. She hadn't wanted others to bully Julilah to get to her.

Tan Xue mussed up Julilah's hair some, making her frown.

"What did you do that for? Aren't you supposed to be a high-and-mighty principal of Vuzgal Academy? It took me twenty minutes to get my hair sorted!"

Tan Xue had a devilish smirk on her face as she raised her hand again.

"No! Not the hair!" Julilah pathetically tried to cower in her seat, sending Qin and Tan Xue into laughter.

"Mean!" Julilah pouted.

"Do you miss home?"

"Alva is our home," Julilah said without thinking.

Tan Xue felt her chest tighten and her eyes itch.

"Are you okay?" Julilah asked as Tan Xue coughed, her throat feeling tight.

"Ah, nothing, just a cough."

"I told you to get your lungs checked. You've been working in the smithy for so long and with all kinds of enhancers." Julilah's worry soothed Tan Xue's heart.

"I went to see them. I'm fine." Tan Xue shook her head as she pulled out food.

"You got breakfast? Look, there are even hash browns." Qin glanced at the perfectly preserved food that seemed to have just come from the pan.

"I know you two. You have plenty of materials and tools in your storage rings, but you eat all the food you have stored and forget to get more," Tan Xue admonished them with her chopsticks.

The two girls ducked their heads as they readied their chopsticks under the table.

Do you think I can't see what you're doing, food assassins! She would need to be quick. Sudden strike!

"Hah!" Tan Xue's chopstick shot out, and she grabbed pancakes, putting them into her bowl and adding some bacon before the other two realized what was going on.

"You!"

"Big sister Xue!"

Like fish and snakes, their chopsticks flashed out, grabbing food and placing it into their own bowls. Some didn't even make it to the bowl as they dived in.

The teachers, and others who were watching them, coughed and looked away, as if a food fight wasn't happening between three of the first generation of Alva crafters.

They quickly cleared their plates and sat back in their chairs.

The plates went into Tan Xue's storage ring, and tea appeared on the table.

"Thank you for breakfast, big sister Xue!" the two said together.

"Though I wish I'd had an extra sausage," Qin said under her breath, just so they could hear.

Julilah stuck out her tongue and grinned before taking the teapot and filling their cups. Qin and Tan Xue drank first, and Qin served Julilah.

The three of them sat there, satiated.

"So, I don't get why we are doing this in Alva and not in Vuzgal," Julilah asked.

"Confidence," Tan Xue said. "Most of our crafters have learned crafting through Alva, and they have not tested their skills against anyone outside of Alva. Here, they can go against one another and gain confidence in their own abilities. They might even not focus on what others can do, as long as they can do better than they did this year and place better according to their fellow Alvans."

"Everyone here, although they don't come from the same place, have gotten the same teaching and training. Anyone outside, they have different teachers, different techniques. Confidence doesn't sound like such a big thing, but if you are nervous and if you have never done something before, you'll be more likely to make mistakes, and you couldn't put your full effort forward," Julilah surmised.

"There is another hidden benefit. The stadium and arenas are another way of training. We have the crafter dungeon, classes, recordings from other crafters, the library, and multiple workshops. With the arenas, people can fight one another. Maybe people are motivated if they are competing against one another?"

"They can see how strong they have become, how strong everyone else is, as well, to build confidence in what they're learning and show off to Alvans as a whole. We have a large crafting population, but we have people from all walks of life. As we've said before, getting to show off our abilities to others is a rare opportunity. Confidence, fighting will, fame, and pride—all of those can raise people up." Tan Xue smiled.

"What if they lose?" Julilah asked.

"If they lose, well, what have we been teaching? It doesn't matter your background or your ability in the past. With hard work and putting one foot after another, you can succeed. Constructive criticism is just that," Tan Xue said.

"If you can find your weaknesses, then you can address them and turn them into strengths," Qin finished off. "It is very different from the other realms and the academies. Any failure or loss there is taken so personal, as if it is someone else's fault that you are doing bad."

"There can be blood feuds and jealousy. They're just using their family or group's power to attack those who bested them in some way. It's pretty stupid," Julilah said. "Erik and Rugrat's lives were on the line just because they did well and created a type of cloth in the competition!"

"Well, no one said the world had to make sense. The law of Strength rules the Ten Realms. If you are strong, you can do as you want. The Alchemist Association crushed those chasing Erik and Rugrat because Erik was capable and was the student of Zen Hei, one of the Third Realm heads."

"The first matches are about to begin! There are so many people watching. Traders, people from the Adventurer's Guild, crafters, farmers, and librarians. Look, aren't there a lot of people from the military?" Julilah said.

"Aren't there a lot of crafters among the army as well? The crafters make their gear, and we go to their events. This is a way for them to support us and see new crafters who they will rely on to make their gear," Tan Xue said. "A lot of them still commission private weapons to be made, and they also have a lot of ideas for new gear that they share with us."

They looked over the arenas filled with people. Those who couldn't make it to the stadium or the separate arenas were in the different taverns across the dungeon's floors, watching the events that would go on for the next few days.

All of Alva had come together. Entire families had entered competitions or had their relatives and friends in the stands cheering them on.

People came to learn, to be awed, and to support one another.

Among them, Domonos and Yui were in one of the military booths. The two brothers sat beside each other in the tailor's arena.

"I never thought I would be so interested in clothes," Yui said.

"From our underwear to our armor, everything is touched and organized by the tailors. Did you hear about the new stealth covers they are working on for the sharpshooting and special teams?"

"Stealth covers?"

"It is essentially a large, multi-layered sheet. The layers insulate the person or people underneath, while the external material and formations work together to make you blend into the surroundings. It's hard for someone to pick you up with sensing spells, even if they know where to look," Domonos said in approval.

"The teams will be able to get closer to their targets. If you're on the run, you can go to ground and hide, let the enemy pass you, then double back and head in a different direction. Will the layers work in the winter and summer?"

"They are rated for the colds of the Fourth Realm's north and the sandy wastes of the Second Realm's deserts," Zhou Heng said.

The two brothers stood up and nodded to Zhou Heng.

"Please, there is no need for those formalities. I'm just a tailor."

"You might be 'just a tailor,' but we both know how much you and your people have put into everything we wear and have even altered and adjusted future gear based on our feedback. What you and your people have done allows us and our people to do what we can," Yui said as they made room for Zhou Heng.

"If it weren't for your support and highlighting this fact to so many people, I wouldn't have the number of tailors I have now. Not many people think being a tailor is an exciting job."

"One needs to be exact with their actions and no less demanding with their studies. I have long heard and experienced the end results of the tailors, but, today, I'm excited to see how tailors work behind closed doors," Yui said.

"I think that fighting techniques and weapons are much more interesting than our meager skills."

"Meager? I think you are doing yourself a disservice. While we have many resources to pull from across the realms—information and even materials—most of it comes from the tailor department!" Domonos said.

"The first match is about to begin. Studying diverse materials, is this how smiths pick ores and the right enhancers to use with them to increase the properties of the weapons?" Yui asked.

"Precisely. The competitors will have to pick out different types of materials to use in different types of clothes. Clothes can have hides that are dried out or treated in special vats. They might need to be weaved together or blended. Each creates different base materials. With smiths, a large portion focuses on smithing the weapon. Forging techniques are incredibly important. With tailoring, making the cloth is the most important part. There are dozens of techniques to create cloth, but there is a truly massive amount of raw materials that one can use and combine through those techniques," Zhou Heng explained.

Competitors walked out from the entrances into the arena. People cheered and some waved to the crowd; others walked to the different examination rooms that were closed off from one another, but their roofs were open so the magical rebroadcasting devices could look in and display the information in the sky above or use their sight spells. There were other competitors who smiled or gritted their teeth, showing all kinds of emotions as they entered the honeycomb of rooms.

"Once you have created a type of cloth and said how you were able to create it, you can do tests to find out its properties. Hopefully, it will be the kind of material you require. Then, using sewing techniques, one can turn the cloth into clothes."

"Formations have to be sown in as well, right?" Domonos asked.

"That is correct. The power that a piece of clothing can handle is usually very low, but simple formations are best. You were talking about the stealth sheets before?"

The brothers nodded.

"We used several layers to reduce the thermal footprint of the person underneath, and the outer layers have properties that make it easier for them to change colors. The formations are on a special layer that has fine metal threads. That way, more power can be fed into the formations. They sense the surrounding area and simulate the exterior cloth. It mimics the ground underneath the soldier. If someone was able to calculate depth, they would see that the area was higher than the others, but it isn't much of a height increase if it's one person lying down with a sheet over them."

"Most sensing spells look for disturbances in mana, a peak or a loss, or a difference in the terrain." Yui nodded.

"Yes, Domonos said." Zhou Heng smiled, and Domonos grinned.

A gong sounded, and the competition started.

Yui and Domonos looked over to watch. The tailors were going through the diverse materials. They used different kinds of spells, some on their eyes, fingers, or noses.

Their hands moved quickly, separating out the different items. Some were stalks, others seemed to be no more than balls of fluff from different parts of beasts, and others were even pellets of different colors.

They were organized into piles. Sometimes, there was just one material, but others had four or five. Each of them was organized according to the pieces of clothing they were being asked to make. Testers would come in once they were done. They would tell them why they had picked the combination of materials they had and how they would process them. The leaders were quick with their assessments. Some showed signs of appreciation as they checked the information against the records that Egbert had stored and compiled in the library. Some had even come up with new permutations or materials that they thought might work. They would be tested out while other competitions were happening, and the results would come out at night.

"So many different combinations; there is not just one answer for every question," Yui said. "That must increase the difficulty greatly."

"Yes, there is a new line of thinking among the tailors. Using all the best materials for a single piece can be heaven and hell. If it succeeds, then you ascend the heavens; if it doesn't, you lose it all. There is a hidden benefit from failure and repetition: mastery."

"Master-level crafting?"

"No, mastery of one's current skills. Working on one item again and again. The stitching the first time might have been crooked or you might not have tied it off securely. Your sizing might have been off. If you do it repeatedly, your skills grow. Instead of needing to rely on outlines and referencing your notes constantly, you can size up the materials with your eyes. You can see where the thread will fray and where the stitching will be hard. If you create more cloth from those fine materials, the material might be a lower quality, but your workmanship will improve, and you can try again if you fail."

"Teacher Zhou's words are wise." Domonos cupped his hands.

"We came from the lower realms. Right now, we have a lot of materials, but we want to teach our students to be proud in their work and prudent in creation. There are some fantastic designs for dresses and suits, but the traders can only sell a few dresses or suits. Not everyone needs them. Instead, it is better to make simple pants and shirts. If one is to make the best pair of pants over the best suit, the person with the best pants will be much more successful. The materials should meet the needs of the user."

"I have seen many fine clothes from your students, though?" Domonos asked.

"We don't say that people shouldn't make great shirts or pants or that they all need to be the camouflage the army wears. Suit the materials to the user. Jeans will be jeans will be jeans. Change the sizing, and that is it. Shirts are many people's way of expressing themselves. That is where style comes into play."

"Come, let's keep watching. They are making shoes next."

"I have to ask where you came up with your boots. They look more comfortable than the shoes I wore as a Young Master," Domonos said.

"Making shoes is an art. After staring at the shoes that Erik and Rugrat used, seeing their rough outlines and designs from their memories, and comparing them with Rugrat's gun magazines, we came up with much more rugged designs. We have the rand at the base, the lugs, outsole, insole, toecap, upper, collar, tongue, and eyelets with different types of string and in some cases tightening formations to secure the shoe. One has to find the best materials for the underside of the shoe and stitch them together and then stitch the diverse materials to create the shape of the shoe, paying attention to padding and weatherproofing. The form has to fit the foot, and the soles need to be comfortable and long-lasting so the wearer can use them over an extended period without fail."

Zhou Heng was glowing, in his element and excited to talk about what he spent his days doing.

Yui and Zhou Heng started talking about shoes and boots, pointing to their own footwear as Yui was enlightened with his insight.

Domonos looked around the arena. The first competition came to an end. People left the testing rooms either excited or dejected, and a myriad emotions played out over their faces as they headed back to the resting rooms. The arena was switched and quickly prepared for the next competition. Some people in the crowds headed down, and others went in to take their spots.

People talked to one another, explaining what had happened, showing off their own skills, and teaching others.

Yui talked about formations and the materials in boots, how they could make a person faster, while Zhou Heng talked about the stability of the shoe versus the additional formations that could overwhelm the base materials and destroy them.

There was still so much to learn and to craft.

"Ah, Tan Xue, good to see you," Glosil said as he saw the smith enter the same booth.

"Glosil, have you come to see the formation masters and blueprint draftsmen in action?"

"It caught my interest. I go through so many information books, and there are always new spell scrolls. I realized that I never saw them getting made."

Tan Xue laughed, seeing the awkward expression on Glosil's face mixed with excitement.

The gong sounded, and the mana in the area surged. Under the control of so many powerful Masters, the mana of the Ten Realms was suppressed!

Glosil's eyes widened. "They take diverse materials and process them into paper, sometimes using fibrous materials such as wood chippings or different reeds, sometimes even hides. The materials can be aligned with different attributes. Creating a spell scroll from a material that matches the scroll will improve its Strength!"

"Look at how fast they go through the materials. Some of them are coming up with multiple kinds of paper to use as a base for their scrolls," Tan Xue said.

"If you have more options, then you can think of the best spell to use on them. Fastest is not always the best, though it is thrilling to see how their fighting spirit is ignited when they are up against one another and there is a time constraint involved."

"Some have started to work on the formation!"

"It is so elegant," Glosil said with a breath. "What are they doing with those paints?"

"Once the materials are picked out for the scroll, the materials and methods to inscribe the spell vary. With formations, people carve the arrays into metals, rock, wood, and other solid materials. Carving into the scrolls would ruin them, so the creators must use other tools. They make formation inks and threads."

"Inks and threads? Ah, I see! So, like how metals can be inlaid into the carved-out formations to increase their power and the conductivity of power?"

"Exactly, Commander," Tan Xue said. "Look—that person there is combining the blue utteka root and nova shoot to create an ink."

The spell scroll creator worked his ink block. Combining the juices of the two plants, he created a deep purple that had flecks of prismatic colors and blue within. He drew out a brush and dipped it into the ink, wiping it on the ridges of the ink stone to remove the excess.

The mana in the area gathered and calmed under his control. He closed his eyes before he raised his hand and released the brush.

It drifted into the air, above the freshly created spell scroll.

The tip of the brush bent in the air, and lines appeared in mid-air.

"Air creation! Impressive!" Tan Xue said quietly, as if the crafter might be disturbed by her words over two hundred meters away.

"Air creation?" Glosil's voice was low as well.

"It is a kind of prototyping. With all crafts, many people will work on multiple prototypes before they start on their true project. With air creation, one can create the spell formation for the scroll in mid-air and break it into components. Then the crafter can press them to the paper, creating the spell formation in one go. The ink is inlaid at the same time. There is a smaller chance for faults as it will all dry at the same rate and there will not be more ink in some places compared to others."

"Ah, so it is like creating a stamp of the spell formation?" Glosil asked.

"Yes, just like the spell scroll printing press. The special inks are made, then the stamp soaks in it and stamps the papers. It is insane to think of how many spell scrolls we now make."

"Ah, there is always a need for stockpiles, though we have been holding off making more. If we keep making them at this rate, it will take years to use all the scrolls."

"Won't they be used against the Willful Institute?"

"Yes, though we have to look at future expansion. We don't want to waste spell scrolls or leave them sitting in the corner. How many different spell scrolls will be made next year? How many will we find a use for? We have a large stockpile, but our printing speed is so damn high it would be a waste. We started a contract with the traders, creating low-key, useful, daily spell scrolls for them to use and sell. Keeps the equipment operating, and we know there will be no issues with it. Passively create an income, and if we need to fight, we can switch back to making our own items."

"I didn't think of that. It is smart, and it means that Alva can make more money."

"I feel like it is an Alvan thing. We'll make money any way we can and repurpose everything we have—civilian to military, craft to craft. Look at those blueprint draftsmen!" Glosil pointed to blueprint creators who sat away from the spell scroll creators, like a silent shadow. It was hard to notice them in the back, but once seen, their eyes would bulge out at their drawings.

Some had papers all around them; the spell formations had been broken down into components. They noted the exact specifics that each of the spell scroll crafters had done: where they laid more ink or their threads were thicker. If they used different styles of brushstrokes or their stitches were laid out in a distinct way.

Even working with them for so long with her own creations, the detail and their ability to dissect complex items…was shocking.

"If one talks of the backbone of Alva, it is not our armor, our healers, or our formation masters. It is our farmers, builders, librarians, and, overall, the members of the blueprint department," Glosil said in a solemn voice.

"If it weren't for them, we wouldn't have the plans for buildings. We wouldn't be able to create our workshops or our armor and weapons. Formations would be nebulous. Instead of the information sharing we have access to in Alva, we would have to implement the same disciple and master methodology as those in the Ten Realms."

"Everything is recorded in the libraries and open to everyone. Instead of having to create an answer to everything, one can go to the library and research solutions that others have made and even see the breakdown of spell formations and how they've evolved. People have gained inspiration from all kinds of things."

They sank into silence, watching the spell scroll creators draw out formations in the air, those who made needles dance upon the wind with the slightest movement of their fingers. Blueprint draftsmen were silent in their corners; sheets continued to flow around them as they modified their drawings according to the changes the crafter underwent.

It was beautiful for casual observers, impressive for those with an insight into either craft, and terrifying for other Masters. Expert draftsman and spell scroll creators had all achieved high in their Mana Cultivation, so they could feel the mana movements.

"It is as if the Ten Realms is breathing with them. I haven't seen such powerful control over mana anywhere but the fighting arenas," Glosil said.

"This is their battlefield," Tan Xue said.

The timer was running out, and the creators started to combine their spell formations with their spell scrolls.

Tension rose, and everyone held their breath. Under the fierce concentration of the spell scroll creators, ink touched the scrolls, soaking deep into the fibers. Mana surged, drawing into the spell formation. Mana stones crumbled into dust, and power flowed into the inks. Needles dove toward their own scrolls, piercing through like fierce sabers and spears. Then, like sentient creatures, the needles dove and rose like great sea beasts fighting against the sea trying to hold them down. The stitched formation was drawn through the scrolls. As the thread prototype was pulled apart, it was needled into the scroll. The spell scroll creator's eyes turned bloodshot; the world had disappeared for them, and everyone saw their determination.

Glosil leaned forward, his eyes flickering between the competitors. The blueprint draftsmen were going through paper, sometimes using floating brushes and pens to write on several pages at the same time. The competitors gritted their teeth, exploiting all their potential and displaying the limits of their skill!

Spell scroll crafters showed dejected expressions when they failed. Scrolls were burnt up, and inks combusted or changed colors as the creator didn't think of some combination of ink to their scroll that ruined them both.

Others nearly collapsed in relief as their scrolls were completed.

Blueprint draftsmen talked to the creators, pulling more information to add greater detail to their drawings.

More people failed, but the majority succeeded.

They were all doing their best, but some of them went above their abilities and were unable to sustain it.

Glosil saw people who had failed staring at their new materials.

"If at first you don't succeed, try again!" one yelled out, their voice sounding out in the arena. Others called out after them.

A new fire ignited their hearts.

Like maddened beasts, they reached out and grabbed the remaining materials as if they were nothing more than weak sheep in front of wolves.

Glosil's heart surged at their determination. His lips pulled back, revealing his teeth as he hit his fist on his armrest. *That's right! Never give in!*

"You can do it!" someone in the crowd called out. The silence that had fallen across the arena changed as people cheered, supporting their crafters.

"If at first you don't succeed, try again!" some chanted.

"Do your best!" others yelled.

Glosil's heart thumped out of his chest as the mana around the arena surged. It had been stirred up with the excitement of the supporters and the fighting will of the crafters.

The crafters redoubled their efforts, sitting taller. Their bloodshot and tired eyes showed a new light as they fought on.

Time went on as crafters turned into legends; they held nothing back, showing everything and giving their all.

The gong sounded again. Just like that, two hours had passed. The rooms were opened. People had half-finished scrolls; others had failures.

Although some of their faces were stiff, when they stepped out and saw the audience standing in their seats and applauding their work, they couldn't help but stand taller.

Many grasped their fists emotionally toward the crowds in thanks.

Glosil released his fists, the smile wide on his face. "I think these competitions might make Alva stronger than any fighting competition the army has."

Delilah and Fehim sat down at one of the large cafeteria areas around the arenas. Different screens showed ongoing competitions, highlights from previous competitions. and results as they were reported.

The two of them were close, but their duties took them in different directions. It was hard for them to meet up.

"The cooks of Alva are fierce! Did you see the one who was creating the spicy fish soup? They must be so strong to toss so much liquid and meat with just a flick of a hand! She didn't miss a drop," Fehim praised.

"It was incredible. There are so many things our alchemists could learn from the cooks," Delilah agreed.

"Maybe one of them can make your pills and concoctions taste better," Jia Feng teased as she came up behind them.

"Principal Jia Feng! Please join us," Fehim said.

"Thank you, Alchemy Department Head," Jia Feng said dryly.

"I'll drop the titles then?" Fehim asked.

"Please," Delilah and Jia Feng said at the same time. They all laughed as Delilah poured a drink for Jia Feng.

"We were just watching the cooking competition. There were so many different dishes."

"You're telling me! Thankfully, we have some arts from the military to consume more food and turn it into pure energy." Jia Feng patted her stomach. "It is so good, but a lady has to watch her figure."

"It is a hard endeavor." Delilah smiled into her drink.

"I won't need to eat for a week! Though there were some items I wouldn't mind a second taste of," Jia Feng said in a low voice. "So many items can be created in each craft. I think that, next year, having it last two weeks and having multiple categories would be fairer. Right now, we have to limit them due to time, and it isn't fair to everyone. Some might have a magnificent pie, but they are competing against all kinds of different desserts. It is hard to get a clear winner."

"For the first year, things are going rather well," Delilah said.

"Yes, but that is due to most of the teachers helping out. We've gotten so much support from Alvans. Seeing all the different crafts has opened people's eyes. Those who were hesitant and disinterested are taking a look—it is breaking down the walls."

"What is the next event you are going to?" Delilah asked.

"I have some more judging, unfortunately," Jia Feng said.

"We do as well," Fehim said.

"I forgot I volunteered." Delilah winced.

"Welcome to adulting. Thankfully, there will be re-runs and we can watch it all later!"

Taran was in one of the viewing rooms over the arena. He leaned against the railing as the different crafters walked out to the large platforms.

It wasn't individual crafters but teams of up to ten people.

There were farmers, alchemists, formation masters, laborers, and woodworkers. Some people wore branded clothing; others wore random clothing.

It seemed as if the building companies had at least one team here. It was a good way to advertise their building speed. Many people underestimated builders. They thought of them as nothing but laborers, unaware of how much planning went into putting up a building or how to work with the environment to create the best building for the area. They had to make sure it was structurally sound—warm in the cold and cool in the warm—and that the room layout made sense to allow people to move around and make the greatest use of them. Those were the basics. Once they had done that, they needed to add in ways to manage clean water, waste, and formations embedded into the walls. Builders were the most practical of crafters, as everything they created would be used in the real world. Working in teams, they had some of the strongest mages and Body Cultivators. Their team leaders were trained by blueprint draftsmen, and some had backgrounds in different crafts so that on complex projects they knew when to best utilize different crafters and prepare for them. Simple on the outside, but only because they made the complex look easy.

Taran's eyes moved to the new groups. The different areas had materials laid out for the building. There were stone, metal, pre-made formations, and then, in several areas, there were different trees.

Everyone was assembled. They stood in the middle of their large squares, dirt under their feet.

There were a lot of building crews and their families who were watching. Crafters who focused on growing their own materials were there out of interest as well. It was more of an exhibition of abilities than the other competitions.

The gong sounded and people moved. The building teams had already broken down what they were going to do. Laborers and mages quickly excavated the soil; others checked on the supplies. Their team leads checked the plans as everyone worked on creating the foundations.

The academic teams were a lot slower, moving methodically and checking every step.

People stood around. Without clear leadership, they all offered advice, drowning out one another. Some groups had clear leaders, and Taran noticed the farmers made up the core of the organized teams.

They started to work with their trees; they had picked out plans to work on as well. They took the trees and planted them at different locations. Most of the supplies were mana-gathering formations and mana stones. They got the trees planted in the correct positions, checking their plans multiple times.

Taran's eyes drifted to the building companies. The leads checked the plans a couple of times and gave their team members instructions. They had done this so many times that they were already accommodating for things they would need to do later. They laid pipes down for water and waste. Formation links were added to connect the building to the energy grid.

With the foundations complete, those with high Body Cultivation put in the metal framework. The mages bent the framework into shape. Then molds were created, and stone chips poured in. A few fusing spells later, and the foundations were created. Supporting walls were added, and the basement was finished off as they moved to the second floor.

"Huh, they are using molds instead of growing out the stone. I guess there isn't a ready source of stone beneath the building, and this way there is less mana expenditure. It takes more time." Taran looked over to the growing groups.

Formations were placed around the trees and activated. Farmers checked the trees, rotating through them. Alchemists tapped into the trees, injecting concoctions or dropping it on the soil. Woodworkers checked the plans and the trees; they worked beside the farmers, telling them how they would like the trees shaped. The farmers and alchemists worked as one.

There were various kinds of trees. Some stretched their limbs across the ground, snaking together and creating floors. Others spread branches upward, creating the second floor; they weaved together, creating walls and stairs. Openings were left between the branches. Where there were gaps, wooden, weaved walls appeared with windowless openings.

Farmers and alchemists placed the windows, and the trees grew around them.

The resource cost was heavy, and there were so many concoctions! The farmers and alchemists had to alter their practices constantly to allow the building to grow properly.

The builders seemed to move slower than the growing groups, but their buildings were going up faster. It looked tiring, and there was always something going on. Constructing a building didn't mean staying ahead of the materials' growth speed but following the process step by step.

Taran watched, appreciating the different styles. He wrote some notes;

a new door seemed to have opened in his mind.

If a building was broken, the materials could be used again to recreate the building. If the still-growing building was broken, then with enough resources and time, it could repair itself. The growing building acted like its own ecosystem, requiring constant maintenance. It could be slightly offset, and even normal buildings required maintenance over time. The growing houses took five to ten times as much energy to create. Each would be expensive.

The growing house group finished ahead of time and were talking with one another as they checked the building.

After a few minutes, the trees started to grow again, and the first-floor trees expanded the building outward.

Taran sat up. *They could make the building grow again?* Regular buildings could have additions, but they were much harder to construct. The trees opened to one another; instead of destroying walls, they adjusted to the new shape. With new blueprints, the builders would need to build a new house, and the growing group would need to hire a team and adjust the trees in place already.

Taran sunk into thought before he pressed his lips together and sighed as he wrote in his notebook.

Although the growing groups had a good idea, they didn't have the planning or coordination of the builders, possibly because they could adjust their building and didn't have to worry about the smaller things that were always part of the builders' plans. They had systems built into the house to supply water, clean the waste, supporting the trees. People might drink more water or have more waste than one tree-house could sustain. They didn't have a basement. Their heating and cooling system wasn't as effective, and if not maintained, the house would fall apart and rot. The trees would recover with time, but they were not as strong as regular buildings. For bunkers, they wouldn't be as useful. If the builders gave them some tips and worked together, they could be much better. A good starting idea, but it would require time to mature.

Taran was pleased as everyone finished their buildings by the time the gong sounded.

In just a few hours, they had made these houses. Working as a team really could help.

After watching the competition with Tan Xue, Julilah and Qin had a new outlook on everything. They went to as many competitions as they could to show their support and learn. They spent their nights judging separate formation competitions.

"There is so much to see, but I'm exhausted," Qin complained.

"I heard from Jia Feng that there is a new formation department head in the Kanesh Academy," Tan Xue said. Qin frowned and followed Tan Xue's amused gaze to Julilah.

"I was going to tell you later, but…" Julilah pulled out a crest and put it on her chest with a grin.

"You!" Qin stared at the senior formation master crest. "W-what? When?"

"Uh, a few days ago. I have the most qualifications apparently, other than you, but you have the Vuzgal position."

"When do you start?"

"Right after the competition!"

"Oh." Qin sounded dejected. "So, where is your new workshop?" She picked at her fingers.

Julilah frowned. "Why would I get a formation workshop away from you?"

"I thought that…with your new position…you might leave." Qin pressed her fingers together.

"You're too silly. You think you're getting rid of me that easy?" Julilah put her arm around Qin and pulled her forward. "I just needed more resources for my projects. Aren't we always running out with only your resources?"

Tan Xue snorted.

Qin's eyes widened. "What is your resource allotment?"

"Add twenty percent to what you get." Julilah's eyes were practically glowing. "Alva pays more."

Qin showed a small smile.

"Just don't forget to call me senior every day. How could I get that if you are in another workshop? Are you okay, Qin? Your color doesn't look so good."

Another critical hit. Please, sister, your wounds are too vicious! I'm older than you by nine months!

"Come on, the smithing competition is up next!"

Julilah dragged her through the stadium to the right arena.

They were a few minutes late, and the competition was underway. Smiths stood in the face of the ferocious flames, framing their strong backs, arms, and legs. Their muscles popped out as they refined ores with enhancers.

"On the outside, their actions are so violent, taking on the heat of such flames with their bare bodies, using their Strength to bend metal to their will. When you look at it from another point of view, they are turning their bodies into tools to shape the metal. Their actions are forceful, but it takes precision and ability to shape such fine items," Qin said.

"We match formations to the items, but they have to be in touch with the materials on a much higher degree—something from nothing—while we are adding and enhancing what is already in front of us," Julilah said.

They heard and saw the rhythmic strikes of the smiths as they made the metals sing. Their high Body Cultivation allowed them to work with the greatest flames and draw out more Strength from their bodies. Their Mana Cultivation was equally high to cast spells and see what was happening within the Metal and introduce mana. Their high cultivation in both areas meant they could create incredibly powerful items.

Delilah and Jia Feng sat in Delilah's office. Egbert sat in a chair as well; he wore a jersey the tailors had created on the second day of the competition. The jersey supported the Alva academies, though Egbert had taken it one step further—he had added flags showing his support of different crafters. He looked as if he were one massive collage.

"Egbert, why are you still wearing the jersey and flags?" Delilah asked. "The competitions ended two days ago."

"Ahem, well, I might have been a little liberal with the glue. You see, the flags stuck to the jersey, and some of the glue went through the jersey and uh... Well, it might be stuck to my bones."

Seriously? He'd glued everything to his body by mistake? How was this guy still operating the dungeon core and library?

She closed her eyes, taking a breath before staring at Jia Feng.

"The competition was a great success. We had about seventy percent of the students participating in the matches. Registration is up across both academies. Traders are talking to more of the crafters than before. Some people want to host competitions throughout the year to test out their skills," Jia Feng said.

"Do you think we will be ready for the one in Vuzgal?"

"I think so. This was great for their confidence. As for how they will place, I cannot give any guarantees. And we need to keep in mind that there will be people who want to make Vuzgal look weak."

"Well, it depends on the atmosphere, doesn't it?" Egbert picked at his shirt.

"What do you mean?" Delilah asked.

"Well, if we make it a competition of Vuzgal showing off their power to everyone, then it will be hard to hold that position for a long time. If, on the surface, it is an exchange of pointers and allows crafters to show their skills and teach one another, then if we lose sometimes, it will be nothing much. There are plenty of crafters out there, and it is good that we get to meet more powerful people. Vuzgal shows its power in being able to tempt these people. Play the neutral party with good rewards, pleased to invite anyone and everyone."

"That could work," Delilah said.

"Though, we should never let our Experts fight in these competitions," Egbert said seriously, looking up. "If our Experts enter the field, then all the academy's honor will be on their shoulders. If we make this a competition of the juniors, do it by age, and then we could have an edge. If we have all kinds of people coming in and challenging us, we'll fall apart. A two-hundred-year-old skeleton challenging us? We have been studying for just a few years. As our crafters fall, people will look down on us. We need to manipulate the rules to appear stronger; otherwise, we reserve our Strength and stop our strongest from competing. That way, we are mysterious and have unknown depths. Personally, I think we shouldn't let our people compete; we can control everything more."

"They aren't going to be happy. They want to compete and show off their power," Jia Feng said.

"Well, we have a stadium here, no?" Egbert said.

"This is Alva. Even if they fail here, then it is not in the eyes of outsiders," Delilah agreed.

"Okay," Jia Feng agreed hesitantly.

"Everything we do outside the dungeon is under the greatest scrutiny. We have to watch our steps. Projecting our strength outward gives us cover."

"I know. I keep forgetting just how the Ten Realms operates after spending so much time in Alva."

5 Rudimentary Design

Rugrat quenched the metal. Steam rose around him as he put it on its side. He checked the different blueprints of the new rifle.

It was formed from a single piece of metal.

As it cooled, Rugrat felt Experience enter his body. He grimaced. There were no notifications telling him he had reached Expert level.

If he could prove the metal's effectiveness, he could learn more formations and make them stronger next time.

"A bull pup?" Erik cracked open an eye.

The mana fluctuations in the smithy seemed to slow down as Rugrat felt the suction force from Erik's body decrease.

"Longer barrel for greater acceleration." Rugrat had an integrated stock with a thumbhole. The magazine was seated to the rear, near the shoulder. The barrel ran forward, reaching four separated pieces of metal with sections of runes with embedded gems to power them.

Staring at it, Rugrat felt proud; his blood surged in his ears. He pulled out a round. It was formed from Mortal mana stone, and he'd traced formations upon its surface.

"I don't know complex runes, but this should be enough! These higher level smithy rooms, even here in this dungeon, have testing grounds. Should we see how it does?" Rugrat asked.

"Right behind you." Erik laughed, eager to see the power of the weapon.

Rugrat opened a door, and they walked into a large sturdy room reinforced with formations and had targets along one side of the wall. He pulled out a vise and put the rifle into it. They retreated, and Rugrat put down a mana shield.

"All right, let's give it a shot." Rugrat grinned and pulled the string attached to the trigger.

Power flushed through the rifle. The metal melted, the runes distorted, and the gems exploded from the power coursing through it. The round amplified the power all around it, turning into one large bomb before it exploded. Metal shot off in all directions, embedding in the walls and the ceiling, striking the mana barrier.

"Ah, my formation skill isn't that high," Rugrat said.

"No worries. Creating takes time." Erik patted his shoulder. "Come on, tomorrow we're heading to the surface. We've got a meal with everyone else tonight."

Rugrat glared at the smoking ruin and nodded, letting out a sigh.

"Yeah, I only worked on it for two days. My speed is getting better at least." Rugrat deactivated the formation and cleared up the remnants of the rifle. Erik bent to give him a hand.

"You know, the crafting system is prejudiced as hell," Erik said.

"Huh?" Rugrat looked over.

"You only progress if you take on higher challenges. Crafting is geared toward one person making powerful artifacts. Mainly weapons and defensive items." Erik rested on his knee. "Like if you were to craft a spoon at the Novice level and a spoon of the Expert level, is there a need?"

"What do you mean?" Rugrat asked.

"A spoon is a spoon—you use it to eat. A Novice-level spoon might be rough, but it works. An Expert-level spoon, it works, it might look amazing, it might be reinforced, but the ability to have more formations and have an innate ability—it doesn't need them. Nearly all crafters make weapons and armor, but they could as easily make high-level spoons. Though making spoons isn't glamorous, there are some additions that can be useful, and one spoon is pretty useless. Mass production is undervalued. Few crafters do it because mass production is synonymous with crap and bad items that are liable to break."

The two of them sank into thought.

"When you think about it, the weapons, the armor, the ammunition we used on Earth—hell, even the vehicles—all of them were mass-produced," Rugrat said. "We've started that with the ammunition factories and production lines to create armor, concoctions, and weapons."

"In the Ten Realms, formation masters work with others, but the other crafters rarely work with one another. Smiths might make cauldrons for alchemists, but they don't make armor that will inject concoctions into a person's body so they don't have to drink liters of potions," Erik said.

"But the people in Alva work together," Rugrat said.

"They do, to an extent. They don't see the overall value in working together, though. They use information from other crafts to advance their own, but there are a handful of projects where there are departments working together," Erik said. "Simply, the Ten Realms rewards skill levels to those who create. It doesn't reward people who keep doing it."

"If we could promote them working together, then we might make more useful items, but then it comes to what you said—if people aren't crafting items that are a higher level, their crafting levels will stagnate. We could have hundreds at the Journeyman stage and not one Expert," Rugrat said.

"That is the Ten Realms's problem, not ours," Erik said. "Though I guess we haven't tested out one thing. If we have all of those low-end parts put together to create something more, like all the parts in a truck or a weapon, if the end product is a higher level than the sum of all its parts, will one's skill level increase? For mass producing, the only thing we can reward people with is more money. Entice them with that and have factories built to produce the items they put forward. A thriving business creating and managing factories."

"Yeah," Rugrat said, not really listening to Erik. He continued to clean up the rest of the failed experiment, wondering just what the issues were.

What he needed was to check with the formation masters and see what they thought.

Lucinda was the last to arrive.

"Okay, let's get out of here," Erik said.

The group headed out of the inn they had been staying in and headed over to the elevator that would take them out of the dungeon.

After paying the fee, they boarded a large elevator with iron bars. They could see over the entire dungeon as they rose.

"Dungeons for training grounds. The Ten Realms is extreme." Yuli glanced over to a group of students in one corner. Their armor and gear were badly dented and broken, but they held their heads high. In the depths of the dungeon, there were plenty of ways a person could advance. There were many fights to be found, and powerful beasts and resources were abundant. The dungeon was a land of death, but it was also a land of opportunities.

"In the Fourth Realm, the dungeons are too small, and entire sects are willing to lay waste to one another so that they can claim them and increase their Strength. Here, they're academy training grounds. Why don't people fight over them more?" Tian Cui asked.

"They do. Just instead of waging wars, they wage tournaments and use the challenges to take resources and power from one another. Betting is the way that resources and places are taken. If someone is unwilling to bet, unwilling to prove their strength, others will use that weakness and attack them through different means. Academies thrive here. The academies with the strongest cultivators, the largest and most powerful dungeon areas—they win," Storbon said.

Light came in from above, and they covered their eyes at the brightness. Erik felt a headache coming on as he squinted. It was more sun than he had seen in weeks.

The noise came next as they heard the bustle of the massive city around them.

The elevator bounced and locked. The gates opened in front of them, and the press of people walked off.

They were checked by the guards and allowed past the defenses into the campus of the Arcane Academy army.

People marched into the elevators, classes of fighters who were on a research trip led by a senior or teacher.

"The academy system is similar to a sect. The more missions one completes or the ways they assist the school will gain them credits that can be used to go to classes, to buy equipment, or to access higher-level books and resources. If you earn enough, you can increase your standing, going from the basic to the advanced, elite, and Expert-level classes with increasingly powerful professors. The competition is strong, and people are looking to take the spots of one another all the time," Lucinda said.

"And I thought hearing about regular college was hard," Rugrat said.

"All right, we need to head to where Melika's teacher is," Erik said.

No one argued. They had left the people at Knugrith for three reasons: They didn't want them to alert Lord Vinters, or whoever was behind what had happened at the tower. They also didn't have any kind of debt to these people. If they kept them along longer, they might become more trouble than they were worth. Also, it would be expensive. If they brought them along, they would have to pay for their travel. People in the Ten Realms were always looking for an advantage. Melika's request had generated a Ten

Realms quest; the experience was always useful, and it gained their interest.

They got onto their mounts and headed to where Melika and her teacher had been staying.

Lee Perrin reviewed the information his students had compiled.

"It looks like this has been going on for some time, people being kidnapped and taken down to the dungeon, but we still don't know who the group is."

"It has to be the Faded Scroll!" one yelled.

"We don't know that for sure. The evidence seems to go that way, but we can't just barge in and demand answers. They are still an academy." Lee silenced the large man with a look, who meekly sat back down in his chair.

"Now—" Lee was interrupted by his sound transmission device. He held it up and listened.

"Teacher, a group of people showed up to the inn you were staying at. They have a girl matching Melika's description with them!"

Lee's chair fell to the floor, and he ran out of the room.

The others looked at one another then ran after him.

Her "teacher" wore simple clothes, his hair swept up in a ponytail, his beard a mix of gray and black that made him appear kind when smiling and a grizzly bear if he were angry.

He knelt, concern covering his face as he caught Melika and studied her. A sound-canceling spell fell over them all. No one else in the street could hear the two groups.

"Be ready for anything—set spell scrolls to stun, then we run down to the dungeons. Easier to lose them down there," Erik said through his helmet.

"You okay? What happened?" the teacher asked Melika.

Erik and Rugrat looked at each other as they used internal comms.

"Fucking Aussie?" Rugrat asked.

"Sounds like it," Erik said.

She was crying and explaining to him about being kidnapped, the orcs, the dungeon, and being saved. Her emotions got the best of her, jumbling it all together.

Her teacher hugged her. "This group saved you?" Her teacher checked her eyes.

She took deep breaths, calming down. "Yes, they killed the orcs, destroyed the tower, and got a quest to bring me to you."

The teacher frowned. "A quest?"

He glanced at one of the people around him. "Calm down." He waved. "Melika, tell me everything, from the beginning, from when you were in the inn."

She painted a picture: Bored of staying at the inn, she had gone for a walk. She'd explored the city. At night, she returned to the inn. On her way back, she'd felt sleepy and collapsed. Next, she was in a cart underground with other people, all waking up. They were carted by guards, who replied to their questions with beatings. They were taken to the tower fortress. They met adventurers who had been captured by orcs. Others who had been kidnapped as well.

She talked of Lena, her grotesque appearance; people being carried away; then new orcs coming out of the tower. Suddenly, the orcs went crazy. People jumped out of the tower and fought the beasts. Then it burst into flames as the group fought the orcs around the cages, pushing them back.

The fighting, the orcs running, and then fleeing the orcs tunnels.

"You're safe now." The teacher hugged her. Melika's little frame sagged, relief causing her to melt. He let her cry, getting it all out.

"I need to talk to those who helped bring you back. Go with your senior sister."

"Okay," Melika said.

He handed her off to a woman in plate armor who pulled her into a tight hug.

The teacher cupped his hands, bowing his head to Erik and his group. "Thank you for returning my student to me. My name is Lee Perrin. I am in your debt."

"No debt here, teacher. Just got a quest from the Ten Realms and completed it," Erik said.

"I have a duty to protect her, but I didn't do so. Even if it was just for the quest, thank you."

"No problem. We done here?"

"I have one question. Do you know who did this and why?" Lee asked.

Erik switched to the internal comms. "Should we give him the information linking Vinters?"

"That Vinters mother fucker has a date with a five-five-six through his skull," Rugrat said.

"This ain't the First Realm. If we roll on Vinters, there is no knowing what shitstorm we might stir up. Looks like Lee and his people should have enough power to deal with Vinters and not get fucked in the process," Erik said.

"We'd need months or even years to mount an operation here. Information network, figure out Vinters's power and backers. I vote we give it to this Lee guy," Storbon said.

"Shit, if I were him, I'd want Vinters's head on a plate too," Rugrat agreed. "Ask him if he knows Australia."

Erik stepped forward and pulled out a bundle of papers from his storage ring. Lee's people tensed, and he slowed his movements, holding out the papers, letting them see and relax.

"Person who ran the place kept records. Lord Vinters was her contact. Don't know if there were others behind him or what. All of it is there."

Lee took the papers from Erik. "Thank you. May I know the names of my student's helpers so I might thank you later?"

Erik and the others stiffened, their fingers closer to their triggers.

"No worries, mate. Anonymity is a powerful protection in the Ten Realms. Thank you for what you've done. If you hadn't, then…" Lee's voice trailed off. "Anyway, I must ask if you will make a move against Lord Vinters. I ask as I know that i and my students would like to pay him a visit as well."

"He's all yours," Erik said.

Vinters's guards were strong enough to kill them without breaking a sweat, but maybe Perrins could do something with the lineup he had.

"Thank you. If you are ever in trouble or are looking for a teacher, please contact me. The favor I owe you is not small," Lee said and glanced over to Melika.

Lee took out a token and held it up so they could see it, and then threw it to Erik.

Erik and Rugrat scanned it with their domains before Erik caught it.

"This is my sound transmission device information. Thanks again."

"The Ten Realms is not as forgiving as Australia," Erik said.

"Australia?" Lee's eyes sharpened, and he stood straighter. He turned back to his group and waved them back.

They turned and started to leave the street.

"Mount up!" Storbon said.

The special team got onto their mounts, turned around, and raced off in a new direction.

They reached a totem and paid the fee, disappearing in a flash of light.

The next day peeked over the city as Lee Perrin walked out of the Fighter's Association with Wei Shi.

"Teacher, why did you let them go?" Wei Shi asked.

Lee Perrin recalled the weapons those people were using, the armor and their masks. It looked like he might not be the only person from Earth here either.

Wei Shi was still staring at him, and he replayed in his mind what she had just said. "They were no threat to us. They helped your junior sister. I wasn't going to keep them."

"You had more questions for them, though."

"Do you think they would appreciate me demanding answers from them when we were staring at one another with possible violence?" Lee asked. "Talking about violence, how are our preparations?"

"Everything is ready. We're just waiting for you, Teacher Perrin," Wei Shi said.

Lee stood, and Wei Shi led the way out. The next room had even more people in it, swelling to nearly fifty or so.

They grew silent.

"Let us teach Lord Vinters why no one messes with my students."

The killing intent in the room grew as their anger boiled over—anger at those who dared to slight their teacher, who dared to attack one of their junior sisters, and who had tried to experiment on her.

"Let's start." Lee turned toward the door.

They mounted up on flying beasts, riding out of the Fighter's Association and up into the sky, toward the private residence of the Vinters clan.

Several people on flying beasts rode in the sky.

Lee Perrin heard students, teachers, and spectators gathering in the street and talking excitedly.

"Just what is going on for such a group to come together?"

"Don't they know fighting in the streets is not permitted? The professors and deans won't have to lift a finger to destroy them."

"Look, there is the disciplinary professor from the Faded Scroll!"

"Ryland Porter is here now. He will teach these people about flying over our heads! This is the territory of the Faded Scroll!"

Lee Perrin saw the man ride over.

Announcing his own arrival. Aren't people supposed to become humble in their old age?

A man stood upon his beast, followed by several elders with severe expressions.

Ryland brought himself to a stop. He glared at the group. "What is your business?"

"One of your people kidnapped a student of mine for an experiment. I seek answers," Lee said, using the power of his body to amplify his voice.

People watching the scene muttered among themselves.

Ryland gathered his strength to speak, studying the group flying around Lee.

"You are welcome to come along, Mister Porter. After all, I have some questions I would like the Faded Scroll to answer as well."

Lee felt the auras around him surge, the flash of association emblems, those from powerful academies, and others.

Ryland paled and bobbed his head. "Please let me know how I can be of assistance." The proud and upright disciplinary elder looked panicked.

"Well, that will make things easier," Lee said.

6 Rest and Recuperation

Storbon led the way to the closest totem. Selecting a random target, they teleported.

Three totems later, wandering two cities and changing their appearances twice, they arrived in another Sixth Realm city and finally checked their notifications.

Quest Completed: Mysterious Teacher

Take Melika Nemati to meet with her mysterious teacher.

Requirements:

Lead Melika Nemati to Blue Crystal Palace in the Faded Scroll Campus unharmed.

Give him information about Lena Lindenbaum's operations.

Rewards:

1,250,000 EXP

36,696,860/108,500,000 EXP till you reach Level 61

The team stepped out onto a main road. Four- and five-story buildings were the norm. Stores filled the ground floors, with more businesses advertised above and living areas above them.

Wide sidewalks accommodated the foot traffic and stalls. Roads catered to carriages, pulled by all manner of strange beasts.

In the middle of the road, large carts were pulled along rails.

The street was filled with movement: people doing quick business, steam rising from food stalls as food was snatched and money rapidly exchanged. Fine cloths were hawked as people were custom fitted with clothes by Journeyman crafters.

Expert crafters rode in their carriages. People watched them with respect and envy, though they were a frequent occurrence. Not a rare sight like in the lower realms.

"It's like frigging New York here, except with a better transport system, or South Korea with the stores. Damn, there are so many stores."

The group walked down the street, and people broke around them. Those who tried to pass through the group were met with a glare and thought better than test their luck.

"Well, you've got to remember that fighting in these higher realms is forbidden except in matches and down in the dungeons," Yuli said.

"What does that have to do with the stores?"

"Fighting isn't how you gain power here. Wealth, your status, crafting level, getting into the academies, and placing well. Just how many crafters are out there? If Experts are no longer rare, then shouldn't Novices and Apprentices be rather common?"

"You think the general population are all Apprentices?" Lucinda asked. "Remember that Alva is a strange case, even in the Ten Realms."

"I know. We take the time to teach our younger generations. Look." Yuli pointed down a street where there was a large building.

"Junior academy?" Lucinda read the name on the building's gates.

"Unless I miss my mark, the people who have the means send their children into these junior academies. They must train all the time to get entrance into the main academies," Yuli said.

"Remember when we were in Korea? Actually, you weren't on that station, were you?"

"Nope, I met you after that," Erik said as they continued forging a path down the street. They went over a bridge at the intersection, leaving the junior academy behind.

Every square meter had a different sight.

"Makes me think about Korea. Kids had prep school in the morning, regular school in the day, and then more school at night. Just a few hours of sleep, and then do it all over again. Did that, day in and out. All of it was to get better grades to get into university. Depending on the university that the person got into, it could change their whole future," Rugrat said.

"Just like the academies here," Storbon said.

"Still, doesn't make me feel any safer in the streets," Rugrat said.

You don't feel safe with enough damn explosives to blow half a damn city apart? Maybe no one should feel safe. It was easy to hide anything in a storage ring, and the fear of repercussions kept everyone from fighting it out.

"You know, there aren't many healing houses around. I thought there would be more in the higher realms," Yao Meng said.

"Medicine pays," Erik said. "A healer's position in the lower realms is much higher than up than here. A healer or an alchemist in the Fourth Realm is like a damn lord. Up here, they're hangers-on. Without war and the fear of dying, healers don't make as much. People who temper their bodies are few and far between."

"People aren't willing to endure the pain of tempering, so they only focus on their Mana Cultivation." Tian Cui shook her head.

"Alvans are a more determined lot. We'll take anything we can get. Up here, they can choose. Anyway, healers, they're retainers. A clan or family will train them to extend people's lives, but alchemists have more power. That is why there isn't a healing association. Alchemists can create potions for any kind of cultivation and give you pills to increase your power in a time of peril. Heal you when there are no healers around."

They wandered through the streets and, for the first time in a long time, just watched.

"The cities are so big that the large carriages have their own roads to connect the city," Storbon said.

"Those beasts must have been raised just to run these routes. There are no drivers; they've been trained to run from stop to stop. They even have aerial beasts. Look at that tower." Lucinda pointed at a spire that jutted into the air with circular discs at different heights.

A large aerial beast flapped his wings. Slowing his momentum, he landed on the disc and disappeared.

"Raising aerial beasts is much harder than ground beasts. I wonder how they raise them." Lucinda spoke aloud.

"Look at the lower levels. The beasts going in there are a lower quality, worked hard. If I were a betting man, I'd say they were trader birds," Yao Meng said.

"Why do you think that?" Erik asked.

"Harder worked. They're hardier, and they're landing lower. Also, look at their backs and legs—they've got gear hanging off them. The higher-up fliers, they don't have things hanging off their legs."

"So?"

"So, who is liable to hang gear packs from the sides of their carriages: the wealthy transport carriages or the merchants? If they can sneak in more goods, they'd do it."

"Aerial beasts are expensive, and traders all move by ground," Lucinda rebutted.

"Cost versus profit. Look at how many towers there are around the totems. Remember those warehouse districts?" Yao Meng said.

"Yeah."

"Bet they offload their goods there, put them on birds, and transport them across the city. Other places, a clan might have stores in a city, probably in a few cities because they'd cut into their own profits with too many stores in one place. Here, there are multiple stores under the same clan. All of them need items to sell, so the supply system changes. Carriages move large quantities; birds do smaller quantities over short distances because it's not as packed as the ground. Maybe they only move expensive items. Birds are expensive beasts, after all. Though, if someone is willing to pay, sure thing! They can get it faster."

"Mana stones make the world turn," Tian Cui quipped.

"And I'm in deep need of something to drink and eat. Keep an eye out for good food places," Rugrat said.

"The foodie of the South," Erik said.

"I like my food. Drinking Stamina concoctions gets boring fast."

A general grunt of agreement rose from the group.

The group found a restaurant.

"So many restaurants, completely different from the Fourth Realm. There are a few of them in each city in the Fifth," Tian Cui said as they waited for the waitress to come back with their orders.

"Even have beer packed with damn medicinal ingredients. Feels like it's doing more good than bad." Rugrat frowned, staring into his cup.

Yao Meng tapped his cup against Rugrat's and then the table. Rugrat tapped his as well.

"Tastes way better than the swill from the lower realms." Yao Meng grinned, tilting the beer back.

"Not as good as the stuff back home, though. Hey! Are you chuggi—you!" Rugrat clamped his lips on the mug as he raced to catch up with Yao Meng, who was downing the beer in one gulp, a competitive shine to his eyes.

He finished with a gasp, then Rugrat a second later.

He squinted and shifted around before letting out a burp. "Tastes like beer!" He grabbed the pitcher and poured more for Yao Meng and himself.

Erik held up his cup. "You all did well. I could not be prouder." He tapped his mug against theirs. They mashed them all together before hitting the table and drinking.

They were all visibly relaxed, as if they could only now put down some of their weight.

"So, why do you think that there are so many cooks up here?" Yuli asked Tian Cui.

"Plenty of ingredients around, ton of people looking to learn crafts. Erik said that the alchemists are a massive power up here and in the higher realms. Cooks can make a lot more products than alchemists. It might not be as potent, but it can give a long-lasting buff, can be kept for a long time in a storage ring."

"Wouldn't work in the lower realms. The ingredients would be too expensive compared to the regular wage, and not everyone has storage rings to keep the meals ready," Lucinda said.

They talked among themselves, discussing the Sixth Realm, the other realms, and just general conversation.

"What's the plan, boss?" Storbon asked.

"Check out the Sixth Realm some more. We were stuck in that dungeon for so long dealing with that orc problem. The dungeons are the frontier for the academies. I want to learn more about the academies."

"Are you thinking of joining one?"

"Why would I want to do that?" Erik asked.

"Your teacher is a member of the Alchemist Association. If you were to join an academy, you'd get a lot of benefits...could increase your level faster."

"You've got to be wary, Storbon. These academies aren't like ours. If you join an academy, you're not just going to learn from them. You'll *be* one of them."

"Don't you have to leave the academy after a certain amount of time or pay a lot to remain in it?"

"Yes, but once you leave that academy, you'll need a job, something that requires your skills. Academies make deals with powerful sects and groups in the higher realms. Say you want to be part of Sect A, then you need to go to Academy One. Sect A only hires people from Academy One."

"So, the academies train up people and then feed them into various sects?"

"Yup. Rugrat's analogy was pretty accurate. Based on which academy one goes to, it decides which sect they will work in for the rest of their lives."

"What about the associations?"

"The associations are their own thing, and they have their own academies; they don't even try to hide their intentions. They recruit some people from the lower realms. In the Sixth Realm, it all changes. They recruit the strongest fighters from the Fourth Realm. They pluck the people with the greatest potential in the Fifth Realm. Groom them in the Sixth and Seventh Realms. Beyond that, I don't know what happens." Erik drank from his cup.

"There must be millions of people in the Sky Realm, not even mentioning the Celestial and Divine Realms beyond."

"And few, if any, come down."

They sat in silence, nursing their drinks.

"So, joining an academy binds you to that academy and their allies."

"Pretty much."

Storbon sat up. "Boss, I don't mean anything by this, but you and Rugrat always make it seem as if you're weak and powerless. I've seen you train and fight. You're strong. Sure, in actual combat, you use techniques or spells, relying on your rifle or on the spell scrolls. You taught us to use our consumables first. Mana, Stamina. Once it is spent, it is much harder to get back than ripping a spell scroll or reloading your rifle."

"Well, yeah, if you use all your mana and Stamina, you're going to feel like a bag of shit. Once you consume that, your overall combat power plummets. With the weak thing..." Erik pinched his brows together.

"I didn't mean anything by it," Storbon said again.

"I'm not angry, just thinking. If I got pissed off at every little comment of me fucking up, I'd never had made it into the army. Certainly wouldn't have survived getting attached to a Marine Force Recon Company." Erik showed a glimmer of a smile before he sighed. "There is always someone stronger. I heard someone say this: 'What is your maximum weight, someone else is just warming up with.' It has to do with exercise; whatever is the most you can lift, someone else can do it with ease. Might be because we're competitive motherfuckers, always looking for that edge, for more strength. Other part is, well, it keeps you humble. You think you're the strongest, the best that there ever is or was?" Erik rolled his eyes. "Couldn't get a head that big down the fucking street."

Storbon snorted.

"Screw the street. I just want a smithy to myself. Got a new plan," Rugrat said.

"Blind the local population with your 'smithing attire?'" Erik raised an eyebrow.

"Hey! Appreciation of the fine male form!"

Erik saw an approaching waitress laden with plates. Everyone started to clear the table to make way for the food.

"Beer! Oh, goddess of drink!" Rugrat said, relieving her of a pitcher of beer.

"It's not blue ribbon. Pass it over!" Erik argued.

As Rugrat tinkered in the smithies with Tian Cui and Storbon with him, Erik and the rest of the special team collected information on the Sixth Realm.

"Well, that sounds interesting." Erik pointed to a poster, and Lucinda took a closer look.

People in the lower realms could read, but most of their information came from criers reading out the latest announcements. In the Sixth Realm, filled with information and technique books, there was simply too much happening in the massive cities for a crier to tell everyone what was happening, so they only announced the most relevant information

Around the city, there were walls of information. Formations displayed illusions that updated with new information, a mix between television news and billboard advertisements thrown together in a hologram. Less gripping news was posted on the wall underneath.

"Great news!" a crier called out. "Young Master Wei has returned from his studies! At only twenty-two, he has become a low Expert tailor! Upon his return, he marched into the Taaj clan's headquarters. In the name of righting previous wrongs against his clan, he has challenged any of the Taaj clan's members five years older and younger than him! He will take them all on at once in a brilliant tailor competition! You can purchase your tickets at the Quansho arena!"

"What is the bet?" someone in the crowd asked.

"Young Master Wei has declared that he will reimburse the Taaj family four Sky mana stones if they are able to defeat him. If he is to defeat his peers of the Taaj clan, they must give up their tailor stores in the Taihe district!"

Gasps and exclamations went through the crowd.

"What do you think?" Lucinda whispered.

"The Ten Realms is not a peaceful place. The rule has always been that the strongest make the rules and take what they want. It seems that there is little fighting that goes on in the higher realms. Most turn toward crafting and cultivation to increase their levels instead of killing beasts. These competitions, it's how the Ten Realms remains stable."

"Maintain stability?"

"The academies, the sects—they don't want to lose people at this level. It takes a lot of investment to raise someone up to this level and more for them to maintain or progress further. Having them die, they'd only fight one another over a matter they couldn't let go."

"They want to milk their people for everything they can; they don't want them to die early. In the lower realms, they would be powerhouses. They're pillars for the academies and sects."

"Right. With the competitions based on any kind of skill, even crafting, it keeps the competitive state alive. Having massive arenas for others to come satisfies their vanity and allows them to show off their power," Erik said. "It stops the sects and academies from falling apart. Probably makes them stronger as well, though it has the same critical flaw as the rest of the Ten Realms."

"Wait, stops them from falling apart? What's their flaw? The sects and academies have stood for hundreds of years!"

"Just take a look at the Willful Institute. On the outside, it is a powerful sect, right?"

"Yeah."

"What about inside? Think of all the factions and clans that make up the sect. Competition, competition, competition!"

Lucinda frowned, confused.

"There is healthy competition, done for fun and to motivate people. Like how we had in the military. People mess with one another, but at the end of the day, they'd stand next to one another in a heartbeat and trust them completely. Then there is the other side of competition—a competition that is for face. Trying to make the other group lose something that is dear to them and embarrass them publicly. That kind of competition means that the strongest can only stand at the top. They need the power to suppress others and secure their position. It also means that while the people are suppressed and pressed together, there is friction. There are only so many resources, so many special techniques. Not everyone will get them. Large and small competitions lead to great feuds and issues. In the lower realms, sects regularly fall, not because of an external source, but because of internal strife. If there is not someone powerful enough to suppress all others, then the sect collapses as groups fight over everything, tearing the sect apart."

"I understand. These open competitions mean that there are less actions in the dark between groups. The competitions allow groups to suppress one another without causing massive disruption in a sect. The sect gains more stability, though they still lead to inner strife that mounts over time."

"Bingo. The groups are not united. They're competing for their own interests, under the banner of a larger group, something that we have been using to our advantage." Erik started to walk away, and Lucinda followed.

"Are you going to leave Alva?"

Erik faltered half a step. "Bit of a sudden question."

"You and Rugrat like exploring, and you've given other people power. Kind of feels like we're holding you back," Lucinda said, no judgment in her tone.

"Rugrat and I had a hole in the ground. It was the people from the original Alva and those who joined us later who transformed Alva, Vermire, and Vuzgal into what they are today."

They walked away from the poster-covered walls. The crier was talking about the latest competitions when the flashing formation switched to a new bulletin.

The crush of people thinned.

"Rugrat and I are not leaders. Sure, we can take a squad out, carry out a mission, and come back. That's easy. Manage a city? All the traders, the varied groups coming in? Manage a military? Run a school? The basics, we can pitch in and help. Alva isn't some new, meek, little existence anymore. There are teachers and other people better suited for those roles. Once the Willful Institute is dealt with—well, Rugrat and I are just two mercenaries given a second lease on life. There's so much to explore in the Ten Realms. Best to leave the running of Alva to Alvans. We'll be around to help if needed and to visit, but..." Erik raised a shoulder in a half-shrug.

"You want to go and see the Ten Realms. I get it," Lucinda said. "What about the leadership? You said it—in the Ten Realms, the strongest person is the leader. That's the case with you and Rugrat, if Delilah takes over for real."

"If someone attacked Delilah, what would you do?" Erik stopped and faced her.

"I'd protect her." Lucinda didn't need to think before answering.

"What if it was any other leader of Alva?"

"If they want to get to Delilah, or any Alvan, they'd have to go through me," Lucinda said.

"Alva needs the best leader, not the strongest bully, at its head. The army, the academies—all of it is so Alva can stand on its own two feet, so that no matter who or what might threaten it in the future, it won't be destroyed."

"Is that why we're still hiding?"

"Yes. The longer Alva can remain hidden—the more Experts it can train in crafting, in fighting—the larger its reach can become. Lord Aditya has the right idea with Vermire. Right now, we're burrowing so deeply into the infrastructure that is the Ten Realms that removing us would hurt much more than leaving us be."

"Has that been your goal this entire time?"

"Yes, so when the day comes that Alva is revealed, its foundations, its people are so solid that they can't be shaken by any sect, academy, or association."

"Thank you for being our lord," Lucinda said.

"Just doing a job." Erik smiled.

"You gave people a home, an education. I don't think it's just some job. Even if it is just a job, thank you for taking it on. You made something"—she searched for the words—"fucking awesome."

Erik laughed. "Fucking awesome, huh? I like it. Come on, let's go recon the Sixth. Or else Elan will have both our asses."

"You know, like good work on those agents, but hell if I could do it. Secrets, playing people, all that? Shit sounds tiring."

The two of them walked down the street, just two more people heading somewhere in the massive city.

Conqueror's Armor

Sergeant Bai Ping and his mage squad looked around the secret testing area. Bai Ping had fled to Vuzgal after his city was attacked—a victim of yet another war they hadn't been part of. He and several of his family members had joined the Vuzgal Defense Force looking to get stronger. Others had joined the administration, became traders, and assimilated into Vuzgal, which protected them. What had been a fresh start turned the low-powered Bai clan into a large clan in Vuzgal.

They had found a home for themselves and had expanded rapidly. Vuzgal was firmly against favoritism: If someone was unable to do the job, they would be dismissed. A few of his family members had tried to skirt these rules and found themselves banned from applying to administration jobs, both the person trying to get a job and the person trying to get past the rules to pull them into a position based on family instead of ability.

Bai Ping devoted himself to the defense force. He had made it through the ranks: from private—learning how to use a rifle and becoming an expert at using mortars—a mage, a medic, and an engineer. Then he was picked for a leadership course. He was already a corporal at that time. He had become a sergeant and started at the bottom all over again. He had just reached the position of mage sergeant when he and his squad was summoned to carry out a series of tests on new equipment.

He had studied in Kanesh and Vuzgal academies. He had opened his mana gates and formed his mana core, tempered his foundation, and reached Body Like Stone. He had served in the clearing of the Water floor.

Another group walked into the area: a sharpshooter squad.

Bai Ping grinned as he saw a familiar face in the lead. “Bolton, good to see you, man.”

“Basic training feels like years ago.” Bolton laughed as he shook Bai Ping’s hand.

“It was just over a year ago,” Bai Ping said.

“Looks like you took all the training you could. Beat me to mage squad sergeant,” Bolton said.

“It’s all a marathon. You know which position you want to settle into yet?”

“Nah, not yet. Still having fun doing different jobs. The time in between turnover is nice;lets me get to know my squad, get integrated, and then switch later on without too many issues,” Bolton said. “You ever think that we would be the ones teaching and training others?”

The two of them laughed and shook their heads. Bai Ping looked over to see the different squads greeting one another and talking amongst themselves.

The door to the secret training area opened again, and six people walked in.

“Atten-chun!” Bai Ping called out. Everyone snapped to attention, and he saluted Domonos and Glosil, who both marched over.

“As you were.” Glosil saluted. Tan Xue, Taran, Julilah, and Qin Silaz were with him. All of them were heavyweights and leaders in their respected fields, but they had all come for this test.

“Gather ’round,” Glosil said.

They created a half-circle, and Domonos cleared his throat.

"You are all here for the testing of the new prototype of Conqueror's Armor and the testing of the updated support formations. I'll let the crafters go over it." He turned to the side, letting Julilah and Qin step forward.

"The new support formations are rather simple. They are separate formation plates that can connect in different ways to the battlefield. Say you need more powerful shields, add in another shield formation. Healing in an area of effect, add in a healing array. Increased Strength or Agility, just a formation away. The formations are about the size of a dinner plate. There are two versions: One can be stacked together, reducing the overall area it covers and making it easier to transport, and the second is placed on the ground. It can create a larger effect and supply more power, but it has limited mobility," Julilah said.

"The Conqueror's Armor incorporates formation sockets and a linking ability. The formation plates need to be put together to act upon one another. This makes them easier to operate and means less to worry about on the battlefield. With the Conqueror's Armor, they focus on individual buffs, increased spell effect, decreased spell cost, and increased Agility or Strength. The buff is overall smaller than the formations Julilah mentioned. Though, with the linking ability, they can 'stack.' This means that if your squad is wearing linked armor, your buffs apply to one another. So, say originally you have a buff of increased Strength by one percent. If you have a squad of ten people and are all wearing that one percent Strength buff, then you all get a ten percent increase of Strength," Qin said.

Bai Ping frowned.

"Some of you might be wondering what will happen if there are a hundred people wearing the same armor in range of one another. Well, in that case, everyone will buff one another," Glosil said.

Bai Ping sent a look at Bolton. He had the same stunned look on his face.

Just how powerful would we be?

"The armor comes in a set with a chest plate, groin protector, as well as shoulder and upper arm protectors. Each piece will be at the Journeyman level. The breastplate will hold the linking formation socket. The arms and skirt, the little drop flaps that protect your sensitive parts, will each have a formation socket that you can change at will. That means one formation socket on your left arm, one on your right arm, and one on your skirt."

"The helmets will remain the same. Their formations are integrated to allow them to operate properly," Taran said.

"Upgrading the formations is just like your weapon formation sockets: Put in the updated formation, and you're good to go. To upgrade the armor, you just need to get new plates from the assembly line." Qin waved her hand, and a set of armor appeared on a mannequin.

It wore the same expressionless helmet, tan carrier, groin protector or skirt, and upper arm protectors. She pulled out another display that held the plates without the carriers.

The outside of the plates was plain metal, except for the formation sockets that were embedded into them.

"Please take a look," Qin said.

The group of VIPs stood back, and the two squads stepped forward.

"Smart. All the formations of the armor are done on the inside, so if it is hit from the front, it won't necessarily be messed up," Bai Ping said.

Bolton turned the formation socket and pulled it out. "All of the formation socket is contained in the lower few layers, and high-strength defensive plates are added to the front."

They went over the new armor. It wasn't that much more advanced than their current armor. The carrier, other than the collar, was the same as what they used already. In public, they used simple Apprentice armor to make people think that their gear's level was lower than it was.

"It might not be stronger than the armor we have right now, maybe even weaker because it doesn't have the reinforcing formations, but the way it's used…" Bolton shook his head.

"Smart, just smart, taking what we have already and giving it a much greater capability." Bai Ping held his chin and looked at the armor as their two squads studied it.

The VIPs walked back over.

"Questions?" Domonos asked.

"What is the range that we can link to other sets of armor?" one of Bai Ping's men asked.

"About forty to fifty meters, depending on terrain," Qin said.

"If you're underground, it will be cut down severely unless you're all in the same area," Julilah added.

"Though there are plans to seed Expert-level linking plates among the companies, not just with the leadership. Have a few sergeants, corporals, even privates with them; spread them out to make sure the network of armor is always linked," Glosil said. "Those command-level plates will link together with all sets of armor within a four-hundred-meter to five-hundred-meter radius. Meaning that *all* armor within that range will stack their buff on top of one another."

The men and women started to chat among themselves. Domonos cleared his throat, silencing the room once more.

Bolton raised his hand. "What about the slimmed-down versions of the armor, like what the special teams use? With just the short plates for the front and back as well as side panels? Why are we using this larger, clunkier set of armor?"

"This is a prototype. We are using old armor plates to test it out. It is our plan to use the new slim-design armor plates once we have a finished formation socket and formation design," Qin said.

Domonos looked around for more questions. Seeing none, he stepped forward. "Your squads' task is to test the hell out of this thing. I want to know its strengths, weaknesses, ways to use it, formation combinations you think are useful. How it operates with the area-of-effect formation systems. Based on the information you give us, it will allow us to develop these systems to be used by all of our forces."

Bai Ping, Bolton, and their people stood straighter. If the gear passed or failed and how it was utilized would be aided with their efforts. Their brothers and sisters would rely on this equipment; they had to make damn sure it was the best equipment they could use before it ever saw a battlefield.

8 Lord's Return

"All right, time to head back. It's been a good vacation," Erik said.

The rest of the special team grinned as Erik checked the screen in front of him.

Do you wish to travel to Vuzgal City Totem in the Fourth Realm? YES/NO

Erik hummed along to "Paradise City," making Rugrat join in.

A flash of light covered them, and they appeared within Vuzgal's totem defenses.

Erik pulled down the scarf around his face, looking up at the large tower in the distance. The police officers were handling the entrance into the city, and the army stood behind them, ready to support if needed.

Erik paid the entrance fee, and the group relaxed.

They passed through the toll stations and headed into Vuzgal. They changed disguises and walked into a bar. Erik flashed a medallion to the barkeep, and they were sent to one of the reserved rooms.

The door closed behind them before a clicking noise came from the round seats. They opened in the middle, revealing a set of stairs leading downward. Erik led the way, getting rid of his extra clothing and items. Tian Cui removed the disguising formation as they headed into the depths of Vuzgal.

"Nothing like being home and hiding in a basement," Yao Meng said.

"Good to be back. I wonder how the training went with the new special team members," Yuli said.

"You wonder what might happen to that Vinters guy?" Tian Cui asked.

"Nothing good, by the teacher's expression," Rugrat said.

They walked down through several layers, presenting their medallions to the different skeleton guards who protected Vuzgal's undercity.

A door opened before them, and they walked out onto an incline. From it, they could see men and women training, fighting one another in large training squares. In other places, there were workshops that never stopped working. Multi-story fields rested upon one another, growing all manner of food. Miners and machines were cutting into the rock.

It was a small underground city. Pillars supported the ceiling and Vuzgal that lay above. Glowing formations gathered and contained mana from across the city, funneling it toward a massive structure that reached from the ceiling to the floor. It was large and squat. Several other structures reached up to the ceiling as well.

"What are those?" Yao Meng asked.

"The large one in the distance is the under-castle. It is built right under the castle and pillar above. The smaller ones that look like fortresses are the underground facilities of the military. We can train down here so others won't learn our secrets," Rugrat said.

"Bigger than I thought it would be." Erik released Gilly and got on her back.

"Good to be back," Rugrat agreed.

"What do you think about that Lee Perrin?" Erik asked.

"Aussie for sure, though we're not the home for reclaimed Earthers. He's got his people. Seems nice enough, but don't need to recruit everyone." Rugrat shrugged.

They wandered down the incline and toward the underground section of the main castle, as people stared at them.

"We've only been gone a few months, and people have forgotten who we are already," Rugrat moaned.

"Who could forget you?" Elan said as he rode over on a purple-and-green-scaled beast that looked something like a reptilian ostrich.

Erik looked around his room, the sun coming in through windows that reached up to the ceiling. His bedroom was the size of most apartments back on Earth. Thankfully, the bed was normal-sized. He had pulled out gear, putting it to the side as he cleaned and worked on it. He had reloaded his magazines and organized his gear in his storage rings to be ready to fight at any time.

He studied his clothes. His brown shirt and gray pants showed a lot of wear and tear. They were Apprentice level, and with his movements in a fight—although his skin could take the rubbing and falling—his clothes were much weaker and fell apart faster.

He looked over to the academy housed in a portion of the Castle District. The district was truly massive. It fit the academy, the administration offices of Vuzgal, and two combat companies with plenty of room to spare.

His eyes moved to Vuzgal. It had grown again, rapidly increasing.

"Things keep changing around here. Looks like the retirement fund is doing good." Erik stretched and turned from his window, walking across his massive bedroom, and left his apartment to head for the heart of

Vuzgal—the administration offices.

Erik scratched his beard as he walked, staring at all the people moving from one place to the next. The frantic and panicked movements he had seen among the staff when Vuzgal had started to build out their administration were toned down. People knew what they were doing now; they had direction.

People glanced at him but kept on going, frowning at his unkempt hair and beard.

Erik grinned as he kept walking.

"Sir, do you have an appointment with someone?" a receptionist asked as Erik walked past her desk.

"Nope, just here to bug Hiao Xen." Erik smiled.

"Acting City Lord Hiao Xen is a busy man." The woman raised her voice. People looked over, and she looked down on Erik.

"Yeah, don't want him getting into trouble now."

The woman seemed confused as Erik continued walking and waved to her.

"S-stop! You can't go on!" the woman said.

Erik turned and glanced over to her, then at his storage rings. *I look like some pawnshop owner from New York* Erik searched through the storage rings as the woman marched around the desk and stood in front of him.

"If you want to make an appointment with Hiao Xen, you need to talk to one of us and we can talk to his assistant to book you in. He is a busy man, and his schedule is filled most days."

Erik kept rummaging. "One second." Erik kept looking.

"You—" The woman coughed but Erik didn't pay attention.

"If you continue to make a scene, I will have no choice but to ask you to leave."

"There it is." Erik held out a medallion.

The woman seemed to shake in anger as she glanced at the medallion and then *stared* at it. Her face changed to pure white. "T-this—"

"Don't worry, I know the layout," Erik said. "Good work. But sometimes you just need to give people some time to sort themselves out." He turned and walked past her.

The woman numbly walked back to her counter, and Erik heard her colleagues talking to her in hushed tones.

"What was that medallion? Why do you look so pale?"

"I-it was the city lord's medallion."

"He's a city lord? How can that be?"

Come on, the beard's a bit rough and the hair is long, but they're not that bad, right?

Erik pushed his hair into a better form as he walked through the halls. People continued to stare at him, their expressions turning into panic.

He reached Hiao Xen's reception.

"Hey, Dougie, how are things?" Erik walked up to the desk.

The young man looked more refined, his hands expertly moving over papers, highlighting things, and continuing on. His hands faltered as he looked up. His frown turned into confusion. "Erik?"

"Come on, the beard isn't that bad. Is he busy?" Erik asked, gesturing toward the door.

"Uh…" Dougie tilted his head to the side and shrugged.

"All right, I'll get a damn haircut." Erik rolled his eyes.

"He doesn't have any meetings for another two hours. He's all yours." Dougie tapped a button under his desk.

The door unlocked.

"Thanks, man." Erik pushed the door open and closed it behind him.

Hiao Xen looked up from his papers. "Erik?"

"It's just a beard. Is it so hard to figure out who I am?" Erik muttered and walked over to the desk that had expanded and was covered in all means of information books. Several enchanted pens wrote words on different pages as Hiao studied Erik and Erik studied him.

"How have you been?" Erik opened his arms.

Hiao Xen, smiling, stood and hugged him. "Busy, very busy, though your people are very good at their jobs." Hiao Xen released Erik and guided him to a set of couches.

"Which people?" Erik asked.

"Oh, the people from the Adventurer's Guild, Trader's Guild, military, police, academy, bank," Hiao Xen said.

Erik shrugged and sat down. Already some people saw the connection between the different guilds and departments of Vuzgal. It wasn't unusual for traders to work together and varied groups to form a deal. Everyone and every group had their secrets; it would be uncommon if they didn't.

The truth of Alva would come to the surface at some point. By then, hopefully, they would have enough strength to take charge of their own destiny instead of having someone lording over them and telling them what to do.

"Don't worry. Not many people have picked up on the different groups. They operate independently, after all, but they interact with one another as if they are united or connected by something. I can only see it from where I sit. I'm sure that the associations are starting to put things together, if they haven't already." Hiao Xen pulled out tea and two cups, serving Erik.

"What will the associations do, knowing that we work together?" Erik asked.

"The associations won't care. As I have said before, even if Vuzgal is attacked, unless they lose out on the deal with the new person moving in, they won't lift a finger. They are a neutral party in all this, though they record and take notes of everything." Hiao Xen passed the tea over to Erik.

"Thank you." Erik sniffed the tea then sipped on it.

Hiao Xen pulled out a letter and placed it on the table. It had a complicated stamp of what appeared to be wax sealing it shut. "This was left behind by someone from the Sha." Hiao Xen pushed the letter over.

Erik's motions stilled as he looked from the letter to Hiao Xen.

"It is safe, but I don't know what is written inside. A lady came to Vuzgal. She was here for a while, studying and learning, but she didn't cause any issues. There are many such people in Vuzgal. She came to the gates with a recommendation and a meeting made by the Blue Lotus. She introduced herself as a messenger from the Sha.

"I met with her, and she said her master is interested in Vuzgal and its people. It piqued his interest. She gave me this letter to pass onto the city lords. From what I can tell, her master is *the* Marshal."

Erik set down his tea and picked up the letter. He stared at the fleur-de-lis seal, took out a knife, and opened the letter. He read it.

"Complete this test, and I will debate if we can work together. Bring me a sample of your gunpowder."

Erik read the few lines again.

Quest: The Marshal

The Marshal, leader of the Sha clans, has extended an invitation to you.

Requirements:

Reach level 60 and ascend to the Seventh Realm

Head to the Sha clan headquarters

Provide a sample of Gunpowder

Rewards:

750,000 EXP

It sounded simple, and it was. But to know what gunpowder was, they had to be from Earth, and the Sha was testing him to see if he was as well. They also knew about his weapons being related to theirs. If he brought them gunpowder, what did they want with it? Did they want them to make more of it? Did they want to take it for themselves? They had only sent one person with the message, but there must be others in the shadows, watching. Whoever met him would have to be at least level sixty. Then there was the fleur-de-lis, which was a French symbol. He would have to check, but he didn't think it was a common symbol in the Ten Realms.

Erik put the letter in his storage ring, a complicated expression on his face.

"Something wrong?" Hiao Xen asked.

"Just confused by what I read. If I think about it too much, it'll become more complicated. Best that I keep it in mind, but no need to worry about it now. Got enough to do," Erik said.

Hiao Xen nodded and didn't pry any further. "You seem to have advanced again. Your rate of improvement puts me to shame!"

"Fighting allows one to advance faster, but it is not an easy path." Erik drank from his tea.

"No, it is not, and I like the world of business and management. Are you interested to hear of the changes that have occurred since you have been gone?"

Erik leaned forward. "Might as well get into it."

Hiao Xen cleared his throat and told Erik about everything that had happened in Vuzgal in the last few months.

9 Alva Production

"So, what are you all doing in Vuzgal? Shouldn't you be down in Alva?" Rugrat asked Taran, Tan Xue, Julilah, and Qin.

"We're all working on a new project together: the Conqueror's Armor," Tan Xue said.

"Conqueror's Armor?"

Taran quickly explained.

"We're working on the stacking arrays too," Qin added.

"With those kinds of buffs, with all our forces working together, we can increase the range; that will be some scary buffs," Rugrat said. "Good work!"

"We are running into a problem, though. There are fewer people who want to work on Journeyman-level gear. Everyone wants to work on higher-level gear, so they can get Experience and increase their skill level," Taran complained.

"I know that only too well," Rugrat said.

"What happened?" Tan Xue asked.

"Expert-level smith. I just can't get there," Rugrat admitted.

"It can take a lot of time," Taran comforted him.

"Reaching the Expert level in crafting is no longer about copying what others have done before but doing your own thing. Creating your own path. I thought about making something similar to a railgun, but it just melts apart," Rugrat said. "But enough about me. This project of yours sounds interesting. We need more people to help out. I can lend a hand if you need it."

"You're diverting. This isn't some small problem you've run into; it's something that is messing with you and annoying you," Tan Xue said.

"Well, worrying about it is not going to make me an Expert." Heat entered Rugrat's voice.

"I'm not saying that." Tan Xue gave him a hard look.

"Sorry. Just frustrated, you know?"

"We've all been there, lad." Taran patted his shoulder.

"So, these new sets of armor and formations—how are you producing them?"

"We're creating two new modified manufacturing lines in the weapons factories. We are already producing more armor plates than we have soldiers who require them. The spare plates are used to test out our new production line. Creating those factory lines bends the damn mind," Qin said.

"Once we have the lines modified, we can create as many sets of armor and formation plates as we need," Julilah said.

"Gets us all back to working on our own crafts," Tan Xue said.

Rugrat held his chin, frowning and biting his lip. "Something has been annoying me for a long time. Why don't other people set up assembly lines? Most crafters just do enough items to increase their abilities and increase their skill, grinding out weapons to get higher."

"Creating the first piece of armor, creating the factory line—it takes a lot of time. You get the most amount of Experience making it the first time, and it decreases as you progress. That's why weapons are rated by the rank of the forger: The higher their level and the level of ability they use on the item, the higher the item's power. Copying other's designs teaches us the basics. Producing our genuinely own items, we have a greater growth that can change how we do everything," Taran said.

"Factories aren't used in the realms. Say a sect is producing a sword. They have all their students making the same sword; some are bound to come up with modifications and updates. The sect will always have that sword and different deviations of it. Their factories are their students. As their students increase in power, it gives rise to the entire sect, as they have a stronger person who can assist the sect, gaining access to more resources and channels that would have been closed to them before," Tan Xue said.

"The main reason we use factories is due to the low numbers we had previously and our requirements to create massive numbers of equipment. Our population is exploding, and people are coming up with new ideas and plans all the time, which is developing Alva at an incredible rate!" Qin said.

"How many of those ideas were mass-produced?" Rugrat asked.

"They are mass-produced if the traders see a demand for it in the market and the crafters of the schools are unable to fulfill them. The cost to have people take time off school and their craft to build factory equipment is high. People say that the best time for one to develop is while they are young, so plenty of people look to push themselves up the ranks of crafting and reach their peak before settling down," Qin said.

"That's fucking stupid." Rugrat blinked, and the others gave him bizarre looks. "Come on! Does that mean people over a certain age are already declining, that there is no way for them to push on? Like, think about that. I started smithing in my thirties. I am now thirty-four and have more ideas than ever before. Maybe in sects and places where there is a limited education, that might be a thing. If you are told 'follow this path; this is the only path, and you will reach a great height,' most will follow that. We don't have a path, so we're always creating new ones. There is no one way to the higher realms or to higher crafting."

Rugrat shook his head. "With that system, people have determination, they have willpower, but it doesn't matter. If you go up a steep incline and every hundred meters, a hundred pounds is added to your back and you can only take that one route, you will fail eventually. Some sects might give you better paths where the incline or the weight is lower, but they will still fail. We just point to the mountain and say pick your gear, adjust your weight. Don't blindly run up the hill; take your time. As people learn, that weight lessens, the incline gets a little less steep. It might be slower, but they can get much higher than the person taking the steep incline."

Everyone fell quiet.

Rugrat laughed to himself. "Hell, who knows. We might meet one another along the path and teach each other different paths one can take. In the Ten Realms, the apex is reaching the Star system of crafting. Does it really matter, though? If you can make one person a powerful shield, can they defend everyone? Aren't they carrying so much weight that they might crumble under it? No, that's ridiculous and dumb." Rugrat's eyes opened wide. A fire seemed to have ignited inside them and burned brighter.

"What if we are not looking to get to higher mountains? The academies teach people according to different levels, teach them the basics and more complicated information. Now they're told copy this, do that, and it creates this. Well, some people can do that, and some can only go so far. Others thrive under greater pressures. They thrive when they find an answer to a question that might not have been asked." Rugrat snapped his fingers.

"The Ten Realms puts progress above all, that you should constantly try to make things at a higher crafting level. You could, but that doesn't mean that a Journeyman- or Apprentice-level item is useless. Really there are a lot of Novice and Apprentice items, like our heating and water treatment systems that can have a massive effect," Qin said.

Rugrat turned to her and saw that she had a troubled look on her face.

Taran played with his cup. "This glass is of the Apprentice level. We're in the Fourth Realm with a massive amount of resources, but the glass, plate, cutlery—all of them—had to be made by crafters. It doesn't make sense to create Expert-level glasses, knives, and forks. Not many people take up those crafts because they do not progress much further than the Journeyman level; there is no demand."

"Though take the glass. We can use it for weapon sights, can use it to focus light. We could create screens that relay information, insulate doors and houses. Could use it to create telescopes to stare at the stars or microscopes to look at samples," Rugrat said.

"We can use a formation to create a weapon sight, though?" Julilah said.

"What if we had the glass magnifying what is in front of us and then had a formation to increase that zoom or to create a second mode that allows us to see mana life or heat signatures? Then it would be a Journeyman-level piece of equipment instead of an Expert-level piece of equipment. Also, if the formation ran out of power, the aiming sight would work no matter what."

"What are you thinking, Rugrat?" Tan Xue asked.

"Instead of crafting mountains, we have questions, ideas, problems, let's say. A rolling problem would be how we can increase the effectiveness of our military. There are many problems there: We have armor, clothing, food, training, weapons, and more. Through *all* those efforts together, you can create a trained soldier. Qin, Julilah—you're on the right path, using all the strengths and abilities you and Alva have to push forward. It's brilliant! You took different problems or ideas and created solutions that work and can work together, not just increasing their effectiveness, like one plus one equals two, but multiplying the effectiveness of both systems together to create ten or twenty times increase in power. The people of Alva are great and smart, and the limitations of the crafting system are dumb. Crafters can increase the power of some people, but inventors—what they can come up with can greatly affect the entire world."

Rugrat sat back in his seat, as if the air had fled his lungs.

"Crafts other than smithing and formations aren't really used together. There are few benefits for them to do so, other than creating items for one another. That cross-pollination of ideas—just what could happen?" Rugrat seemed to be breathless. The fire in his eyes had turned into a raging storm; his eyes flickered back and forth, looking at things to improve, ways to push forward, anything and everything that could be advanced.

"That is a good idea, but will crafters go for it? Won't it hurt their own progression?" Tan Xue said.

"Contracts and patents. Someone comes up with an idea and produces it. For ten years, it is their idea and they can create as many as they want of the item. Every subsequent item that they create is also covered under a ten-year patent. Now, they can hold on to that patent or they can produce it, get a factory to make the item, then traders sell it. The crafter earns a percentage of the product's value. They work on their different ideas, and the item passively brings in income."

"Though our ranks might drop," Julilah said.

"The crafting levels only matter for Experience. They don't necessarily mean people can earn more money. Crafters are some of the people with the greatest debt. If you could figure out how to pay your way out of that debt *and* create your own private workshop and unlimited materials, do whatever you wanted? I think we might need to revise the whole ranking system in the schools. Right now, it is based on the skill level the Ten Realms says that you have."

"What about a whole new department to deal with it? With teachers who know what the hell they're talking about and have created practical products? Hah, we should call it the applied sciences, taking the knowledge from the academics and turning it into real-world solutions," Rugrat said.

They all fell silent around the table.

"It could create instability within the academies and drop the ranks of people, as Julilah said," Tan Xue said.

"Yup, it could," Rugrat agreed.

"How could we mark the people who are in the academies for these projects?" Qin asked.

"They would have their own academic projects. If they create something within that time that is their own creation, then why the hell not?" Rugrat said.

"Use the academies to teach them, create their foundations, and leave them the freedom to create their own applications for what they have been taught," Taran said.

"Is anyone going to want to do it, though? People might feel that they are wasting their life away. Trying to make products and not increasing their skill level," Julilah warned.

"Not everything succeeds; we all know it. Although they might only create products at the Apprentice level, they could have the knowledge of an Expert. That is how one's skill level doesn't relate to their potential or true ability."

"If we can get more factories going, we could have crafters focusing on building the prototypes and an influx of factory jobs to take the original design and mass-produce it. Then we don't have to fear that a crafter will find something new to work on and never make that item again. As they create new items, we can have others reproduce their original creation. Where are we going to find people to do that?" Taran asked.

"You're thinking inside the box. The crafters don't need to. The traders can build the factories and pay the crafters to create the items and assembly lines. Also, there are crafters who like building but might not like inventing. There are all kinds of people and personalities. Again, working with others with different mindsets and skillsets," Rugrat said.

"They already look for solutions among what the crafters create, but few are willing to work with them and instead wanting to push ahead more," Qin said. "But won't it decrease the competition within the crafting departments?"

Rugrat bit his lip.

"The trade is if we want people to increase their crafting ability or to focus on inventing new things to increase our overall strength," Taran said.

"Does it have to be a choice? Can't we do both? You know, give incentives for people who are looking to do different jobs?" Rugrat asked.

"If we need something, we could have people bid on it with gear they have created," Qin said. "It would create competition between the crafters, like how traders will have auctions to create competition between the buyers."

"The person with the best item for the job wins." Julilah nodded.

"It might be like a spoon: The person who can make it the cheapest and in the largest quantities will win over the person who can make the most finely handcrafted one," Rugrat said.

"It will make it so that crafters and traders need to work together to make it viable, and if they want to make more profit, then they need to know other markets or people to sell it to," Qin said. "Teams of traders could go to crafters and pay them to create something for them. Or crafters could go to traders before creating something to get the traders to back them."

"I forget that your dad was the head of a massive trading company," Tan Xue said.

"You know what, there are some people who are more inclined to create functional machines over just increase their crafting. Also, there are crafters who have reached a certain stage and are unable to progress further. If they can create factories and know how to adapt the items created by the academics into applications..." Taran shook his head. "I think creating a system that is based on their inventions instead of their skill level is flawed."

"Taran—" Rugrat started.

"Hear me out. I don't think that people shouldn't create useful items. I just think that it could create a mess in the academies. People can create all kinds of items. Some will hit the market well, and others will flop. Crafters create things. Some might have a sense of the market and people's needs; others might not have a clue. The academies should remain a place where people go to learn and increase their overall crafting ability, to study and grow their knowledge. If someone wants to take their time and turn it toward creating new items, they are free to do so. If they can do it at the same time they study, great. If they can't do it while they're studying, we have four semesters a year. At the end of a semester, people can put their education on hold. This is already a thing. They can do whatever they want, and next year or even decades later, they can go back to the academy to take dedicated classes."

"Keep them separate. An academic route and an applied route. They can influence one another, but the academy only offers one service, and then another department offers contracts for crafters to bid on?" Tan Xue asked.

"Exactly. If we try to do too much, it will adversely affect both systems." Taran nodded.

"Do you think that will be enough incentive?" Rugrat asked.

"Able to do something for their fellow Alvans, work on their own projects and ideas, and can earn a large sum of money out of it? Yeah, I think that by itself will be enough for many people. Remember, for every Expert crafter we have, we have nearly two hundred Journeyman crafters, and that ratio only increases. There are crafters who have turned their hands away from the academy and are pursuing their own knowledge and looking to pay back their loans. This gives them a clear route. Creating the factories and how things will operate together is their own puzzle. I can think of some crafters who would be interested in it," Tan Xue said.

"What if the rate we create Experts decreases?" Julilah asked.

"That is for other groups and people to talk and worry about." Taran snorted. "What does it matter how many high-level crafters we have if we can have five Journeyman-level crafters, let's say, creating a Master-level piece of equipment?"

They all sunk into their own thoughts. The fire in Rugrat's eyes had dimmed, but with their discussion, they had a starting point.

"Well, then, do skill levels really matter?" Julilah asked.

No one answered right away, trying to form answers.

"The system benefits crafters who work alone or in limited partnerships. It is like medieval industry." Rugrat saw the confused looks and cleared his throat. "In ancient times, there were people called artisans. They were like crafters. They would learn certain crafts and train others to complete them. Due to a lack of resources and the power structure at the time, with kingdoms, the people at the top could purchase crafted items, though many couldn't. There were knights, people who had complete armor. Compared to normal people, they were unkillable and highly trained. With that system, some people could wield power much greater than others and gain greater benefits. Later on, systems changed and spread power to others. People could rise and fall easily, but there were more people rising, and most people had more power than they thought. Instead of making finely crafted weapons and armor, rifles and firearms were created. The lowest of the low could use a firearm and kill someone who had been trained for decades," Rugrat said.

"So, we are the people with the lowest power but the best weapons?" Qin said.

"Using technology to make up for the gap." Rugrat nodded.

"You're forgetting something," Taran said in a low, serious voice. His eyes fell on Rugrat. "The way that people from Alva freely share information with one another. Crafters normally work in isolation and want to hide their techniques but show off their wares, but people who tell others their groundbreaking theories and show their data and proofs will gain greater praise. I still think that academics should be broken up, but maybe we should relax some of the rules so people can go and check out higher level classes?"

"We should take it to Jia Feng first and have Elise and the treasury weigh in on it. They'll each have their own perspectives and ideas," Tan Xue said.

"More meetings. Love it," Rugrat said.

The others smiled and laughed. There was a knock at the door.

"Come in!" Rugrat yelled with the others.

The doors opened, and the waiting staff brought in the food they had prepared. The aromas made the chopsticks shake in their hands in hunger.

Rugrat looked out over Vuzgal. Even now, late at night, the Sky Reaching Restaurants glowed and the Battle Arena was lit up. The totem continued to flash as people arrived and departed. The crafting district never stopped or rested; the gates out to the dungeons had foot traffic even at this time.

Vuzgal had turned into a city that never slept as people worked at all hours.

"Dig in!" Taran said as the staff finished laying out all the food. They set upon the table, their chopsticks fighting for food. Their fine hand control turned it into a true battle as the staff looked on in shock. They quietly left and closed the door.

Rugrat drank his beer as he competed with Julilah, finally getting the gyoza before he tossed it back into his mouth. Julilah pouted and captured two pieces of thinly cut meat before anyone could defend against her attack.

They all grinned, eating their food, and then charged back into the battlefield that was the table, using all their eye-hand coordination skills to try to steal the food from one another.

Applying Pressure and Incentives

The brightness of the totem teleportation faded as Erik and Rugrat looked around.

"Seems bigger now." Erik whistled.

Quest Completed: Dungeon Master

You have returned your dungeon to its former glory. Advancement quests are unlocked. Grow your dungeon's power!

Requirements:

Increase your dungeon core's grade to Sky Common

Increase the Strength of your minions (Complete)

Rewards

40,000,000 EXP

Dungeon Master Title IV

Quest: Dungeon Master

You have returned your dungeon to its former glory. Advancement quests are unlocked. Grow your dungeon's power!

Requirements:

Increase your dungeon core's grade to Sky Grand

Rewards

60,000,000 EXP

Dungeon Master Title V

Title: Dungeon Master IV

Control over the Dungeon building interface

Grade: Sky Common grade (Can be upgraded)

Ability: Dungeon Sense, 100 km radius (Can be used 6 times a day)

Increase all stats by +1

Able to bestow title Dungeon Hunter (8/13 remaining)

Can create Dungeon Master (Costs 5 Dungeon Hunter spots)

Dungeon Overlord mode. Consume the power of the dungeon. As the power consumes you, you will be unable to unleash immense power.

81,209,360/108,500,000 EXP till you reach Level 61

"You were saying?" Rugrat said.

"They expanded the floor again to accommodate more people. The Alchemy garden has taken over what was most of the fields, which moved down into the Earth floor. They now supply food for most of the Beast Mountain Range, all of Alva, Vuzgal, and our network of Sky Reaching Restaurants," Erik said as a streak shot toward them.

"Egbert!" Rugrat yelled as the streak dodged around him and appeared in front of Erik.

"Seems you're excited." Erik laughed as he pulled out two large crates from his storage ring.

The flames in Egbert's eyes danced, and he stared at the crates as if they were filled with the most precious materials.

"Romances from the Sixth Realm," he said breathlessly before the crates disappeared, and he cradled his hand.

He turned, but Erik's hand was on his shoulder.

"Before you disappear, status of the dungeon?"

"Construction on the Water level should take five or six months. We have a lot of projects going on. The residential floor is expanding once again. With the dungeon cores, I was able to create new training areas. There is the military training area. It has a horde training area where endless waves of monsters will attack people as they protect a position. If the pillar is broken, then they lose and are teleported out. If they break their medallion, then they exit. Then there is a small-level dungeon. The monsters and walls change. It is up to the team to clear through the dungeon however they desire. Then there is a large-scale dungeon that is still being worked on. In it, there is a forest, and the forces inside must create a base and hold the position against beast hordes. All are being expanded, and all give out dungeon points. These can be redeemed at the end of training from one of the dungeon point kiosks. The crafting dungeon is the same size as the crafter dungeon in Vuzgal. I have been feeding pure mana into all of these dungeons to increase the speed in which they expand."

"The Beast Mountain trial?"

"It is complete and will start in two months. People will no longer face the beasts from within Alva's dungeon. I am using the same testing areas from before, so people will need to fight in different environments. Then there are different tests to see one's character. Illusion spells will bring out their inner demons and reveal who they truly are."

"Where are these all positioned?" Rugrat asked.

"Well, Alva's current area of control has greatly expanded. Using the teleportation array, these dungeons are seeded throughout the Beast Mountain Range. All of them are deep so that no one will find them unless they dig for months. And there are formations to sense around the dungeons. It has effectively increased how much we can see in the Beast Mountain Range at any given time," Egbert said.

"Good work. Have Elan meet us in the dungeon headquarters," Erik said.

"Can do!" Egbert freed himself and turned into a flying streak again.

"You know you can go to the barracks and relax?" Erik said to Storbon and his special team without moving.

"The job isn't done until someone else gets here to make sure you two don't get into trouble," Storbon said.

"I thought we were respected dungeon lords or city lords?" Rugrat complained.

The members of Special Team One kept scanning the area.

"Headquarters?" Storbon asked.

"Lead the way. I know you won't let me," Erik said.

"I wonder if this is how people felt when we were protecting them," Rugrat asked.

"Probably, though we also know how freaking annoying the package could be if they started to get their own plans and do their own thing," Erik said.

"Yeah, nice and slow, take your time, better to get there than end up dead," Rugrat agreed.

"You're always the happiest little rays of sunshine, aren't you?" Yuli asked.

"I think if they were laughing and joking all the time, then someone is seriously screwed," Yao Meng chipped in.

"Maybe they're just sadists?" Tian Cui asked.

"Hey!" Rugrat finally got out.

"Sadists—where did that come from?" Erik asked as they left the totem and its defenses and headed toward the center of the floor.

"Well, you trained us, and I've seen how you train," Tian Cui said.

"Masochist is what you're thinking about when they're training themselves. Thrive off pain," Storbon said.

"Tough crowd," Rugrat muttered. "Erik is the one who likes breaking his bones; I just take the pills!"

"And you burst your mana channels when training, and now you train harder than before. You reached, what, the Mist Mana Core stage, and you're waiting for the impetus to form your Liquid Mana Core?" Lucinda said.

"She knows too much!" Rugrat said in a hurried whisper.

The others laughed. The tension from the last half-year started to drain away.

They had become closer in that time. They had gone out as polished blades and come back as if they were blood-covered blades hidden in a sheath. They hid their killing intent and their power incredibly well. All their fighting techniques had been modified and altered to increase their lethality.

They reached the dungeon headquarters. The guards saluted them as they passed. People stopped what they were doing, and a nervous-looking assistant led them forward.

"Is she in?" Erik asked as they passed the door to the council leader's office.

"She should be." The assistant stared at Delilah's assistant.

"She's in. Would you like for me to announce you?"

"Does she know that I'm in the dungeon?"

"No. She only knows that you have returned to Vuzgal."

"What's the use of being a dungeon lord if you can't bug your student?" Rugrat asked.

Erik laughed and walked over to the door.

The assistant unlocked the door. He opened it, finding Delilah rubbing her eyes.

"Have you been reading books all night again?" Erik said in a chastising voice.

"No, I mean yes, uh, Teacher?" Delilah nearly jumped out of her desk, taken back to when the two of them had worked together for several months—her learning the art of Alchemy, while he tested out his theories and ideas.

Her tired brain snapped together.

"Teacher!" Her face nearly split with her smile as she ran over and hugged Erik.

He took the impact, smiling as he hugged her back.

They hugged for a few moments before pulling apart.

"So, just how strong have you gotten now?" Erik smiled.

"I am still in the early stages of Expert in Alchemy. There has been a lot to do, and each level is hard to gain," Delilah complained, and then her eyes darted back to Erik. "Did you...you made it into the Expert level of healing?"

Erik nodded. "I made it into the Expert level. I'll be chasing after you now!"

Delilah smiled and then seemed to remember something. "Oh, Grand Teacher has gone to the Seventh Realm. He reached the level of Master, and the Alchemist Association has made him a professor. He gave me these to pass onto you and Rugrat." Delilah pulled out the Master-level pills and a letter.

"I feel that the second wasn't meant for Rugrat," Erik said dryly, seeing through her.

"Well, you two are in the most danger. I have plenty of resources, and I am in the safety of Alva. You two are out there fighting, so..." Delilah shrugged and pressed it all into his hands.

"The letter tells where he will be and how to reach him. The Master-level pills can be ingested and will rest in your bones until you are gravely wounded. Then they will allow you to recover enough to run away and increase your power."

Erik stored them away. "I always knew he would achieve his dreams with the Alchemist Association." Erik smiled, thinking of the time he and Old Hei had spent days working on their Alchemy skills with Old Hei pouring out his knowledge. The two of them had become closer than blood relations.

"I have a meeting with Elan shortly, but are you free for lunch or dinner?"

"I'm free for dinner—over at my parents', if you're interested. Bring Rugrat too."

"Yes! Free food!" Rugrat said from the doorway, having arrived unannounced.

Erik shook his head as Delilah laughed and hugged Rugrat.

Seeing her doing so well made him proud—and think of himself as some kind of uncle.

"All right, off you two go. You'll mess around here and distract everyone otherwise!" She shooed them forward. People who hadn't seen the lords or the council leader interact before were surprised as she organized them and got them moving.

It reminded him of some officers he had met when he first joined. He had always thought they were hard-asses when they were training or in the field. It was only later that he discovered that everyone had their own personal life, and what they were like at work might be completely different from how they were at home. A hard-ass commander on the battlefield and a loving husband and father when at home.

Erik and Rugrat bid their goodbyes and headed off to the conference room like two good dungeon lords.

"It's kind of weird, our position in all of this," Rugrat said.

"What do you mean?"

"You know, like the lord bit. Like we found these places and started things, and now everything can run without us."

"And we wander off to other realms and come back, and people still defer to us," Erik said.

"Yeah, feels weird." Rugrat stared at Erik, his brows pinched together.

"I think that is our upbringing. In the United States, our leaders changed all the time. The person at the top here isn't always changing. It is kind of like the royalty in the UK, where someone holds the highest position and then there are people who come in underneath them. The difference is that while most royalty on Earth are just figureheads, royalty is real in the Ten Realms. The leaders tell everyone the direction they want to go; they are the guiding light, and the people under them need to create and walk the path the royals have set."

"Don't really want to be like royalty," Rugrat said.

"Yeah, me either. But at this point, we have our fingers into so much of Vuzgal, Alva, and the rest that we basically own eighty percent of everything. Look at it this way: We created the system, and now we're the guardians of it. We hope people will do better because of what we've done. We give people information and see what path they can come up with. We can use what we know and have seen in other places to create a path for others. It is weird because we're not used to it, but do we have another choice? If we change things, we might feel better, but it could destabilize everything," Erik said.

Rugrat exhaled. "Yeah, it just feels weird, you know?"

"Yeah, I get that. It works, so why mess with it?" Erik shrugged.

Tian Cui opened the door to the meeting room. She swept the room with her eyes before she gestured it was clear.

They walked into the room, finding Elan waiting. Beside him were two women and two men. They looked like plain and simple people, which made Erik raise his guard.

Elan's spies.

Elan rose with his people, they bowed deeply, cupping their fists.

"Lords," Elan said.

"Come on, Elan. You know we're not bowing kind of people," Erik said.

Yuli closed the door. She and Yao Meng took up guard outside while Lucinda, Tian Cui, and Storbon moved to seats along the wall.

These people might be heavyweights in information-gathering circles, but they were nervous meeting their true masters.

"Qin and Domonos send their love. The two of them are working like crazy. I met up with Qin and Julilah in Vuzgal. They had classes to teach, but they'll be back down soon to complete work on the armor," Rugrat said.

"Armor?" Erik asked.

"Conqueror's Armor. Don't worry. There's a demonstration this afternoon; I'll take you."

"More things to do. All right, Elan, how are things shaping up?" Erik asked as he and Rugrat grabbed seats.

Elan and his group dropped into their seats as well.

"This is Miss Evernight, who you've met before. She is my agent on the ground dealing with the Beast Mountain Range and all things in the First Realm. This is Mister Liu. He deals with the Second Realm. Mister Yi operates in the Third Realm, and Miss Wen deals with the Fourth Realm." Elan indicated to the people in the room. "I am operating agents in the Fourth Realm, and I will be setting up new departments for the Fifth, Sixth, and Seventh Realms. We have people operating in just the Fifth and Sixth at this time."

Erik nodded to Elan and examined the others once again. On the outside, they looked like simple, easygoing, low-level folk. If they were running the agents and operations across an entire realm, they were anything but simple.

"It is good to meet you all. Shall we go over what is happening in each realm?" Erik asked.

Evernight looked up. Both Erik and Rugrat had beards; they wore simple pants and shirts identical to the rest of the Alvan army. On their arms, Erik wore a patch that marked him as part of the special teams. Rugrat wore the same.

As someone completed a new course, they were re-badged with their new qualification. Now that training had been going on for so long and constantly refined, people had to go through the training step by step and couldn't jump ahead based on open slots in different advanced courses.

She had seen them briefly once before when they had appeared in front of Aditya. Erik had healed the man's leg. Aditya had known he was talking to people higher up in Evernight's organization, but he hadn't known he was dealing with one of the *leaders*.

The two men were relaxed and laid-back. Their beards softened their appearance, but there was a predatory look in their eyes as they assessed the people in the room. Evernight had seen enough mercenaries and fighters in her life to feel the chill on the back of her neck, and her back straightened. These were wolves.

The air in the room seemed to come to a standstill, falling under their control. They smiled, dispersing some of the tension.

Elan introduced them all, while Erik and Rugrat sat down.

If Evernight didn't know who they were, she wouldn't have noticed the small changes that hinted at their hidden power; she would have forgotten they were in the room as the briefing started.

She talked by rote response, her attention remaining on the two men at the end of the table.

Rugrat rubbed his tattoos while Erik scratched his beard. Their eyes flickered as they absorbed everything. Although they looked lazy and uncaring, nothing made it past them. Rugrat was working on a blueprint while he listened. Erik wrote out alchemical formulas and studied the diagrams of different beasts' biological structure.

The realms were not calm. In the First Realm, Lord Aditya was quickly turning the alliance of outposts into the Beast Mountain Range nation. King's Hill was rising to prominence. People were launching attacks from different kingdoms and groups. They were trying to undermine them, but it wasn't working out.

Alva operated in the dark, and the Beast Mountain Range nation operated in the light. With the Adventurer's Guild, Trader's Guild, and crafters, they were rapidly accelerating how fast the nation developed. The military and Adventurer's Guild trained up selected Experts, turning them into Alva's people, first and foremost.

The Beast Mountain Consortium was being organized and formed in secret. It would unify the outposts and create a central power that would be the spiritual backbone of the new nation.

Over time, the situation would stabilize.

In the Second Realm, the Adventurer's Guild and Trader's Guild forged new paths into different regions, one supporting the other as they expanded. Most of Alva's trade occurred in the Second Realm. The Willful Institute that could be found in the Second Realm was being systematically cut off from their allies; other kingdoms, sects, and groups that the Willful Institute had stepped on had been enabled and assisted. Using their informants, they had only exacerbated the tensions between the two groups, putting them at one another's throats.

The intelligence department, run by Elan, was the nerve of Alva, the council the brain, and in this operation, the Trader's Guild and Adventurer's Guild were the hands.

The Willful Institute focused on their old enemies as tensions flared and didn't pay attention to the small "mice" that were slowly destroying their supports.

The same thing was happening in the Third Realm. Hundreds of Alvans were of the Alchemist Association. Sky Reaching Restaurants were located in every Division Headquarters and proliferated throughout the Regional Headquarters, creating bases for Alva in each city. Some were only manned with members from Alva, and the rest hired externally. Using the restaurants and a few Wayside Inns, traders and adventurers blossomed. The First Realm was their headquarters, but the Fourth Realm was where they had the greatest strength.

The Blue Lotus's endorsement of Vuzgal meant that although many sects coveted the city, few were willing to act on their desires. Pissing off them and the Alchemist Association didn't seem like a wise choice. The Fighter's and Crafter's Associations had also come over to their side. If someone wanted to take the city, they would have to offer incredible terms to the associations.

"The noose has fallen around the Willful Institute and is tightening as we remove their resources and motivate other groups to act against them," Elan said.

Evernight thought how they had infiltrated the nations and groups in the First Realm was advanced, but it was nothing compared to what was happening to the Willful Institute. The lower nations should be happy they didn't have any designs on them and only cared about the Beast Mountain Range.

"When will it all kick off?" Erik asked.

Rugrat looked up from his tattoos, his eyes cold as the sense of ease evaporated around him.

"That depends. It will take a spark. There are two things that might happen: Others start a fight with them or we start the fight," Elan said.

"What about the nations in the First Realm?" Rugrat asked.

Elan glanced at Evernight.

"They sent out groups of fighters and assassins to attack traders moving through the Beast Mountain Range," she said. "The military is growing in strength. With their training in Alva, they can reach the level of adventurers who live in the Third Realm. Those with potential have the option to be directly recruited into the Alva army."

"That would be a good way for them to have some Experience. We should see about having those who pass initial training in the army serve in the Beast Mountain Range to get some Experience." Rugrat looked at Erik, who nodded.

Evernight continued, "We have the army that is reserve, and within that, we are creating a reactive force that will go out and hunt down the enemy before they ever reach the Beast Mountain Range. We can use them as scouts, spies, and assassins as needed in different nations."

"Well, instead of using a new force, you could use some people from the special teams. We need to rotate them around and teach them about the different realms. Have them operate in different realms—become Experts on them," Erik said.

"They are the best of the best," Elan said.

"Yeah, and you need it for dangerous operations. Though I have one rule." Erik held up a finger. "No secretive bullshit with them. If they're going on a mission, you can tell them and *consult* them on the mission parameters. They must all agree to the mission, and they have the right to change it if they so desire. No offense, but you gather the information, and they need to act on it. I trust your information and their judgment as to whether they can act on it or not."

"Too many times spooks come in and tell us a mission, and they have a skewed vision of how it will come out—too many damn action movies," Rugrat muttered darkly.

Movies? Evernight kept her judgments to herself as Elan nodded.

"Understood, lords." Elan bowed his head.

Rugrat and Erik's body language turned weird at the mention of "lords" but they didn't say anything.

"Have we got any information on people from Earth?" Erik asked.

"There have been some instances. Evernight?" Elan said, and everyone turned to her.

"People from Earth are new to the Ten Realms, so they will appear in the First Realm. A few incidents have gained our attention. Although our net around the Beast Mountain Range is dense, it is much thinner in the lands beyond. We have found a total of seventeen people who might have come from Earth. Twelve of them have died. Of the remaining five, three advanced into the higher realms, and we are searching for them through other sources. Two remained in the First Realm. One operates as a commander of an army; the other is a slave of a nation. Advances in materials have occurred again and again from that nation. Based on our information, they appeared in the same areas, so we have expanded our search area to where people have appeared.

"We have also have information about a group of possible Earthers we found by mistake. Queen Ikku is moving her forces toward the Beast Mountain Range. I thought they wanted to attack us, but they seemed to be searching for something. I checked into it deeper, and a group of people, some who are fighters using crossbows and are terrible with blades, escaped with a group of weaker people and are protecting them. It was said that they had been gathered by Queen Ikku."

"The man who is a slave and this group—what have we done about them?" Erik asked.

"We were waiting for your orders," Elan said.

"Brief a special team. They are to secure that man at all costs. I want another special team ready to meet with this group of people from Earth. You said Queen Ikku is moving her people toward the Beast Mountain Range?"

"Yes," Evernight said.

Erik glanced at Rugrat.

"She has to be following them," Rugrat said. "If I were looking to disappear, I would want to go somewhere where it is hard to track down people. We have people moving all over the place. Outposts are being shifted around; more people live and trade above us than ever before."

"Perfect way to get lost in the crowd," Erik agreed. "All right, have your people figure out who these people are and locate them. Once you find them, tell us. They're running scared. If you make contact, it could be an issue. If you can't get Rugrat or me, get Matt or Tanya to meet with them."

"It will be done." Evernight nodded.

"Anything else?" Erik asked.

Evernight pressed her lips together, thinking of Aditya. She raised a hand at the last second.

"Miss Evernight."

"Lord Aditya…he has served faithfully and worked for Alva for the last few years without complaint. His subordinates already know about Alva and have even trained here, but he has been kept in the dark." Evernight stared at the table in front of her, not knowing whether she had spoken out of turn. She felt the heat in her face as her stomach turned over.

"Well, we have met him, and he has done a lot of good for us," Rugrat said.

"Elan?" Erik asked.

"He has done everything we asked of him and gone beyond. I think it's past time," Elan said.

"All right. Miss Evernight, in four days, bring Aditya to Alva. Make sure everything is prepared," Erik said.

Evernight shivered. She wasn't sure whether it was fear or excitement, and she bowed her head. "Yes, Dungeon Lord."

After all the other heads had left, there was only Elan, Erik, and Rugrat left.

"I'm guessing you want the details about the Sixth Realm now?" Rugrat asked.

"It wouldn't hurt," Elan said, pen and paper ready.

"All right, well, we should start from the beginning." Erik stretched in his chair.

It took a few hours for them to get through everything, telling Elan about the academy cities. The dungeons underneath them were like a whole second world. The orcs and the testing carried out by Lena. They dumped all her journals they had gathered. They'd made duplicates with special spell scrolls.

"We also ran into a guy called Lee Perrin. Sounds like an Australian, a place on Earth. He had some people with him who called him a teacher. They were all plenty powerful. If you could have some people keep an eye on him, we might find an opportunity to bring him to our side," Erik said.

"To make it to the Sixth Realm, he must be one hell of a fighter. Do you think that he was power-leveling?" Elan asked.

"Honestly have no idea. There are different ways to grow one's Strength. Seems he found a really good one," Rugrat said.

"I will see if I can get some information on this Lord Vinters too.

Sounds like the dungeons are a wildland down there."

"Perfect for exploitation. Could have a whole bunch of mines in there or people collecting resources," Rugrat said.

"We might have needed that in the past. Now, not so much. We haven't used up twenty percent of the overall space on the separate floors. The Water floor is largely unexploited as well. Going to take us some time to develop all that," Erik said.

"Makes sense. Sorry, I'm used to us having to make secret bases all over the place."

"Yeah, it was my first thought too," Erik said. "Also, Elan, talking about secrets, what about your son Wren?"

"What about him?" Elan looked up.

"You haven't asked once for him to become an Alvan; you didn't want to cloud our judgment, I know. I read the reports from Evernight about his interactions in the First Realm and work in Vermire, Chonglu, and now in King's Hill. He's not the little shit who attacked us back then," Erik said.

Elan didn't say anything.

"We would be willing to give him a shot at being an Alvan and for the Silaz Trading house under him to become a member of the Trader's Guild," Rugrat said, cutting to the point.

"Thank you. I know in the past—"

"The past is the past. He has grown up, having to rely on himself and develop out the trading house. We can only give him a shot. Whether he makes it through recruitment or not is up to someone else."

"I understand. Whatever the decision, I won't fight it."

"Good." Erik tapped on the table and stood. "Now, the next thing we need from you is information on the Seventh Realm. We need to deal with this Willful Institute crap first, but I want us to be ready. The Sha have their eyes on us."

"Yes, sir. I am leveling up some of my agents so they can enter the Seventh Realm."

Calm Before the Storm

Delilah and Erik walked together. They wore relaxed clothes, and although people stared, with just a different set of clothes, few people recognized the duo.

"How is the family?" Erik asked.

"They're good. My mother is at the school working as a healer. Two of my brothers—John and Jamie—have joined the army; Joanna followed them too. My father is a confirmed farmer. He works on the farms and the Alchemy gardens." Delilah smiled as she looked up at the ceiling and the roof of mana stones. "Nolan followed him, and Kyle is a cook and Greg is a tailor. Suzy and Rachel are still figuring out what they want to do. Zhiwei was in the military, but she is now expecting John's child. She is resting at home, but she spends most of her days in the library and has become a student of pure magic."

Erik laughed, a wide smile on his face. "Looks like the Ryans are going all out!"

Delilah smiled, proud of her family. They reached the low tables and chairs that filled the first market square. There were restaurants, bars, and stores around the square. In the middle were chairs and tables with staff ready to take their order and bring them meals from the different vendors. All of them sold a variety of meals and items, allowing one to have a truly different style of food.

The square was packed with people having meetings over lunch or catching up with friends, fellow students, workers, and compatriots.

An attendant came over with menus. The man opened his mouth to speak and stuttered when he saw Delilah's face, putting his hands to his side and starting to bow.

"Please, don't. I'm just looking to have a private meal," Delilah said to the waiter.

The waiter didn't seem to know what to do. He nodded and cleared his throat.

"Thank you." Erik held out his hand for the menu.

"Your brother is working in the kitchen. I know he would like to say hello. If you want?" the waiter asked.

"Kyle is working today? Only if he isn't in the middle of something," Delilah said guiltily.

"I'll let him know discreetly." The waiter smiled and cast a side-eye at Erik, seeming curious.

Delilah quietly pulled out a formation that would show an illusion over their mouths, so nobody could read their lips and would stop their conversation from reaching others.

She saw a similar formation in Erik's hand; he activated it and placed it in his pocket.

"I wonder if he knows who you are, Teacher." A playful smile rose on Delilah's face.

"Hmm." Erik made a noise in his throat, raising an eyebrow. He read the menu, not caring to join Delilah's sharp tongue.

"Teacher, how was the Sixth Realm?" Delilah watched Erik closely.

His eyes stilled, seeing memories instead of the menu in front of him.

His eyes flicked up to her before he took a deep breath and lowered the menu.

"The Sixth Realm is filled with academies based upon super dungeons. The planet is broken into two parts: the academies and their training grounds. The academies compete on the surface for fame and fortune, and they wage secret, hidden wars within the dungeons for resources. The people there are powerful. The members of the academies are no weaker than the elites of the Alvan army, and their genius students could have the strength of our special team members—maybe higher. They have all condensed their mana cores, with some reaching the Liquid Mana Core stage. Body Cultivation falls behind, but there are many with Body Like Stone, and Experts have Body Like Iron."

"So, we beat them in Body Cultivation," Delilah said.

"Having a higher cultivation in one area is far from 'beating' them."

Delilah winced. The academies had to have tens or hundreds of thousands of students, sometimes millions; their techniques and combat ability had to be much higher.

"We don't focus on our power in a one-on-one basis but our many fighting as one."

Erik's words calmed and reassured her. His eyes were like clear water, soothing her soul, and she nodded.

"Those with the greatest aptitude might pass higher into the Seventh Realm. One in ten thousand makes the marks to get higher training and lessons. Their power is hard to understand. Many of them fight in competitions, and their abilities in their given craft or fighting ability are the highest. Those who reach level sixty can enter the Seventh Realm, but they will not be held as geniuses, getting the resources and support of forces in the Seventh Realm."

"Why are so few people allowed in the higher realms?" Delilah asked.

Erik's brows pinched together, and he glanced over to the side.

"The Fourth Realm is a barrier, and the Seventh Realm is as well. The Fourth Realm is a competition grounds; the Fifth is where the winners are sorted. In the Sixth, they're groomed, and in the Seventh, well, rarely do people come down from the Seventh Realm. People ascend to the Seventh Realm, never to return." Erik's eyes flicked to hers. A chill came over her. "It is said that the people in the Seventh Realm can't return to the lower realms because of mana deprivation."

"Mana deprivation?"

"The Seventh Realm is the start of the Sky realm. Have you studied the books we have on mana gathering?"

"I have. There are the three primary stages: Vapor, Mist, and Mana Drop or Liquid. Then the core stages: Vapor Mana Core, Mist Mana Core, Liquid Mana Core, Solid Mana Core. Then the Mana Heart," Delilah said.

"What is the greatest issue of increasing one's Mana Cultivation?"

"Mana. One needs an incredible amount of mana to increase their overall cultivation."

Erik nodded. "That is part of it. Not only does one need mana, they need a high mana density." He pulled out a bag of saline solution and held it up. "Think of the saline solution as mana and the bag like your body."

He pulled out a bucket of water and put the bag in the water. "What happens cultivating our mana as we go up realms?"

"The higher the realm, the easier it is to condense mana in our bodies as the mana is more concentrated and of higher purity," Delilah said.

"Like how this water is around the bag of saline here; everything is in balance. Now, what if we absorb more mana than can be found around us?" Erik poked holes in the saline bag underwater.

"It is harder to increase our cultivation," Delilah said.

"Right." Erik lifted the saline bag out of the bucket. As the first holes were revealed, saline began to spill out. As more holes were revealed, saline spilled out faster.

"If we have reached a point where the density or pressure of mana inside our bodies is higher than the mana pressure outside of our bodies, then we would start leaking pressure, like how this bag is leaking saline all over the place. If we go to a higher realm, though"—he put the bag back in the water and squeezed it; it drew water in through the holes—"then our bodies are like a vacuum, dragging in more mana from around us."

Delilah stared at the bucket, her mind turning into a buzz.

"On one side, Mana Cultivation is a chore. On the other, it accelerates rapidly so that one's cultivation will soar," she said in a low voice.

"The density and purity were nearly ten times stronger from the Third Realm to the Fourth Realm. What must it be from the Sixth to the Seventh? If someone with a high mana density inside their body were to go to a lower realm and not be able to contain all of their mana?" He raised his saline bag. It was draining faster than before as there was more water and saline in it.

"Then it starts to drain out *fast*."

It all disappeared into his storage ring, and a smile appeared on his face. "Unless the bag, or person, can be reinforced."

Delilah was quiet for some time. "Body Cultivation?" she whispered.

"I think so. Body Cultivation is about altering our bodies with the mana and power of the Ten Realms, increasing the strength of the container and our control over attribute mana. The two are clearly linked." Erik's eyes shone.

Delilah snorted upon seeing that look. "It seems you found a new challenge for yourself, Teacher."

His grin widened, and Delilah noticed someone coming over.

"Mister West." Kyle bowed deeply to Erik.

"No need for that."

"You saved me and my family, sir. It's not something we'll forget easily," Kyle said solemnly.

"Right time, right place," Erik said.

"It's good to see you, sis." Kyle turned to Delilah with a tired smile before it got awkward.

"You too! You're always working," she complained, standing and hugging him.

"Hey, just doing my tests so I can get into the Sky Reaching Restaurants. Trying to make manager!"

"Then I'll have to go to some other realm to get your soup dumplings?"

"Well worth the trip." Kyle laughed. "You have a good lunch. See you later!"

"Bye, Kyle," Delilah said, and Erik waved.

"So, what should we eat?" Delilah asked.

"Anything but soup. Gets up in my beard, turns into a mess."

"Yeah, your hair got a little long," Delilah said.

"I need to get it trimmed a bit. Look like I was on a remote island for some years." Erik grinned.

Delilah shook her head, smiling.

"So, dating anyone? Or aren't you interested in that?" Erik asked. "I'm not really one to give advice—bad with relationships, just ask my ex-wives. One plus is I never have to hear about them again in the Ten Realms. Though you're young. You should go for it. Work isn't everything."

"Teacher!" Delilah sputtered.

"What? Shouldn't I want what is best for my student?" Erik asked innocently.

"Y-you!" Delilah didn't know what to say.

"Come on, look, aren't the Silaz boys both good candidates? I could put in a good word? Storbon is a good and strong boy too. Think of him as my own boy. Glosil is too serious, doesn't seem your type. Yao Meng? He's a good guy and funny. What about Gong Jin? He just got command of his own special team, and he's the tough, reliable sort with a heart of gold," Erik quickly rattled off.

Delilah closed her eyes, her lips moving. She shook her head as unwanted images and thoughts filled her mind. "Teacher," she hissed in a low voice, cutting him off. She took a breath and glared at him. "I am not interested in anyone right now," Delilah said forcefully.

Erik saw no malice in her expression. It was the look of someone who cared deeply. "Delilah, I am just your teacher, but you're like a daughter to me. Don't hold back your own life for your job. I have done it before, and I threw myself completely into my work. I don't blame anyone but myself, but looking back, I wish I had taken those opportunities, that time I needed to explore my options, to try out a relationship."

Delilah was stunned as she sat back and thought about his words. The waiter came back over, and they quickly ordered. Delilah felt as if she were in a haze, focusing on his words. She seemed to return to reality when the food arrived. She found her eyes had fallen on a group of soldiers marching around the dungeon headquarters.

"Alva's population has grown rapidly in a short period of time. Our external branches have nearly doubled in size since Rugrat and you left. With our foundations, we have absorbed all these people seamlessly. Though war is coming with the Willful Institute, I know there is no turning back now. I am worried about the price we will need to pay and what the outcome will be."

"Good," Erik said.

Delilah looked at him with more questions.

"A good leader leads from the front; a great leader leads from the front and plans for the future. Every movement now, they ready their next moves and create new paths." Erik sat back.

"With this war, the Adventurer's Guild will be revealed to have a power behind them, at the very least. At the most, Alva itself might be revealed. We have grown our strength in the darkness. If we are attacked and under siege from every side, we can retreat into the depths of Alva. We have been stockpiling resources for years; we have training floors and dungeons. In Alva, people have reached level sixty. Who says we can't train people to level seventy or one hundred? Completely cultivate the body and one's mana with enough time?"

Even if they know where Alva is, they will have to dig through kilometers of rock and break through multiple defenses. If we retreat from the main living floor and moved into the lower floors, then it would take decades, if not centuries, for our enemy to even reach us." Erik's words left a heavy silence in the room.

"What if we win?" Delilah asked.

"We sell the cities we capture. We don't need them. The resources and promises we can get in exchange for them are worth much more. We recover and ready ourselves, train until we have forces to infiltrate the Seventh Realm. We learn about the Seventh Realm. We push forward, striving up through the realms. Unravel the mysteries of the Ten Realms—why are we here, what are the Ten Realms? What is at the peak of the Ten Realms? Who made this place? For what purpose?" Erik's words grew faster, and his eyes shone brighter.

Delilah's heart sped up, and her hands tightened in excitement.

Those same questions had crossed her mind before, though she had dismissed them as questions she would never learn the answers to. *What if we can make it to the Tenth Realm? Then what? What would we see?*

"As a leader, our responsibility is simple. Listen to the needs of our people, plot a path for the future, and if *anyone* dares to hurt those under our command or under our protection, we make sure that they never threaten their lives ever again. Even if we have to go up against the strongest sect, the most powerful beast—even the Ten Realms itself—we will fight for them with everything at our disposal. That is our oath. That is our purpose."

"Attacking one of our adventurer teams—they didn't attack the Adventurer's Guild, they attacked Alva," Delilah said.

Erik nodded.

"They nearly killed Domonos and tore him apart. They stepped on our necks across the realms. They attempted to kill you and Rugrat. Killing our people was the last straw. Now our strength has reached this point. If we do not attack, then we could lose our people's confidence. If we are attacked, it is okay to wait, but we must never forget."

Delilah's fury built in her stomach, anger that made her muscles tense. She also felt fear and despair, as she knew that in any war, there were casualties on both sides.

"Right now, we can only increase our abilities and prepare for whatever our future is," Erik said quietly.

High Elder Cai Bo wore gauze clothes that made her look mystical as she surveyed the city outside of the window. She examined her reflection in the glass, seeing the iron-crafted Willful Institute medallion on her chest.

"Henghou City wouldn't have reached its current state without your efforts, High Elder Cai Bo." A plain-looking man entered the room. He clasped his fists and bowed to her as the doors closed behind him.

He looked to be in his early forties. His movements were elegant, and he wore a fine set of armor that didn't seem to have joints and flowed together as if it were a second skin.

"Low Elder Kostic." Cai Bo's voice came out with a pleased tone. "Please rise."

She turned from the window and moved to a desk that stood in front of the low elder and sat down easily. "I have received alarming reports that our root sect's tributes have decreased."

Kostic's face turned dark as he waited on her.

"It seems that many are handing over the minimum required resources." Her voice was light, but the pressure in the room seemed as heavy as the tower they were in.

The Willful Institute was spread over three realms, with outposts in the Fifth Realm. Being spread so far apart, they had been given a large level of autonomy. Competition was seen as a great motivation; the strongest would rise and get more resources. Those who gave more resources, the best geniuses, they would be rewarded with more slots for progression in the future and greater training arts and advanced items from the higher realms. Factions went against one another, but it mattered little as long as strong people were pushed higher.

With fewer resources, the geniuses in the higher realms couldn't advance, and the sect would stagnate. What mattered was the power of their strongest members. They had been able to get people into the Sixth Realm, and there were even some members in the Seventh!

"Do they not acknowledge their position? I will go down there and deal with them personally to make sure they remember!" Low Elder Kostic said.

Cai Bo raised her hand lightly, stalling Elder Kostic.

"It is only a few of the sects that have slowed their contributions. Make a note of those that are meeting the minimum requirements. If they are not paying me, are they increasing their payments to others?" Cai Bo's words were light, but there was a coldness to them.

If they dared to pay other elders before her, they would learn that she was not someone to be forgotten. If their contributions dropped, it must be because they are paying off other elders, increasing their power. Did they think her blind?

"Should I check which elders have been away for training in seclusion recently?" Elder Kostic hinted.

Smart. If they could see who was hiding in seclusion, hoping to use their extra resources to gain more power to take over his position or gain more followers, he could restrict their power. This way, he would find out who was going against him.

"It is always good to know the location of all our elders…for *safety* reasons." Cai Bo's eyes flashed.

Kostic bowed deeply and backed away.

"I heard that your grandniece was able to progress into the Fourth Realm," Cai Bo said.

Kostic stopped, and a wide smile appeared on his face. "It was only by High Elder Cai Bo's teachings that my little niece was able to reach the Fourth Realm. It is my hope that she can repay your kindness in the future tenfold," Low Elder Kostic said gratingly.

"They call her Mistress Mercy, do they not?" Elder Cai Bo asked.

"A playful moniker from the lower realms," Kostic said with a laugh.

"How are you related?"

"She is my sister's granddaughter, thus the different last name. I was interested in supporting her after hearing her exploits."

"Interesting. Still, there are many enemies of the sect who we might need your grandniece's talents for. There is a good position for those who can make the enemy reveal their secrets."

"If you are ever in need of her talents, I am sure she would be most pleased to serve." Low Elder Kostic's expression was cold. The corner of both their mouths lifted slightly.

"Make sure she doesn't fall behind in her training." Cai Bo turned away from Elder Kostic and stood. As she walked to the window, Low Elder Kostic bowed and backed out of her office. The doors opened and closed behind him. High Elder Cai Bo continued to look over Henghou, focusing on her empire.

Something was happening. She could feel it through the network she had created; oddities were appearing.

Chapter: Alva's Technology Sector

Rugrat reached Jia Feng's office. The older lady was putting some books into her storage ring as he arrived.

"Rugrat! Good to see you. Do you mind if we walk and talk? I have to head to a class I'm teaching," she said as she checked the notes and information on her desk before walking around it.

"That would be fine with me. Had too many meetings in stuffy rooms and around desks." Rugrat laughed.

Jia Feng smiled, her eyes shining. The corners of her eyes showed laughter lines. "Perfect!"

Rugrat opened the door for her and followed after.

"Taran told me about the idea you had with the applied side of things. I think it is a great idea to have teachers on the academic side who have not only been taught the different theories and ideas but have used their knowledge in a practical way. 'Applying' it to their everyday lives."

They walked down the stairs of the academy headquarters, passing other teachers, nodding and greeting them as they talked.

"I don't see the need to adjust much else on the academic side. How are you going to start having people applying their craft, though?"

"Contracts. The military will pave the way. Every year around the time of the crafting competition held internally by the academies, people can show off their skills in a timed event and show us what they can build. It creates a competitive platform for the greatest technologies. The academy and Alva propose what will be the technology focus in the events, and people build all year to create those things that people require."

"Okay, but there are some people who are better at creating complex equipment that will take longer and be much better than the items created in a few hours or days." Jia Feng nodded. "Though that creates one item. People will not do it all the time if they have one opportunity."

They exited the main teacher's building and walked across the grounds. Jia Feng's brisk pace went against her short stature, and people made room for them both.

"Government contracts. We need something in the military. We create contracts for people to build items; they can get low-rate loans to support their efforts. The best item is picked from what is supplied. People looking to create their own items for a perceived need will present a plan to the bank. Based on the perceived viability of it, they can get loans," Rugrat said.

"How will the bankers assess the plans? Will they have crafters on staff to check the plans and see if they are viable, not only in terms of profit and loss and return on investment but make sense? Will people need to provide a blueprint of their technology? What is this patent you are asking about?"

"Uh, well, the blueprint and the hiring of crafters for the proof of concept, uh, I didn't think of that," Rugrat said.

"Bankers deal with money, not crafting. Might need to have people on staff to assess plans—or patents, as you called them"

Rugrat explained patents. She had questions about different kinds of patents, how they would work if a company paid for people to develop an idea, if someone developed it themselves, changing people's access to the patents, and how payouts would be split to the different crafters on different projects.

"What about the workshops? Will they be working in our workshops or others?" Jia Feng asked, turning around at the entrance to her classroom.

"They would be able to rent them from the school, but I am hoping that we can create more independent crafting workshops. People can work there for a fee. If people want to, they can buy their own land and create an office or a crafting workshop," Rugrat said.

Jia Feng held her chin and bit her lip, silently collecting her thoughts. "I think it is a great idea and will develop the crafters from Alva even further. I think that you are underestimating the ability of the traders, though. If they sense money can be made, they will be the first people to start employing more crafters to work together. They hire out crafters who are looking for jobs to help them out. There are crafting workshops in Alva already that are owned by the academy. Talk to Elise and the treasury—Matt as well as Taran. Taran set up the factories with Matt for the military. Elise's Trader's Guild is hiring out crafters who are done with school. And the treasury will need to put in strategies to encourage more people to work together on projects that will create powerful gear but won't increase one's skill level.

"There are some brilliant crafters who aren't well-suited for academics; they have gone out to learn in the world. There are crafters who dabble in other crafts. Some of them have probably thought about mixing their crafts together, but there are no clear benefits to them. There are people trying to become Experts, and there are those who know they will not be able to get higher than Apprentice or Journeyman unless they have a fortunate circumstance. These are the people who will become the backbone of your plans, become inventors and factory creators. People have families who they need to support; they need money to increase their cultivation and provide for others."

"Okay." Rugrat felt as though he had been dunked in cold water. He had rushed ahead, missed key steps, and forgot people to talk to.

"It will be slow to start, but with time, it will increase. It takes one to start everything." Jia Feng smiled and patted Rugrat's bicep—she was too short to reach his shoulder.

"Thank you," Rugrat said, calmed by her words. He grinned.

She nodded and squeezed his arm as she turned to head into the classroom.

"Needs someone to start it all. I don't know everything. Gonna need some of the heads of departments to help. Then involve the students to help with researching and building the factory. Wouldn't that be the best example of applied science?"

Jia Feng checked behind to Rugrat. He shivered as sparks and fires burned in his eyes; his mouth turned into a determined grin. His hands moved as if grasping the handle of a hammer.

"Thank you, Miss Jia Feng. I have work to do!" Rugrat turned around. People pushed to either side as each of his strides created waves of mana and air that brushed through people's hair as if an unstoppable train had passed them.

13 Congregation of Experts

The flash of teleportation faded as Blaze and Jasper led the Adventurer's Guild's branch heads out of Alva's totem.

Their identities were verified by the soldiers before they passed the walls. Blaze led them across the city that had grown once again, leading them to the military district. It was filled with factories that mass-produced the gear for the Alva army. They were checked again and given a group of guards to watch over them and escort them to a private field.

Stephan glanced at the academy tower in the distance, wishing to get some time among the books there and talk to Tanya about what he had learned about pure magic.

He looked over at the squat factory buildings, unimpressed. The guards who were watching his group were wearing Journeyman armor. Not one piece of Expert-level gear among them. They had their rifles, but how could that be compared to the power of magic? They were just inert tools.

He didn't try to find out their levels or cultivation. It was rude to pry, and he felt it would be worthless. In the fights at the Battle Arena, the soldiers had reacted quickly, but they were buffed by being in the city and able to increase their Strength retroactively. In Stephen's eyes, they were too reliant on gear that could fail.

He looked down on them and their abilities. Fighting together as a party made sense, but their squads—how did they get anything done? And they lost all the benefits, dividing loot up so much.

They were led to a private testing area.

There were nine people talking to one another, six men and three women crafters by their clothes. They all seemed to know one another well. Eight hardened-looking men and women who wore Alva Army uniforms—their shoulder patches denoting them as officers—created their own group, glancing at the group of nine. Behind them, two army squads milled around, wearing their complete body armor, minus their helmets.

Stephan surveyed it all, his face expressionless. He rubbed his storage ring, eager to pull out a book and read instead of dealing with this waste of time.

The Alvans stopped their talking and looked over to the approaching Adventurer Guild party.

"Lords!" Blaze and Jasper called out, snapping their feet together. Their arms went to their sides, and they bent to a full ninety degrees, bowing to two rough-looking men who sported beards and worn clothes with the group of military leaders.

The two men seemed simple, but Stephan's pupils constricted; a coldness in his stomach raced up his spine. It was as if he were facing two wolves with nothing but his fists. Before them, he felt powerless. The other branch heads also seemed struck by the force around the two men.

Blaze cleared his throat, the noise like a bolt of thunder next to their ears. They all bowed deeply. Even Derrick was pale-faced and showed signs of a cold sweat.

"Blaze, Jasper, seems that you've raised some good fighters," one of the men said.

"Their performances at the Battle Arena were impressive, I heard," said the other.

Blaze and Jasper rose, and the rest of the branch heads did the same.

The four men hugged one another while those in the nine-person group greeted Blaze and Jasper easily. It was clear they were all good friends.

Stephan felt that he was on unsteady ground. He used his sensing spells, and light sparked deep in his eyes as he looked around. His body shuddered.

This mana density. He knew Blaze and Jasper were powerful, but He couldn't see through their levels or skin. *Just how advanced* is *their Body Cultivation?*

Stephan quietly moved beside Kim Cheol. He had undergone the greatest Body Cultivation, reaching the impossible height of Body Like Iron. None of them had believed they would get so strong without a sect's support.

"Cheol, how powerful are they?" Stephan asked quietly.

"Their Body Cultivation is higher than mine," Cheol said.

"They have bodies at the peak of Body Like Iron?"

"Close. I can barely sense Rugrat's mana. Erik's is on the same level as yours. I can't—" Cheol stuttered as Erik looked over and then went back to his conversation. Cheol's voice was hoarse and strained. "His Body Cultivation is at least a stage higher than mine, maybe two. He's like a beast in human skin."

Stephan shuddered.

"What did you find?" Emilia asked. The branch heads grouped together, staring at Stephan, whose eyes were shaking.

"Dual cultivators, of body and mana. Past core formation, and both have above Body Like Iron. I can't tell their levels," Stephan said.

"Seems that you haven't spent much time with the soldiers," Derrick said in a low voice. "We are relatively powerful. The best in our respective cities, and we ranked highly in the Battle Arenas. I was here a month back for training. I sparred with the soldiers every time. When I had started, I was stronger than them, then we were on the same level, then I was suppressed, and then I couldn't even stand up to ten moves. That was in the last six months."

"You have been one of the fastest among us to increase your fighting ability," Joan rebutted.

"When we started training, I could compete against their lieutenants in power. Guess what rank my power is equal to now?" Derrick asked with a wry smile. "I can barely hold my own against their youngest sergeants. Some corporals can even defeat me."

"Corporals are one step up from the most basic privates," Lin Lei said in a low voice.

"You all know my combat strength. I'll tell you this. It is not that I am too weak; it is that the soldiers are training demons in human skin. They are treated to special meals, powerful training, unlimited access to the academy, and anything else they want to learn. Their equipment is basic, but there are thousands of them, not just six, like us."

"Don't they rely on their weapons too much?" Stephan asked.

"Don't I?" Derrick patted his blade.

"But theirs are complicated. We have all seen how complicated equipment is prone to failure and can break if not in the best conditions," Stephan pressed.

"Well, looks like we'll see how tough their gear is," Emilia said grimly as the three groups were pulled together, and the two squads in the middle of the training area stopped talking and pulled on helmets that hid their faces.

Qin stepped out in front of everyone.

"Today, we will be demonstrating the power of the Conqueror's Armor. It is a new version of armor that is based off the plate armor from before but has a greater integration of linked formations."

Qin pulled out a front/back armor plate from her storage ring. She turned it over and showed them the formation lines. "This is a linking formation that connects the wearer's armor to other linking formations. It is based off the stacking formations that Formation Master Julilah worked on and the socket technology currently employed on weapon systems.

"Now you might be wondering how this is useful. These linking formations also connect to the other formation sockets of the armor plates, such as your backplate and both side plates.

Some people started moving around, putting the pieces together.

"If you can link the effects of formations to one another, then you can effectively stack their effects. Say you have two sets of armor linked together, and each formation gives you a one percent increase to your agility. Backplate, side plates, that is a three percent difference for one person, but linked, that is a six percent increase to agility."

She saw it sinking in.

"Now, how many are there in a squad, in a platoon, in a company, in a regiment?"

She had them now.

"Sergeant Bai, would you be able to take off your armor and hit the target with a bow?" Qin asked.

"Yes, ma'am." Sergeant Bai pulled off his armor and his helmet, setting them to the side. He pulled out a simple bow and arrow, and he fired at the target. It was a special target that recorded damage.

1293

"Could you put on a linking medallion?" Qin asked.

The man pulled out a necklace and put it on. It lit up, and power covered his body. The buffing light disappeared, and he fired another arrow.

1706

Yui arched his eyebrow. It was a thirty percent increase of power. "With your armor, please?"

Bai Ping got into his armor and then fired his arrow.

2172

The target rang out again.

"Sergeant Bolton, would you and your squad activate your linking formations and go for a run, please?" Qin asked.

Sergeant Bolton and his people ran away from the target, reaching the other side of the training area five hundred meters away.

"Sergeant Bai?"

He fired another arrow.

3051

People talked to those beside them in low voices.

"Each of these sets of armor have been enhanced with Strength sockets at one percent. One squad of seventeen will give an overall boost of sixty-eight percent to one another. Two squads will have a boost of one hundred and thirty-six percent of one's original output." Qin's word's left silence in her wake.

"Okay, so how do you see this operating?" Rugrat asked.

"It uses small formations to create a network of buffs. The more people wearing this armor, the more buffs applied. The buffing formations are in your socket design, so they can be upgraded and changed according to the battle. This is just the first type, the Journeyman level one formation type. We are crafting it out now, but it is designed to be created by the mass-production factories."

"A Journeyman-level set of gear—are you using it as a testbed to reach Expert?" Rugrat asked.

"Journeyman level is the best suited for this, as we can produce it faster and it is more stable. We know more about gear in that range. With the way the buffs stack, we don't need to have Expert armor for all the different parts. Say you have a squad of sixteen, including the sergeant. If they all have a buff of just one percent Agility increase, then they would enjoy an overall buff of sixty-eight percent to each person. That is a way larger buff than you would get for a piece of Expert-level armor.

"If a whole company were linked together, three hundred and sixty-eight people, that means your Strength and Agility would be nearly *fifteen times* what it was originally. Expert armor would only help one person, but this, working together, the effect is much greater."

"There is a limit though—range." Taran stepped forward.

"The Journeyman-level armor has a range of about one hundred square meters, but if you make an Expert-level armor plate, it can reach one thousand meters. Instead of making all the plates Expert level, you create one backplate and give it to the leadership," Taran said.

"It might be more effective to seed them randomly. That way, if the leadership is taken out, they won't lose the distance," Glosil said. "How is the production time?"

"With the right factory refit, we can make three sets of regular armor for how long it would take to make this set of armor," Taran said.

"How long to refit a squad?"

"We could refit them in two days once the new lines are operating," Taran fired back.

"Can the formation sockets be changed?" Rugrat asked.

"Sergeant?" Taran waved Bai Ping forward. With a rip of Alvan rip-tape, a section opened, showing a formation socket in the shoulder; another ripping noise and a second socket formation on Bai Ping's hips was revealed.

"We have worked with the tailors to alter the carriers, to increase the ease of access to the formation sockets. The sockets can be altered in seconds," Qin said.

"What was the necklace?" Erik asked.

"The necklace is a backup. If the linking formation in the armor is broken, the necklace will still function. It can be worn around the neck or in another piece of clothing, even added to boots. It reduces the power to fifty percent. But even if you are without your armor or your armor is broken, it will function," Qin said. "Also, Julilah has something else to add."

Julilah stepped up. "The interlinking formation works not only on the armor but for the stacking formations." Julilah pulled out a table and put down a large cylinder that had a series of shelves, a handle on one end, and runes that glowed with power.

She turned a handle at one end, and the cylinder clicked, unlocking the shelves. She pulled out small formations from within the shelves.

Pulling the handle, she drew out the mana stone power core at the center of the U-shaped formations.

"This is the stacking formation?" Yui asked.

"Yes. Combining separate formation plates, a formation that would be fifty meters long is transformed into ten formation plates."

She pulled out a small pillar of larger formation plates and put down formations around the large pillar. "In these mana-gathering formations, you can dump mana stones to power a barrier as powerful as one of the secondary mana barrier towers in Vuzgal. The formation plates can be switched out, changing their function and ability." Qin pulled out four plates and put in three new ones. "Now, it will buff anyone in range with the right medallion with increased spell effect of fifty percent."

Everyone was captured by her words.

"The cylinders could be changed, but they would take more time as you need to pull out the power core to change the plates. They are about a fifth as powerful as these larger plates. Their issue is with power consumption. Though we have created power cores where you can tear the dead one out and slot in a new one, much like a magazine on a rifle. If staying in one place, then you can hook up a mana-gathering formation and dump in mana stones."

The group watching shifted, their brows pinching together, absorbing every word.

"So, linking our formations together, we get overall buffs, increasing the effect of our base stats. An all-around buff to every attribute?"

Julilah and Qin glanced at each other and then at Yui with smiles on their faces.

"Yes," they said at the same time.

"That won't be a simple doubling of power. It will increase our fighting capability massively." Stephen was floored.

"Yes," Qin repeated.

"Power consumption?" Domonos asked.

"High, really damn high," Julilah said. "At maximum consumption, the portable formations will burn through an Earth-grade mana stone every ten minutes. The larger emplaced formation will go through a hundred Earth-grade mana stones every ten minutes. The linking formation is the power hog."

"The armor will not consume much power. It can operate at maximum capability for thirteen hours. It is one of the reasons we put in formations that are the lowest energy consumers," Qin said.

"If you were to put in the strongest formation sockets, they could hold?" Rugrat asked.

"About two hours. It would take twenty Earth mana stones to recharge the armor." Qin anticipated the next question.

"Sergeant, what are your thoughts, soldier-to-soldier?" Erik asked.

Bai Ping seemed a little stunned. Qin hid her smile. Erik and Rugrat didn't act like sect heads who seemed to know everything. They asked questions and didn't see themselves higher than anyone else.

Bai Ping was caught off guard by the question. He paused before finding his voice. Leading men and women and turning them into soldiers was one thing—talking to a legendary figure in person, who was asking him a question…?

He cleared his mind and pulled off his helmet out of respect. "The armor is useful. Overall, the defenses of the rear plate decreased, so more materials were needed to increase its strength. With our current strength, the armor is not an issue. The formations are accessed easily. It allows us to change for different circumstances. There will be a learning curve, and I am not talking about just deploying the armor." Bai Ping grimaced.

Erik indicated for him to continue.

His expression was solemn. "When we cultivate the body, our Strength, Agility, Stamina, and Stamina Regeneration increase. That jump, though powerful and allows us to do a lot more, takes time to get used to. It can take up to a week to get used to those changes."

A spark appeared in Erik's eyes, and he nodded. "If your attributes increase by two or three times the original, then instead of helping, it could be a massive hinderance."

Bai Ping nodded.

"It's the first time I have heard of a buff being too powerful." Rugrat laughed.

"We could balance it out," Qin said.

Everyone looked over.

"Increasing a single stat can create a massive imbalance. If you have a high Strength, then won't you need Agility to employ it correctly?" Qin said.

Bai Ping cleared his throat. "With shooting the bow, I could pull back farther and launch the arrow more, but when trying to run or do complex movements, the extra Strength can be more of a hindrance than an aid."

"If all the stats were boosted, then people could adjust for it easier," Glosil said. "Instead of worrying about a single change, they could take their overall abilities and multiply it."

"Would there be a way for the user to adjust their formation? They could train for three stages—basic, moderate, advanced—and could adjust through all three. That way, they could train for three different levels of power," Rugrat said.

Qin glanced at Julilah. "That should be possible, but why would we want to limit it?"

"Erik, do you want to do a demonstration?"

"You just want people to punch me," Erik muttered, but he stepped forward.

"Erik will be your enemy sergeant. And you lot"—Rugrat glanced at the people behind Sergeant Bai—"will be my targets. As I 'kill' you, you will switch off your formations, change up the variables."

Everyone looked forward eagerly. They all wanted to see how strong Lord West was.

How can they want me to fight him? Damn, just how powerful is he? What if I hurt him?

"Uh, sir." Bai Ping cleared his throat, not sure what to say to save Erik's face and not have to fight him.

"Don't worry. If you beat me up, I get beaten up. Won't take me long to recover. Just try and not hit me in the face, all right? Airways suck to fix." Erik flared power through his body, ready for combat.

Everyone watched closely. Rugrat had a wide grin on his face.

"Right now, all of the linking formations are active. Have you trained at this power level before, Sergeant?"

"Yes, I have, Lord Rodriguez."

"Good, then you should have an advantage. Though I would suggest you get ready. Erik's a fucking ass if he gets you on the ground."

"That sounds weird, man," Erik muttered.

"You know all those holds and wraps and crap—it freaking hurts! Anyway, get ready. Three, two, one. Beat him up, Bai!"

Erik summoned power from the realms. It flowed through his mana channels, into his muscles. Bai Ping drew in power as well, but it didn't have the same effect as he charged Erik.

Erik was in a boxer's stance. He covered up as Bai threw a punch. Erik was pushed back and took a few steps to stabilize.

Erik nodded when Bai Ping peeked at him with wide eyes.

It's like punching a fucking shield!

"Come on, Sergeant. If your enemy has an opening, you take it!" Erik yelled.

Bai Ping punched out again, putting all his power into the attacks but making sure to not leave openings to exploit.

Erik moved to the side and smacked out with the back of his hand. He struck Bai's forearm, pushing the punch wide.

Bai Ping punched out again and again. The shock of the punches shifted Erik's hair with the breeze.

Erik's eyes never wavered. They seemed unfocused, as if he were focusing on another sense.

Bai kicked out at Erik's knee.

Erik raised his leg; he took the hit and tilted.

Bai advanced to take advantage, ready to punch as Erik was tilting.

Erik pushed off the ground with his foot and threw himself away. Bai Ping lunged forward and punched.

Erik shifted away. The attack missed, striking the ground. Bai left a crater, shattering the ground.

Erik put his hand to the ground. Fire appeared underneath, and the small explosion gave Erik the force he needed to get back on his feet. The mana in his veins seemed to dim, and his skin hardened; black veins traced his skin, and he seemed to expel heat.

Shit, he wasn't using all his power.

"Bang!" Rugrat said.

Bai Ping lost connection to one of his people. Erik advanced in a blur and struck out at Bai.

Bai lost his momentum, turning to the defensive.

"Come on, Sergeant! You should know some combat techniques. If you don't pull them out, it's going to hurt you a lot more than it hurts me." Erik still had the time to talk as he jabbed at Bai.

Blades of mana appeared in Bai's hands, and he jumped backward, using a gliding technique. He threw the blades at Erik.

"Bang, bang." Another two people were disconnected.

Bai struggled to maintain the spells as he drew out more power from himself to sustain it. He couldn't rely on the formations now.

It halted him for a half second, and Erik punched out; two fireballs hit the mana blades. Bai Ping had to fight to get used to the power fluctuations and the fireballs aimed at him.

Rugrat "killed" three more people. Having to adjust to the new power balance and having different stats boosted at different amounts made it confusing for Bai Ping.

He threw out mana blades and sent out trapping spells, imbuing the Fire attribute into his attacks.

The flames didn't affect Erik in the slightest. He took the hits, showing red marks from the point of impact one second and then returning to normal the next.

Bai Ping forgot about Erik being a lord as they fought it out. If he stopped for even a minute, Erik would kick his ass.

Shit!

Erik kicked him, sending him backward. Bai hit the ground and rolled, coming back up. He punched out, sending mana blasts. Erik had been advancing; now Bai had to throw out a mana barrier to cover himself. Spears shot out from the ground, and Bai Ping cut them down with mana blades. He kicked out, and the stone spears exploded and melted.

More people "died" until there was just a squad left.

Bai Ping was trying to adjust when Erik's Earth spell trapped his feet while he was trying to back up. He staggered. Erik punched him three times in the vest, and each strike rattled Bai.

It felt as if he were being shot.

He was holding back in his punches? Shit!

Bai dropped to the ground, and Erik backed up.

"Thank you for going easy on me, Lord." Bai cupped his fists, fighting for breath.

"None of that. Get your breath back," Erik said. "Not bad, Sergeant. Training is going well."

"On one side, we see that Sergeant Bai Ping was getting fucked up with the power changes. On the other, Erik was adjusting his power throughout. Going from seventy-five percent to twenty-five percent power and then back up to fifty percent to finish off Sergeant Bai. Right?" Rugrat said.

"Yeah, about." Erik nodded.

That was only seventy-five percent of his power? Bai Ping coughed as he got his breathing back under control and his body recovered from the injuries he'd sustained.

Those watching talked with their eyes before staring at the unassuming Erik.

Shit—he wasn't even using armor or formations. It had felt like he was punching an armor plate. Body Cultivation was hell to go through. Just how much had he cultivated his body already?

"Say that we start losing people. As they die, their armor goes offline. Think of how they will now need to adjust for every person we lose. Massive boost one second, no boost the next." Glosil's words were hard and brutal.

Bai Ping stood straighter. It was the role of the Alva army to defend the people of Alva, by defeating the enemy or laying down their lives if it was called for.

It was the reality all soldiers dealt with.

"With the settings, we could adjust them, so at basic, it adjusts for a squad's worth of buffing, moderate for a combat company, advanced for a battalion. Even make higher stages, if needed. As time goes on, the basic buff will increase from a squad buffing power to a combat company and so on," Rugrat said.

"We could do it," Julilah said. Her voice was quieter than it had been. The two women seemed to shut off as Glosil presented them with the cold truths of what their formations would be used for.

"Sergeant Bai?" Erik asked.

"Sir?" Bai said, confused.

"Do you think the different levels of power would make it easier to manage?"

"I think it would. We can train to work on the higher levels of power," he said after a moment's thought.

"It might be harder for others to adjust to the changes, but it shouldn't be too hard for us," a woman's voice called out.

Erik grinned.

Bai Ping saw members of the special teams walking over.

From the shadows behind the main group, the special team in charge of protecting Erik and Rugrat stepped out.

The cold expressions turned into grins as people greeted one another, smacking shoulders.

The special teams were a level beyond many others, but seeing them, he felt as if they were beasts in human skin. There was a deadliness around them that chilled the air. Even when completely relaxed, they were a spring, ready to act and react in a moment.

"What did you mean, Roska?" Erik asked.

"The special teams train on separate floors, dealing with all kinds of variables. There is no knowing if we will be working in the middle of an ocean, forest, jungle, mountain range, or burning desert. We have to accommodate for all those factors. Having training where our power is increasing and decreasing randomly would be good. De-buffs are a common weapon."

"You and the members of your special team are training maniacs," Erik said.

"You're not?" Rugrat spoke in a quiet voice, but everyone heard him.

The two men chuckled.

"Yeah, well, fuck it!" Erik said. "Okay, anyone have any other points?"

The questions moved from the leaders to the captains.

As the questions died down, the leader of the Adventurer's Guild raised his hand. "Will this gear be issued to the Adventurer's Guild?"

Glosil stepped forward. "No, it will not."

"Why?" Blaze didn't seem to be worried in the slightest, and there was a smile on his lips.

"The army works in groupings of units. There are strict rules, and our tactics are based on working together as a single force. To armor everyone would be a great expense, and although an overall buff would work for the army, most of our people are at the same level of power, so there won't be too many changes. You have people from the First to the Fourth Realm in your organization and all kinds of different fighting styles…" Glosil trailed off.

"Naturally, when fighting in large battles, we would follow the examples of the sects and others, creating separate armies for people of different levels and capabilities. It makes it much harder to organize." Blaze nodded, and the other guild members seemed at greater ease.

"The war against the Willful Institute is coming closer every day. The army and the guild will work together in the coming fights. The guild will be the vanguard, and the army will support you—information, weapons, gear, supplies. There are some people who have not only our trust but position to act." Erik walked forward, his eyes looking to the men and women behind Blaze and Jasper.

"Blaze and Jasper can't do everything. They might be the head and shoulders of the guild, but you are the blades. You will be the ones in the field leading the guild forces," Rugrat said.

Blaze turned around to the group. "So, for the next week, you better open up your ears. You will be training and working alongside the army and have the attention of the special teams. We will continue our operations against the Institute, but you will learn how to properly train and command our guild into a fighting force. The guild and the army are two sides of the same blade. Do not forget that."

Bai Ping was caught by the image: Blaze and Glosil stood shoulder to shoulder, while Erik and Rugrat stood behind them and to the side.

"Captain, it will be an honor to fight beside you," Glosil said.

"Hah! The last time we had a real fight, I was a village head, and you were the leader of the town guard." Blaze let out a raucous laugh. The two men shook hands and hugged each other.

They turned and glanced at Erik and Rugrat.

"Sergeants Storbon and Gong Jin, front and center!" Rugrat barked out, making all the military members unconsciously straighten, pulled back to their days of basic training.

Storbon and Gong Jin walked out from the special team members.

They stopped in front of Erik and Rugrat and saluted. "Sirs!"

Erik and Rugrat came to attention and saluted them back. Their arms fell to their sides, and their smiles appeared again.

"It's overdue, but I'd like to congratulate you two on becoming captains. Both of you will lead your own sixteen-person squad of special team members." Erik and Rugrat pulled out rank tabs and handed them over to the two new captains.

"Do us, Alva, yourselves, and your fellow soldiers proud," Erik said.

"The lives of your men and women lie heavy on your shoulders, though you will bear that weight and succeed. In the hottest fires, the strongest metal is forged," Rugrat said.

"Return to your teams," Erik said. They exchanged salutes again, and the two men went back as the others ribbed them, laughed, and demanded to see their medals.

"Sorry, needed to attend to a few things," Erik said to everyone. "Please take a look at the gear. Examine it for as long as you need. This gear will be key in the oncoming war." Erik turned to the crafters. "Masters Qin, Julilah, Taran, and Tan Xue, thank you."

Erik clasped his fist to them in the traditional Ten Realms salute.

All of them looked surprised and bowed to Erik.

"We ain't much, but when we work together, nothing in the Ten Realms can stop us," Rugrat said. His voice was sober, but it created powerful ripples in everyone's hearts.

14 Military Actions

While Yui had been focused on preparing for capturing the Water floor, Domonos had formulated plans and continued to gather intelligence against the Willful Institute.

Glosil had supervised but had turned it into a test of the brothers' abilities.

The group sat in one of the barrack's planning rooms.

Domonos cleared his throat, and people's conversations came to a halt. He looked out at the members of the Adventurer's Guild, the leadership of the Dragon and Tiger Battalions, Glosil, Erik, Rugrat, his father Elan, and his trusted subordinates in the Second and Third Realms.

All of them stared at him attentively.

"The situation within the Willful Institute is fractious. They are constantly competing against one another to get a better position. It is not unknown for people from the same region to attack one another. We even have information on some groups in different regions attacking one another through proxies to steal their supplies and gear. They stand under one banner but are loose sand and rocks smashing into one another. We have scouted out the major cities controlled by the Institute and are working on plans to take each city. We are breaking their trust between one another and their cohesion." Domonos's eyes swept the room.

He pointed to a map of a city. "This will turn from a strategic trade war into a fighting war quickly. That is the nature of the Ten Realms. When it does, it will happen fast. Once they see they are losing their power, they will not go quietly. They'll lash out. In most places, they haven't even heard of the Adventurer's Guild. Instead of attacking some unknown, they'll attack their rivals, seeing them thriving with the support of the Adventurer's Guild and Trader's Guild. Either they won't have enough to pay their taxes and their administration will fall apart, or they will fight. I believe that they'll choose the latter."

Members of the Adventurer's Guild bristled at his words.

"In this situation, the less the enemy knows, the better. If we give them a single target, it will be harder to deal with. It could even unite them."

His words sunk in, and he continued.

"We have three operations planned, hidden operations. The first will act on the periphery, aiding those fighting the Willful Institute. Second, we will have the Adventurer's Guild actively attacking the Institute locations. We pull in the support of the locals who are against the Institute. Hidden in the ranks, we have Alva army support. Third, we create a reason for Vuzgal to attack the Willful Institute; we deploy our fighting force beside the Adventurer's Guild and others who ally with us. We attack the enemy, under the complete control of Vuzgal."

Domonos tapped the map again. "Those are methods of attack, but for the overall operation, there are three stages: infiltration, destabilization, attack.

"Infiltration has been handled by Director Silaz. Destabilization is ongoing by his forces, the special teams, as well as the Adventurer's Guild and Trader's Guild. When we attack, it will combine all the forces in this room and the allies we can pull to our side, even people who hate or just want to take advantage of the Willful Institute's weakness.

"If you look at the files in front of you, there are plans for how we intend to coordinate these plans. There is also specific information on the cities and strongholds we have gathered through departments."

The meeting continued, with the varied groups talking about tactics, coming together and integrating with one another.

In the darkness, a hidden force was mobilizing, a wolf sneaking up on its unaware prey that could only see the tip of its tail.

Yui passed Roska's security team, entering the range of a sound-cancelling formation. Rugrat was leaning on the banister overlooking the first training grounds. New recruits were running around the exterior doing exercises to keep fighting fit.

"I remember my training days like it was yesterday. Embarrassing as hell, but there were some good moments in with a lot of shitty ones." Rugrat smiled at Yui.

"I just remember getting my ass kicked. Officer school was no joke." Yui nodded, coming to stand beside him.

"You say that like I don't remember teaching you."

"Hey, I know where the training came from. It fucking sucked, but we needed it."

"You didn't turn out too bad, and the training has gotten better over the years. Hell, it's been years already. I'm getting old!"

"Don't look a day over twenty-five."

"Thanks, makes me have real gravitas when I look like I've only just started growing hair on my balls."

Yui snorted and chuckled.

"Well, got people to do and things to see, so, how are the backup sites?"

Yui's smile evaporated, switching to focused professionalism. "A plan is in place for the dispersal of personnel across the one hundred and eighty-nine backup sites. Each site can hold one thousand people at a minimum. With all the action against the Willful Institute, we haven't been able to capture as many dungeon cores." Yui's voice halted.

"Spit it out."

"Well, the thing is that we have to rely on the special teams to recover dungeon cores. We have a population of nearly four hundred thousand Alvans. We have enough room for two hundred thousand people in the backup dungeons. We need people with a dungeon hunter title to get cores to increase our capacity. I know its beneath you, but—"

"Erik and I have the Dungeon Master title, so we can raid dungeons and steal their cores, increasing the number of backup sites. So, you need a hundred more? What type of dungeon core?"

"We're using Grand Mortal-grade dungeon cores."

"Okay." Rugrat bit the inside of his lip.

"We have the location of several suspected dungeon core sites. Most of the locations are remote, and people don't venture into them. We've left the dungeon where it is, or we've made it smaller or larger and inserted the blueprints we have."

Rugrat glanced back at Roska's team members responsible for protecting him.

"Well, shit, there isn't much I can do right now. Any new weapons are at the back of the line. Might as well put me to some use. Might annoy my protection detail on the surface, but they're eager to do something as well."

"Thank you, sir." Yui sighed.

"I've told you before I ain't no sir and it's no problem. Gives my lazy ass something to do." Rugrat leaned on the banister; his eyes fell on the names carved into the wall.

"I heard that nearly all of the bodies of the dead on the Water floor were turned into undead," Rugrat said.

"Yes sir."

"Why?" Rugrat asked.

"They didn't want their bodies to be wasted. Most of them wanted to have their bodies awakened again. To serve as undead. We added it to the dog tags so their wishes can be respected."

Rugrat was quiet for some time.

"On Earth when you die, there are only two things you leave behind: what you've done and your bones. Even centuries or millennium later, your bones will be found. They never disappear. It is the last thing we have that shows we ever existed. In the Ten Realms, they take that away some days outside a storage ring, and your body will collapse. Different views. On one side is a marker of your existence; on the other, it will be gone otherwise, so why not make use out of something? Making use out of it will be a marker that you once lived. Protecting the later generations." Rugrat rested his elbows on the banister, raising his hands to his mouth, muffling his last words. "Undead are a testament to your life, a walking tombstone."

Yui didn't comment, his eyes focusing on the names carved into the wall.

From the Tiger's Mouth

Kanoa adjusted his hood in the rain, checking the rest of the people in the group as they all passed the guards at the gate.

They pushed forward into the outpost. Thankfully, the main roads were fused stone instead of cold, wet mud.

He was soaked and felt the chill of a cold coming on.

The rest of the group gathered around him, and they pushed on. Their eyes darted here and there.

"Don't worry. We're in the Beast Mountain Range now. This place is controlled by the King's Hill Alliance, so it will slow down Queen Ikku some," Kanoa reassured them as he led them to a tavern a guard had told them about.

"What about the other groups?" one of the civilians asked.

Walking into a city with a group of fifty-four people would have raised alarms, so they had split into groups of nine, with at least two guards in each one.

"We will meet in King's Hill and then disappear. There are plenty of trading caravans heading everywhere," Kanoa said.

They entered the tavern and pulled back their wet layers, welcoming the warmth.

Kanoa felt a little better.

"Rooms for nine, please," Kanoa said.

"Two silvers and forty coppers," the man at the tavern's table said.

"Food?"

"Four silvers total."

It was more expensive than in other outposts, probably because they had to import it all. He gritted his teeth and passed the man four silver coins.

The owner smiled as the silver disappeared and two keys appeared. "Second floor, third door on the right. Do you want your food now?"

"Yeah, that would be best," Kanoa said.

"Sit wherever." The man waved to his tavern. A few people were sitting and talking, getting out of the late-afternoon rain.

A trader sat in one corner, working on different books. He glanced at Kanoa and the others, his eyes falling on their shoes. Confusion passed the man's face, but it quickly disappeared. He wrote down more numbers then sat back in thought, using the reflection from the bar and the pad of paper on his lap to sketch out the shoes the group were wearing.

Evernight had just returned to King's Hill. Night was coming, and Aditya was away at a meeting about trade agreements with the outposts and King's Hill.

She entered his office. Observing, she smiled. One of these days, she might get her own office, but this was comfortable enough, for now. She sat at her desk and glanced out of the window.

As night came in, light formations lit the city. It truly was a city now, boasting a population of forty thousand people and a floating population of thirty thousand. In the First Realm, there were few independent cities that could boast such numbers.

She looked over her region, the domain under her protection. She knew every alley, every backdoor gambling hall and tavern. Her network spread throughout the Beast Mountain Range.

A satisfied smile appeared on her face. Thinking about Erik and Rugrat and their questions, her smile grew wider.

Even with their dominating presence, they were reasonable people. They didn't jump to conclusions and valued the information she and the other agents gathered. They even went so far as to thank them for their work.

She stretched out as if to capture the excitement in her heart. Her sound transmission device shook, and she paused at her full stretch. Her smile disappeared like a flame in winter.

She listened attentively before sending several different messages.

Looking out at the rain, she sighed. "Looks like I should take a coat." She pulled one out from her storage ring and moved to the middle of the room. She activated a teleportation formation that not even Lord Aditya knew of.

She appeared in a basement. Around her, there were crates and four doors.

Evernight checked the crates out of habit, making sure the weapons, armor, and supplies were all accounted for. She moved one of the crates, checking a formation hidden behind it to ensure that no one else was in the secret tunnels under the outpost.

She opened a door and closed it behind her; it looked like part of the wall of a large, open area. She walked across the floor. *I hate walking over trap formations. Scares the hell out of me.*

She kept walking, passing through tunnels and hidden doors until she finally emerged from a stable. She exited and closed the door behind her.

A stable hand was waiting for her outside.

He put his forefinger and thumb against his other forefinger, creating a crude "A."

"It is mighty cold this time of year," Evernight said.

"It might be cold, but the shadows stretch longer every day," the man said.

"They do, but the night does not come earlier," Evernight replied.

The man bowed his head and then quickly pulled out a package. He handed it to her and indicated for her to follow him.

He led her through the stable to another disused stall. He opened a hidden door, and they walked into an office where there were two others. One wore the garb of a trader; the other, a mercenary uniform.

The stable hand closed the door behind her, and she tore open the package and studied the images inside.

The shoes' craftmanship was much higher than anything she had seen in the Ten Realms. The sewing and the shoes reminded her of the boots used by their military.

Evernight stared at the three people. "Report."

The trader stepped forward. "A group of nine people entered the outpost late this afternoon. I made those sketches of their shoes and reported to my cell leader, who told me to check the other inns. Altogether, six groups of nine people entered the outpost today.

"All of them seemed to be in good health and had footwear not from around here. At least, not from the First Realm. Their levels aren't high enough that they could get into the higher realms."

Evernight could smell the alcohol on him, but sobering potions kept him completely alert.

The mercenary stepped forward. "That's fifty-four people in total. There are about sixteen fighters among them, with at least two per group. The rest seem to be smart people. I had some of my people listen in on them. Some were talking in medical terms about things no common First Realmer would know. Their main weapons are crossbows. They are moving fast and light. A few of them had tattoos."

Evernight couldn't help but raise her eyebrow. Rugrat had introduced tattoos, and they had taken off. Some formation masters and scroll makers had turned them into an art form and created formations on one's skin. The buffs were limited, but they used a person's own power and could glow with power. Few other groups used them. Most had scarification instead.

"It appears they are on the run from Queen Ikku."

The mercenary finished his report and stepped backward.

"Shit." Evernight hissed, recalling the report she had read about a group of people fleeing toward the Beast Mountain Range.

She pulled out her sound transmission device and sent out some messages. She felt the information network that stretched across the realm coming alive as information flowed back to her.

In a matter of minutes, she had the latest information from those around the empress and the odd rumors going around.

Evernight closed her mind, checking the information she had pulled together and the conclusion she had made.

With a deep sigh, she used her sound transmission device.

"Evernight?" Director Silaz's voice came over the sound transmission device, sounding immediately alert.

"We have a situation. A group of around fifty Earthers just entered one of our outposts. They are wearing high-quality boots, have tattoos, use crossbows, and talk advanced medical terms for the First Realm. They are being chased by Queen Ikku. It looks like she drew them in and wanted to enslave them, but they escaped. She has made alarming advances rapidly, and after the people ran away, there have not been any more advances. She only told her closest advisors about new advantages and then turned sour. Linking it all together, it makes sense."

"You need to defuse this group and prove their ability to trust us. Potentially, they are military figures. They are probably tired and angry, possibly armed," Silaz said.

"Yes, sir," Evernight said.

Silaz was quiet for a moment.

"Erik and Rugrat are going to want to know, and they are the best people to defuse the situation. One moment."

Evernight's connection went dead. She and the three other agents waited. The mercenary sat down and cleaned his weapons. The stable hand left and came back, checking the area while the trader went through information slips and read textbooks from Alva. It was one of the few places he could do so openly.

"Which groups are in inns that we control? Who is their leader? Are they military or civilian? What are their plans? Find out for me," she said to the agents.

The three of them put their heads together, with the mercenary heading out to talk to some of his people while the trader and stable hand sent messages out.

A few minutes later, Evernight's sound transmission device buzzed.

She activated it, once again cut off from the outside world.

"Erik and Rugrat are mobilizing and heading your way. They should be there within the hour. Keep the Earthers there. Make sure no harm comes to them. Roska and her special team will be with them for protection. Confirm their identities, and make sure they are Earthers. Organize a place where they can meet away from prying eyes." Director Silaz's words were heavy, as if carved into stone.

"I will make the preparations and ensure nothing bad happens to them," Evernight vowed.

"Good. They'll be with you shortly." The connection went dead again.

Evernight curled her fists. She felt as if her brain cells were on fire. She'd have to carry out her job without the outpost leader knowing anything.

They had cells in all the outposts now. It was a good way to raise intelligence agents with a safety net in place. Once they graduated from here, they could be sent across the Ten Realms.

She needed to bring in these groups and set up a meeting. Even if everything went well, she still needed to make fifty-four people disappear and leave just enough of a trace to lead Queen Ikku on a wild chase. *Right, let's get the meeting prepared first, then we can move to extraction.*

She snapped orders to those in the room and then contacted different agents under her command. The outpost shadows shifted under the cover of night.

Kanoa was down in the tavern. He nursed the beer slowly. It wasn't the best beer he had ever had, but it had the bite of alcohol that relieved his mind and body.

Just one beer. He couldn't afford to lose his focus or edge.

He quietly surveyed the room. The patrons had left some time ago. The tavern owner was cleaning the area quietly, and most of the staff had gone home.

There was one way up to their rooms. Kanoa watched downstairs while Miller was upstairs. If they were attacked, Miller would wake everyone and escape out the windows. They had scouted the area and found three routes, pressing them into the brains of their charges.

The people under his care had changed a lot from who and what they were before. They would think he and Miller were alarmists before; now they accepted what they were saying and thought of their surroundings as they did. Back on Earth, they could just be civilians, but here in the Ten Realms, where the powerful ruled and stole from others, there was no such security.

He had trained boys and girls into iron-face soldiers. He had little mercy for those who complained and whined because they were uncomfortable, too used to their leisure lifestyles. He was a hard man, but they needed a hard man.

Certainly didn't make any friends that way. Kanoa grinned and took another tiny sip of his beer.

The tavern owner walked to the door and opened it. Kanoa looked over his mug. His dark eyes flickered to the two men who entered. His nose flared as the two men scanned the room and locked onto him.

Fighters—they're spacing to cover each other.

His eyes flicked to the tavern owner, who closed the door. He didn't lock it, Kanoa noticed, and headed into the back of the tavern, closing the door behind him.

The two men pulled off their hats and cloaks.

Kanoa's eyes widened and then thinned, staring at the all-too-familiar carriers covered in magazines, tools, and with patches on the front that denoted blood type and units.

"So, who did you serve with? I was with the Marines—United States, of course," Rugrat said.

"A hello would have worked," the other man said.

The marine shrugged.

Kanoa held his crossbow at the ready under the table, his thoughts in a mess.

"My name is Erik West. This fine redneck creation is Jimmy Rodriguez, but we call him Rugrat. We served together. I'm an army medic—yeah, I know, weird, but I'm guessing you know how the military works, based on your boots. We landed here—three, nearly four, years ago. Got the Two-Week Curse when we were working a security contracting gig in Africa. Got shipped back stateside and then to wherever the hell this is." Erik grabbed a seat and straddled it. Rugrat did the same.

"You got anything to prove it?" Kanoa asked.

"Sure, but don't shoot me." Erik pulled a cell phone out of thin air. He tossed it onto the table. He kept away, not crowding Kanoa.

Kanoa grabbed the cell phone and looked it over. "Shit. What do you want?"

"We want you to help train up our fighting forces. The people under your protection can study in our academies, though they'll need to pay for it. Tuition costs did follow us over, unfortunately," Erik said.

"I worked my way up to Captain One-oh-One, Airborne," Kanoa said. "How do I know you're not slavers or will sell me to Ikku?"

"Well, if Ikku saw us walking around here with this gear, she would probably try to capture us too. We can make an oath on the Ten Realms, if you want," Erik said.

"Don't shoot me," Rugrat said.

Kanoa eyed him as a rifle appeared in Rugrat's hand.

He held it by the barrel and threw it on the table with a heavy thud that made everyone wince. Rugrat pulled a magazine from his carrier and tossed it over as well.

Kanoa pulled out his crossbow, keeping it aimed at the two. He had his right hand on the bow and used his left to turn the rifle over. It was rough but looked to be based off the FAL. He pulled back on the cocking handle, checked the chamber, and studied the mechanisms inside.

He checked that the barrel was clear and the firing pin was there. He released the cocking handle and aimed the gun away, dry firing it with a satisfying click.

Kanoa kept an eye on the two men as he checked the magazine and the rounds inside before slapping it into the rifle and pulling back on the cocking handle. He loaded a round into the rifle.

Still, he held his hand on his crossbow, not trusting a weapon he hadn't disassembled personally.

"Where were you based? Where did you serve, and what is your name? Don't want to be calling you Cap throughout." Erik grinned.

"Kanoa Nalani, from Hawaii."

"Hawaii is pretty far from Kentucky," Rugrat said.

"The island boy wanted to jump out of planes. My parents weren't best pleased when I signed up." Kanoa relaxed some more. "You make this?" He pointed at the rifle.

"Yeah." Rugrat nodded. "The firearms from Earth work in the lower realms but need stronger materials to handle the powerful rounds and powder we use. Also integrated them with formations to increase their force output."

"I think I know what might make you trust us—another gun." Erik pulled out another rifle. Erik unloaded it and racked it back twice, ejecting the loaded round before he turned the rifle around.

Kanoa realized that he didn't feel threatened as Erik cleared the weapon, seeing the rote functions that had been burned into the other man's brain.

Erik stood and extended the rifle. "She's my personal. Been through a lot with her."

Kanoa took the butt of the rifle. His increased strength since arriving in the Ten Realms allowed him to hold it easily. Erik retreated, and Kanoa pulled the AR platform rifle back.

"Shoots a six-point eight round. AR platform uses the piston system—keeps it operating for longer—with an ACOG mounted on the top and a red dot on the side rail. I had to mark in the red dot because it doesn't work in the Ten Realms," Erik said as if he was detailing the features of a car.

Kanoa looked at the HK on the side of the magwell and turned it over. "German engineering—can't beat it." Kanoa smiled and pointed his crossbow in another direction.

"Okay, so I'll listen." Kanoa's smile faded, and he peeked at the two men with a cold face.

"If you trust your people, we will supply you all with plate carriers, magazines, and rifles. Gear that you can use and defend yourselves with if we fuck with you. Then we come to an agreement. At the very least, hear our pitch. We'll smoke screen Ikku, and get you on your way," Rugrat said.

"How the hell did she capture you anyway?" Erik asked.

"Welcome to the Ten Realms quest. We went looking for a totem and were in her territory. She had some people from Earth, knew the stories about people coming from new places. She acted all nice. Then she tried to get us into contracts that would basically bind us to her forever as her slaves.

Didn't like that idea much and got the hell out of there before she knew we knew something was fucked," Kanoa said.

"Shit, ours took us to a totem as well. If Chonglu was more of a bastard…" Rugrat trailed off.

"Lucked out, man," Erik said. "We'll need oaths that you will never tell anyone where you got the gear or anything about us or our organization. Nothing more unless you want to join Alva."

Kanoa's eyes narrowed. "Guess I'm going to have to trust you. You must have some pull and power to get this tavern under your control."

"Tip of the iceberg," Erik said. "First, something to assure you. I, Sergeant Erik West, swear on the Ten Realms that I am from the United States of America, Earth. I wish to assist you and your people and will not harm you and your people unless you are actively trying to harm me or my comrades. If I break my oath, then might the Ten Realms strike me down."

A golden glow wrapped around Erik.

Rugrat followed with the exact oath, and the golden glow fell away.

"You want to come down from the stairs now?" Rugrat turned to the stairs.

There was a noise, and a moment later, Miller walked down the last few stairs, holding his crossbow. "How did you—?"

"Ten Realms. There's a lot of tricks you can learn. Now, how about this cooperation?" Rugrat smiled.

Things moved quickly then. Kanoa told them everything he knew about their enemy. Then they formulated a plan, utilizing the support of Erik and Rugrat's people.

A masked woman entered the tavern. She listened to Erik and Rugrat and went off to prepare everything.

"Okay, now we just have to convince the other groups," Kanoa said as the door closed behind her.

"Your people are in these places." Erik pulled out some paper and passed it to Kanoa.

Their information network was quick and efficient. In less than a night, they knew who they were and where they were staying, as well as the leadership. Kanoa was interested to see what they have done.

Kanoa spent the night going from one tavern and inn to another. Erik and Rugrat had given him rifles, and he passed them out. At the first tavern, he took one apart completely. It was a crude weapon, but it functioned and there were no traps embedded inside.

"Are you sure about them?" Badowska said in his thick Russian accent.

Kanoa stopped thinking on the duo and snorted. "You know, some shit you just can't fake. Down to their bones, they're soldiers. I trust them."

"Okay," Badowska said. That was enough for him. They had been on opposite sides on Earth, but here, they were two guys in the same foxhole. When the shit hit the fan, they'd banded together and fought side by side. It was a quick and dirty bond that was as strong as steel.

Kanoa patted Badowska, thankful for the other man's trust.

Erik and Rugrat remained in the tavern, though Roska and her people who had been protecting them from outside the tavern were now posted up inside.

"I've got some of my people watching. No one in the surrounding area thinks that anything is different." Roska shared a table with them. They were eating soup with bread the tavern owner had made.

"Looks like everything is ready," Rugrat said.

"Everything is going smoothly. Some real clandestine, secret spook shit." Erik snorted and dipped his bread into his warm soup, soaking up the juices.

"I didn't realize it earlier, but Queen Ikku used to be my queen. Alva Village was within her domain," Roska said. "Never thought I would be running an operation to hide escapees from my ex-queen."

"We live in a weird world," Rugrat said.

Roska grunted as she ate her soup.

"How long until Ikku's people reach the Beast Mountain Range?" Rugrat asked.

"A day or two, I think."

"We got to them just in time then," Rugrat said. "They'll ship out with the traders in the morning, spread out over the outposts, and split Ikku's forces. It'll get them nice and confused. Get them to disappear into the forests. The traces will be spread across the Beast Mountain Range. With our agents creating 'spottings' of the group across the First Realm, Ikku's forces will be dogs without a scent."

Lord Salyn gritted his teeth. The rain from last night had continued into the day, and he and his men were covered in mud. A third of them rode on mounts, and the others did their best to catch up.

The group of nearly a hundred people slowed as they reached the outpost gates.

"Move aside in the name of Queen Ikku of the Shikoshi Kingdom!" Salyn demanded.

People moved out of the way while complaining in low voices that they were forced to do so.

A whistle went up along the wall. The outpost guards readied their weapons; those on the higher walls readied their bows and spears for anything.

Salyn sneered as he touched his blade. He had chased Ikku's helpers across half the empire and through three forests before reaching the Beast Mountain Range. The group was slippery and smart; even with non-fighters, they were able to make fake trails and keep ahead of Salyn and his people. They had even counterattacked and scared off their mounts, forcing most of their forces to run on foot.

They were at a boiling point, and now some worthless outpost thought they stood a chance against his fighters.

An outpost guard stepped forward. "Please wait for your turn to enter. The auction is still some days away. There is no need to have a problem," he said comfortably.

"Who cares about your auction? Tell your lord that I am here with the full force of Queen Ikku's power. We are tracking saboteurs who attacked the queen. Step aside or do not blame me for my actions!" Lord Salyn pulled his blade out and held it at his side, facing the guard.

His own force moved, ready for a fight if it happened.

"Let us not be rash. My lord should be here soon," the guard said.

"He best have an explanation for why he stops Queen Ikku's personal force!" Salyn roared.

A few minutes later, Salyn heard armored soldiers marching. The gates opened wide, and a tanned man wearing gear better that Salyn's own walked out. He wore a smile, as if greeting his best friend on a sunny day. Each of his guards wore their own high-level, custom armor, fanning out to protect him.

Why couldn't he sense their level? And how could there be people this strong in a backwater like this?

Salyn's wariness increased as his eyes scanned the walls, then focused on the outpost lord.

"What is the meaning of this?" Salyn hissed. "You dare to stand in the way of the envoy of Queen Ikku?"

"I do not know of queens or envoys, my lord. I am sorry. I am just an outpost lord. It seems that there is an issue here. If you want to enter the outpost, you will have to pay the fee. If you are wanting to go to the auction, you can go around and take the road to King's Hill if you do not want to enjoy our hospitality. I am sorry, but we live off trade, and, currently, you are holding up the traders." The lord held out his hands to the traders and people waiting to enter the outpost.

"I have been sent to track down and capture a group of people who attacked Queen Ikku. If you stand in my way, you will face the power of her wrath," Lord Salyn said.

The outpost lord's smile didn't falter, but it gained an edge as the placating and easy smile of a simple man never changed. "I am but an outpost lord, but this is an outpost of the Beast Mountain Range and the King's Hill Alliance."

The guards behind the lord and those on the wall unsheathed their weapons in one movement, ready to attack in a moment.

"The kingdom of Thilu's Lord Russo stood where you were some days ago, demanding as you did. He lost the right to enter the Beast Mountain Range and lost three-quarters of his forces. He didn't reach our walls." The lord chuckled and opened his arms. His face didn't change, but a dominating air came from his body and the guards behind him.

Salyn's eyes constricted, feeling their strength wash over him. Many of the guards were stronger than his own elites, who had been riding for weeks. These guards had just woken up after a good night's rest.

He bit back his words, putting on a smile and sheathing his sword. "I am sorry about my actions. It was unbefitting of me. My men and I are tired and tense. We have been on the road and away from civilization too long. I hope you can forgive my sharp and unruly tongue." Salyn bowed his head to the lord.

"Ah, we all have had those days. I hope you can find those you search for." The lord's smile had never changed throughout the conversation, making Salyn feel a mix of rising fury and a chill.

Salyn had his people put their weapons away, and the guards on the walls did the same. Salyn paid the fee and entered the outpost.

"Drev, find me those saboteurs as fast as possible. I will find some food," Salyn said to his second-in-command.

"Yes, my lord." Drev saluted.

Salyn headed to find somewhere warm, dry, and with something to eat with his personal guards as Drev coordinated the search inside the outpost.

Salyn sat in a private room eating, when Drev came to make his report.

"We have found traces of the targets. It looks like they came into the city in several groups and from different ways. This morning, they all left by different means. We are two days behind them, though they didn't all go in the same direction and separated out, taking different caravans to other outposts."

"Your thoughts?"

"Some groups headed toward King's Hill. It is a super-outpost that has reached a population equivalent to a city. To reach it, one needs to pass through the Beast Mountain Range. It is a hard journey. If one is to leave the path, there is no guarantee one could survive long."

Salyn looked through the window. "Where did the strong Experts we saw on the wall come from?"

"They are part of the Beast Mountain Range guards. They were trained in King's Hill. The outposts banded together after a large fight and created an alliance. King's Hill is their center and connects them all. The outpost leaders put forward their own guards to join the new guard unit. They come from all the outposts, making them a neutral party in outpost conflicts. They are well-trained and supported."

"How has a backwater group of guards become so powerful?" Salyn's eyes were sharp as they cut to Drev.

"The Beast Mountain Range is a place of peril. There are many mercenary groups who put their lives on the line to earn a living here. They are rough men and women, but due to the constant fighting and high pay, if they succeed, they become very strong. Some of them become guards who must weather beast tides, protect traders and their outposts, and give justice. Although the mercenaries are strong, the guards must be even stronger to suppress them or else the outposts would have been taken over by a mercenary band. It has happened before. The best of these guards were pulled together, given powerful training aids, and gained discipline, creating a structure that allow the guards to fully employ their strength."

"So, all of the outposts are controlled by them?"

"No, each outpost has its own guards. The Beast Mountain Range guards are just support and rotating guards. They protect the roads and support the local outpost units, if necessary."

"Sounds like you respect them," Salyn asked.

"They live in a hard place. The guards are as strong as I am, but they work for the King' Hill Alliance and are organized into a true army. Calling them guards is to underestimate them; they are true warriors."

"So, it will be hard or nearly impossible for us to force the locals to help us." Salyn smacked the table in frustration. He stood and moved to the window. "The routes other than the one to King's Hill—what are they like?"

"There are the main routes, but there are many roads and routes between outposts. Some caravans might head away from the Beast Mountain Range toward other villages and towns if the weather or roads are bad. If our targets run, they can go anywhere," Drev replied.

"With the route to King's Hill, they're boxed in. Okay, we will head out as soon as possible." Salyn turned around to Drev's frown. "Something wrong?"

"The roads are well made, but they still go through the Beast Mountain Range. We will need to be at our best condition if we want to rush through. We could hire the guards to escort us, but it is expensive and we would have to travel at their pace," Drev said.

Salyn snorted. "You think too little of our people and too much of these guards. Have everyone prepare. We will set off in two hours."

Drev moved his lips, as if he had something more to say. He cupped his hands and bowed. "As you command, Lord Salyn."

16 Light at the End of the Tunnel

Kanoa waited as the guard passed. The sound of footsteps faded away. The trader who was ferrying them to King's Hill checked the area once again and waved them forward. They left the rest deployment area at the side of the road and quickly escaped into the forest.

It was cold, still wet from the last few days of rain. They reached a group of boulders in the middle of the forest. They were covered in moss, untouched by time.

The trader moved a rock out of the way and pressed a medallion against an engraving.

Kanoa scanned the area, covering the civilians who were huddled together. He'd convinced them, but they were understandably scared about trusting someone new.

The ground shook and some boulders moved aside, revealing stairs leading down. The trader waved them forward. They passed through a series of doors and found three people waiting for them around a teleportation array.

"Captain," Rugrat said in greeting. "All right, step into the teleportation formation and then we'll be off to the races. I'll hold your hand if you want?"

Kanoa sighed. "You got into all kinds of shit with your officers, didn't you?"

"Once or twice." Rugrat grinned.

Kanoa stepped onto the teleportation array with three civilians and Rugrat. The trader turned around and headed out. Kanoa heard the boulders moving back into place as a flash of light consumed him.

Kanoa had his rifle ready to snap up to his shoulder.

He scanned the area, noticing the defensive structure around the teleportation array. The air was warm; the men and women at the defenses wore modern military equipment and toted firearms, though they had lines of formations on their weapons and gloves. They were relaxed and laid-back.

"Please vacate the teleportation array and step forward. New arrivals to the left for medical check and familiarization courses. Returning citizens, to the right. Welcome to Alva." The words were monotonous and bored, as if the speaker had been drained, body and soul.

Kanoa stared at the little imp holding paddles and standing on a box.

Kanoa stepped out of the way of the teleportation array and saw more of his people appearing at different teleportation arrays.

The imp sighed, filled with suffering and unwillingness.

Kanoa's eyes went wide as a flame appeared and the temperature increased. He felt a chill watching the enslaved creature repeat his instructions, waving his paddles from the left to the right entryways.

"What are you doing here as a greeter, Davin?"

"Hey, Rugrat," the imp said, his entire body slumped.

"Did you make a mess in the Wood floor again?"

"I tooted one time! How was I supposed to know it would set the field on fire?" Davin waved his paddles and pouted, like a five-year-old child who couldn't have possibly done wrong.

Kanoa coughed slightly and lowered his guard. *Okay, so not indentured servant, but a fire-spitting imp on time-out?*

"What was it this time?"

"There were some pies out for free, and because the people from the cooking trades are so nice, I couldn't let them go to waste so I had to show my support for their hard work!"

Rugrat turned to a guard.

"There was a large test being held by the cooks. The pies had only just come out of the oven. They were so hot they had to be handled with gloves, and they were put near the window to cool them down."

"They were just the right temperature!" Davin said.

"You're a Fire imp—everything hot is the right temperature. Most other people would be sent to the hospital with burns!" Rugrat said.

"I was just passing by. How was I to know?"

"It was the seventh floor," the guard said deadpanned.

"Right, it all makes sense now," Rugrat said. "Keep up the good work, Davin, and stop eating everything!"

Davin made hurt noises, and his face crumpled some more.

A large skull head appeared in front of Davin.

"Are you slacking again?" the head asked, its eyes glowing with mysterious fire.

"No! Not at all, Brother Egbert! Please vacate the teleportation array and step forward. New arrivals to the left for medical check and familiarization courses. Returning citizens, to the right. Welcome to Alva." Unlike before, Davin's words were filled with cheer and happiness, as if he were only too happy to please others.

"Right." The head disappeared from mid-air.

"Mysterious and creepy. Stop putting on a front, Egbert!" Rugrat yelled into the air. "Hard to find good help these days." Rugrat led the way.

Medics cast spells, checking everyone. "You have an issue with your heart. You should go to the hospital for further testing." The medic wrote out a note, passing it to Kanoa.

"What do you mean?"

"Your knees are in bad shape. Your back is a mess. Did you break your collarbone and one of your fingers?"

"Yeah, just pains of the trade," Kanoa said.

"Well, we can get that fixed up easily, and you have some scar tissue leftover that will be simple to fix. Also, it looks like your arteries are partly clogged, so you'll need to flush them out. Easy enough, happens a lot of the time," the medic said with a smile.

Kanoa walked forward and looked at Rugrat.

"Ah, just a partly clogged artery. A few healing spells and you'll be fine." Rugrat waved it off as they entered an auditorium.

"Like I could've had a heart attack? And what did he mean about my wear and tear?"

"Bit of healing, and your knees will be like when you were sixteen. Spine all in the right place—no more aches, pains, squeaks, and creaks. Also, heal your heart and circulatory system up good. Just clears you out. I was a big chew fanatic; I'm all good to go now. Got a whole new set of teeth—not one filling!" Rugrat opened his mouth and pointed at it.

Kanoa checked, seeing nothing but pearly whites.

"Oh, whoops, you've got a quick presentation first."

A lady was waiting for them all at the front of the auditorium. "Please take a seat. Once everyone is ready, we will begin the introduction to Alva," the lady said.

"We have replaced some of your people in the varied groups with our own. They'll act like you and keep running, make it appear that you've disappeared into the Beast Mountain Range." Rugrat tilted his head to the lady. "You might find this useful."

"Thanks." Kanoa was still not sure about all of this, on alert against anything. Kanoa and the other military members sat around the civilians, watching the doors.

"Hello, and welcome to Alva. First of all, we require you to take an oath on the Ten Realms to not share any information you might learn. This is the oath. Please review it and let me know if you have any questions."

Behind the lady, a set of words appeared on the wall, outlining the content of the oath.

Kanoa went through the oath with everyone, and then the lady started talking of Alva, going through its founding, the different institutions, then property ownership, loans, taxes, and so on.

Kanoa was a little surprised by the founding, but the main points were similar to what they were used to on Earth. It was clear Rugrat and Erik had affected the changes in Alva.

The civilians, starting to see something that reminded them of home, began asking questions and coming out of their shells.

When the information session was over, they were given temporary resident cards and led out of the auditorium and past the defenses around the teleportation array.

Kanoa stared at the growing city that lay underground. It was dark, simulating night, but he could see lines of light above his head. There had to be hundreds or thousands of glowing crystals growing from the ceiling. It looked like an artificial night sky.

He took a deep breath and realized just how dense the mana was. He could feel it flowing into his veins, making him feel alert and full of energy, clearing his mind.

Lights could be seen in different windows as buildings grew from stone and metal or trees and bushes while factories worked through the night.

"Well, shit." Sung stopped next to Kanoa. The military members grouped together so others couldn't hear them and made sure no one else got close.

"What's the plan, Captain?" Badowska asked.

"We give it a shot, see what the truth is of this all," Kanoa said.

"This might not be too bad." Miller looked around.

Kanoa grinned, and some of the others chuckled. All of them stepped back from the hyper-alert state they had been in for months, relaxing minutely.

"I heard they have showers, and we've got food vouchers," Sung said.

"Move in groups still. Always have the civvies covered. We'll check in a week and see how things are going," Kanoa said.

The group nodded and then broke up. They gathered up their charges and headed toward their temporary house, what looked like apartment-style housing.

17 Truths and Misdirection

Tanya cracked an eyelid open and looked around the dusty room.

What was that noise?

"Mrhmmk." She rubbed the dribble from the side of her mouth and blinked a few more times, taking in her office and staring at the book she had fallen asleep on. She smacked her lips and cleared her throat as she woke up.

She blinked slowly. Her eyes focused on the wet spot on the book. She stretched her hands and paused mid-stretch, as if struck by lightning.

I drooled on a book? A library book?

"No! Nononono! I am not getting in shit for defacing a book! Egbert will kill me!" She jumped up and ran around the room. Grabbing a rag, she moved to the book, dabbing it as if it were the most precious item in the universe.

I could use my Clean spell? No, shit, don't—that would remove the ink from the pages and turn it blank! Egbert would murder me!

The wet mark wasn't shifting, and her panic increased.

Tetsu watched her running around and got up, jumping up and down, excited to play. He was nearly twice the size of a regular Doberman, with that goofy I-want-to-play-too-human look on his face that dogs got when excited.

"Calm down, Tetsu. I can't play right now!" Tanya said as she ran through ideas in her head.

She closed her eyes, focusing. "A hairdryer would work. I need something warm. Not a Flame spell—could set it on fire. Is there a way that I could create a hot element that is strong enough to dry out the pages?" Tanya raised her hands; the air around them shimmered as she combined mana and attributes together.

Flames appeared first.

"Nope!"

Then Metal shards shot out over her hand.

"Okay, more Metal, circulating Water and Fire to create a circulating breeze and increase the Fire attribute for more heat." She kept her eyes closed, and the air in front of her moved; it turned red and seemed to have reflective particles within.

There was another knock at the door.

Shit, I totally forgot there was someone at the door!

"Who is it?" Tanya put her hand under her magical heater.

"It's Rugrat. I wanted to talk to you about your recent studies. I made an appointment."

"Oh, yes." Tanya looked around and then took out a key; she threw it toward the door. Using air manipulation, she turned it in the lock; then with Earth manipulations, she used the door to shift the doorknob, opening the door as she sent a blast of air to at it.

It happened in some hurried gestures before she focused again on her book.

Tetsu bounded over to Rugrat, eager for someone to play with in his excited state.

George, who was in his dog size, sniffed Tetsu.

Tetsu tapped George's neck with his head, his tongue hanging out, wanting to play. The two of them wrestled and started jumping around like two puppies again.

"Make sure you two don't break anything," Rugrat said to George.

"What are you doing there?" Rugrat asked, turning his attention to Tanya.

As Tanya raised a page of the book, she moved her hand, manipulating the spell around the page, and the water started to evaporate. "I am using a heater spell to dry the book," Tanya whispered.

"You defaced a bo—"

Tanya's hand clamped over Rugrat's mouth, and she looked around.

Rugrat nodded. She removed her hand and worked while Rugrat walked to the door and closed it quietly, locking the door.

He waited as Tanya painstakingly dried the pages. She waved her hand and sighed as the spell fell apart and the book's pages dried.

"Holy crap, I nearly died of a heart attack." Tanya slumped into a chair, her back covered in a cold sweat.

"Definitely not." Rugrat shuddered.

Tanya clicked her tongue, and Tetsu came over. "You two go play in the yard," she said.

Tetsu jumped up and down.

"I can't come now. I will play with you later."

Tetsu lowered his head, and his tail dipped.

"You have George to play with!"

Tetsu looked up and over to George, whose tail wagged as his tongue hung from his mouth.

"All right, don't get into too much trouble." She opened the door using more mana. The two hounds ran out, and she closed the door behind them without standing up. She sighed and brought out some fruit juice. "Drink?"

"Please." Rugrat cleared papers off a chair and put them on top of a full desk, making sure nothing fell before he sat.

She chilled the juice with Air, Water, and Metal magic and inverse flames that drew the heat away.

Rugrat took it, watching the spell fade away before staring at her.

"Okay, so what are you interested to learn?" Tanya said, the sweet juice clearing her throat as she glanced over to Rugrat.

"Pure magic. Explain to me what you think it is." Rugrat leaned on the armrest and stroked his beard.

Tanya played with the piercing through her lower lip, staring at the ceiling to pull her thoughts together. "Pure magic is a name that others have given it. What I am looking to do is study the fundamentals of magic. Primarily, what is mana, what are attributes, how do the two work together—then the system of ley-lines, dungeon cores, and the various ways those fundamental components are utilized in different ways." Tanya glanced to the corner of the room and nodded, sure in her answer.

"Okay, so what have you found out about magic? Small words, please."

"If mana is fresh water, then attributes are the salt creating sea-water. There is very little freshwater compared to sea-water. Mana flows throughout everything; it is sunshine and water—the power of the Ten Realms. Everything has adapted to it. Attributes by themselves are nothing, just impurities lying around. When combined with mana, they change the state of mana, let's say. Going with the water idiom, you have steam, water, and ice. Combining these different attributed mana, or different states of water, you create a spell. A spell is a combination of attributes, powered by mana to create an effect that the attributes and the mana could not create on their own. So"—Tanya held out her hand—"use your Mana Sight and watch my hand. First, I will create a Fire mana attribute layer around my hand. Fire mana creates an immense amount of heat, but it can also pull it away. It is why people with a high Fire attribute have greater resistance. Same for the other attributes. Now I have some Wood element, and I'm going to add in some Fire element."

A flame appeared in her hand.

"So, it's like a circuit: The attributes are different parts, but linked together, they create something greater than the sum of their parts, and the mana powers it," Rugrat said.

"Traditional spells are more like that." Tanya dismissed her original flame, and a spell formation appeared, showing the same flame. "Spell formations are a means of quantifying spells. It is like the math of magic."

"I thought you were against traditional spells?"

"Against them? No, I think they're an incredible discovery, though I also think they are outdated. This burns three times the amount of mana for the same effect. To increase the power, you need to put in more mana. If I were to just use Water and Metal elements, I could create a highly oxygenated area instantly through electrolysis. It costs much less mana overall, but the effect is the same."

She cast the spell version and then her own modified version into the air, creating two larger flames in mid-air.

Rugrat studied the flames and half-closed his eyes. He raised his hand and a flame appeared, identical to her pure-magic version.

"It is more like cooking than it is like spellcasting, though I can see how it would be faster to cast. What about higher-grade spells?" The flames disappeared.

"That is a problem. Spells are useful when it comes to large spells. They create a path for the mana and the attributes to follow. I am not saying that we should use the spell structure. I think it is a useful guide—training wheels on a bike, if you will. Once you master the spell, you can take off the training wheels and cast a spell without needing the complete structure. You can cast it faster, adapt quicker, even alter your spell mid-cast."

"If you alter a formulated spell mid-cast, there can be a severe backlash," Rugrat said.

"Yeah, because you are stuck in a rote system that casts mana and attributes together. If you deviate from it, it will collapse. This attribute spellcasting is simply combining attributes in different ways and then powering it afterward with mana to create an effect. It's interesting that you mentioned cooking. At the basic level, it is like cooking—but isn't cooking, when you get deeper into it. Chemistry, perhaps?"

"So, you're breaking down magic into its attributes, studying the reactions, and then using your knowledge to recreate spells without the formulas. Where do attributes come from, though?"

"Pretty much! Though one distinction to make is that elements and attributes are somewhat interchangeable. Elements are the basic and pure building blocks. Everything else is made up of different attributes. Humans are made up of all five elements—all creatures are—but some have a greater Fire attribute. Elements are all around us. We all have a different Affinity—control—to different elements. Someone who has spent their days working in a field, say, will be able to control Earth, Water, and Wood much more than say a smith, who would find it easier to manipulate Wood, Fire, and Metal. In my research, one's environment changes their control over the different elements. Now, a great way to increase one's elemental control is to increase their body's elemental attributes. Confused yet?"

"I'm holding on, barely. How can you increase your Affinity for the different attributes?"

Tanya pulled out a book from her desk and turned it toward Rugrat, reading out the title. "The Fundamentals of Body Tempering." She smiled as Rugrat's brows pinched together.

"Think about it. You and Erik have tempered your bodies in the different elements, changing the attributes of your body and increasing your Affinity for the elements. I read the notes that Erik made on learning that body tempering and Mana Cultivation were of the same path. That one tempered their body with the elements, making it stronger, leaving purified mana to increase one's cultivation without fear of mana rejection. It clicked for me. The two systems are treated as different items, but they are two parts of the whole!"

"So, Mana Cultivation is like increasing the power of your battery, and then your elemental Affinities are the different parts you can create a circuit with? Playing with those power board things was way back in high school."

"That's exactly the idea. Looks like your teachers would be happy."

"I'm not so sure about that. I gave them enough troubles." Rugrat grinned.

"I know that only too well." Tanya sat back and played with her eyebrow piercing. "Always liked reading, but school was more of a pain than anything to me. The only thing I really enjoyed was meeting other weirdos like me and getting together to play games. I was a factory worker. I didn't care about the work; I did it so I could live comfortably and play my games in peace. Here, where magic is real, it's terrifying, but the nerd part of my mind is excited. Sure, the system is not the same as what is depicted in fantasy books, movies, and games—and the stakes are a lot higher—but the possibilities to learn something new, the ability to cast spells, it's awesome."

"Just have to make sure that it is practical as well."

"Well, yeah, like min-maxing in real life doesn't make sense. Look at you and Erik. You trained in Mana Cultivation first and are ahead of Erik, but you are still tempering your body, learning from his lessons, and he is doing the same from you. Both of you are not only fighters; you are crafters, medics, and adventurers. If you were to only train your Strength, then you would have too much power to usefully apply. You need to increase your Agility stat to get greater control. If you don't have enough Stamina, then you can throw out a really powerful punch, but you'll be drained. There are game-like elements to the Ten Realms, but it is the real world. Things change. Even the Ten Realms system isn't completely accurate. It tries its best, but it is just a system. Every system has good points and bad."

"Basically, spells are like writing an essay on how to do math. While creating spells with the attributes is doing the actual math. Two units of water and one unit of metal equals reinforced ice blade."

"Breaking the Ten Realms code."

"Like when science changed from observing the surrounding environment to trying to quantify it."

Pan Kun walked along the wall of King's Hill. He held up a hand in greeting to some of the guards under his command who had been escorting traders.

They returned the gesture as they walked through the gates. Their fellow guards took the entry fee and allowed the traders to enter.

It was midday, and there were still more trading caravans coming in from the distance or circling around the large walls that protected King's Hill.

He came to a pause next to one of Aditya's servant girls.

"Nice day for a stroll, miss?" Pan Kun said in a respectful voice.

"Looks like you've come for the show as well?" The servant girl was unremarkable: straw-like hair, simple clothes, and slightly tanned skin. She looked just different enough that someone wouldn't take her for Evernight.

"I have my orders. I think you made them, after all," Pan Kun said.

Evernight smiled slightly and kept watch over the wall, a bored girl wasting her time off.

"I hear that the Beast Mountain consortium will open their doors in a week or two," Pan Kun said. "There are already hundreds of people from the area looking to join. Seems that someone leaked what kind of resources they will have and who will be leading it. I also heard that people who perform well in the sect could earn positions in the military."

"Well, there are always more people creating trouble out there," Evernight said.

"And there are plenty of recruiting offers for my people to take," Pan Kun said with a wry smile.

"You've seen their training facilities and just how powerful they are. If you were given a chance in the future…?" Evernight asked.

Pan Kun thought of what he had seen in Alva. The men and women who walked in the streets were stronger than him, but they were just farmers or crafters.

He remembered seeing the Alva army training, advancing and shooting, creating a wall of bullets as they charged forward across smoke and destruction.

Pan Kun's heartbeat increased before guilt intruded. He glanced at the headquarters of King's Hill. "I feel like I would be betraying my friend."

"I understand. But be aware that if you increase your power much more, you're going to need a new charm to cover it. It looks like they're nearly here."

Pan Kun squinted and used an enhancing spell on his eyes. He saw a group of ragged people moving past the inner-city gates. There were just a handful of mounts for the entire group. Their armor was covered in scratches and a dried mixture of blood and mud. A savage air surrounded them as they pushed forward. "What happened?"

"Thankfully, they didn't contract any of our people to help them. Seems like they might have encountered some enraged beasts along their travels." Evernight shrugged.

Pan Kun felt a chill in his bones. Alva's fighting power was scary, but it was nowhere as terrifying as their intelligence department. If they chose to strike, their enemy might not even know who they were actually fighting.

The group spread out and started browsing King's Hill.

"Looks like our guests have arrived, Major General Pan Kun." Evernight's words drifted to his ears as she left the wall, reminding him of his recent promotion. As the Beast Mountain Range army grew, so did his rank.

Pan Kun looked at the group from the Shikoshi kingdom as they headed to a tea house.

What are you planning?

It is not at all what I thought.

Salyn held his tongue as they paid their fees and entered King's Hill outpost. There were noble and powerful families riding on stone roads in their carriages. Traders were everywhere, selling high-quality items of various kinds. People pressed in together as the streets were reduced to foot traffic. There were so many people.

They were in the middle of the treacherous Beast Mountain Range, but they had items that would be hard to find in the capital city.

He studied the weapons, armor, resources, textiles—all of which were of the highest quality, reaching mid-Apprentice level. Only nobles were able to get regular access to mid-Apprentice-level items. Here, they were as common as stones. There were even high-Apprentice-level items being sold in some of the stores.

Salyn studied the people browsing the different wares. Nobles and powerful figures from several different kingdoms that Salyn knew of were there.

"There is a tea house up ahead we can stay at," Drev said.

"Check on the situation of King's Hill and find out just where those rats are." Salyn shot a look at Drev.

Drev left with most of the fighters as Salyn found a tea house and sat down. One of the guards ordered for him as he sat back, watching the movement around him. He couldn't help but overhear a conversation a couple of tables away.

"I heard all the tickets for the main auction have been sold already. Three gold coins a ticket, and they're all gone! People sure have money to burn!" someone was saying to their friend as they admired the action in the city.

"That is nothing! I heard that three other auctions were started up as there were so many goods people wanted to sell or trade. An entire building was dedicated to people who want to barter their goods or services."

"That might be interesting for many people, but how many auctions can you find in the First Realm that boast genuine high-Apprentice-grade equipment?"

"Apprentice? I've heard rumors of Journeyman! I thought that was gear the outpost leaders are keeping to themselves."

"It's the alliance. You know, how they're all working together."

"Alliance, my ass. Lord Aditya controls the Beast Mountain Range. Should have done this years ago! Why are they selling such precious gear? Aren't they afraid outsiders are going to turn around and use it on us?"

"If they're willing to sell it, doesn't it mean that it isn't as useful for them and they're keeping the best gear for themselves?" The other man laughed and drank his tea.

Salyn was brought out of his eavesdropping as his tea arrived. He dismissed the server and took the cup, letting it cool before he took a sip.

He appreciated the tea, letting it settle his nerves. He glanced out at King's Hill. It looked more like a city than an outpost. Their fighting force was strong, and they were able to pull out all these people from their kingdoms just for some kind of auction. Salyn clicked his tongue.

It took some hours and a meal later before Drev returned.

He came in with a tired expression, twisting Lord Salyn's stomach.

"People confirmed that the groups arrived some days ago before heading off in different directions. None of them took the same route," Drev said.

Salyn sighed and tapped his finger on the table. If the queen found out that he had hesitated for even a moment, she would come for his head.

Salyn felt every ache and pain from the past few days of hard riding.

"Make sure everyone gets a meal in them. See if there is an apothecary in the city to heal our people and stables we can buy mounts from."

"Thank you, sir." Even Drev, the hard man, seemed moved.

"We only have the day. We will leave as soon as we have supplies."

"Yes, sir. I'll do my best to expedite supplies. I won't be done until"—Drev gauged Lord Salyn's mood—"midday tomorrow?"

"Too late. We must push on faster for the queen!" Salyn said righteously.

"Early morning?" Drev asked.

"Well, if that is the best you can do, there is nothing my yelling at you can do."

Good man.

"As for the apothecary, there is no need for it. There is a healing house."

"All the way out here? They are a luxury that the nobles can pay for in the large capitals and important cities."

"No, really, sir. They're real healers, too—spells and all. Called the Alva Healing House. They serve the mercenaries, the general people. I talked to some guards of different nobles; they went there to see if it was worth anything. They don't charge much, but they healed the guards up completely!"

"What was it called?" Salyn felt cold sweat on his back.

"Alva Healing House," Drev said.

Alva Healing House—Alva village? It couldn't be.

"When was it created?" Salyn asked.

"It started three, four years ago in Vermire, an outpost under the control of Lord Aditya. He is the head of King's Hill and the leader of the Beast Mountain Range Alliance. He's the ruler around here."

They were simple farmers, nobodies. How was it possible they had become healers?

"Lord Salyn?" Drev asked.

Salyn realized he had been quiet for a while. "Get the men ready to move. I'm going to look around."

Drev bowed, and Salyn left the tea house. His two personal guards followed him.

"Find out where this Alva Healing House is," Salyn hissed to one of them.

They ran off and Salyn wandered the city, apparently taking in the sights. Meanwhile, he was scanning for any of the Alvans he recognized.

"Lord, I have found its location. Do you think it is *those* Alvans?" the guard asked.

"Best to check and make sure. Take us there."

Salyn stood in an alleyway, watching the Alva Healing House. He'd seen severely wounded people being brought in from outside the city. Some of the strongest beasts roamed the heart of the Beast Mountain Range. It was easy to be critically or even fatally wounded if one made a simple mistake.

His guards entered the alleyway and wore cloaks to hide their identities.

The three men stood there and watched as a young boy went up to the front of the healing house. Healers were assessing the wounded and those waiting.

"Hey, boy," Salyn yelled to a kid walking by.

"Mister?"

"I'll give you a silver coin if you run up to the healing house and yell something for me."

"A whole silver? What do you want me to do?"

Salyn whispered in the boy's ear.

He nodded and held out a hand.

Salyn pulled out the coin and pressed it into his hand.

The boy's eyes went round before quickly putting it away. He headed over to the healing house.

"Look! There's Blaze and Elise!" the boy yelled out. "Blaze and Elise!" He ran away from the healing house.

Salyn's eyes locked onto the healers as they turned to where the boy was pointing. The boy ran off, and the healers looked around, searching for "Elise and Blaze."

They frowned, glanced at one another and went back to work.

An official-looking lady stepped out. She looked around and then headed back inside.

There was a chance they were just staring at the noise. Some people did that, but they seemed excited. Even one of their higher-ups made an appearance before disappearing back inside.

"Lord?" one of his guards asked.

He didn't know how they had done it, but maybe some of the survivors had become healers and worked here in anonymity. Blaze and Elise had to be alive as well. Salyn would have to make plans for how to deal with them, just in case.

"Let's go. We have a tough ride ahead of us." Salyn studied the front of the building again and turned around, moving deeper into the maze of alleys.

Erik read the report and looked at Elan. "Is it *that* Lord Salyn?"

Rugrat put down the papers with a grim look.

"Everything matches up. I didn't realize it before." Elan pressed his teeth together with a dark expression.

"You can't see through everything. It has been years since we defended Alva. So much has happened it is easy to forget," Erik said.

"What we need to worry about is what is he going to do next?" Rugrat said.

"Well, he has limited options. Alva was a hidden village. There are no records of it, which is why we didn't connect it to *this* Lord Salyn. My agents are trying to find out more information on this Lord Salyn as well as his operations," Elan said.

"Nothing to do but sit on him and wait," Rugrat said.

18 Earth Knowledge Meets Ten Realms Reality

Rugrat stared at the new building in front of him. "Mana Cultivation Training Facility," he read out the sign above the door.

There were people moving through the doors from all of Alva's various sectors. A group of soldiers formed outside and marched toward the barracks, while a group of woodworkers ran up the stairs with excited expressions.

Rugrat went up the stairs and entered the large foyer. There were shops on either side, and he went up to the front desk.

"Hello, how might I help you today?" The man behind the desk smiled.

"What is with the stores?" Rugrat asked.

"They have all that one might need: Alchemy concoctions to increase the rate that one absorbs mana or increase one's concentration, materials for crafters who are working in the special crafting workshops. There is also a small library that holds books on common cultivation practices and reference materials," the man said helpfully.

He had let his cultivation fall behind, and Erik was right behind him in terms of Mana Cultivation. With so much happening, it was easy to let it slip.

"I'll take your highest rated training room for"—Rugrat checked his timepiece—"say, four hours?"

"Are you sure, sir? With the higher mana density, it can take more time to get used to. The lower mana densities are gentler on the body. You can train in them for longer with greater control. Also, they are much cheaper," the man warned.

"It shouldn't take me too long to adjust." Rugrat smiled.

"Okay." The man drew out the word, unsure of Rugrat's confidence. "It will be one Earth mana stone per hour for unrefined mana, two for refined mana from the dungeon core."

Rugrat pulled out his Dungeon Lord emblem. "Unrefined, please." He wanted to check out the validity of Tanya's research himself.

The man eyes widened. "I am sorry." He made to bow, but Rugrat stopped him.

"I'm just a dude. No need for all that bowing."

"Uh, yes, sir." The man was shaken up. He quickly grabbed a key and passed it to Rugrat with both hands. "Your key, Lord Rugrat."

Rugrat coughed, and his face went red. *That sounds so damn ridiculous.* "Uh, yes, thank you. Have a good day." Rugrat grabbed the key, checking the markings on it.

He passed the front desk and entered the training facility, staring at a map on the wall. They had broken it up into two sectors. On the left, there were the crafting workshops; on the right, there were individual and group training rooms. The two sectors met in the middle where the highest density of mana was. In a big circle, there were rows of training rooms, each sealed and isolated from one another.

He headed into the training facility. He held up his "key," which was just a piece of metal with formations engraved inside.

The door opened, and he stepped inside. It felt like stepping out of the airport in Texas, right into a wall of heat. Instead of heat, though, it was mana. Maybe it wasn't really like Texas. It was so damn hot.

Rugrat grimaced as he walked past the different rows of training rooms. People took their pills and concoctions, quickly opening the doors and rushing into the rooms. A green light turned red, showing the rooms as occupied.

There were formations all over the training rooms. The walls around the facility stopped the mana from leaking out and kept it concentrated. The doors in and out were like air locks, the formations a force field retaining the air.

It was an impressive feat of engineering, taking the construction crews, formation masters, and Egbert working together to make it a reality.

People staggered out of training rooms. There was staff on hand to check on them. Some wore expressions of frustration while most were ecstatic.

He moved through the different rows. He had to use his key on different doors. Each set of doors was like ascending to a different realm. As his body relaxed, his mana gates opened, and the mana within his body started to circulate faster. He stood outside of his training room.

Area of High Mana Density

You have entered an area of high mana density.

Mana Regeneration is increased by 4.0x

Damn. Was that how people from the Tenth Realm were supposed to be able to cast powerful-ass spells? With that kind of Mana Regeneration buff, they could load up their stat points into a mana pool, and the higher mana density would refill the pool quickly without the need to drop lots of points into Mana Regeneration. Rugrat sank into thought.

The common thought was that people from the Seventh Realm didn't dare to come down to the lower realms because they would lose their power.

There was something wrong with that. The idea of the internal pressure of one's mana system and the world around them—that sounded like crap. Rugrat didn't want to lose mana by going up in the realms. He had focused more on his mana pool than his regeneration due to the availability and increase in mana density.

That had to be the crux of the issue.

People in the Seventh Realm and higher were relying on their environment to recover their lost mana. It made sense; humans were born and designed to rely on the forces of gravity to live. Look at our digestion system, he thought. Our inner balance. If they went to higher or lower gravity worlds, after generations, wouldn't they alter their bodies to get used to the new environment? The thing that would hold someone back in the higher realms wasn't their lack of Mana Regeneration but their lack of mana pool! When they left the mana-dense areas, their Mana Regeneration dropped, and then they were a big balloon with a tiny pump!

That is a weird mental image. Like a space hopper and a gnome cranking on a tiny pump. Rugrat snorted and put his key to the door's lock. It opened with a click, and he walked inside. The room was like a prison cell. There was a chair, a washroom, a desk, and a bed.

"Hello, cultivator, your rented time has started. On the wall, you will find a health sensor. Please take this off the wall and place it on your chest before you start cultivating. It will send updates to our health staff to make sure that you do not overtrain and lead to injuries upon your body and mana channels."

Rugrat winced, thinking of how he had crippled his own mana channels in the past. He spotted the piece of metal as the voice continued.

"Once you have placed the sensor on your body and it is linked, you can hit the green buttons around the room. These will increase the mana density up to the predicted level of the Seventh Realm. Please refrain from taking training aides before you start your first session for the first hour. You should know your limits after that time."

Rugrat put the sensor on his chest and sat in the chair. There was a green button beside him. He pressed it, and all the buttons turned red as runic lines increased in brightness. He took a deep breath as the mana density started to increase rapidly. He used his Organic Scan to look through his body and see what was happening inside.

His mana core had reached the peak of the Mist Stage. Next, he had to combine the mist and start to fill his core, creating a Liquid Mana Core.

Rugrat's face relaxed, becoming emotionless. He breathed, focusing his mind; he felt his fighting will rise from his bones. Around him, the room started to fill with a blue mist.

Dense, unrefined, attribute-filled mana. Rugrat approved. He started to open his mana gates. It was like a dam opening.

The mist around him started to shift, drawn to his fifteen mana gates. Rugrat felt his blood boiling, feeling endless power within his body. His mind was clearer than ever.

Compress! Rugrat ordered his body. His mana veins flexed their strength as he circulated the mist mana.

Again! Compress it again! I can handle liquid mana! Come on!

His circulations increased in speed, and the mana density within his mana channels rose. He held back from forcing the mist into his core. It shone brighter as it was forced together.

Rugrat started to feel himself reaching his limits.

The mana in the room rushed through his mana gates. His mana veins were outlined in the mist, making him look like a primordial machine covered in runes.

Rugrat gritted his teeth, but his lips raised in a grin as he opened his eyes. "Refine!" he yelled out, staring at the ceiling.

It felt like a bomb went off in his body. Instead of being pushed deeper into his innermost core, the mana he had been compressing was refined through his mana veins. It flowed into his bones, through his muscles, his nerves, and his very cells, soaking every part of his being in the elements and mana of the Ten Realms.

Rugrat felt as if his body had been struck by lightning, crushed by its own weight. He saw visions and illusions, but he persisted. The power ran through his veins, through his soul.

Staff Sergeant Jimmy Rugrat Rodriguez, Second Reconnaissance Battalion, United States Marine Corps. Staff Sergeant Jimmy Rugrat Rodriguez, Second Reconnaissance Battalion, United States Marine Corps.

Rugrat recited the mantra over and over again. Steam rose from his body as impurities were expelled from deep within.

Mana escaped through his body, but most of it passed through and entered his mana veins. The color started to change as the mana was purified repeatedly.

Rugrat's mind went blank as he kept up his mantra. *A marine never gives up! Are you a marine or are you an army brat? Come on, Erik has done this dozens of times. Are you going to let him win? Come on!*

His veins were like worms, and he pushed onward. The pure mana passed through his body without issue. He directed it through his inner mana channels, compressing it more. His body fell into a rhythm as the element-dense mana tempered his body and the pure mana compressed further.

He couldn't hold it back anymore as the pressure within his body was reaching his peak.

"Liquid Mana Core, here I come." Rugrat grinned and gritted his teeth as a mist of pure mana was drawn into his mana core.

A sound like an emptying sink rose from his stomach. More threads of mana mist reached Rugrat's core. It was a whirlpool in the middle of his stomach. All his mana channels led to his core as the mist started to condense.

Then, in a moment, they transformed from mist to liquid. The drops occurred in different places, but they shot into the middle of the core.

Rugrat continued to cycle the mana within his body to purify and condense.

He pulled out a Mana Concentration pill and threw it into his mouth.

He crushed it with his teeth and drank it down with a Mana Regeneration potion.

A ripple ran through his mana channels, originating from his mana core. He smiled as a golden glow surrounded him. His body was the tinder, and the mana was the spark as his body changed internally.

The shifting mist in the room turned into a raging maelstrom as whirlpools appeared around Rugrat's mana gates. He exercised his full domain, removing all his limitations as the mist became a deeper blue color.

Through the chaos in the room, everything was orderly within Rugrat's body. The mana that had been a raging, out-of-control flood was now a tame irrigation system, supplying Rugrat's body with everything it needed to undergo a complete evolution.

Rugrat's body glowed—his gates, veins, and core outlined. One could see a grinning devil through the mist as he stretched his Mana Cultivation muscles.

"Liquid Mana Core!"

He laughed into the air as he drew in more mana. But the raging storm that had appeared around him was relaxing. He had a drained look on his face, even while his eyes glowed with power.

He wouldn't have been able to condense this much mana if his body weren't tempered enough. It could take him months or years if he were using the ambient mana in the Earth realms. No wonder the people in the Sky realms never wanted to leave. If they had all that mana, they could easily increase their Mana Cultivation.

There was a noise from the wall. Rugrat looked over.

"Ah, crap! Just when it's getting good, times up. Oh, how I love meetings!"

Kanoa looked around, searching for Rugrat.

"Where is he?" Miller scanned the area. They had brought some of the civilians and a quarter of the military members from their group for the meeting.

"He should be here soon," Kanoa said, once again glancing at the fully armed men and women on the wall. The heart of the Alvan army was behind the wall. All their supplies, ammunition, weapons, armor, medical supplies, even rations. The main manufacturing facilities were all here.

"Sorry I'm late!" Rugrat yelled.

Kanoa turned around. Rugrat looked drawn and tired, but he gave off the feeling that he was full of energy. A wave of power rushed over Kanoa.

"Whoops, sorry! My domain is a little all over the place. Just made it into Liquid Mana Core stage. I consolidated, but with any title change and cultivation increase, it takes time to get used to. All right, come on then!"

Rugrat led the group to the gate. They had to hand over their gear; none of them had any storage rings. Then they got bright-yellow badges that showed they were visitors.

A few more sets of doors, and they were inside the facility.

Big place, but the different buildings are operational. Kanoa observed the area. Guards patrolled here and there. Wagons came in and dropped off resources, while others headed out. There was a group of recruits going through their kit. The Ten Realms natives were all stunned by their new gear, but the fear of their instructors limited their curiosity.

"In here, we make the core supplies for our armed forces. We also have a large development group who work on different gear and upgrades that can be used by the army. Right now, everything is done in-house, but I am hoping that in the future, innovators will make their own and try to sell them to the military. We've already got some promising projects from different people." Rugrat reached a warehouse and walked inside. The space was broken up into different areas. There were mechanical-looking creatures in one area, clothes in another, boots in another; ammunition was in its own stored area.

Then there was an area tucked away in the corner that Rugrat led them to.

The board had a question mark on it.

Rugrat sat on a table. "You are all from Earth, from across military branches and civilian jobs. I don't even know what you all do, though I had asked for people who might know of military projects. I wanted to bring you here and show you what is going on. First, there are people who look into different innovations we can develop in every way we can. Also, while we're aiming to increase our ability, there is only so much that the four people from Earth can remember."

Kanoa felt the others shifting behind him. They had nearly been enslaved for their knowledge by Queen Ikku. They were hesitant to work on anything.

"Back on Earth, military might was more of a buzzword than a tactical factor. If someone was pushed into a corner and their enemies were coming for them in every direction, you can bet they're going to use their strongest moves. Bye-bye, so sad. A lot of the governments on Earth cared more about their GDP over the readiness of their fighting forces, which meant they were operating with gear that is twenty, thirty, sometimes forty years old. In the Ten Realms, there are no nukes, but there is military might. How strong you are, or the group you are a part of, is your protection."

Rugrat pulled out the two mainstay rifles of the army. "This bolt action rifle is our main weapon. We are in the process of upgrading most of our main-line forces with newer semi and full auto rifles. We have distributed grenade launchers, standalone six-shot systems, and underbarrel versions. We have mortars, armor, and more. All this gear is good, but we have a problem. Advancement. As we reach higher into the realms, these weapons are less effective, which means that we have to be predictive, scaling, and adaptive.

"We predict the conditions in the higher realms and their abilities. We scale our weapons to defeat enemies on that level. So, we might need to adapt our weapons, or our tactics; we might need all-new weapons—there are too many factors to know for sure. Now, that is hard, but, thankfully, we have a whole other world to draw inspiration from."

"What if we don't want to work on weapons?" someone asked.

"That's fine. There are plenty of jobs out there. Think of this as me trying to sell you on the army. If nothing else, you'll look at us favorably, and if you can give a hand, you won't be afraid to let us know how we can do better. There are not just weapons in the army. Nutrition, training, cultivation, and tactics are all items we can work on. Heck, even beast taming, beast raising, Alchemy, healing—these crafts directly link to the army and our operations."

"So, we don't have to be part of the military or your crafters?" another asked.

"You are temporary citizens of Alva. If you take the final oaths, you pay your taxes and adhere to our laws; you are under our protection and a full citizen of Alva. You are free to leave at any time, no matter what. You can stay here for up to six months with that status. If you become a full Alvan and pay your way, you can be here forever. There are a number of people who are still temporary residents. Full citizens can come and go as they please, with no worry about being escorted out."

"You kick people out who don't want to be your citizens?" someone asked angrily.

"This is Alva. If you want to come here, you are welcome, but we have limited resources. If you want to stay, awesome, but we need your help to maintain everything. If you don't, well, we don't want freeloaders; we want people who are driven to push onward."

"Have you needed to kick out many people?"

"Not personally, but there have been over two dozen people who were going to be removed. Over half of them decided to join Alva, but they had to get an intern citizenship, meaning they had to pay more taxes and there is zero tolerance with any misdemeanors. It's crappy, but we want engaged, driven people to join us."

"That's outrageous! You pick and choose your citizens?" another yelled.

"If they want to join us, that is up to them." Rugrat shrugged.

"I heard that you are the lord of all this," one of the civilians, a teacher, asked.

"Yeah, Erik and I are the lords of Alva, Vuzgal, and their subsidiaries."

"Doesn't that make you dictators?" the teacher asked.

"Don't think of Alva and everything here like a city or a nation or whatever. Think of it like a company. Erik and I are the founders, though there are all kinds of departments that see to the needs of the people, future expansion, and so on."

"So, everyone needs to work for you?" The teacher started to get more outraged.

"Pretty much," Rugrat said.

"How can you do that? Putting everyone to work whether they want to or not, forcing them into servitude! How are they better than slaves?"

"Have you been watching the Ten Realms? This is not Earth. The strongest rule here."

"Because you are the strongest, you can make the rules?"

"No, because I *own* this place, I can make the rules." Rugrat raised his hand, and a pillar of stone shot out of the ground. Everyone gasped. He lowered his hand, and the floor flattened.

"I am a dungeon lord, and this is my and Erik's dungeon. We control it completely. Same with our subsidiaries. We are a company the size of a small nation. Thankfully, our focus is on helping people and making sure that those under our command are treated in the best possible way."

"How can we be sure of that?" the teacher snapped.

"There's the door. You can leave if you want. You can't reveal anything about Alva, but you can do whatever else you want. This is the way things are. Accept it or leave."

"Rugrat, what about the council? Are they elected?" Kanoa asked.

"In a way. The council manage everything. They are leaders in their own fields of study. They have held their position for four years. Other than the leader of the military, they can be elected and changed in different circumstances. At the end of the four years, those who have the greatest ability within the department can appeal to their fellows; those with the most votes get the position. Each council member fights for their department and works with the other council members to advance Alva as a whole," Rugrat rattled off.

Over the next few hours, Rugrat and the people from Earth talked over the systems in place in Alva and their subsidiaries. He held nothing back.

Kanoa watched it all. Really, the Ten Realms was nothing like Earth. What they were used to was gone, but there were still a lot of people trying to hold on to that. Those who were too rigid would collapse. The people of Alva were pleased with the system, if not overjoyed. Sure, it wasn't perfect, but they were immigrants to this land. If they wanted to become Alvans, they would need to wholly embrace what Alva was. Thinking of it like a company, that made more sense, and having people with the highest ability and the support of others reminded him of the ranking system in the military. It wasn't perfect, but it worked.

Rugrat led the group out of the compound. He hoped to recruit some of them to help with the development of military hardware. There was a war coming, and he wanted to be ready for it.

Instead of recruiting people, it was turning into some damn political debate.

Rugrat headed to the workshop to find two people waiting there.

"Kanoa? Badowska?" Rugrat asked.

"So, I hear you have some space in your military. I might be older, but these old bones got a new lease of life in the Ten Realms," Kanoa said.

"You don't have any tanks or mechanized forces. Can you say you are army without a tank?" Badowska said. His thick Russian accent and partial English made it hard to fully understand him.

"You sure? If you want to help, you need to become citizens," Rugrat said.

"We haven't been sitting on our asses this whole time. We have been out and in the middle of the Alvans. They aren't fanatics or idiots; they know what Alva is and are more than happy to put their full strength behind it. You've not only created a safe place.; you've created a powerful community. Sure, we could keep running and berate you for not having a democratic society."

Badowska grunted in derision.

"But this system works, and it's clear to me that although you aren't the best lord, you are an honest one and someone I'd trust watching my ass," Kanoa said.

Badowska shrugged. "As long as you not wearing American flag booty shorts, *da*?"

"It'll grow on you."

"I do not want booty shorts growing on me."

Rise of the Beast Mountain Range

Lord Aditya returned to his office.

"How was the envoy from the Marcella kingdom?" Evernight asked.

"They wanted better trading terms. I put them in contact with some traders who might interest them and kept them personally invested with some extra trinkets." Aditya sat down.

He looked out of the window at the large complex that was being built within the latest round of expanding walls around the city.

"The sect hasn't finished construction, but Consortium Leader Quan has already filled the teaching positions. The Adventurer's Guild is also building out a branch within the city. The auction will be starting in a few hours." Evernight stood.

"How about things beyond our borders?" Aditya watched as she walked toward his desk.

"The same as they were this morning. We shall see how people's attitudes are after the auction." Evernight smiled. "Before that, don't you want to learn about your real masters?"

"What are you hiding?" Aditya watched her suspiciously.

"Come on, you have a meeting before the auction." Evernight pulled him out of his chair and led him to the secret ladder.

Aditya's hands grew clammy. "We're really going to see them?"

"Of course. Come on." Evernight dropped down the ladder first.

Aditya swallowed and then followed after her.

They reached the bottom of the ladder, and the bookcase above rotated back into place.

After some twists and turns, they reached a room with different connecting tunnels. A city interface was placed against one wall. On the other side of the room was a teleportation array.

"Okay, your oaths are all good, so we won't need to do that again." Evernight waved him over to the teleportation array.

He gritted his teeth and balled his fists, stepping over.

Evernight activated the formation. In a flash of light, they appeared in a bright area.

Aditya looked around with hooded eyes against the sudden light. He adjusted quickly, seeing the odd guards and the defenses. His body shook; it felt as if he was soaked in a warm bath.

This mana density! Training in here for one day would be like training for a month in the First Realm. No, three months!

Evernight was well known and greeted a few people.

When they stepped out of the defenses around the teleportation facilities, Aditya saw Alva Dungeon spread out in front of him.

Even the people on the street were stronger than him, and there was high-Journeyman-level gear for sale in the market—in large batches.

They passed a group of police officers who nodded to them and a group of soldiers marching through.

Aditya had thought his own forces were impressive, but they were just imitations of the regular soldiers.

He was burning up. He had been fed hints and information for so long but had never seen the power behind him. Now that he saw it, he was even more stunned than he had expected.

They reached a large, round building in the middle of the city. It was covered in formations, and a pillar of light shot into the skies above.

It pierced through the blue "sky" and spread through formations to a ceiling of mana stones. Aditya shuddered at the casual display of so much wealth.

There were mana stones growing on the roof! *On the roof! Are we underground?*

He had been so focused on what was around him that he hadn't looked up.

"Come on, Aditya!" Evernight teased as she pulled him into the building. They passed some guards, who watched them both. They headed up past offices.

"The dungeon core used to be just a single building. But with the expansion of the city, the buildings were pushed back, and we created a new, larger building around the dungeon core, adding in offices and meeting rooms."

She guided them in farther and stood straighter.

Aditya did as well.

"Someone can make you act official? Looks like they are really powerful," Aditya joked.

She shot him a look, pressing her lips together to force down the smile.

They reached another door with guards and opened it. To the left side of the room, there was a massive cylinder that went from floor to ceiling. The room was one section of the cylinder. There were formations all over the place; inside the cylinder was the pillar of light. It branched out through several formations and headed through the building, back down into the ground. It captured Aditya's attention before he saw Evernight bowing to the two occupants of the room.

Aditya glanced at the two men who wore simple but comfortable clothes. Both had short haircuts and sported freshly shaved faces.

They gave off a feeling of quiet, controlled power.

Off to the side, there was a wolf with wings that seemed to be made of flames, and he nipped at a large, lizard-looking creature that dodged his attack and bit back.

Aditya bowed with Evernight.

"Lords Erik and Rugrat, this is Aditya, the leader of King's Hill, its associated alliance, and Vermire," Evernight said. "Aditya, these are Lords Erik and Rugrat, celebrated soldiers of Alva, the saviors of Alva Village, and the creators of Alva, Vuzgal, and all associated guilds, academies, and subsidiaries."

"It is my honor to meet with you," Aditya said.

"How is the leg doing?" Erik said.

"Uh, it is fine," Aditya said.

"Don't need to talk into the floor there," Rugrat said.

Aditya looked up at Erik, who had stood and was walking toward him. He put his hand on Aditya's shoulder and used a spell.

"Y-you are the one who healed me?" Aditya said, seeing Erik up close again.

"It healed fine. Your Body Cultivation is progressing well." Erik pulled out a pill and gave it to Aditya. "Go to the healing house and have them watch over you as you take this. It will suck, but it will allow you to temper your organs." Erik used another spell.

Aditya felt his body rejuvenate. He operated just like the healers in the healing house. *I was healed by the lord of all this?* Was he like the people in the healing houses or were they like him, mimicking his methods?

"Try to get up and walk more often. Your back is getting bad," Erik warned.

"Yes, thank you, Lord Erik." Aditya's breathing was harsh and strained.

"You did Body Cultivation. I guess I should do mana, huh?" Rugrat touched the bracelet on his wrist. Each of the pieces was actually a storage ring.

Aditya shuddered. Storage items were rare in the First Realm, but

Rugrat had enough to create a bracelet! Elders and powerful figures in sects had several storage rings. It wasn't until the Second Realm that the middle class got them. In the Third Realm, nearly everyone had storage rings.

Rugrat walked over as he examined his bracelet. He pulled out a book and scroll. He pressed the scroll against the book, and with a flash of mana, words appeared on the scroll, and he put the book away.

He took out a salve and passed it and the scroll to Aditya. "These should help you out. Ask the people at the healing house to apply it for you. Should open some of your mana gates and increase your rate of absorption. The scroll is based on what I have learned about Mana Cultivation. Do you have Organic Scan or a way to look inside your body?"

"No, I don't," Aditya said.

"Erik?"

"One sec." Erik checked his storage rings and pulled out a book. He tossed it to Rugrat.

Rugrat passed it to Aditya. "Here is a technique book on the spell. That should work. Also, here is a formation necklace to help you if you are attacked."

"And here are some pills to help you recover from grave injuries." Erik walked over with the pills.

"Do you have a sound transmission device?" Rugrat asked.

"I do," Aditya said.

"Good. If you need help, there will always be someone to answer."

"What are your plans for the future of King's Hill?" Erik asked.

"My first plan is to grow the power of the sect and the army, which will create security for the outposts and bring everything under one control. With the sect, we will get the people on our side and draw in more from the surrounding areas to support us, sending their children over to train and become stronger. The younger generation will have a favorable outlook on the Beast Mountain Range since it is the place where they learned and transformed from children into adults.

"Unlike the kingdoms, outpost leaders in the Beast Mountain Range gained their positions by being great and powerful leaders, instead of politicians. Their own personal strength and backing isn't small. Most of them have come to our side, and those will follow. They all crave position and power. Giving them places within the sect allows them both"

"How many of the outpost leaders have come over to your side? Come on, let's sit." Erik moved the conversation to the seats.

"We have most of the outpost leaders; I would say four-fifths of them at this point. Some are holding out for better terms or positions." Aditya sat.

"So, through giving the people and the outpost lords more opportunities, it makes them united," Rugrat said.

"Yes. At that time, we will create our own region. We announce that Beast Mountain Range is our domain; we say that we are allied against the beasts overrunning the surrounding area. If we unite people in words, it is easier for them to unite in reality. King's Hill will become the capital. All the guards will become Beast Mountain Range guards. We will boast a strong sect that's open to people from across the lands and focused on learning how to fight alone and in groups and training healers and crafters. People are excited about the Adventurer's Guild showing interest in the area. It would be a clear path to the higher realms. Proving yourself in the sect could lead to a higher and greater position. Even if not, you could become a great crafter because there are rare materials in the Beast Mountain Range one can buy for cheap to train with. Healers would be advanced as there are always wounded people. They would be learned and tested. On the surface, that is." Aditya smiled as Erik and Rugrat's gaze sharpened.

"Under the surface, while people are training, we are picking out those from across the Beast Mountain Range who show promise through different competitions and avenues. These people are recruited to your force. On the surface, they are Beast Mountain Range people, the sons and daughters of powerful nobles. In reality, they are your loyal people. With time, we will gain control over these surrounding kingdoms and groups, or at least nurture an even greater embedded intelligence network across the First

Realm." Aditya smiled as he saw the surprise in Erik and Rugrat's eyes as they smiled.

"You have been working hard," Erik praised.

"He's getting as sneaky as the intelligence department head," Rugrat said to Erik. He grinned at Aditya, who felt a new energy in his veins with their praise.

"So, that happens internally. What about externally?" Evernight prompted.

"Trade," Aditya said, gaining everyone's attention. "Trade is the basis of all agreements. If we can trade with others, we draw them closer. If they fight us, they might gain something in the end, but they will lose any possible revenues of trade. We planned the auction to happen as soon as possible to bring the attention of the kingdoms to us.

"The groups closest to us are coveting our outposts. They have multiple borders with other groups, so we have been focusing on these other groups for trade. What will possible enemies nearby think when they know our good friend is standing at their backdoor? What if we have three friends along different borders? We've used ourselves as bait with the Zatan Confederation—but didn't they suffer a miserable defeat? With this in mind, freely selling to everyone, even our greatest enemies, will hide their swords for now. If we show we are docile and open for trade, they will come and will think twice about attacking us, as other nations reliant on our trades will attack them to keep their trade routes open. We shift the focus outward to other troubles instead of the Beast Mountain Range,, and we stay hidden and safe in plain sight."

"A constantly neutral force on the surface while we move affairs around under the surface," Evernight said.

"Over time, that weight will increase, or maybe as people see one feather, they don't notice the smaller feathers you have spread around. You're using the auction as a smoke screen to bring in trade interest as fast as possible with goods that you know the surrounding kingdoms' elites will *have* to fight over," Erik said.

"Yes, my lord." Aditya bowed his head slightly.

"Damn—plans in the future and in the present. Aditya, I am glad you're on our side," Rugrat said.

"Our relationship was an unsteady one when it started," Erik said.

Aditya winced and bobbed his head.

"You have proved that although you are a schemer, you aren't malicious. People in the outposts are safer. There are more jobs. You have spread healing houses to the outposts, created schools of crafting from what you have. While you have talked about the secondary reasons of the sect, the primary one is that you hope to help the people in the Beast Mountain Range and the surrounding areas succeed. They also line up with your secondary objectives nicely."

"So, Phillips Aditya, would you like to become a citizen of Alva?" Rugrat pulled out a medallion and slid it over the table in front of Aditya.

Aditya glanced at the simple medallion. He heard his heart in his ears; he felt anxious, afraid, and excited. The medallion and what it represented were not simple. He had worked for years for Alva without knowing it. Now, he could become one of them.

For the first time in a long time, he felt that he belonged somewhere. When he was in the worst positions, they were there to support him. Even just now, Lord Erik and Lord Rugrat had taken the time to check on him. Hadn't Lord Erik repaired and healed his leg?

He felt a door closing behind him, on his hunting party, his friends who had abandoned him in the First Realm. It was time to move past that anger and on to something more—a new future, a new possibility.

His fingers curled around the medallion, the edges of the metal firm in his hand. "If you'll have me," he said in a hoarse voice.

"Phillips Aditya, please stand," Erik said.

Erik and Rugrat stood in front of Aditya.

"Please raise your right hand and repeat after me: I, Phillips Aditya," Erik paused waiting for Aditya.

"I, Phillips Aditya."

"Of my own volition, swear upon the Ten Realms."

Again, Aditya repeated Erik's words.

The oath passed in a blur, and he stood straight and proud.

"And to follow the orders of the Dungeon Masters Erik and Rugrat as long as their orders are reasonable," Aditya said, finishing the last of the oath.

The golden light of the Ten Realms covered him as he lowered his hand.

"Welcome to Alva. I am sure you have a lot of questions and want to see more of the dungeon. Evernight can show you around," Erik said.

"Thank you." Aditya bowed to them both.

"Lords," Evernight said in closing and pulled Aditya with her out of the headquarters.

"Okay, we'll check out the barracks and the academy, then we have to get back for that auction. Don't worry—now you have that medallion, you can come down here and train through the teleportation formation. You could even buy a house or apartment down here. Oh, Council Leader Delilah will want to meet with you at some time. Also, Jia Feng might want to talk to you about the sect, and Elise will go over trade. Might be best to add you to the monthly council leader meetings." Evernight was mostly talking to herself as Aditya recovered from everything that had happened.

He rubbed his storage ring. Inside were the treasures Erik and Rugrat had given him.

"Come on, Aditya. Lots to do now!" Evernight said, close to his face.

It made him jump, waking him from his daze. "Hey!"

"Looks like your brain is turning over again." Evernight laughed and led Aditya on a whirlwind tour.

On the other side of Alva, Elan watched as a group of about fifty people joined Alva. From kids to adults, everyone completed their oaths. Among them was a man in rough pants. His hair was shaggy, and it looked as though he had been walking for weeks. There was an easygoing, disarming smile on his face.

Elan was proud of the roguish-looking man. *He's changed in the last few years. Got to know the world more, made friends.*

He glanced back at Yui and Qin. The two of them smiled, and Qin was the first to open the door.

Wren's eyes glided across the room effortlessly—until they reached the rest of his family. His movements became stilted, and he pushed his hair back out of his face, staring at them all in surprise. "What? You said you went to the higher realms!"

"Well, we have. Qin works in the Fourth Realm, didn't you know?" Yui laughed.

"What is with all this hair? Are you trying to lure more girls home?" Qin pouted.

Elan chuckled as Yui pulled his brother into a headlock.

"Welcome to Alva, little brother. You shaped up well. Need a haircut!"

"Get off me, you brute! How did you get even stronger?" Wren complained, but his eyes were shining.

"Welcome to Alva. There is a lot for you to learn, but if you want to keep running the trading group, I suggest you head over to the meeting in the Trader's Guild's bar. Lord Aditya is going over there too," Elan said as Yui released him.

"Lord Aditya—you know people call him the King of the Beast Mountain Range?" Wren said.

"Yes, I heard. I was the one who created your information network."

"Ah, yes, Dad." Wren laughed.

"Come on, you can bug him all you want later."

"I just got off work!" Qin complained.

"I can't slack off for too long. What would the troops say?"

"Just say that the director of the intelligence department stole you for a night. I don't think they would mind."

"I have a lot to do!" Qin said.

"I'll pay for dinner." Elan sighed.

"Great!" Qin jumped up and clapped her hands. It was easy to forget she was still a teenager.

"Yeah, the troops would be scared that you'd start telling me everything they did last weekend." Yui smiled.

"Now, come on. We own the Beast Mountain Range. With your contacts and the trading house, it would be perfect to work with Aditya. Even take the trading house up a few realms." Elan put his arm on Wren's shoulder and dragged him away.

"Nice hair, Wren!" Qin yelled as he disappeared out the front door.

"Good work on the trading company!" Yui said.

"Hey!" Wren said as he was whisked off, and his siblings quickly departed.

20 Raising King's Hill

Aditya finished greeting the highly influential representatives from various trading houses, kingdoms, and empires.

He walked into his own booth at the highest point in the auction house, looking over the hundreds of people who had come to participate.

His eyes glanced over the Alvans he had just met a few days ago. There were so many of them in every facet of the Beast Mountain Range.

He couldn't help but feel awkward.

Compared to Alva, King's Hill was a little lackluster. The farmers and cooks were stronger than their envoys and even their highest-ranked guards. It was no wonder the Zatan Confederation were played to death by Alva's forces. If these men and women knew just how powerful their backer was, they wouldn't dare to put on airs around the staff of King's Hill. They would be meek sheep, and even the kings, queens, emperors, and empresses would send their children to the Beast Mountain Consortium.

The items for sale were rarities in the First Realm. There were sets of mid-Apprentice-level armor, even pieces of peak-Apprentice gear. There were alchemical concoctions to heal and to aid in one's cultivation. Blueprints to create weapons, armor, and gear—even if they were only partial blueprints—created a storm of interest. They were the scraps from Alva to help develop their position in the First Realm.

On the surface, Aditya was the lord of the Beast Mountain Range, but underneath, he was a recruiter who would pass on the most promising applicants to Alva. No wonder they wanted people who would be fiercely loyal and hard-working. They didn't need people who were a high level; they could train them. Having loyalty—that was a currency that couldn't be bought.

Lord Erik and Rugrat had talked to him as if he were almost a peer. They had treated him with kindness. Aditya rolled his shoulders back and sat straighter. There was a new hardness in his eyes; underneath, there was a fiery passion.

Just how far could he build the Beast Mountain Range under their orders? What tasks might they have for him in the future if he proved himself? Could they train him in fighting, give him an education in crafting? He had never had a formal education. If he had a teacher, what would that be like?

The auction house was an inferno; people silently cursed one another and turned bloodshot stares on fresh enemies when someone won a victory in the fierce duel for money.

The winners wore excited smiles, breathing heavily as their eyes dared others to compete with them before their attention fell on their new property.

Silver and gold were their weapons; their tongues, their tactics. Money poured into the coffers of the alliance. The outpost leaders, many whom were part of the King's Hill administration, couldn't help but smile as their eyes filled with shining lights.

He had to bring the whole of the Beast Mountain Range under his control. Then they could push to increase their power. With greater deeds, he could show his loyalty. Evernight had said that he could even own a home in Alva. *Think of that!*

Aditya's worldview and goals had shifted over the past couple of years, going from a ruthless outpost leader to a man filled with plots, ideas, and complete loyalty to those who trusted and had backed him.

He touched his storage ring and smiled.

They might be two odd men, but they are good men.

Lord Salyn postponed his departure from King's Hill to get information for Queen Ikku. He sent a report about the growing power of the Beast Mountain Range. It was far from the Shikoshi kingdom, but the auction had gathered many elites and their power was sure to grow with time.

If they remained neutral, it would be for the best. And then the empire could join the other groups in competing for the different goods and items that the Range sold.

His gaze moved unconsciously to where the Alva Healing House was located.

They had to be related to Alva Village. Perhaps he could try and influence the queen into attacking? She was prone to her outbursts.

Salyn bore a dark expression as he and his group headed out of the city. The hunt was back on. They were well supplied, rested, and had new mounts. He would track down the traitors and drag them back to the queen.

Insight into Body Cultivation

It had been three weeks since the auction and a month and a half since Erik had returned from the Sixth Realm.

It might have been a realm to educate people, to grow their power, but that was only on the surface. In the massive dungeons underground, academies waged war against one another—for resources, for places of higher concentrations of mana. At the same time, the dungeon was fighting back, the beasts and creatures in its depths tried to claim the lives of students and citizens under the academies that were as large as cities and nations.

Erik walked into the Body Cultivation ward of the hospital. The rooms were separated out; medics checked the formations outside the different rooms and monitored the men and women inside.

Erik checked the information on the different readouts. He turned quickly and collided into a medic.

"My notes!" the lady yelled as papers flew up in the air.

"Sorry about that." Erik bent over to help clean up.

"Don't worry about it. I was rushing and not looking where I was going. I just came from class, and I'm late for my shift. Too many questions." She didn't look up as she gathered her notes and tried to get them in order.

Erik passed her the ones he had retrieved.

"Thank you!" she said with a cheery smile. Her eyes creased in half-recognition, but she dismissed it with a shake of her head before hurrying off.

Erik smiled to himself and kept looking through the ward.

He found a library that was filled with texts on the human body, theories and information on Body Cultivation, and everything in between. Several medics in the room sat in chairs or at tables.

Many of them had finished their primary education and were now intern medics. They were following a qualified medic, turning theory into practical skills.

There were medics from the army as well as civilians. They communicated with one another freely, talking about different scenarios.

Erik found some new papers, books, scrolls, and a chair, and he started reading.

Theories of Body Cultivation's Effect Upon Human Musculature: Unraveling the Cleansing of One's Muscle Stage.

Bit of a wordy title. Makes me think of papers academics would write.

Erik opened the papers and started to read. Either someone from Earth had written it, or their medics were more advanced than Rugrat and Erik in the medical sciences. Erik leaned forward, excited to read more.

"Excuse me," a woman said.

"Sorry, just one moment." Erik held up a hand, enthralled by the paper.

It was as if explosions went off in his mind. The papers took his ideas and thoughts and condensed and clarified them.

"Huh." He sat back in the chair.

"Was it useful?" the woman asked.

Erik looked over. It was the woman who had dropped her notes.

"Yes, it was. Sorry about that. I just wanted to finish reading it all. Sorry, what is your name?"

"Melissa Bouchard, from Paris, France," she said.

"Ah, you must be with the new group. Sorry, I didn't know everyone. I'm Erik, Erik West. Are you working here now?"

"Good to meet you. I've heard good things. There were a lot of people in the group. Yeah, I took up the position of medic. I wanted to learn the practices in the Ten Realms and came across information on Body Cultivation. Using the facilities and talking to the medics, and those who had undergone body modification, I've been applying my knowledge from Earth to Body Cultivation. I wrote that paper."

"'Body Cultivation is an active process through which one changes their overall cells. With the power of mana, one can change their genetic code, creating mutations known as 'constitutions,''" Erik recited, turning to face Melissa.

"Maybe we should talk somewhere that isn't the reading room?" Melissa glanced at the people looking over at them, and they bowed their heads over their books again, not wanting to show disapproval around Lord Erik.

"Right." Erik followed her lead out of the room.

"You were interested in the state of research into Body Cultivation—I'm your guide. So, please." Melissa waved for him to keep talking as she guided him through the hospital. It had grown outward and upward, turning into more of a campus than a hospital. The real healing went on in the Beast Mountain Range, Vuzgal, and within the Adventurer's Guild.

"So, how is research on Body Cultivation going?" Erik asked.

"It is one of the tri-alterations. Some call it the tri-force. Think of a triangle, with Body Cultivation at one corner, Mana Cultivation at the other corner. In the middle of the triangle, you have mana. At the peak, you have techniques. Your body plus mana equals fighting techniques; your Mana Cultivation plus mana creates spells. The two types of cultivation combined with mana create much stronger techniques. Now, around this triangle are the five elements: wood, fire, earth, metal, and water. This is the system of the Ten Realms, the basis of true power. Everything else relies on ability or proving you have a higher level or better technique." She opened a door, and they entered a clean office with papers and notes on the desk.

"Okay, that is a good way to organize it," Erik said.

"That is the start of all research: create the genus, categories, and subcategories. There are multiple techniques one can learn that are broken up by the school of crafting or ability they fall under. That is not what we are talking about, though. Mana gathering is broken down into the different stages of cultivation. My fellow researchers created their own training ground to increase the speed of Mana Gathering Cultivation. Alvans were blindly increasing their Body Cultivation—tempering their body with the elements and growing stronger. They were looking at the result and the gains they get from the Ten Realms, not studying and understanding the process. We are still studying just what happens in someone's body when they temper it. So far, we have made some major discoveries."

Erik listened to her every word, enthralled.

"First, when one is going through the stage of 'cleansing of body,' they open their cells for modification. It is like they open new gates in their cells, like how insulin tells cells to absorb glucose. It creates and opens those new gates. It changes your very cells." Melissa shook her head.

"It makes sense," Erik said, thinking of the changes in his body.

"Tempering your body is about withstanding the elements, by the texts from the Ten Realms. We put some 'activated' cells from the cleansing body stage under a microscope and introduced them to environments with a high concentration of different elements. Do you know what it looked like?"

"What?"

"Like one of those videos where cells multiply hundreds of times in a second. A powerful evolution; a war between the cells was waged. The cells, under these terrible conditions, grew and evolved!" Melissa shook her head. "What craziness is that! Cells evolving within a single person, not once or twice, but hundreds, thousands, tens of thousands of times. There are reports of those who collapsed when they were tempering their bodies. They suffered grave injuries. Some were deformed, and others died! Now, with modern cultivation, most people use mild alchemical solutions or perform the tempering with the assistance of a healer to make sure that there are no issues. How is it so simple?"

"It is rather dangerous and painful," Erik argued.

"Painful? Yes, of course. Your body is changing on a genetic level, with you in it! You are not merely feeding your cells; you *change* them on a basic level. You unleash your cells' ability to be altered with poison. You tempered yourself with the elements of Fire and Earth, reaching the height of Body Like Sky Iron! If someone hit you with a baseball bat as hard as they could, it is hard to say how badly that bat would be bent!"

"When you say it like that—"

"It sounds crazy? Well, it is! What is happening in the Ten Realms is *incredible*. Things that are simply impossible to do on Earth happen here all the time. Anyway, we are getting off topic." Melissa leaned forward and pointed at Erik. "Those cells you tempered with the elements, they are like bacteria that you could find in the Arctic or in the permafrost of the poles. The most virulent of viruses. They reach a point where they can not only survive in extreme environments, they can use the power of those environments themselves."

Erik's forehead wrinkled as he thought on what she was saying. "So, tempering the body is tempering one's cells. Somehow, we don't turn into puddles of goo if we suffer through it, and we can control the elements around us and go into areas with high concentrations of them."

"Right. We surpass the limits of any normal human being. Though that is not the end. The second thing I discovered is potential!"

"Potential? What do you mean?"

"The potential of the cells is much greater than they were in the past. Individually, they are much stronger than before; their smaller inner systems are greatly refined. The cell walls are tougher, but they accept a greater amount of the elements inside. The nucleus changes. Instead of it just being reactive, we can control it!"

"What does that mean?"

"Usually they just do their own thing. We have no real control over them. On Earth, if you had a cut, you had to wait and let it heal itself, right?" Melissa held out her hand to Erik.

"Right."

Melissa chuckled. "Well, now, in a way, you have control over your cells. In the cleansing process, the nucleus links to your mind. When you want to cultivate your body, you can consciously open the gates of the cell to accept the powerful elements into your body. We have only just discovered this, and we have no idea what it would even mean!"

"So, the cells are under my control?"

"Possibly? When you are cultivating or when elements enter your body through tempering, they alter you so you can take in more in the future. It will take more testing to see if this is something that is happening naturally, consciously or unconsciously. We know that there is a conscious control you can exercise on your mana system."

"How we have to compress and refine through circulations?" Erik asked.

"Right!"

A weird smile appeared on Melissa's face as she pointed to a piece of paper hung up behind her desk. It was the mantra of body cultivators.

"The foundation tempered, the soul grounded, the mind forged." She drew out the last three words. "Based on the texts we have been reading, the mind is altered with tempering of the metal element. Not only that, but one will undergo a Body Rebirth. A rebirth! Isn't it right there! Maybe that is the stage where you will gain conscious control over your cells. You could prioritize what your body heals. You could alter the structure of your cells, maybe even alter yourself. Cells make up your entire body. What changes could you create?"

Melissa's eyes burned into Erik's as his heart thumped like a war drum and his blood raced through his veins.

"Though those are all just my theories and hypothesis! There is nothing to prove it yet." Melissa laughed, and the heat in Erik's limbs cooled, regaining more of his control.

"The last discovery we made also has to do with the cells. They create new lysosomes. These don't break down chemicals like they do on Earth; they broke down the elements and release purified mana. Specialized vacuoles store the elements and supply them to the cells. Once the body is tempered with the correlating element, these two cell structures form. The greater one's tempering, the more the element can be processed and stored by a given cell."

"Can someone temper themselves with all the elements?"

"They can, but there is a reason for the Body Cultivation mantra. It seems that our bodies will naturally follow this path of incorporating different elements."

"You said something about constitutions being mutations?" Erik asked.

"A family that occupies one area for multiple generations has the same training aides and such over a long period of time, and their children's bodies will be more efficient in absorbing the element populating their area. Constitutions are related to the body, not one's mana system. If I have a Water element constitution, my body will find it easier to pull in mana with the water element as it can temper my cells faster; it gives me a greater resistance and control over it. As a side benefit, I refine out that water element in mana faster, using purer mana in my Mana Cultivation."

"Then your Mana Cultivation would soar because you have purer mana than everyone else to condense!" Erik slapped his leg. His head spun from all the information.

"I was thinking on a surface level about what the Ten Realms could give me and the benefits. Of course, if there are changes, they have to come from somewhere. The Ten Realms just reports the changes. I didn't think I was changing my actual cells." Erik snorted.

"No one did. There is simply too much to study in the Ten Realms. It is why I go to the academy. I can't do it all by myself. Researching and studying what is happening will allow us to crack the Ten Realms. This brings me to my main point. None of this would have been possible without information. Without data, I couldn't prove any of this."

"Are you asking for more funding?" Erik asked.

"No, I'm asking for more subjects and to be approved for testing facilities."

"What do you mean by testing facilities? Laboratories, microscopes?"

"Maybe, but a big part of it is that other than what the Ten Realms tells us, we don't know what the effect is on the people who have tempered their bodies. I want to build a gym."

"A gym? Like with weights and such?"

"Yes, weights and such." Melissa's face bloomed in a smile. "What I have talked about are the basic breakthroughs we have made in the area of body tempering. I have not talked about our discoveries. Come with me."

She led Erik out of the office and down the corridor. They passed through a few secure doors to a hall that had medics talking to one another and watching what was happening in one of the rooms through a window.

Seeing Melissa and Erik, they moved to the side.

Melissa and Erik smiled and nodded. Melissa waved toward the window, presenting a room where a man lay on the ground. There was a complex formation below him; an IV fed into the man's arm, and metal shackles dug into his skin.

"Don't worry—this was voluntary. We used a numbing agent where the spikes are inserted," Melissa assured him. "This was actually an idea that came from the military. What ways could we create to artificially temper a soldier's body as fast as possible without any side effects?

"The healing formation on the ground heals the patient. The IV bag contains an alchemical formula to numb the soldier and boost their cognitive function."

"The spikes?" Erik asked in a deep voice.

"Weapons created by the smiths. They are hollow and inject poison into the patient's body."

Erik looked at the patient lying there with their eyes closed. Several medics circulated their mana right next to the formation; another was ready, next to a control panel that could change the effects of the formations above and below the man.

Impurities dripped out of the man's pores, staining his clothing as steam rose from his body.

Erik would have accepted the same thing. It seemed more comfortable than the temperings he had done in the past.

"With this system, we have things under greater control. From a few hours to a day, one can cleanse their body and be ready to push forward along the body tempering path," Melissa said.

"What about elemental tempering?" Erik asked.

"Take a look." Melissa took him down the corridor, and they looked through another window. A woman stood on a formation that was releasing waves of heat. She wore old-fashioned armor covered in Fire-based attack runes.

In each of her shoulders, an IO had been driven in. An intraosseous infusion was injected into the marrow of the bone. Even if the veins collapsed, the IO would keep functioning.

The woman dropped to the ground into a push-up position and then stood up and jumped. She reached some ten meters in the air before crashing back down and repeated the burpee.

"Squats!" A training instructor was there with medics, overseeing everything.

The woman got under the bar and squatted the massive weight. She yelled with every explosive movement upward. She completed five sets of ten. Her body steamed as water vaporized from her skin.

"Pull-ups!" the instructor yelled.

The woman groaned and grabbed the bar. She stared right ahead as she pulled herself up, lowered herself, and did it again. Her face pulled into a snarl.

Erik mentally nodded to her. There was a state of mind one could reach when they were fighting against their body and against other's thoughts. An inner dialogue where you would curse yourself out to get that little bit more. *You got twenty? That was cute. Come on, you have five more to show how strong you are. Got that five. Come on, that pain is a gain! Five more!*

"We found that combining tempering with working out increases the speed one could temper their body. When working out, your body is at a peak state. Your cells sympathetically activate. You can absorb more power and repair faster as you go. Utilization of the elements increases after physical exercise in high-element areas. She is being pumped with healing concoctions. The formation is pumping out the Fire element, and the armor is actually a weapon. There are spikes inserted into the patient, forcing more Fire element into the depths of their body. It is barbaric and cruel, but with the numbing agents, the patients don't feel the pain and the healing concoctions push them on."

"So, you want a gym for people to work out when tempering?" Erik glanced over to her.

"No, I want a gym to test the changes that people undergo. I need to gather data. We have titles for the different stages of tempering—Body Like Stone, Like Iron, and so on. Is that really true? Even if it is true, how much stronger and faster are people? What is the actual impact of one point of increase Strength, Stamina, or Agility? Is there a way we can increase that more through tempering? Is it on a cellular level? What are the best cell mutations? Can we replicate those in different people?"

"This is way above my pay grade." Erik shook his head.

"It is a whole new world and system. It isn't surprising to be overwhelmed. Right now, we're grasping at everything, trying to find out anything we can. There is so much to learn out there. Also, there is something that you might find useful." Melissa pulled out some papers from her storage ring and passed them to Erik.

"These detail the information we discovered about tempering one's body with the Metal element. Unlike the previous temperings, it needs to be completed over time. Working out and doing explosive exercise do assist, but if you reach a meditative state, it speeds up the process. If you are sleeping, it slows down, though. It seems that one needs to be awake but in a relaxed state. Also"—she pulled out a pouch, put it on top of the papers in Erik's hands, and opened it, revealing several spikes—"each of these are formation-enhanced tempering needles that will inject the Metal element into your body. They increase in power to temper your body."

Erik put it into one of his storage rings. "Thank you, but I have a question for you."

"Please." Melissa smiled.

"Why?" Erik left the word hanging as Melissa frowned, multiple thoughts rising to the surface. "Why did you join Alva? Why did you put in the time to research this? What are you looking to get from it? Why are you okay with everything?"

"A few simple questions," Melissa drawled, getting the time to think. "Although it is not a democratic society in Alva, it is not a bad one. Ability beats all in the Ten Realms. If you can show results, you will be able to get higher. Look at you and Rugrat. You could be warlords and try to control everything. Instead, you got people to represent the people. You listen to others; you have your own goals, and you go out and complete them. Is it a perfect system? No, of course not, but it works. We are safe here, and we are with people who understand us. People have opportunities here they would not have in the other realms. There is a roof over our heads, clean water, food, safety. I accepted those things freely when I was in Paris. I didn't think the military stood for anything but to cost more taxes and parade around with their weapons. I thought they were a backwards system." Melissa turned and leaned against the window, thoughts and memories in her eyes as she sighed.

"When I entered the Ten Realms, it was different. I nearly died in the first two days. Luckily, there were other humans from Earth in the area. Kanoa and the military members grouped and pulled together the civilians. There were a number we didn't get to in time. We thought we had found a place with Queen Ikku, but she was going to use us as slaves. She had a binding contract that would have done so. We ran and escaped. I talked to Miller about it—why the military members were putting their lives on the line for us civilians and if they would be better off without us."

Melissa's eyes trembled and dampened. "You know what he said? He said people sleep peacefully in their beds at night because rough men stand ready to do violence on their behalf. He had dedicated his life to the survival of others. If he died, then he would do so gladly to protect the lives of those behind him. To protect his beliefs and those who believed as he did."

Erik nodded, agreeing with it. "When I was angry with the military, I saw them as a throwback to times of old. The reality is that with them as a foundation, I was able to reach higher. If not for those men and women standing ready to protect, we would never progress; we would never advance the sciences, gain education. We would fall into those times of old instead of reaching for higher pursuits."

"Well, I do this to support those men and women who protect me. I do this because I'm good at it. It is a whole new field of discovery; my team and I are pioneers. Who doesn't want to create a new field of study? Each day, we learn something new."

She was just a lady living and working in France before she had to come face-to-face with the ugly reality of the Ten Realms.

"You've certainly given me a lot to think about. Egbert?"

"Boss man?" Egbert's voice appeared from mid-air.

"Work with the Body Cultivation department to build new training facilities on the separate floors. Get with the smiths to create gym equipment. Rugrat can draw it up for you. He spent enough time there."

"Right on it, boss!" There was a popping noise, and he was gone, though the skeleton could listen to nearly everything going on in the dungeon.

"Thank you," Melissa said, getting herself back under control.

"No problem. There is an upcoming fight with a powerful enemy. We'll need our soldiers to be the strongest they can be. Increasing one's cultivation with these new methods will be faster than increasing a person's overall level," Erik said.

"There is one other thing I should tell you about Body Cultivation. Activation. When we were doing our testing with the cells, we found that with an increase in pure mana, the cell would be 'ignited' in this state, and its abilities were much greater than before."

"Okay, so again, the relationship with the mana and Body Cultivation—the higher the Mana Cultivation, the greater potential we can ignite in our cells?" Erik asked.

"Exactly, though there is a secondary way to activate them: being in a high-dense mana area. We have only completed some simple tests, but it is looking promising," Melissa said.

"All of this is promising. You've certainly been busy over the last couple weeks," Erik said.

22 Tactics Transformed Through Technology

There was a knock at Glosil's door as he reviewed the latest reports on the recruits across the Alva army. "Come in." He put the report to the side.

Newly minted Captain Kanoa opened the door and saluted Glosil, who returned the gesture.

"Captain, good to see you. Please, take a seat. Is everything going well?" Glosil asked.

"Everything is good. Thank you, sir." Kanoa sat down.

Glosil smiled. Kanoa, like the rest of the military members from Earth, had arrived nearly two months ago. Last month, most of them had joined the military with the stipulation that they could challenge the various tests. After a week of familiarization, they challenged every test. They were qualified as medics, sharpshooters, artillery gunners, and engineers. Most of them had been active in their service, reaching the peak of their professions. Those who had retired remained sharp, even afterward. With healing, they were as healthy as a twenty-year-old and with the knowledge of hardened warriors. Glosil had taken complete advantage, tapping into that knowledge pool to augment and enhance the Alva army's ability.

"I sense a 'but,'" Glosil said.

"But air assault and waterborne assaults. Alvans haven't trained for either. The Water floor took months of training before that operation was carried out."

"I'm listening."

"As you know, sir, there are multiple ways to get to the battlefield. Tactics have been developed to use ground transport to reach the enemy, dismount, engage them, complete the mission, and then mount back up and exfiltrate the area. Leading assaults with an Air or Water component hasn't been explored yet. I believe this is part of the secretive nature of Alva's Army. We head in close to the ground and under cover to strike the enemy. If we were to use air vehicles, we would stick out and blow our cover. Also, few of Alva's opponents have been located close to a shoreline."

"Though there is no way to say for sure if this will remain the same in the future," Glosil finished for Kanoa, intrigued. "I'm guessing you have a plan?"

"Stepping up two new units, trained in the same way as the others, but their focus will be on Air and Water assaults. Ground, air, water—we cover them all, and all the units have training in those so that they can support one another. Say there is a ground assault going on. We have the water assault company moving in to the rear of the enemy, and the air assault comes in and flanks them. The enemy fights the force on the ground, only to have their side torn apart by the other two forces."

It made sense. It had taken months for Yui to train and prepare his people for the Water floor. Most of what they had learned was from Rugrat's notes on beach assaults, fighting on the water, and so on. Though there were few missions where they would need to rely on ships.

"I don't think we need a navy. All our battles, except for the Water floor, have been on the ground. If we can add in an air force, it will increase our mobility, but training a specific force just to fight from the air—we just don't have the people or the time," Glosil said.

Kanoa nodded. "Well, then we don't raise airborne; we just add more training courses. Army, navy and airborne units back home were all using helicopters and fighters to support their people. What if we raised an air force whose only focus is to support the army units?"

"That could work. We wouldn't have to break up training or split off people for different units too much. We keep our combat force consolidated instead of splitting up into groups too small to do anything." Glosil fell silent, thinking.

"Okay, what would you need to raise a supporting air force?"

"Birds. We have a number of different birds being raised across Alva. We can use those as the mounts for the aerial force. On Earth, we needed helicopters and other types of aerial transport. We could make them with enough time, but the birds have some great advantages. First, each team member could have one bird to transport them. Entering and exiting a helicopter are the most dangerous times. Instead, we can just jump on a bird, and we're lifting off in seconds. Faster exfiltration. Also, birds can be healed and just need to be fed. We don't need to perform costly maintenance in terms of materials and time. The team on the ground can manage most issues themselves. Finally, birds are quiet, and you don't need to learn to pilot them. We can insert and exit silently, with the birds taking care of the flying while we take care of the fighting."

"I have read about medical evacuations that were primarily taken care of by helicopters. Also, close-range support. If we were able to train birds, we could have medical groups on standby to rush into the fight, get the wounded, and get back out, increasing the chances of survival. We could also mimic the bombers and attack helicopters of Earth. Add in machine guns under the beast's wings and storage rings on their stomach that can drop bombs. Even if they're not capable of that, they can remain in the sky, feeding information back to command. Give new firing solutions to the artillery forces on the ground, even," Glosil said.

"You know about helicopters?" Kanoa was a little shocked.

"Erik and Rugrat told us everything they knew. Same with Matt and Tanya. I thought it was crazy, but I've learned there are a lot crazier things around."

"Yes, sir. We have the birds. I have been talking to the beast tamers, and there are several beasts we could raise to be insertion mounts, bombers, or quick-response medical transport."

"Can we not use one kind of mount?"

"We could, but they would be limited. The ground unit panthers are perfect for getting in and out of an engagement. Also, they have been raised in large numbers to fill the needs of the army. The birds, although they are raised and sold to traders, are luxury items. They have not been raised in large numbers. The fastest ones have been bred the most, while other birds were left alone, the aggressive ones especially. Who wants a mount that is angry?"

"I'm guessing we do?" Glosil smiled, getting a grin from Kanoa.

"Damn right we do. We need their aggressive nature to dive at the enemy, to go into dangerous situations. If you can tame the strong-willed ones, they will be better than the docile ones."

Glosil sat at his desk, turning it over in his mind. "Bring it up at the meeting at the end of the week with the Silaz boys. I think you might get your airborne unit."

A whining noise filled the air. Rugrat and the rest of the testing group were in a bunker, using spells and gear to watch the test bed platform and the target.

There was a *tzzing* noise as the target was struck.

Everyone watched the weapon. The heat-dissipating formations pumped the heat away, their glow dimming so one could see a barrel between formation blocks with a chamber at one end.

"The power consumption is still much higher, but the barrel variables are lower," one of the people in the room said.

"Yeah, Phil, it is much more stable than the air-enhanced weapon system, but the requirement for power and formations is too high to mass-produce it," Rugrat said.

"Over the last couple weeks, we have come up with the enhanced air gun and a railgun. The air gun uses a modified round, an artillery shell. Once the round is fired, air formations are triggered, shooting in a massive amount of air. The artillery shell, combined with the air formations, greatly increases the overall velocity of the round. Though the timing has to be perfect or the airflow will slow the round. Or worse, it will highly pressurize the barrel, and when the round is ignited, the barrel could explode. The railgun uses metals that, when introduced to an electrical charge, create magnetic forces that shoot the round forward at great speeds. I never knew that metal could be turned into a magnet before," Taran said.

"We have mostly fixed the issues in the enhanced air gun version. We are testing the fourteenth version, and it fired ten thousand rounds without fail already," Julilah said.

"Though the overall power of the air gun is less than the railgun," Rugrat said.

"You just want a science-fiction rifle in a fantasy world," Phil said as he checked information on his clipboard.

"Yes, Phil, I want a *laser* gun. Can we do that?" Rugrat paused.

Phil looked up and tapped the pencil to his chin. "I don't see why not. Though we are in atmosphere, so the power of the weapon will be greatly decreased and be even more prone to overheating than your railgun."

"We have two issues. One, power." Julilah guided them back on task. "The railgun takes a massive amount of power to shoot. And two, the weapon tears itself apart because of the forces acting upon it."

"We already have charged magazines. What if we were to create cartridges that didn't have gunpowder but mana stones?" Rugrat said.

"We would need to work that out. If we could use Earth or Sky stones, that should solve our issues, I think. Julilah?" Taran asked.

"It could be possible, though that means every round we fire is going to cost a ton."

"We're raking in the stones. To enhance our military, I think we'll be happy to do so," Rugrat said.

"Why don't we use crystals to power all the weapons?" Phil asked.

"One, they are, as Julilah said, expensive as hell. We'd be burning money to shoot. Two, we can mass-produce a ton of gunpowder. Railguns are expensive and time-consuming to make. As our military continues to expand, we will create more rifles and rounds. They are not outdated yet. For the lower realms, there are few things that are their equal.

"Three, with formation sockets on our weapon systems, we can update them all the time, increasing the way they enhance the weapon. The systems work, and they are reliable. Adding crystals would be a waste. There is so much we can upgrade on them still," Rugrat said.

"And we would need to build a system like the air gun or railgun for them all, which takes development and time. I think I have a solution to the second problem we have with the railgun—wear and tear. Controlled air buffers. Create a powerful air cushion in the barrel. It keeps the round in the middle of the barrel when it is fired instead of scraping along the barrel," Julilah said.

Everyone sunk into thought.

"Normal rifles work on the use of explosive force. Railguns don't. It doesn't need to be a completely enclosed system," Rugrat said.

"The air flow could also decrease the overall temperature of the weapon. First with the lack of friction and then expelling air from within the barrel," Phil added.

"We would have to keep the system separated. With all these formations, we won't be able to add in formation sockets to start with. The metals and materials making the weapon will melt with so much power running through them."

"Looks like we have an idea for prototype twenty-three!" Rugrat announced.

"More damn prototypes." Taran rolled his eyes.

"At least we have the air gun. The rounds are large enough to be stamped with formations. They can shoot faster and longer with the cooling effect of the air system, and the speed of the round has increased by ten percent compared to our regular rifles, with thirty percent less recoil," Rugrat said.

"We are creating a new factory for them to assemble the machine guns as we speak. Should be starting production in another month." Taran rubbed his face, feeling tired.

"How is production going on the Conqueror's Armor?" Rugrat glanced over to Julilah.

"We replaced a regiment's worth of armor with the new versions. It will be another month to upgrade our serving members' armor."

Rugrat made to speak but got a sound transmission. He listened to it before smacking his head. "How the hell didn't I think of developing an air force. Dammit. At least Kanoa talked to Glosil. Well, damn, we could use the air gun for weapons on the birds. We might need new bombs for the bombers. I should talk to Han Wu," Rugrat muttered to himself.

"If you two idiots start making bombs together, do it somewhere like the Metal floor. You're likely to blow up the damn dungeon!" Taran said.

"More bombs? Do you ever get tired of explosions?"

"Tired of explosions? Pfft! Nope! The bigger the better!"

Taran, Phil, and Julilah looked at one another and shrugged.

"Since the others from Earth arrived, we have had an explosion in the areas of research and technology. They are rapidly advancing in different crafts," Taran said.

"We just need to know how to coax the Ten Realms into understanding our skill levels. We're still figuring out all the rules for the Ten Realms. Healing without any aids. Using the principles of shooting and our knowledge to take out targets at a long distance, mixed with skills to take out people at close range with great accuracy. As long as we apply that knowledge within the Ten Realms's parameters, it will give us a clearer and easier route of skill progression. Though I am not sure that is for the best," Rugrat said.

"How so? I know we have the whole debate of application and academics going on right now, but if we find a way for people to increase their skill level faster, isn't that good?"

"It is good for experience and egos, but it is not good for learning. In the Sixth Realm academies, they call it specialization. Someone will specialize in one area. Say healers—they will specialize in broken bones or colds. They will just do that one thing. They learn all the spells that can heal a person's bone in the best way possible. They reach the stage where they can heal a person's bone in one touch. They are Master-level healers because they have demonstrated to the Ten Realms their ability in that one area. Academically, that is awesome, but in reality, they are pretty damn useless. Take our medics: If we had one learn how to do one thing, then how the hell are they going to talk to one another if they are dealing with a gunshot wound? How are they going to heal them? Sure, that is fine for research—find those spells, teach others, and then they can do it as well, though you can see how in learning the system, the Ten Realms allows us to manipulate it. Look at the tech we're coming up with!"

"As time goes on, I think that the practical applications will have a greater weight than the theoretical academic advances. Still, we should teach general principles up to Expert. Beyond that, people have to specialize. But that knowledge, when distilled into the practical, aren't they two sides of the same coin, empowering one another?" Taran said.

"Yeah, I just hope we don't lose our edge of taking knowledge and applying it in new and different ways. Just talking to the other military members, I've found there are so many things I am missing. Phil is an integral part of this team with all the ideas he has come up with," Rugrat said.

"Well, let's leave those questions to the council and teachers to worry about. We can just make the guns and tech," Julilah said.

"Maybe I am thinking on it too much. Making guns and explosives is much easier!"

"Says you!" Taran shot back.

23 New Tempering Path

The weeks rushed by. There were just over five months to go until the Second Annual Fighter's Competition in Vuzgal.

Erik and Delilah walked through the Alchemy garden as Delilah kept him up to date with everything that was happening.

"More inventions are created every day. The traders are certainly loving it, and although there are people taking a break from their academic pursuits, some of them have advanced their class with their new inventions. The Ten Realms gives Experience to everyone involved in a group project. Not only increasing one but multiple skills as people have to understand the parts they are creating and how they relate to the other components."

"What does that mean if they make a Journeyman-level item?" Erik asked.

"Some of them might get Journeyman in their main skill, and others will get lower-ranked contributions. Whatever the level of the item is, no one can achieve a skill level higher than it," Delilah said.

"Okay, that is interesting. I was scared it would stagnate people completely. I thought only the main people working on the item would get Experience. Like with weapons and formations, the smithy gets their Experience, and then the formation master gets theirs from the Ten Realms."

"I think it might be how everything is assembled. The one smithing item to one formation is simple. With these new inventions, there can be multiple parts, and they can be altered and refined and then combined with other components to create a complete device. It lines up with the Experience gain; there is a burst when creating the parts and a larger one when all the parts are put together and function. It can increase with time as components are changed and the overall design becomes better. Then, all the parts contained within will send Experience to the original creators as their parts were able to create an item with a higher level of ability!" Delilah couldn't hold back her excitement.

"There are new things happening every week across Alva's lands." Erik chuckled as he continued down a path out of the Alchemy garden.

"It only seems to speed up as things go on," Delilah muttered.

"Well, you have new helpers as well. Lord Aditya is under your direct command, and I heard that he is helping out where he can."

"He and Lord Chonglu have helped out a lot. With them both being controllers over lands and people, they're a great resource. Though, what are your plans for them?" Delilah asked.

"Well, Hiao Xen is on loan to us by the Blue Lotus. That time will come up eventually. Chonglu has had a front-row seat to the operations within Vuzgal, kept in the loop by Elan, and attends the meetings with Hiao Xen."

"You're grooming him to take over the position?" Delilah nodded. "He is well suited. He has been training and tempering his mana and body. He is one of the strongest fighters we have in Vuzgal. He has been training with the Alva army based there to increase his capabilities. His wife's position lends him strength as well."

"Aditya will join Alva completely to train as he wants and do what he wants. We have a lot of people filling in positions. Leaders are hard to find." Erik sighed as they passed through the formations that contained the Alchemy garden.

"There is always more happening in Alva than what one can see on the surface." Delilah admired the sights around her as they walked.

"How is the integration with the Earthers to Alva going?" Erik asked.

"Mixed reactions. Most of the military members have joined in one way or another. The civilians are a mixed bag. Some see Alva as their new home, opening up new fields of research, delving into the secrets of the Ten Realms that were seen as grounded facts previously. Others…" Delilah had a complicated look on her face.

"We're from the same planet. It doesn't mean that we're alike. In fact, you would be surprised how different most of us are from one another," Erik reassured her.

"Some of them don't really understand. They complain about the Alvan system. They are trying to create protests, asking people to stand for a democratic system. Only three of them. Saying that what we have now is akin to socialism or communism or slavery—whatever that means. Police have been called a few times, but then the protestors go wild and say they are going against their right for free speech."

Erik felt a headache coming on. "What's the Alvan response been?"

"Don't care for it, think that they're idiots, more pissed off than the police. Tell them to get the hell out and go see what the Ten Realms is really like." Delilah shrugged.

"If they don't have jobs and aren't doing anything to help Alva and are living off of our supplies, the law is clear. They are no different from any other intern citizen."

"Thank you. I was going to press that we treat them the same as everyone else as well."

They reached a large house. People were talking and laughing inside.

Delilah walked up to the gate.

"So, any boys or girls you're interested in?" Erik asked.

"Boys! And not really." Delilah sighed. "My job kind of keeps everyone at a distance from me. Though I am happy that I have my position and not Aditya's or Chonglu's."

"Oh, why?"

"Well, although there are a lot of people in Alva, they are all our people. We can walk around freely. We don't have to care about our outside appearances, no matter one's station—well, other than between military members of different rank in the same chain of command. For Chonglu and Aditya, people are always talking up to them. They have to cultivate a certain personality to deal with the outside world."

"What if there comes a time when you have to talk to people who aren't Alvans?" Erik asked.

"Then I hope my teacher is there to back me up." Delilah grinned.

Erik rolled his eyes and mussed up her hair, making her scowl as she pushed away the offending hand.

The door to the house opened. Amelia Ryan, Delilah's mother, stood there. "Erik! What are you two doing out there?"

"Mrs. Ryan, we were just discussing a few things. How are you? I am sorry I haven't been around to check in on you and your family." Erik put on an apologetic expression. He felt that time was constantly slipping through his fingers as he trained or went off to level up and reach higher realms.

"We've got dinner set out. It would be great to have you join us." Amelia turned her head into the house. "Erik will join us for dinner too. Add another place at the table!"

"I—" Erik thought about the training that lay ahead of him, the research he wanted to do in the library, and how he wanted to search out an Earth doctor who was steadily marching upward through the skill ranks now that they knew one needed to heal their patients with just mana in order to increase their skill.

"You don't have any set meetings. Come on. You might have great meals in your storage ring, but you can't have famous Ryan company!"

Delilah grabbed his arm and pulled.

"Hey, aren't you supposed to honor your teacher?!" Erik laughed as he was pulled forward.

"Erik!" Joseph, Delilah's dad and Amelia's husband, appeared behind his wife with a wide smile. He had that hard-worked tan of a man who spent his days working in the fields. There was an earthly presence to him as he reached out a hand.

"Joseph, I heard you were this year's winner of the largest watermelon contest," Erik said.

"Yes! And the juiciest, by Rugrat's opinion." Joseph chuckled. "That redneck was always complaining about never having watermelon. He was like a book on watermelons, knew everything about them. We held the contest last week with just four days to grow them. He about collapsed from a watermelon coma. I didn't think it was possible!"

They laughed as Amelia got them inside and closed the door behind them.

The Ryan family was spread around the house—some in the kitchen, others playing with kids or preparing the table. Delilah was recruited into the kitchen as her mother organized others and picked up the latest addition to the family, showing her off proudly. Joseph found a bottle he had been holding onto for a special occasion.

They talked about Alva, what they were doing at their own jobs, and the latest gossip from the dungeon. Erik talked to Jamie, Zhiwei, and John about the military. Joanna, the last Ryan in the army, was serving in Vuzgal and wouldn't get leave for the next two weeks.

"So, there will really be three new units?" Zhiwei said.

"Just two: Alva Army and Alva Air Force. Captain Kanoa's air force will provide transport in and out of battle and will close support during it. It will be a company-sized force to start."

"Where are the people going to come from?" Jamie asked.

"Transfers and new trainees. People who have a good record with beasts will have a higher chance of getting the positions. They'll have to have completed sharpshooter training to be part of the transport crews and all your artillery courses if you want to be fighters and bombers, at a minimum," Erik said.

"Do you have to do an extra course?"

"Door gunners will be good with the sharpshooter course, now that the course has machine guns covered, though everyone else will need to take flight combat courses that go over tactics, care for the gear, and care for the beast. Anything and everything related to their job. Trust me, it'll be much easier than the courses back on Earth where you're working with machines instead of animals."

Kyle emerged from the kitchen with dishes in each hand. "Hot dishes coming through!"

"All right, everyone to the table!"

"Come on, put it right here. No one needs any, right?" John looked up from where he was sitting with a wide grin.

"I think your daughter will have something to say about that!" Zhiwei passed John their daughter before she sat down.

"You know I couldn't take food from you, baby. Your momma is making things up!"

Jamie and Rachel helped Kyle put the food out while Delilah poured the wine.

Suzy stared at Erik as if he were the most interesting thing she had ever seen. Erik winked at her, causing her to turn beet red, raising Joseph's laughter.

"Stop staring at people, Suzy Ryan. It's rude to stare like that!" Amelia chastised half-heartedly.

"Here, try these potato scallops! Teacher!"

"Do you want some meat?"

"Gravy over here, please!"

"Excuse my reach!"

"You've already got three bread buns!"

They distributed food around the table, talking and laughing. Erik passed food, served others, and was served.

Drink flowed, and they enjoyed the food. Erik forgot about his research and his training for the night as he was taken in by the Ryan household, and he felt his heart open.

Rugrat stared at his plans, rubbing his face and yawning.

"You're still here?" Taran asked from the workshop's doorway.

"Just making some last-minute changes. I'll catch up with you later." Rugrat checked the blueprint, looking for the flaws that were creating issues with his new weapon system.

"All work and no play makes a smith a dull nail."

"That is a terrible saying."

Taran grinned. "I didn't make it up. I'm just using it."

"I've just got some alterations to make."

"Come on, there are chicken wings to eat and beers to drink."

Rugrat sighed. "All right, all right. I won't say just one beer because I have a feeling that will be a lie!"

"Good man!"

They left the workshop and found a nearby tavern. Different shops, restaurants, and pubs appeared in Alva as more people came. Just having one place to eat and devoting the rest of the space to work was sure to make people bored.

Taran talked to the owner and got them a table inside. There was a band playing, but their table wasn't getting blasted by the music, thankfully.

"Pretty packed in here." Rugrat looked around.

"Yeah, if you're single, it's nice to go out somewhere with people from work or meet up with friends," Taran said.

"You ever thought about marrying?" Rugrat asked.

"I was once. Had a kiddo too." Taran pulled his chain out from his shirt, showing a simple, worn gold ring. It was at odds with the works Taran was capable of making.

"I made both of our rings, spent four months of my wages. Worked in the gold with an enhanced iron that shone like silver and looked like a sunset over time," Taran spoke softly.

The waitress came over and dropped off their drinks.

"What happened?" Rugrat asked as Taran took a big gulp.

He spat and wiped his beard with the back of his arm. "Raiders. Fucking scum."

Rugrat drank his beer. He could see Taran needed to get it out and off his chest; he waited as Taran pulled himself together.

"I was working for Lord Salyn. We were fixing the hinges, bars, and other metal bits of his city. My wife worked in the fields outside the city. She looked after our little boy as loud noises would wake him up and send him bawling. We were hoping to save enough money so she could stay home and look after the little one while I smithed. She was slower—having the baby, sleeping less.

"She and the other farm hands were bringing in the harvest. They loaded it onto carts and were wheeling it toward the gates. Raiders attacked from the forests. They cut down everyone in their way, captured several carts, and fled." Taran gritted his teeth, his fist turning white from the pressure.

"There was no need for it. No need to kill those folks. Just take the cart and run. None of them would have fought." Taran took another drink from his mug. "Killed my boy and my wife. I stopped smithing. I stopped doing anything. When Blaze asked if I would like to help him make a village, it was my last hope. Everything I did was touched by her or my boy. I couldn't talk to people without thinking of or seeing her.

"With Alva, I was able to work as a smith again. I let my days slide by. When you and Erik arrived, it lit a fire under my ass. I could finally do something to help others. I've been able to get over my past, become a teacher, and push into the Expert realm of smithing. Not something I thought possible," Taran said.

"Takes a lot for you to stand back up again and keep going," Rugrat said.

"I see that same loss, that same drive in you, Rugrat."

Taran's words caught him off-balance.

Rugrat saw those who hadn't come back from patrol. The moments when he didn't know it already, but his friends had died. Those moments when he knew they weren't making it back. The countless hours he had spent thinking of just what their family was going through, the part of him that thought of what might happen if he didn't make it back. How would it hit his mother?

"We all have our weight to carry." Rugrat tapped his beer on the table and drank from it deeply.

"The thing is, we can't shut people out, just focus on the work, on the next thing that needs to be done. If we did that, then are we really alive or just someone imitating being alive?" Taran said.

"I like working on different projects. I get a satisfaction from it."

"I know, man. I do too. But if you don't have people to share that satisfaction with? Is it really worth doing?"

Rugrat frowned before drinking his beer.

Taran patted his shoulder. "When I saw how broken up you were about not making it into Expert, I wanted to do everything I could to help you. Now look at you! You found another path. Remember that you can go around obstacles, not just crash into them again and again. Your head isn't *that* hard. It's pretty hard, but not by that much."

"Thanks." Rugrat flipped him the bird.

"So, how about that Racquel girl?" Taran asked as the waitress arrived with their wings, and Rugrat stared daggers into Taran.

"Want anything with that?" she asked.

"I think we should be good. Oh, actually, do you have that ketchup?"

"Yeah, one second!" She disappeared.

"She's in the higher realms. There ain't nothing to talk about," Rugrat said.

"Oh, who knows? There are a few women in your life who might make you feel that way."

Rugrat rolled his eyes as the waitress returned with Taran's ketchup.

"All I am saying is that you don't need to be some weird, celibate, short-short-wearing hobo."

"Good to know how you feel, Taran." Rugrat snorted with a smile as he bit into the wings. "*Mmm.* Damn, I missed you, wings."

"You don't seem the hang-around kind of bachelor guy," Taran said.

"Appearances can be deceiving. I like to flirt with girls, don't get me wrong, but any more or being in a relationship, that's a big leap. My momma taught me to treat women with respect. Always make sure that both parties know what the other wants and that they're okay with it. Communication is key. Just because you're nervous or anxious is not a good reason to keep something from a person you care for. You should care for them too. People are people; they are no less than or more than you. They shouldn't be your highest priority or your lowest. You know what I never believed in?"

"What?"

"Two parts of the whole. You are your own whole. Another person is their own whole. There shouldn't be some weird symbiotic relationship going on. You bring yourself, and they bring themselves. Together, you're not one plus one but one times one."

"I understand what you mean. Once you find that one and you devote yourself to them and they devote themselves to you, that is powerful. Damn powerful and hard to replicate," Taran said. "So, why aren't you going on dates and seeing more people?"

"I'm tired, and I have too many damn issues right now. I need to work on me, get me sorted out, and then I can look into a relationship. Also, with this dungeon lord/city lord shtick, it's hard to meet people who aren't freaked out by your position."

"I can get that. I'm just saying, don't shut yourself in. You feel the weight of all this on your shoulders, and it will lead to an early grave if you don't share it."

"I share it with Erik." Rugrat shrugged.

"You two do well to make sure the other is okay. You two are closer than brothers with the same blood in their veins. It is one thing to share it with a brother and another to share it with a lover."

Rugrat ate his wings, feeling lighter than he had in a while and thinking about possibilities he hadn't considered before. "You know what, Taran? You might have a point. Though damn if I wouldn't like to take Racquel out on a real date." Rugrat chuckled.

Taran laughed. "Well, what was she like?"

"A redneck dream. She could destroy beers as if they were nothing but pop. And that body—damn! Her mind was fierce, too! One-liners here and there—I was under fire, man! She could string together a series of jabs so well I was honored to receive them!"

Erik walked through the streets of Alva. Night had arrived inside the dungeon. People were headed home or out to some event with friends and family.

With his Stamina so high, he wouldn't need to sleep for a few days. He kind of missed sleep, but he would hardly have the time for it anyway.

It didn't take him long to reach the teleportation array.

Gilly, where you at, girl?

He felt a response to his link with Gilly. Smiling, Erik pulled out a fresh slab of meat. He threw it casually into the sky. It reached fifty meters high and started to descend. It had just about reached Erik again when a brown-and-blue streak appeared, snapping it from the air.

Erik's smile widened as Gilly chewed on the meat and threw it back before she rubbed her head on her master's shoulder.

"You are getting big from all of the beast meat and monster cores." Erik scratched her head as she stayed there, happy for the attention.

He spent a few minutes giving her scratches before he patted her side. "Come on now. Down to the Earth floor." He walked forward to the teleportation array. Gilly followed him as Erik nodded to the guard.

Light enveloped them. The smell of freshly churned earth reached his nose as the light dissipated.

"Welcome to the Earth floor," the guard on duty said.

"Thank you."

It looked a lot better than the last time he'd seen it—not so much of an apocalyptic-looking wasteland anymore. Fields had grown in, there was a small settlement, and they were raising beasts.

Erik exited the teleportation array and the small-walled settlement outside it; some people were living on the Earth floor. Most of the buildings were related to growing crops and raising assorted plants or nursing beasts with an Earth Affinity. There was one building that focused on Body Cultivation.

Erik jumped up onto Gilly's back. "Let's head to the center."

Gilly quickly took him out of the settlement and toward the true Earth Body Cultivation facility. She picked up speed, following the road through the Earth floor. On either side, orchards and fields spanned for kilometers in each direction. Buildings lay here and there, places for the farmers to rest and work on developing their crops.

Erik gripped hold of his saddle as she quickly surpassed the speed of a sports car back on Earth.

"Woohoo!" Erik yelled, feeling the rush of air as Gilly pushed harder, increasing her speed once again.

Erik saw a few of the Gnome Automatons-nicknamed Crawlers. The old gnomes' assistants were few in number With old versions on the different floors the blueprint office had been able to replicate their plans.

They worked through the night to turn the dirt path into a road to the center of the Earth floor.

The modified crawlers for the artillery units were as scary as hell. They'd doubled in size adding mounted heavy mortar tubes. A crew of four could manage six mortar tubes at the same time. Giving them a serious firepower increase.

Gilly jumped over the mortar crawlers and rushed down the unfinished dirt road, leaving a trail of dirt behind. Gilly showed off all her speed, excited by the open space.

It still took a few minutes to reach the center of the Earth floor. Gilly dug her talons in and raced up the hill. A pillar of light shot out from the hill and into the roof above. Runes could be faintly seen around where the pillar of light reached. There were more runes across the hill.

As Erik and Gilly climbed higher, reaching a flat plateau that broke the hill in two, Erik looked out, seeing vast areas of the floor that were unused.

"Egbert, have you been increasing the size of the floor?" Erik asked.

"Yes. With the dungeon cores, it is much easier to do so. The living floor is slowly increasing at a rate of one meter deeper a week and ten meters wider each day. The floors that are not so populated and have complicated infrastructure are increasing to eighty percent of their limits as fast as possible."

"So, it is going to be massive," Erik said.

"Yes. The individual dungeon cores greatly aid the expansion of each floor, so I don't need to keep moving other dungeon cores around."

"How are things on the Water floor going?"

"Slowly, but it is a massive floor, and there is a lot to be done. I hope it will be complete a month or so after the Second Annual Fighter's Competition at Vuzgal. Though my motivation is somewhat lacking."

"I'll get you some more romance books to read. You're just sitting down there in the freezing cold, reading books, aren't you?"

"I move every so often."

"Flipping the page and opening the menus don't really count as moving."

"What do I need to move for? Not like I'm going to get back spasms or lose my figure. I'm about as slim as one can get!"

"Talk to you later, Egbert. Have fun reading."

"Thank you!" A noise filled the air, and Egbert disappeared.

The plateau cut into the hill.

Erik reached a building that had been built into the side of the hill.

"Sir!" The guards snapped to attention at the doorway.

"At ease." Erik dismounted from Gilly. "You want to come in, or do you want to go off and play?"

Gilly glanced over to the fields and orchards that looked like forests.

"I'll let you know when I'm done." Erik patted her side.

She nudged him with her snout and ran off to stretch her legs and terrify the local residents.

Erik turned to the building and guards. "When I was here last, this was just a cave. Is the new Body Cultivation area set up?"

"Body Cultivation training areas were set up on each floor with the help of construction crews, people from the blueprint department, and formation masters. The most powerful and pure Affinity energies are contained within each training facility. They just finished putting in the new testing and training equipment earlier today," one of the guards said.

"That came together quickly. Construction in Alva was always fast as hell!"

"Now it's spread to Vuzgal as well. That place has more buildings every time I see it." The other guard fell quiet, nervous by his outburst.

"Yeah, it's growing at an alarming rate. I heard we will reach the old borders of the city in just a year and a half." Erik shook his head. "Keep up the good work."

Erik headed to the main door.

"Are we really going to have a war?" one of the guards asked.

Erik paused and contemplated the two men. The other guard looked as if he wanted to hit his fellow comrade over the head, but the guard asking, although expecting to be yelled at, didn't turn away.

"Yes, we probably are. Though we're not going to charge into it like idiots. We have been attacking and undermining our enemy for nearly a year now. It has been slow progress, but their foundations are weaker than ever, while ours"—Erik pointed his thumb at the door behind him and looked upward—"we have never been stronger."

"I heard what they did to Colonel Domonos and the Adventurer's Guild. Those could have been me and my buddies. We've all seen the reports on how they treat people. How they have killed and stolen Beast Mountain badges from people in the First Realm. They stand on our necks and take all the benefits."

"Look after the men and women to your left and right; do your job to the best of your ability. It sounds simple, but it'll get you through." Erik wasn't talking as a lord, but as a fellow soldier who had been in their shoes. "Trust in your training and your officers. You'll be surprised with how fast those reactions can save your life."

"Thank you, sir," the guard said.

The two men came to attention. It was different from before—not just a greeting, but an acknowledgment.

"Carry on." Erik turned and headed into the facility. He passed through the defenses. A man holding a clipboard was waiting for him.

"Medic Larsson, sir." The man came to attention.

"Just call me Erik. Shall we get started?"

"Yes, sir. First, we are going to do some tests to check your Affinity and resistance with the Earth element."

"Okay, what afterward?"

"Afterward, we conduct physical tests. Basically, we'll see how much you can lift, how fast your reaction speed is, and how fast you can run or jog and for how long," the man said.

"All right. Well, let's get to it," Erik said.

He checked his stats quickly.

Name: Erik West	
Level: 60 Race: Human	
Titles: *From the Grave II* *Blessed By Mana* *Dungeon Master IV* *Reverse Alchemist* *Poison Body* *Fire Body* *City Lord* *Earth Soul* *Mana Reborn* *Wandering Hero*	
Strength: (Base 54) +51	1050
Agility: (Base 47) +72	654
Stamina: (Base 57) +25	1230
Mana: (Base 27) +79	1166
Mana Regeneration: (Base 30) +61	73.80/s
Stamina Regeneration: (Base 72) +59	27.20/s

Doctor Melissa Bouchard drank her tea as she marched into the training facility. Medic Larsson passed her the reports and notes he had compiled with the rest of the research team.

He looked pale, and his confident smile wavered.

"How is he doing?" Melissa peeked into the room where Erik was curling weights repeatedly.

"He's a monster. I heard about it before, but this—it's nothing like what I expected," Larsson said.

The other researchers and medics all had haunted looks as well.

"What do you mean?" Melissa asked. The Ten Realms came with many surprises, but she was determined to quantify and pull back the mystery surrounding them.

"We started with the element tests. We increased the Earth Affinity up to seventy percent, and he asked if he could start lifting. Started working out while enduring the Earth element infiltrating his body. We increased it all the way to ninety percent before we had to dial it back. His skin transformed, taking on a stone-like appearance while his veins looked like magma."

"It changed on a physical level? What did he say?" Melissa asked.

"He said he was digging deep." Larsson shook his head glancing into the room again.

"He was lifting an average of five hundred kilos for all three major lifts. Bench, squats, and dead lift."

"What about afterward?"

"He was in a high-gravity training room. Once he was in one of the element-neutral rooms, he crushed it. Lifts went up to over two thousand kilos of force. His reaction times were close to 0.075 seconds.

"So, we can confirm the triple-stat theory," Larsson said. "At ten of any stat, the body reaches the limits of what was seen on Earth. At thirty stat points in any given attribute, that ability is doubled; at ninety, it doubles again. Other than Agility. Strength increases the weight one can lift. Stamina, the speed one can move and for how long. Agility is based upon reaction times. At ten stat points, people have an average reaction time of two hundred milliseconds; at thirty, they have a reaction speed of one hundred and seventy-five milliseconds. It decreases by twenty-five milliseconds each time. Though at ninety stat points, the reactions are not simply reflex-based; they are closer to cognitive decisions. Instead of simple movements, Erik is exhibiting a string of complex actions in response to outside stimuli."

"Is that because of his body stats or his mana stats? People with a higher Mana Cultivation have reported faster problem-solving skills and a higher cognitive speed than others," Melissa said.

Larsson laughed dryly and rubbed the back of his neck. "Never assert anything on hunches. Verification first?"

"Precisely. Though it is a good theory, you need more data to back it up. Have you taken samples?" Melissa asked.

"Yes, though we had to use the formation-enhanced needles and an enchanted blade just to break his skin!"

Staring at the numbers was one thing. But by the standards of people on Earth or people from the Ten Realms, Erik was a through-and-through monster.

He had left the limits of human physiology from Earth long ago. They had only just tested his physical abilities.

"Did he activate any of his spells or mana abilities?"

"No. The readings show he was drawing in mana and the elements in massive quantities, and when he had finished, they dissipated from his body slowly, reaching pre-exercise levels," the researcher said.

Erik finished with his curls and dropped the bar. It landed, creating craters in the ground. He went to the squat rack and grunted as he pushed into the bar. It was made from Earth-grade metal, but it was still bending with the five hundred kilos on each side.

"*Putain*! That's eight fully grown people." Bouchard shook her head and snorted.

"With the high mana, it must feel closer to sixteen."

Erik felt refreshed after completing the tests. It had been a long time since he had felt the pains of working out, and it felt good to move again. The weeks seemed to be evaporating as he worked in Alva.

"Something wrong?" he asked Melissa, who looked at him strangely.

"No. Just you're a genetic freak, you know that?"

"Well, you were the one who told me about the cell changes."

"Fine. Okay, so the next thing we need to talk about is tempering your body with the Metal element."

Erik leaned forward on the table between them.

"We set up training facilities like this one across all of the floors, except the Water floor as it is unstable right now with construction. When tempering your body, it is best to temper everything in one go. Your cells were opened by the foundational cleansing. Now, when you introduce the elements, it is painful, but they enter a transformative state; the more you absorb, the greater the advances. If you had stopped at merely tempering your body to the first stage, getting the preliminary title instead of the advanced second title, it would have been harder to advance all the way to that second title as you'd need to overload the cells you had already tempered, in order to get to the deeper cells. The deeper the tempering and the more cells you reach, the better. If you get them all, you will get the second title."

"Is that why each tempering is harder than the last?" Erik asked.

"Kind of. So, the elemental tempering focuses on different cells and parts of the body. Each part of your cell evolves rapidly, as we've talked about. They each become dominant within your cells, fighting one another. The elements are not at harmony either; each of them is competing—subsuming or being subsumed by one another. It is like magnets, but instead of a negative and positive charge, you have five different charges. The repulsion increases with each one until you reach the fifth, and then everything might snap together. Well, it did in some tests we did with element-heavy monster cores."

"It took me a month to completely temper my body with the Earth element," Erik said.

"And it could take you five months with the Metal element. Not to worry. We have a way around that." Melissa took out a needle.

"One of those elemental spikes?"

"Yup! It's simple, very simple, but effective. If you stop absorbing the Metal element, it will be harder to progress. If you have this needle inserted and powered up, doing a Metal damage over time, then although your tempering might not increase over time, it will not regress. You can temper in high Metal areas, increase your tempering, leave to do other things, and this will keep on going. Also, it might be a way to super-temper."

"What is super-temper, and could it temper my body over time?"

"It could, but the pain would be extraordinary. What I mean by super-temper is when someone gains the title of Body Like Stone, they usually stop their tempering, but they have just reached the first stage. One needs to push further to reach the true Body Like Stone, gaining the Fire Body or Earth Soul. If you temper your body with the Metal element, you could unlock the Body Rebirth, but you won't get the second stage of tempering, Metal Body or whatever it is called. This will keep tempering your body, so even if you relax, you will not automatically go through a Body Rebirth."

"So, it's like a bucket of water on a see-saw. You push the see-saw a certain amount, and the water will come tumbling down before reaching vertical. This needle is like a string. You push the see-saw so it is vertical and then release the string. Then the water will all pour out and smash on the ground with greater power than when it fell off before because it got too high?"

"Weird analogy, but yes. This is your string that allows you to go higher and create a greater impact," Melissa said.

"So, when can I start?"

"You really are a monster," Melissa said under her breath.

"What was that?"

"Nothing. Just head to the Metal floor. There is a training facility there. If you allow it, we would be really interested to study your training methods and see what works and what we can improve on. The more data we have, the faster we can help others," Melissa said.

"Okay." Erik nodded. "Not the first time I've been used as a test dummy."

"That is one thing the Ten Realms doesn't have. People don't share information here, even in the same group. They hide it under flowery texts and extrapolated details, caring more about the presentation to make themselves look better than the overall effect. Of their art or technique, there is little actual research carried out. It is why so many people still die on the battlefields in the Ten Realms, even with access to alchemists and healers." Melissa sighed.

"The healers try to conserve their mana for the highest-paying customer, and it's the same for the alchemist. Our general healing-and-Stamina recovery pill is a peak-Journeyman-level pill, but it costs as much as a low-Journeyman-level pill in materials, and we can mass-produce them in a factory because dozens of healers, alchemists, and others have worked together," Erik said.

"Compared to the world outside, Alva really is a paradise."

"The power of working together and caring about your fellow citizen," Erik countered.

Erik exited the Earth element training facility. Dawn had come and gone, leading to midday.

Erik whistled into the forest as he lowered himself. Working out made him want to see just how fast he was now. Erik looked up with fighting spirit in his eyes as his muscles contracted and then released.

He took off at a sprint, shooting across the plateau. He reached the edge of the hill and ran down it, maintaining his pace and increasing it as he leveled off. The clear path through the floor to the teleportation array lay ahead of him; he dug deep and pushed on. His hair was thrown back as he breathed in twice before exhaling violently. He pumped his legs and arms, feeling the blood thrumming in his head as his heartbeat increased. His body hummed with excitement.

Faster!

Erik threw all his Strength behind his legs and hurled himself forward. His Agility allowed him to react to and compensate for his footfalls, and his massive Stamina pool supported his outburst of energy.

His speed increased again and again as he forced his mind past what was possible in his old life. He pushed harder and threw himself forward more. He raised his own dust along the road as he sprinted.

Gilly let out an excited shrill, and Erik saw her running through an orchard to his side.

Erik dug deeper. Mana flowed through his body. "I reached the limits of my body but not my mana." Erik laughed. As his eyes shone, power flowed through his body. He used so much force his legs muscles ripped apart while tears formed in his tendons. His natural healing, born from his Earth body, fixed the damage before he touched the ground again.

Spell formations appeared behind Erik's back, shooting him forward like a rocket in bursts. Different fires appeared around him, and the flames seemed to be made from dragons and tigers. These untamable beasts heeded his commands; they created a sea of fire around him, increasing his speed again.

Erik took in two short breaths, and a spell formation appeared in front of him. The air along the path exploded outward, making the crops and trees shake. Erik shot through the vacuum he had created, and he hit the ground. Waving his arms to catch himself, he slammed into the ground, creating a divot. He bounced up again. Flames appeared around Erik and he adjusted his position, breaking out forcefully. The same Wind spell appeared in front of him. Wind shot out to either side of the road and Erik yelled. The beast flames around him detonated and threw him forward. He windmilled again, but he didn't fall this time. Erik tried it again and didn't need to wave his hands around that much. With each attempt, Erik required less time to stabilize himself, increasing his speed multiple times.

Erik reached the automatons that had been working throughout the night. He slowed his speed, leaving grooves in the dirt. He smiled as his chest rose and fell rapidly.

Gilly came over to him, giving him a strange look.

"Got a little excited there." Erik patted her as he opened his notifications that had been screaming at him for the past couple minutes.

You have created a new Expert-level technique. What do you wish to call it?

???

Expert

Rapidly increase your speed through utilization of Fire and Wind spells.

Cast: 40 Mana/second

"Let's call it the Quick Step," Erik said.

The "Quick Step" has already been taken. Here are some suggestions.

Fiery Tornado Step

Wind Hell Sprint

Inferno Steps of the Heavens

"Is this why there are so many damn crazy names for simple techniques? Because all the simple names were taken?"

Of course, the Ten Realms failed to answer him.

"What about Mana-Enhanced Sprint Version One?" Erik asked.

Mana-Enhanced Sprint Version One is available.

Mana-Enhanced Sprint Version One

Expert

Rapidly increase your speed through utilization of Fire and Wind spells.

Cast: 40 Mana/second

For teaching yourself an Expert-ranked spell, you gain: 5,000,000 EXP

86,796,860/108,500,000 EXP till you reach Level 61

Erik felt the flow of Experience enter his body.

Erik was pleased with his gains, albeit tired from the dead sprint across the floor.

He jumped onto Gilly's back, and she headed for the teleportation array.

They crossed through to the Metal floor. Smithies and refineries could be seen everywhere as people refined the natural materials into items for the smithies on the living floors. Others were headed out across the floor, placing down plants that naturally refined the metals around them or turned into metals with enough exposure to the Metal element.

"We have to look to the future, not just now. If we take everything from the floors, there would be nothing left in a few years. Creating a balance will assure our ability to move forward without cutting off our lifeline."

Erik and Gilly rode toward the center of the floor where the Metal mountain stood with its constant rain of lightning falling day after day.

Erik pulled out the needle Melissa had given him.

Metal Tempering Needle

Attack: 65

Weight: 0.4 kg

Health: 100/100

Charge: 100/100

Innate Effect:

Increase damage by 5%

Enchantment:

Metal Corruption—Inflict Metal damage on target. Varies on overall charge.

Requirements:

Strength: 21

Agility: 32

"The higher the charge, the more Metal element it will release into the body," Erik muttered. "That way, if you figure out the amount of charge that correlates to your tempering, then you can use a remote charging device to maintain the needle at that charge. If one needle isn't enough, you can use more. Simple—utilizing multiple Journeyman equipment together to create a desired effect."

Instead of having to ascend the entire mountain, Erik found the entrance to the training facility built into the side

"Go and play if you want," Erik said.

Gilly headed off to do her own thing. On the Metal floor, not even the beavers were a threat to her.

He passed through the guards and entered the facility beyond. There was a researcher reviewing their notes at the reception. Erik walked up and cleared his throat.

"What is it, Duncan?" The man at the desk sighed as he kept looking over the files.

"I'm looking to rent out a training room," Erik said.

"What?" The man looked up, frowning, as if trying to place Erik. "You need to complete Earth training first."

"Yes, I did it. Melissa Bouchard gave me this needle." Erik held it out.

"But the only person who has reached that stage is Lord Erik... West." Things seemed to snap together for the man. "Sorry, sir! We have just been manning the facility and running our own tests. We haven't had anyone visit us yet!"

"No worries. I wanted to start in the lowest-density rooms. Test them out, see how effective they are, and go through rooms with greater density."

"Are you looking for any training aids? We have a number of pills and concoctions that are reported to help in tempering the Metal element," the man said.

"I didn't know you sold aids as well. What do you have?"

The man took out a list and passed it to Erik.

Erik looked over the various concoctions. There were recommendations on the sheet; detailed information was listed underneath each concoction.

Some were more relaxed while others were much more aggressive in tempering the body.

"These have been tested out?"

"Trials on different beasts were carried out, and they were researched in the outside world. If there are any complications, then the health monitor in your training room will alert us and we will send in medics right away to assist you."

"I'll take the ones from here to here." Erik picked out most of the concoctions from the first page.

Using Reverse Alchemist, Organic Scan, and his tougher body, he could test out what the concoctions did. They could modify and enhance them later on.

"Are you sure, sir?"

"It should be fine. I won't take them all at once."

The man seemed to be debating it before he took the list back. "I'll prepare those for you right away." He went into another room, only to return shortly with a large box. It was subdivided with different potions, powders, and pills.

"Your room is ready—number one in block A."

"Thank you." Erik took the key and headed into the training facility.

It was laid out like the exact design as the Mana Cultivation facility.

Just instead of mana, it was pumping out elemental power.

Erik reached his room and put the key into the door.

It unlocked, and he stepped inside. A simple room appeared in front of him. Erik laid out the different concoctions on the table.

"It's like a damn motel." Erik took out the health monitor that was packed with formations to check on his health. He stuck it to his chest, feeling a cold ripple as the formations scanned his body.

The coppery smell of metal filled his nose. It reminded him of the times he had smelled that coppery tang; it was so close to blood. He saw the men and women he was working on. Their pale skin in contrast with the bright red seeping from them. Their eyes as wide as saucers as they mumbled or yelled or screamed. Erik yelled back to them, covered in their blood, doing all he could for them. Tourniquets, gauze, iodine, painkillers, and IVs. There were wrappers and shit everywhere as he worked.

Erik gripped his hand and closed his eyes. Mentally, he reviewed how to load and unload his rifle. A shiver ran through his body as he centered himself and thought of operating different weapon systems.

"Shit." Erik surveyed the room quickly and headed back to the individual training room.

Instead of releasing the Earth element, Erik took out the needle he had been given by Melissa. "Time to see how this works." Erik pulled his pants out of his boots and pushed the needle into his leg.

He grimaced as the Metal element entered his body and started to attack him from the inside. He twisted his head, grunting as he worked to focus his mind on something other than the pain. "Fuck! This sucks!"

His Organic Scan showed the Metal element corrupting his body. Cells were dying under the power of the Metal element. His body fought back. The Fire element ignited the power of the cells, and the Earth element fought to recover his cells. Three warriors fought within his body: Earth and Fire were being suppressed by the dominating power of the Metal element.

Its attacks were new to Erik's body; he hadn't built up any defenses.

Erik focused his mind and used a healing spell. It was like

reinforcement for the Fire and Earth element warriors.

The cells were still being cut down, but some recovered. They lasted for a half-second longer than the ones previous. More would reform, stronger than before, but their defense was futile as it collapsed again and again. The Metal element spread to Erik's upper leg.

Black lines ran through his skin. It cracked and bled. Silver peeked through the cracks, and flashes of light shot through Erik as lightning tore up his body.

Erik slumped on the bed and waited there. The power of the needle decreased over time. The spread slowed to a crawl and then halted.

Erik gathered himself as the charge of the needle continued to drop.

He pulled out the charging device and activated it.

The Metal element still infiltrated his body, but it was at a stalemate with the other elements within his body. The area from his leg up to his stomach was covered in silver veins; his skin looked black and burnt as if made of charcoal.

"That fucking sucked." Erik winced at how his leg looked. He put weight on it and felt the weakness within. "Looks like I won't be running for a while."

He headed into the gym and tried training. His legs were about twenty-five percent weaker and hadn't completely tempered. The Metal element had only gotten as far as the skin and muscles. The tendons, bones, and veins had only just started to be affected. "I'll get weaker before I get stronger."

Erik pressed the button for help.

In minutes, a medic arrived at the door with several others behind him. Gong Jin was there as well.

"I'm not going to be able to shake you, am I?" Erik asked Gong Jin.

"You haven't yet." Gong Jin smiled.

"Help me put some IOs in."

Gong Jin sighed and moved past the medics. "I've got this."

The medics and the special team members moved away. The special team members took out seats and got comfortable.

Erik took off his shirt, boots, and pants, leaving just his underwear. "Bit breezy. Should turn the heat up in this place," Erik complained.

"My boss is so fucking weird." Gong Jin checked his supplies. He had an IV stand on wheels and had hooked up four healing and Stamina potion bags, and he pulled out his IO kit.

Erik put Wraith's Touch on his shoulders and below his knees. "You've done this before, right?"

"Yeah. We even came up with this." Gong Jin held out a strap attached to a formation plate with a cylinder sticking out of one side.

"What's that?"

"Advanced IO." Gong Jin put it on Erik's leg. The strap was sticky, clamping down on Erik's lower leg, right under his knee. Gong Jin checked it and activated the formation. The cylinder turned and dug in, piercing Erik's leg right into his bone.

"Huh. Cool. I don't feel shit."

Gong Jin grunted and placed an IO kit on Erik's other leg and the other two on his shoulders. He ran the IV lines from the stand, hooking them up to the IO. "All right, I think you're good to go." Gong Jin admired his handiwork.

"I look like an 80s B-movie alien." Erik waved his IV tubes.

"Happy temperings, boss." Gong Jin left the room.

Erik waved the tubes a few more times, laughing to himself before he hit the other button on the wall.

Metal-attribute mana entered the room. Gas with shimmering silver sparks appeared within; electricity arced between the dust, giving the room an ethereal feeling.

His body had already been weakened with the Metal element and continued to lose its war. Erik opened the friction locks on the IV lines slightly.

The progress slowed slightly, but the Metal element attacked him from all over, changing the color of his body and causing his body to crack. More lightning flashed through his body.

Erik focused. It felt as though lightning and metal shards reached into his very bones.

He used healing spells to stop the power from reaching his head. If it reached his head, he would no longer be able to control his healing spells or examine the state of his body during the last and most critical stage. He used healing spells on his vital organs for the same reason: to make sure nothing could go wrong.

Riding the line between death and rebirth might be terrifying, but fuck if he didn't feel alive!

Brilliance appeared in the depths of Erik's eyes and he closed them, focusing on the situation inside his body. Time slipped by. Below his neck, he looked like a demon rather than a human.

Any patch of skin that wasn't altered before slowly changed, reaching his neck as if meeting an impassable barrier.

Erik shed his skin, and red blood mixed with what seemed to be mercury ran across his body, giving him a savage appearance.

His eyes snapped open. They were no longer blue but pure black with silver specks. Lightning flashed periodically. Purple and green smoke mixed with red flames and yellow rocks in the depths.

He sat up slowly. His face shook with pain as the red-stained mercury fell from his body. The drops hissed as they hit the ground, leaving scorch marks.

Erik gritted his teeth as the reactions repeated within his body. Not being able to move to take his mind off the pain was worse than the pain itself.

You are a United States Army medic. You served five tours. You survived being a mercenary for four years. You just going to give up? Come on, one more! That drive to show himself, to show others what he was capable of, pushed him on.

His body was covered in wounds that continued to open with every breath. The Metal element moved deeper into his body while his potential only increased and the changes within his body sped up.

His cells were sent into overdrive, heating up. They repaired faster, nursed with Erik's healing spells and the IVs. Erik's wounds started to close, and the color of Erik's body began recovering in parts.

He pulled out the box of training aids he had purchased, took out a powder, and sprinkled it on his leg. It entered his wounds, and he heard it crackle. Erik's leg was torn apart with lightning.

"Feisty," Erik said through gritted teeth. He pulled out a notebook and started doing his own tests.

24
By Land, by Air

Kanoa secured his carrier.

"Too high," he muttered, placing the Alvan rip-tape in the right place. He pushed down the forward flap that held some magazines and checked the medical pouch on his side with a casual touch as he grabbed his rifle.

"Who do you think they will give us for the aerial unit?" Badowska asked.

"What are you doing here? Wouldn't you be better with the artillery unit's crawlers? More like your Russian tanks." Kanoa moved in his carrier with the unloaded rifle, feeling the points of pressure and tightness or where it was rubbing more.

Badowska grinned speaking with his thick accent. "We make great army. Tanks with every unit, air force, and helicopters that would make you shit your pants."

Kanoa flipped him the bird. The Russian laughed as he rolled his shoulders around and jumped, making sure everything was in the right place.

"Now there is no you and me, just us. There are many Experts in the army, but for the air force, there are none. Why don't I use what I know to make up for their weakness?"

"You two ready?" Rugrat walked into the room. He wore the standard multicam of the Alva army. It was well-worn and broken in, unlike Badowska and Kanoa's.

"You won't be needing that." Rugrat pointed at Kanoa's carrier.

"Just checking it out. Was getting the pouches in the right place and sizing out the sides."

"The sides pinch like a bitch," Rugrat agreed.

Kanoa ripped the Alvan rip-tape open and slid out of the carrier, dropping it and his rifle into his storage ring. "Lead on."

Rugrat led them out of the room, and they put away their weapons in their storage rings. Rugrat led them to a training square where men and women were lined up in formation.

"Atten-shun!" a woman officer yelled.

The group came to attention.

Kanoa looked over them all, hiding his shock. All wore the standard multicam uniforms. On their shoulders, they wore various emblems, denoting which type of squad they currently served in.

Damn, there isn't a regular soldier or sharpshooter among them. The lowest were from the artillery platoons and had completed mage and mortar crew training.

Kanoa noticed movement on one of the upper balconies. Commander Glosil and his aides were headed away from the training square.

"Captain Kanoa?" Rugrat introduced him.

"Sir." Kanoa saluted Rugrat, who returned it, and then faced the lined-up formation.

"At ease!"

Their movements were precise. Their eyes seemed to unlock as they stared at Kanoa and Badowska behind him.

"Under the orders of Commander Glosil, there have been some recent changes in military organization. I have been ordered to create Eagle Legion. The purpose for such a legion is to operate in the air. To lead air assaults on our unsuspecting enemies, inserting and helping our allied forces in exfiltrating their mission and operational areas."

Kanoa let that sink in as he walked in front of the new recruits.

"In the previous Tiger and Dragon Regiments, everything was built upon combat companies. Within the Eagles, our basic units will be air assault companies and will have the same breakdown as the combat companies, but instead of moving on panther mounts, you will be riding on eagle mounts!" Kanoa opened a beast crate on his hip. A massive three-meter-tall predatory bird appeared next to Kanoa.

It stretched out its six-meter-long arms, and with a screech, whipping its wings, it created a powerful breeze that rushed over the alarmed recruits. Glorious white runes ran through the bird's brown-and-black feathers.

"You will learn how to use mortars, but you will also be taught how to fly gliders." Kanoa opened another crate.

A pitch-black creature made of scales and three times the size of the eagle turned her head before shifting around under its leathery wings.

"And become bombers. Mages will not be solely based on the ground but will fly sparrows." A smaller, hyper-looking beast appeared. "While you cast, your mount will move across the battlefield, making you a hard target to strike."

Kanoa looked at the men and women staring at the three beasts. "We will also be in charge of training crews to work with the kestrel."

He released the last beast. It was between the eagle and glider in terms of size. It moved its wings and shifted on its feet, calmer than the sparrow and not as dominating as the eagle or as cold as the glider.

"The kestrel will serve as the workhorse for our aerial forces, holding two gunners, one pilot, and beast crates to hold people in and deploy as needed. Eagles will be your personal mounts, allowing each of you to enter and exit the operational space. Gliders will be strategic bombers. From these, their pilots will be able to call down supporting mortar fire and correct it; they will be able to drop bombs in close support of our operations. The sparrows will allow us to control the airspace with mage pilots stirring up trouble in the skies, keeping them clear and supporting operations on the ground as well. First Lieutenant Badowska, what is the purpose of the eagles?"

"Arrive undetected at the enemy's weakness and strike them directly and decisively!"

"The army charges across the ground, and we blitz the enemy from the sky. Together, we will outflank, outmaneuver, and destroy any force that dares to challenge Alva." Kanoa's voice rose to a roar as he saw the fighting spirit swell within the men and women in front of him.

"War is on the horizon, and we don't have time to mess around. Officers and senior non-commissioned officers up to Briefing Room Charlie. Those remaining will be under First Lieutenant Badowska's instruction! Attention!"

They snapped to attention.

"Officers and higher NCOs, fall out!"

The units broke up, and he turned to Badowska and saluted him. "You have command."

"I have command," Badowska repeated.

Kanoa turned to go and meet with his new leadership. He took position at the front of the room and waved in the group.

They quickly sat down. The woman who had called everyone to attention came to him and passed him a scroll.

"Thank you." The scroll detailed the people who had applied to join the Eagles.

There were holes in the rank structure, but nothing major. Although it was not a full company, it was enough to create a badly under-strengthened company. They also had members from the close protection details in large numbers. Most of them were just waiting for their chance to enter the special teams or gain more experience in the field before they became officers.

Kanoa's eyes fell on the leaders of the close protection details. Unlike regular units, they could be tasked out independently of their units. Most of them supported operations carried out by the special teams and the intelligence department.

The way they held themselves, that casual focus in their eyes, how they surveyed the room and positioned themselves—it was as if they were in a constant state of laziness but ready to burst out with their full strength in a moment.

Kanoa nodded and stared at the other members. They had been training for months, and there was an eagerness to their expressions.

"Over the next couple of weeks, I and other Earth military members who have experience in air assault will devote our time to teach you everything we know and adapt that knowledge to operating with beasts instead of technological machines. You have been training for months, and I will not treat you like children. We will develop together, so any concerns or ideas, pass them up the chain of command.

"First things first. We have to organize the chain of command, and I will go over any extra duties you might have in your new roles. Everyone will undergo the same basic training. Once that training is complete, people will specialize into one branch: army or air force. We want to invite cross-training between branches.

"You can apply to do this training at any time, with the consent of your leadership and when we are not in combat. It is advised that you complete the training once you complete your engineering class-one training or your close protection detail. We are one military fighting for Alva, but that doesn't mean the air force will be anything but the best branch," Kanoa growled, getting grins and nods from the people in the room.

"Since we need to train all the troops, it means you lot are going to have little sleep and a lot of learning in the next couple of weeks. Take these books and start studying. I will have a chain of command and unit organization in two hours." Kanoa dropped off a pile of books for the group. They were all information books, so they could be absorbed in minutes. The information was dense, so it was liable to leave them with headaches. Absorbing information was one thing; Kanoa wanted to go through everything in person as well.

The information books would make things a lot quicker as they wouldn't need to spend so much time in the classroom and could spend more time on the gear and birds they would be using.

Colonel Yui and Lieutenant Colonel Carvallo looked over the new plans.

"What do you think?" Shi Wanshu asked after several minutes of silence.

"Shit," Carvallo said.

"Fucking firepower," Yui agreed.

"The more the better," Rugrat drawled.

"We have a selection of weapon systems: the rotating Gatling guns that are in current production and belt-fed grenade launchers. We are working on adjustable mortars, though we think that instead of the mortar systems, the long-range artillery cannons would be the best." Taran pulled out plans and put them on the table.

Yui studied the simple-looking weapons.

"Railgun?" Carvallo read out.

"We wanted to use magnets to accelerate a round to a really high speed, which would create massive damage on impact. Julilah came up with a series of Metal formations and Air formations. The impetus is created by Air formations releasing a burst of air behind the round and creating a pseudo-air barrel while the Metal formations pull the round forward at tremendous speeds. We are still testing out different prototypes, but the weapon system should be complete by that time. If not, then we will use artillery shells. Think of them as big damn rounds," Rugrat said.

"Isn't this a bit...much?" Yui asked. Seeing the looks, he quickly corrected himself. "I am not saying I do not want these items, but we're getting ready to fight the Willful Institute. We're just getting used to the weapons we have."

"These will take months or years to mass-produce. We can possibly create them in time for when the fighting starts," Rugrat agreed. "Though we shouldn't stop developing. What's to say we won't run into people from the higher realms who want to attack us. Proactive, not reactive."

"And cause you love blowing shit up," Taran added.

"And cause I'm a redneck," Rugrat grinned. "My own fuckin' artillery cannon. Oh momma! I'm gonna mount Gatling guns on fuckin' everything. Figuring out how to secure it to George already."

25 Cultivation Maniacs

"You look like shit," Rugrat said as Erik walked into the office they shared.

"Spent too much time seeing your face." Erik flipped him the bird. "Where's the coffee?"

"I finished it off. You want to make another pot?"

"Fill it up when you're done, will you?"

"I meant to, just been going over these plans," Rugrat muttered absently.

Erik fired up the Ten Realms's coffee machine, one of Matt's greatest inventions. Erik and Rugrat had bought the very first one and the second one too.

Erik rubbed his face, feeling the ache deep in his bones. He stared at his blackened hands, the cracked skin. Since he had started tempering his body with the Metal element, everything below his neck looked the same and ached all hours of the day. In the last month, he had gone from one tempering needle to three.

He sighed and walked over to Rugrat, staring at the plans in front of him. "What's the problem?" Erik asked.

"The air barrel. If the round touches the barrel, after a few dozen shots, the barrel becomes useless. We need the air barrel to protect the round and the barrel."

"Sounds complicated."

"It is. Never thought I'd wish I had learned aerodynamics."

"How is your cultivation going?" Erik continued to study the plans as he talked.

"Accelerating." Rugrat grinned. He shifted to let Erik see the plans better while he turned in his chair. "I am almost at the mid-Liquid Mana Core level. I heard you've been working on your Body Cultivation diligently."

"How is your Body Cultivation?"

"Avoiding the question." Rugrat clicked his tongue. "I've started to temper my body with the Earth element. I bet I can reach the peak in just two weeks."

"I don't doubt it. The resources, technologies, and processes have been updated and upgraded. Most of the military members are lagging behind as they only get a certain amount of contribution points they can put toward their training. As for my Body Cultivation, I think I have some way to go before I can completely temper my body with the Metal element. I am tempering seventy percent of my body currently. Then my vital organs one by one. Slower is better. I reached mid-Mist Mana Core level. I have a lot of strain on my body, and I don't want to overload it."

Quest: Mana Cultivation 2

The path to cultivating one's mana is not easy. To stand at the top, one must forge their own path forward.

Requirements:

Reach Vapor Mana Core

Rewards:

+20 to Mana

+20 to Mana Regeneration

+50,000,000 EXP

Quest: Body Cultivation 4

The path to cultivating one's body is not easy. To stand at the top, one must forge their own path forward.

Requirements:

Unlock Body Like Diamond

Rewards:

+24 to Strength

+24 to Agility

+24 to Stamina

+40 to Stamina Regeneration

+100,000,000 EXP

Quest: Bloodline Cultivation 1

The path to cultivating one's body is not easy. To stand at the top, one must forge their own path forward.

Requirements:

Unlock your Bloodline

Rewards:

+48 to Strength

+48 to Agility

+48 to Stamina

+80 to Stamina Regeneration

+100,000,000 EXP

Name: Erik West

Level: 60	Race: Human
Titles: *From the Grave II* *Blessed By Mana* *Dungeon Master IV* *Reverse Alchemist* *Poison Body* *Fire Body* *City Lord* *Earth Soul* *Mana Reborn* *Wandering Hero*	
Strength: (Base 54) +51	1050
Agility: (Base 47) +72	654
Stamina: (Base 57) +25	1230
Mana: (Base 27) +79	1166
Mana Regeneration: (Base 30) +61	73.80/s
Stamina Regeneration: (Base 72) +59	27.20/s

86,796,860/108,500,000 EXP till you reach Level 61

Erik stood and walked back over to the coffeemaker as it filled the pot. "Why not use a sabot sheath" Erik pulled out a cup and poured coffee into it.

He heard Rugrat moving around and writing something down.

Erik took a sip of coffee and turned around. Rugrat looked like the devil possessed.

He took a gulp of his coffee and walked back to the plans Rugrat was throwing together quickly before pulling out a sound transmission device.

Erik smiled into his coffee and moved to his desk. The desks created an angle so they could watch out of their office located at the peak of the

Dungeon Core Headquarters.

They had been in the barracks, but the new dungeon headquarters building was the heart of Alva. It was packed with offices and departments, and it was now Erik and Rugrat's living quarters.

He picked up information books and started to use them. They collapsed into dust as he was updated on everything happening under Alva's control.

Rugrat got up from his chair. He snatched his cold coffee and drank it down.

"Where you going?"

"I need to head to Vuzgal. I want to talk to Tan Xue and the formation girls. Don't wait up, hon!"

"I'll get dinner ready for you, dear!" Erik shot back as Rugrat hurried out of the office. "Check in on Hiao Xen while you're up there!"

"All right!" Rugrat jumped out of the door.

Erik snorted and went back to drinking his cold coffee and reading his reports.

Who would have thought that a bunch of people from the First Realm would have been able to do all of this? At the beginning, most things had relied on Erik and Rugrat. Now, their actions were just a drop in a sea. Traders across the realms. An Adventurer's Guild that was more powerful than some sects. A region under their command that could contend with kingdoms. A city that has become a paradise for fighters and crafters in the Fourth Realm.

An advanced military and an information network that reached into the Seventh Realm. A technology sector coming up with new inventions almost every other day. A nation didn't succeed based off one or two people; it succeeded with the efforts of many people working together.

A proud smile stretched across Erik's face as he sipped his coffee again.

"Hey there!" Rugrat saw Han Wu and his group waiting outside his and Erik's office.

"Where now?" Han Wu followed after the jogging Rugrat. The rest of the special team checked their gear, some throwing on their vests and Alvan rip-taping them together.

"Fourth Realm!" Rugrat ran out of the Dungeon Core Headquarters, and a red streak glided down from above. Rugrat jumped onto George's back as he landed on the ground.

The special team jumped on their own mounts, following him to the Ten Realms's totem.

Rugrat pulled on a cloak and used a stealth formation that would make people unconsciously look away from George and the group.

"Vuzgal, I am assuming?" Han Wu asked, in the totem menu.

"You got it," Rugrat said.

Light consumed them and faded away as soon as it had arrived.

Han Wu led the group from Special Team Two as Gong Jin's second-in-command. Gong Jin was in charge of protecting Erik with his half of the special team.

Han Wu flashed a symbol to the guards; they opened the gates, and the group rushed out.

Rugrat headed right for Vuzgal Academy. "Damn. Julilah is not picking up her sound transmission device." He tried Tan Xue.

"What is it?" she asked after the second call.

"Where is Julilah?"

"She is teaching a class. I'm working on a project."

"Thank you!"

Tan Xue hung up with a grunt.

Rugrat called the school and got Julilah's schedule.

Vuzgal had expanded again, and the mana density had increased. Planters throughout the city were filled with plants that would focus one's mind and could passively increase the mana density of the surrounding area.

There were massive residences and manors. Mercenary groups and guilds had their own streets; workshops of different crafts were fully employed.

It was ragtag before, the city was just finding its feet, but now after another year, it had developed and matured. Fighters congregated around the Battle Arena. There were stores with weapons or fighting-based supplies. The workshops were surrounded by diverse materials and tool merchants. Auction houses were in the city. Healing and Alchemy houses were close to the gates to the dungeons and around the Battle Arena.

Construction was still ongoing, but it had moved farther out, giving the city less of an unfinished feeling.

Rugrat entered the towering Castle District heading toward the academy. "I didn't think Vuzgal was as tall when I left," Rugrat said, slowing his speed.

"They expanded. People came from the Fifth Realm wanting to learn at the academy. Give them a higher chance to get accepted by an academy. Not many places are willing to accept coin for teaching. Most places want their students to swear fealty or join their sect," Han Wu offered.

"So, things got bigger?"

"Yeah, with an explosion of Experts coming down. There were plenty of Experts walking around. They offered their insights, but they weren't necessarily the best teachers. A teacher's school was created so high-level Experts weren't just lecturing people but helping them to learn. The graduates were impressive, in just a few months nearly everyone advanced a half-step in their skill. Some passed barriers they had been unable to cross previously."

"How did you get so many experts?" Rugrat asked.

"You'd be surprised how many people need a rare pill or are ostracized because they're different or need resources to carry out their studies or have complicated health issues. Our people have reached the point to help them without having to bother you or Erik anymore.

"I swear that when I blink, everything changes. Where the hell is this classroom anyway?" Rugrat showed Han Wu a slip of paper with the name of the classroom written down.

"Uh, I don't know." Han Wu shrugged. "Davos, do you have any idea?"

"Nah, haven't seen that one before. Simms, what about you? You go to more classes."

"Let me take a look." Simms nudged his mount forward and looked at the paper. "Yeah, I know where that is. Follow me." Simms led them across the academy campus.

Rugrat took his time to look around. "Taller and bigger," Rugrat said to himself. "Seems like I'm always playing catch-up nowadays!"

"You do a lot already, more than the elders, kings, and empresses out there," Han Wu said.

"I'm barely around, and when I am, I'm working on a project or cultivating."

"In the Ten Realms, it is not the power of the weakest person in your group that matters but the power of your strongest. In most of the cities and capitals we infiltrated, there is a ruling group or party with one or two powerful members. They are the pillars of the rulers. Their families gather around, devoting everything to increase their Strength and extend their lifespan while trying to raise new powerful members. The gap between the rulers and their subjects is the difference between the Mortal realms and the Earth realms. It maintains stability. The leaders can demand anything because they have the power over their people to do so. Everyone is scared that someone stronger will come from below and take them out. So, they hide their techniques, hoard their resources, and maintain a distance from their subjects," Han Wu said.

"The strong rule in the Ten Realms." Rugrat sighed.

"You don't seem to get it. You and Erik, you're strong as fuck, dude. I've read the reports and led the intelligence teams into the Fifth Realm. If someone reaches the Mist Mana Core stage or the Body Like Iron stage, they're geniuses in the Earth and Mortal realms. People who have both? As rare as a phoenix feather. Any higher than that, hell, you might only find a few thousand people in the Sixth Realm who meet those standards. The Sixth Realm has a population of several billion."

Han Wu stopped talking as they passed a group of teachers who stared at them.

"Seems that even fighters are coming to our academy," one of the teachers whispered to another.

"The atmosphere here is among the best to be found. Even the fighters of the Fourth Realm can learn a thing or two if they have the mana stones!"

They faded away, and Han Wu kept talking.

"Alvans come from across the realms. Most of us were down on our luck. Alva not only gave us refuge but opened a path to the peak. There are competitions, but they will only grow stronger. Instead of creating a gap between everyone, you spend your time increasing your Strength to protect the people of Alva. You develop weapons so we can defend ourselves."

"And because they're awesome," Rugrat interjected.

"And because they're awesome." Han Wu chuckled with the others. "But, dude, you're a hero to the people in Alva, the members of the military. You've showed us that we can serve the people, not our own interests. What gains might we get in a battle? Fuck the loot. Is that worth more than our brothers and sisters standing beside us? So, when you're worried about not being around, fuck it. You are there when we need it most. And didn't you create the council to look after everything so you two could run off to the higher realms? Battle fanatics."

"Hey, you do the same thing—all your covert missions, retrieval, and information," Rugrat said.

"Dude, I'm just saying to take us along next time!"

Rugrat laughed. The stress from the last couple of weeks and months relaxed. He felt that there had been a beast on his shoulder, driving him forward to complete the next weapon, make the next thing to increase the power of the military.

"This is the place." Simms pointed at the door.

Rugrat moved to the door's window. The classroom was filled with people listening attentively: young, old, shabby-looking, or wearing the finest clothes from across the realm and even the higher realms. Julilah stood at the front of the room, waving her hand as she created a formation script on the chalkboard with a clever manipulation of her mana.

Everyone was captured by her words as she added complexities to the formation.

A bell sounded, and the classes ended. Students moved, some heading to the front of the room to talk with Julilah.

Rugrat stepped back as several doors opened and students left the lecture hall, talking to their peers or hurrying to their next classes.

The flow died down, and Rugrat entered the room.

Julilah was the center of several people as she cleared up her tools.

A few of them bobbed their heads in thanks and headed off, talking to one another, their eyes filled with excitement. They looked as if they could barely hold themselves back from jogging to their workshops.

"Miss Julilah, you are a rare talent. To be wasted in such a place...you could enjoy a life deserving of your beauty and your knowledge as my wife." A handsome, young man gave her an impish smile.

Julilah finished cleaning up. "I don't think being your wife would be the peak of my talents, Lord Venezzio," Julilah said dryly.

"As my adored wife, I would be your firm support to hold you up and push you forward. The Fifth, the Sixth Realm, even—you could rise to the peak!"

"City Lord." She bowed to Rugrat, showing no signs of being influenced. "Did we have a meeting? I am sorry my class ran longer than I thought it would. Shall we get tea together?" She ignored Lord Venezzio as she smiled at Rugrat.

He frowned at her, questioning, but Julilah shook her head.

"Yes, I would enjoy that." Rugrat graciously raised his arm.

Julilah showed an amused expression, holding back her laughter by pressing her lips together as she put her hand in the crook of his arm. She pressed on his arm, making him walk away.

The rest of the special team moved around them like specters as they left the room, scanning everyone.

"Which city lord are you?" Lord Venezzio asked.

"This one," Rugrat said as he left the hall.

They walked out of the building, and Rugrat used a sound-canceling formation.

"He's some silly lord's son from the Fifth Realm. He came here to 'broaden his horizons.' Don't worry. I get a new proposal every other week. People think because I am young and smart in formations, I must be dumb in the way of the world."

"Well, any of these boys catch your eye or should I hit them off with a broom?"

"They'd be a fool to try anything, and I think they're largely innocent in it all."

"Looks like not everything is so simple on the surface," Rugrat said.

"Don't worry. With my cultivation, he is no problem for me. So, why are you here?"

Rugrat put his words to the side. He pulled out a shabby blueprint and passed it to Julilah.

She released him and looked at the plans.

"Do you really want to go and get tea?" Rugrat asked.

"Of course not! To the workshop! There is plenty more to be done. We can drink tea and work at the same time, no?"

"That's what I thought." Rugrat laughed in relief.

"Though this plan, sabot, a covering? How is it supposed to operate?"

"We have the round in the middle. This sabot around it stabilizes it in the air barrel. Then, upon exiting the barrel, the sabot is discarded, and the round is freed, heading for its target."

"A kind of casing, then. The air barrel formations and the sabot work together to create a barrel within the barrel, leaving the round free-floating. As the Metal formations accelerate it out of the barrel, the casing is blown off and the deadly round or payload in the middle is revealed and bang! It smashes the target. This sabot covering will be useless after one use, though," Julilah said.

"Yup." Rugrat nodded.

"Isn't that kind of a waste?"

"What do you mean?"

"Well, formations, if they are maintained and powered, can last forever. This will only be used once."

Rugrat frowned, trying to think of a way to explain it. "Think of it like a spell scroll then."

"It creates a massive effect but is burnt out in the process?"

"Yes, but the difference is that the round is wasted, but the weapon, that remains, and we can load another round and fire it immediately. Actually, you know that heat issue we were looking at? If we needed to, could we create formations that store the heat into metal blocks? We refine metals with an innate ability to contain heat. In rapid firing, they can be changed out in an emergency."

"That…it's wasteful." Julilah half-closed her eyes, calculating and thinking. She looked as though she had tasted something unpleasant. "We could do it. I was thinking about conditional formations. We line the barrel with high-heat-capacity metal blocks. Along the hot spots, we create formations that bleed the heat off into the blocks. As they reach high temperature, they push out from the heat transference formations to secondary formation plates that dissipate the heat. Once cooled, they drop back into place and start absorbing more heat. Also, you could change modes: fire multiple low-speed rounds and the heat is slowly accumulated, or fire more powerful shots and the heat is ramped up. Quickly."

"How many heat sink systems are you thinking?"

"I was thinking of just the one. But if we had multiple, we could cool or dissipate the heat through multiple to keep a steady rate of fire." Julilah pulled out a blueprint and passed it to Rugrat.

There were metal blocks in a row on a slider that went up and down. The formations at the bottom released heat into the metal. The formation controlling the slider turned the heat into motion. Once the capacity was reached on the metal blocks, it would move, driving them up just a centimeter or two, matching the blocks up to three-sided formations that dissipated heat.

It would look like a metal vertebra along the barrel of the gun.

"If you did four of them and made an X shape with them, you could easily aim, reload, and attach grips and grenade launchers underneath," Rugrat said. "For the indirect fire systems like mortars and artillery cannons, we could have nine different cooling systems around the barrel. They're just calculating off angles; they don't need weapon sights, and they'll make a hell of a lot more heat."

They reached Julilah's workshop, and she used a formation to unlock it. Inside, there were more attack formations, and guards roamed the halls. Still, Julilah kept all her items and projects in a special storage ring.

"The new sabot rounds will need a new magazine system," she said.

"It might, but it might not. It depends on what the sabot rounds are like."

Julilah continued looking over the plans and then checked some other plans.

Rugrat studied the plans she had given him. "Where's Qin?" He looked at the other half of the double workshop.

"Under the city. She is working on the Conqueror's line that is going into production. The air force has requested special formations, and she is working on several version twos for the armor. Nearly every Alvan crafter is working on some kind of innovation or working with the military."

"How long do you think it will take to make this weapon system?" Rugrat asked.

"This final version?"

"A workable version."

"Well, we just started to build a test bed for the new system, incorporating the power of Wind and Metal. We can combine that into an upper receiver. We already produce the lower receivers. Those weapons will work, but they will be greatly reduced in effectiveness as they don't have the heat sink system to allow the weapon to fire repeatedly or to fire rounds at a higher velocity. We could add that in later, so a month of testing on the base weapon design while we finish building the assembly lines. Say six weeks to two months until mass production, as long as there are no testing issues. Three to four months if we run into issues. We should complete the heat sink systems then upgrade the old weapons with them."

"Also, we have to look at the manufacture of ammunition and magazines," Rugrat added.

"And that. Also, if we want to make different versions, long-range rifles, and machine guns, another few months."

"So, what? Four months until we can issue the basic weapons?"

"Something like that."

"Conqueror's Armor is already being made alongside the new formation-stacking system. Every soldier has their basic weapon loadout, medical supplies, and ammunition." Rugrat clicked his tongue.

"You're overthinking it. We've got what we've got. When the fight comes, we'll be ready," Han Wu said.

Rugrat nodded. "Well, no matter what, I'll still worry. The more advantages we can get, the better!"

26 Unrest in the Institute

Grand Elder Mendes of the Willful Institute glared at the elders around him. He couldn't help but feel frustrated. His anger caused the mana around him to fluctuate, and his eyes focused on Elder Dean.

"You are telling me that the Adventurer's Guild—a third-rate, useless band of mercenaries—is behind this?" His voice remained quiet but turned colder as he stared at the elder.

"Yes, Grand Elder," Elder Dean said.

"We need to wipe them out," Elder Tsi said, hitting the desk.

Mendes's eyes cut over to Tsi, silencing her. "I am supposed to meet with the Council of Grand Elders in a few months, and I have to tell them that we are unable to pay our tithe because of a group of mercenaries? A group of mercenaries who were grossly underestimated by us. Who have roots in the first three realms and are closing in on three hundred thousand members. Who have stolen missions and contracts from us, cutting off resources that we require to train and grow our younger generation!"

Mendes's anger reached boiling point.

"They haven't attacked us directly. They know that if they did, we would destroy them," another elder said.

Mendes stared at the elder; silence taking over as he turned to his own thoughts.

There had to be someone behind this guild, someone capable of gathering information and learning about their operations. They had struck at several of their ventures, cutting them down. When looking at it all in parts, it wasn't much to cause alarm. Examining them together, it became apparent that this guild was pulling them down. If they allowed it to continue, their city would falter, and their students' progress would slow. They needed those resources to raise geniuses. If they didn't, they would go to other cities in the Institute to gain better opportunities. They needed to draw this group out and destroy them.

"They're willing to go this far?" Mendes shook his head. People were expendable at the end of the day, only worth what one could profit from them. He couldn't see why a group of fighters would motivate the entire guild to take action that could destroy them.

Subconsciously, he had stopped looking at them as a simple band of fighters but as a power on par with his own city.

If the roles were reversed and the guild had killed a group from their sect, he wouldn't hesitate to attack them, threaten them, and take a price from them that would compensate the sect and make sure they could never develop in the future.

"Send out a challenge to the guild. Make it public. Invite them to a competition. We will put our fighters against theirs. We will put resources and contracts on the line and sign an agreement to that effect. We will have the fight in one week. If they do not appear, we will attack their known locations and wipe them out," Mendes said.

If they come to the competition, they are scared of their power, and it will bring their leaders and powerful fighters out into the light. If they do not react, then we can attack, and others won't look down on us.

Jasper looked up from the scroll in his hands and to the messenger who had delivered it. "Looks like we have a fight on our hands." Jasper stood and walked out of the room.

People moved out of his way as he went through the Khusai Adventurer's Guild headquarters. It was the first location the association had developed.

He knocked on a door.

"Come in," Blaze said, his voice coming from the other side.

Jasper walked in and put the scroll on his desk.

Blaze picked it up and read. "Well, looks like some of them are smart enough to figure out who we are. This all started when they failed to punish their students or even offer an apology. Seems it is only fitting they would be the first faction in the Willful Institute that we officially clash with."

"Do you want me to ignore it?" Jasper asked.

"Pass it higher and see what they say."

"It could be a trap."

"Oh, it will probably turn into one. But it remains to be seen who will fall into it." Blaze smiled.

Erik jogged through the Alva army base in the dungeon. Since the army had increased in size, so had the barracks, transforming it into a complete base. He passed different units' training areas. Soldiers checked their weapons, carriers, and storage rings. Groups across the Ten Realms and the units on standby had been given notice. Classes and training continued for most of the army, but there were signs of mobilization.

He passed through armed and armored men and women before reaching the command center. It was a heavily fortified room under the base.

"Put pants on!" Erik yelled as his first sight was Rugrat in his short shorts, blacksmithing apron, and cowboy hat.

"I was in a rush!"

Erik turned to Glosil, nodding for him.

Captain Kanoa was there as well.

Colonel Yui came in through the door, followed by Elan.

"We're all here," Glosil said. The room grew quiet. "Director Silaz?"

"Thank you, Commander." Elan faced the small crowd in front of him. "A few hours ago, the Adventurer's Guild received a message from one of the Willful Institute's branches. This branch is the home location of the group who had attacked the Adventurer's Guild. They issued a challenge to the guild, inviting them to the branch to have a tournament for resources. It's highly publicized, so the guild wouldn't be able to back out."

Everyone looked at Erik and Rugrat.

"Is it a trap?" Rugrat asked.

"They are looking to assert their dominance and regain their losses. Internally, we have found out that the higher-ups are not pleased about the reduced payouts. They are used to their bribes and now not getting them, so they're applying more pressure. This reduces the power of the Adventurer's Guild, and it could recover their resources. It can also elevate their position and reassert their dominance. From their perspective, it is a win-win. Now, if they don't win, things could turn into a mess and they might fight back."

"Do we have a plan for this?" Erik asked.

Glosil stood. "Colonel Domonos Silaz has come up with a plan. Special teams will infiltrate the branch location, getting close to the treasury of the city. Once the fighter's competition is over, the Adventurer's Guild will provoke the Willful Institute, reinforced with members from the Fourth Realm, and exit the city. We will use our contacts and agents to mess with the branch's communication and have the branch attack the Adventurer's Guild. It should drag everyone into the mess. As it happens, the special teams will reveal themselves to be people under the Grey Peak Sect, a local sect with roots in the Fourth Realm who is displeased with the Willful Institute. They will attack the treasury, stealing what they can and destroying what they can't. They'll exit the city and run away. Kanoa and his force will be waiting at a rendezvous, where they will transport the special teams to a secure location. We will weaken their fighting force, hit them in their heart, and rip away their resources. Each attack will open them up more."

"Follow-up attacks?" Erik asked.

"Internally, they are more divided than ever," Elan added.

"Are we ready for this?" Erik asked.

"Colonel?" Glosil glanced at Yui.

Yui stood up at attention. "The Tiger and Dragon Regiments stand ready!"

"Captains?"

Niemm and Gong Jin stood up as one at the back of the room.

"Special Team One stands ready," Niemm said.

"Special Team Three stands ready," Gong Jin finished.

Kanoa stood. "The Eagle Company stands ready."

Erik glanced at Elan.

"The intelligence department is always ready."

"The round's in the chamber," Rugrat said.

"All right. As long as Blaze agrees on the side of the Adventurer's Guild, begin Operation Black Shadow," Erik said.

Domonos's blade sent sparks flying as it met his opponent's shield, getting turned to the side. Domonos followed the direction of the blade, his form blurring as he circled around. The shield user yelled as their shield *shifted* to face him. The two of them increased their speeds and attacks. Each of them used the full power of their bodies and their Mana Cultivation.

Flames followed Domonos's blade, causing his opponent to wince, even with their high Fire resistance. Their shield stopped the sword again and again, with Domonos having to forcefully increase his speed through his movement techniques to avoid being caught by his opponent's sword.

The man stomped a spell, changing the ground around them and creating ripples in the stone that were easy to cross if someone were going slow, but led to one missing their step and tripping if they moved quickly.

Domonos jumped and took a hit on his blade. He flew backward, outside the rippled circle.

He concentrated mana in his legs and arms. Flames condensed on his blade, and he shot forward, buffing his limbs and reaction time to the extreme as he touched on the ripples on the ground, sending him flying forward and picking up momentum.

His opponent yelled as flames covered their body and their skin took on a stony appearance.

Domonos waved his sword, sending out flaming blades that the man broke upon his shield, cutting his sword forward and sending out a bolt of lightning.

Domonos slashed out another blade of fire, the lighting broke through it, crashing into his real blade , slowing his momentum and numbing his hands. He pushed forward the last meter and brandished his sword.

The shield user turned. Their shield guided the blade away as their sword cut down at Domonos.

Shit.

Domonos had telegraphed his attacks, eager to see if the power of his technique and his blade matched one another. His opponent had turned him to the side, leaving him open. Domonos could practically feel his opponent's blade cutting through his armor and digging into his leg.

He heard the noise of the blade hitting his leg armor, enough to scratch. But he knew that his opponent's full strength wasn't behind it.

Domonos stutter-stepped past his opponent and sighed as he lowered his blade.

The sergeant grinned as he pulled off his helmet.

Domonos took off his helmet as well, wiping sweat away with his hand. "You got me good." Domonos smiled as he shook the sergeant's hand.

"Ah, well, you got me three times out of five. Need to get at least some hits in!" The sergeant laughed. "Are you looking forward to the Battle Arena's competition?"

"The year has gone quickly. Just a month to go until we have another competition. I'm sure this year it will be even larger." Domonos pulled out a canteen and drank from it.

"I heard there are a lot more people coming. They all heard about last year's rewards and the abilities of the people training at the Battle Arena!"

Domonos offered the sergeant his water canteen, who took it with a nod of thanks.

"I'm sure it will be as lively as ever. I wonder how the fighters from last year will compare to the new contestants." Domonos chuckled. A messenger walked over now the fight was done.

The sergeant nodded to Domonos, passing the canteen back. "If you're ever in the need of someone to spar with, I'll be around."

Domonos nodded. There was no saluting in the sparring area. Here, everyone was the same, fighting to improve their personal skills. Most of the people were at higher levels than others and were actively looking to get on the close protection details and onto the special teams. The simple sergeant he had been sparring with wore the markings of the CPD and had added more patches to show his training with the air force's birds.

The messenger passed him a sealed letter. Domonos cut his finger and used it on the letter. The seal broke, and he read the contents quickly then took his time on the second pass. He needed to see Roska.

He left the training area and went to some of the more secluded buildings in the military compound.

The area was separate from the main compound and had their own guards. It was one of the training grounds for the special teams. Domonos was stopped and checked. There were all kinds of spells and skills people could use to fake their identity. He passed through and saw special team trainees who were just coming back from a mission, while others headed off on another. The air around them had shifted; there was a subtle change between regular soldiers and those on the special teams. The soldiers were like a shield; you knew that they were soldiers. You could see through their actions and how they acted. Veterans and those who knew their roles were instantly recognizable. They could do things with such fluid ease it was hard to notice it. Silent gears in the machine.

The people on the special teams were like a sheathed sword. They didn't look different from anyone else. They were normal—easy smiles, laughing and joking more often than not. Once they were on a mission or given a task, they came alive. They were professionals to the core, the sharpened blade in the sheath.

Domonos went through the camp and reached Roska's quarters. He knocked on the door.

"Who is it?" she called out.

"Domonos!"

"Come in."

He opened the door. She looked as though she had just come out of the shower as she toweled off her hair.

She's so young still.

When they were in armor, no one could see one another. They had grown up fast in the Ten Realms. Training and growing with the Alva military had accelerated that. Alva was young by the Ten Realms's standards. They did have people who were two, even three, centuries old, but most were under a century old in the military.

Though I can't really say anything; I'm a few years older than her.

"What can I help you with?" Roska asked, oblivious to his thoughts.

"The Willful Institute is moving in the Third Realm. Operation Black

Shadow has been authorized. I have your target and your mission orders." He pulled out an information book and passed it to her. "When will your trainees graduate to the special teams?"

"Another week and they should be ready," Roska said.

"That went quickly." Domonos sighed.

"It rarely goes slowly." Roska smiled.

Domonos chuckled and nodded. "Very true. I have a feeling that things are going to heat up sooner rather than later."

"That's why they pay us the big bucks." She used the information book. A glow covered her then disappeared as the book turned to ash.

"So, it will all kick off where it started. Seems fitting. I'll have a squad move over to begin preparations. We'll be in place and ready. I'll confirm our escape with Kanoa."

"Let me know if you need anything. I'll have a combat company ready to act as a quick reaction force around the clock and a battalion ready to act within a two-hour window."

"We both know how you've been training your people. If it were under an hour, I wouldn't be surprised. Hopefully we won't need it, but knowing that you're watching our asses is reassuring." Roska used a Clean spell, removing the remaining water as she circulated her mana.

There was a chilling sneer on her face. "They fucked with the wrong group of people. Now it's time we taught them a lesson."

Domonos's own killing intent filled the air as well. The two of them glanced at each other, two weapons united in purpose and direction.

27 Taking Resources

Ludnakov wore a cloak that hid his identity and his aura. He blinked away the light from the teleportation scrolls aftereffect.

"Guildmaster." The assassin bowed, staring at the higher echelon of the guild.

When hearing about what the Willful Institute had done—how their students had killed members of the guild and how the elders had dismissed any punishment on their people and had instead awarded them a promotion to a higher realm—the guild wanted blood.

The guildmaster and others held them back, driving some people to leave the guild, thinking that the guild wouldn't do anything.

When the guild started their attack, it wasn't like an attack the assassin had seen before. It was much more vicious, cutting off the Willful Institute from their funds and, therefore, their power. The guild had clashed with the Willful Institute here and there as they were found out. But now, it looked as though it was starting to come to light.

There were twenty people in total, all wearing black cloaks. They pulled down their hoods, and a shiver ran through the assassin's body. He had been highly praised in his branch as being one of the best assassins they had.

Seeing the elites of the guild, he felt lacking in both skill and power.

These people were at least level thirty-five, wore five or six pieces of Journeyman armor, and even had Journeyman-level weapons. Not only was their power higher than his, the way they moved showed their combat standards were higher as well.

He thought people had been exaggerating about how powerful the guild was. *Seeing these Experts—just how powerful is our guild?*

The assassin controlled his breathing as he realized that the guildmaster had asked him a question.

"The Willful Institute has prepared the stage and are waiting for our guild's representatives. They have spread the word through the city that if we are not willing to come it is because we are scared. If we don't show, then the traders we deal with will start to think we don't have the power to protect their goods."

"Looks as if they are ready for us. What about the fighters from your branch?" Blaze asked.

"They are waiting for us in the city," the assassin said. *Why does he want us to have our people from the Third Realm fight? With his group, we could easily defeat the Institute's fighters.*

"Good. Let's meet with them and go to the fight." Blaze waved his hand, and a pitch-black panther with lightning running through its fur stood there.

The others all pulled out mounts.

The assassin gulped and pulled out his simple mount. It quaked, seeing the other beasts.

He smiled awkwardly, calming it down before he got on top and led the party toward the city.

The group pulled their hoods up and once again reined in their auras and power.

There was no hiding their presence as they reached the entrance to the city. Being in the Third Realm, the Willful Institute focused on harvesting and processing ingredients to be sold to others or used to raise alchemists within the Institute.

The city wasn't big enough to warrant a Blue Lotus, although it had extensive fields, while being less than a third the size of Vuzgal.

It didn't stun or dazzle Blaze in the slightest.

They stood in the line to enter the city.

"Shadow Foot, isn't it?" One of the guards peeked at the leading assassin. "Don't think I have any record of you leaving the city. Odd, that," the guard said in a dark voice.

The other guards moved forward. One spat on the ground. All of them wore the emblems of the Willful Institute.

"Looks like you've got some new friends. Couldn't handle things yourself?" The man snorted, staring at the people and the beasts. "Scared to show your faces? Once a loser, always a loser. Who knows when another group might just disappear from your guild?"

The guard's friends stepped forward, and the people around them stepped back.

"Bunch of weaklings."

"Derrick, pay the man," Blaze said.

Derrick dropped from his mount in a fluid movement. He stood above the guard who snarled, stepping forward.

Derrick held out a bag of money and wore a playful smile that could be seen under the cloak.

"Kneel, and I might accept it. You guild fuckers will learn your place," the guard said.

No one moved.

"Get on your knees or you're not making it in. All of you! Just like your dead group. Beg, and I might let you in."

The guard took their lack of action to be fear and laughed. His face twisted into a snarl, and he checked behind at his people. "You know, I heard the group our Young Master killed, they were crying and screaming out for their guild. They died like the dogs they are." He kept an eye on the group, but he didn't catch sight of Derrick's hand as it rested on his shoulder, almost gently.

The man turned back, grabbing his sword before yelling in pain. Derrick didn't seem to exert any power as the pauldron in his hand started to deform, screeching and cracking. The guard couldn't put any Strength into his hand as Derrick clamped down on his tendons.

He dropped to one knee and then both.

The other guards pulled out their weapons but just watched as Derrick *crushed* the high-Novice-level armor as if it were paper.

The scariest thing wasn't his Strength; it was the way his smile never wavered.

"Fucking dog guild!" There was a pop and a crunch, and the guard screamed as his shoulder popped out of place and his collarbone broke.

"Whoops. Sorry about that. Well, we don't want to trouble you too much. Looks like you should go and see a healer as soon as possible.

"I'll leave this with you. Thank you for welcoming us into your *grand* city. I hope you fellows don't get any ideas. I would only be too pleased to redecorate the front gate. You see, I have been meaning to use my brush recently." Derrick's hand holding the money purse touched the hilt of his rapier.

He kept the same smile, but the guards' confident sneers were gone.

Derrick pulled his hand off his rapier, weighed the money bag in his hand, and threw it out.

A guard caught it, and the man on the ground whimpered as Derrick released him. He held his shoulder as he fell on the ground, tears of pain on his face.

"Good choice." Derrick mounted up, and they continued into the city.

"I heard the Adventurer's Guild was a bunch of pushovers who had annoyed the Institute."

"How brazen! The Institute won't let them off easily now!"

"I thought the Institute would win for sure, but I'm not so sure anymore."

"Having a fighter who can crush one's armor with his hands—just how strong is he?"

"Their cloaks were hiding their identities and auras. Are they really just a simple guild?"

News quickly spread through the city. People who had been hesitant to watch the fight between the two groups were now queuing for tickets.

Blaze and his group passed through the city and found themselves an inn. As they arrived, the other patrons quickly paid up and headed out, leaving the inn to the guild.

Guards were posted around the building. Blaze took off his hood and studied his hand-picked group. Each of them were powerful and had potential. They were making their way through the guild's ranks, growing their power and contributions to the guild. They also had Ten Realms contracts that would keep their lips sealed on guild secrets.

"In one hour, you will be fighting the Willful Institute people on behalf of the fellow guild members who were attacked and killed by students from this very city. They believe they can use resources to push us into a bad position. I don't care for the resources; you will crush the Willful Institute's people completely."

The group looked at him with a mix of pride and anxiousness.

One stepped forward, and Blaze indicated for them to speak.

"We aren't switching out fighters? I know we are strong within our branch, but we aren't strong enough to take on the elites of this city," the man said with a sour expression.

"Do they have a greater will? Do they have greater fighting abilities?" Blaze's voice rolled through the room. All their attention focused on him;

his voice didn't have accusation or malice, just questions.

The man gritted his hand, working up his courage. "We have all undergone training through the guild. We are no weaker than them in techniques, but they have higher cultivation of the body and mana. They will undoubtedly be wearing Apprentice-level armor and some Journeyman-level gear. Combat standards don't matter if we don't have the power to land a hit that will hurt them."

"What is your name?"

"Sok Young-Min."

Blaze smiled. A breastplate appeared in his hand, and he threw it to the man.

The man stared at the breastplate. It was actively drawing mana toward it, pulling on the very air.

Sok Young-Min shook as he held the armor.

Blaze knew what he was seeing.

Ice Knight Breastplate

Defense:	241
Weight:	42.3 kg
Charge:	10,000/10,000
Durability:	100/100
Slot:	Takes up chest slot

Innate Effect:

Strength of the user increases by 8%

Increase Agility of user by 6%

Formation One:

Fighter's Instinct—Increase speed by 12%

Formation Two:

Ice's Touch—Each attack has a chance to increase the numbness of an opponent (chance to paralyze and decrease speed (3-5%; stacks up to 30%))

Requirements:

Mana Pool 21

Agility 26
Strength 31

It was a true Expert-level armor. With their basic stats, it would allow any of them to drastically increase their power. The Ice's Touch didn't sound like much, but in a long battle, the effect would increase, decreasing how fast the enemy could move. With their speed changing from what they were accustomed to, it would throw them off, creating more openings.

This was a task that Alva was behind. They wouldn't skimp on the gear supplied to their people. Expert-level crafters had joined Vuzgal and sold them their goods and multiple connections through the Trader's Guild. With the wealth of Alva behind them, they had acquired a fair amount of Expert-level gear.

Blaze pulled out item after item, passing them to the different members of the team.

They were all stunned by the gear.

"Don't forget that the guild stands behind you. The Willful Institute thought we would forget about them murdering our people." Blaze snorted, and the air chilled.

Even the branch heads shifted their weight unsteadily, as it felt like an ancient beast had shifted in its sleep. Chills ran down their spines and set their hair on edge.

"You will be our fist and sword, to show them that the Adventurer's Guild will not stand by and they do as they like."

Everyone stood straighter, feeling the weight and responsibility of the guild upon their shoulders. Those who were from the region held their gear with white knuckles and gritted their teeth.

"Put on your gear and get used to the changes. In one hour, we will show these people what we're capable of."

There was no nervousness in their appearance; they anticipated the fight to come. They were excited to reverse the tables on the ones who had stepped on them before.

Elder Mendes sat in the highest booth in the arena. The other elders chatted idly, their voices mocking when the subject turned to the Adventurer's Guild.

"I heard they dispatched their own guildmaster with only twenty or so people," Elder Tsi scoffed. "If even our lowest elder wandered the streets, they would have no less than fifty people with them!"

"I heard there was an issue at the gate?" someone asked.

"It was nothing. Just them raising a ruckus. I want to see what noise they make when we defeat them in front of everyone. They won't even be able to lift their heads," Tsi continued.

There was a commotion as thirty people from the Adventurer's Guild wearing cloaks walked out into the arena.

At the same time, another group walked through the arena and into the boxes reserved for them at the bottom.

Mendes hadn't greeted the visiting group and had even placed them in the bottom-most box, showing them no respect and slapping them in the face.

Instead of raising a ruckus, the Adventurer's Guild settled into their box.

A man removed his hood, his body still hidden as he glanced up to Mendes. The two made eye contact; the man was unperturbed as he looked away from Mendes.

There is no tension in his expression. Seems he doesn't know how high the heavens are. Mendes dismissed any threat from the Adventurer's Guild leader. He would soon destroy him and tear out his roots, making sure that there was no way for him to recover.

"Look at them. Truly ridiculous, hiding in their cloaks. Must be concealing their scared expressions. There was no need for us to send out our best!"

"Truly, if we sent out best students, it would only tarnish our reputation, using so much force to defeat an ant."

The elders ridiculed and laughed at the Adventurer's Guild's people.

Even Elder Mendes scoffed at the guild and sat back to enjoy the show.

"Do they not care for face, accepting their position at the bottom of the boxes without complaint?" someone said in the crowd.

"What do you expect? They are just a guild. The Willful Institute has connections to the higher realms. There are rumors that some students reached the Seventh Realm."

"It seems that they are finally realizing what kind of power they slapped. It is too late for them to do anything but accept their fates."

"It is a shame they were too bold and spat in the face of the Institute. I was thinking of joining them at one time."

Mendes let people discuss the Adventurer's Guild's fate.

He indicated to the referee standing at the main stage to continue.

"Thank you, everyone, for coming. On one side, we have your Willful Institute's ten competitors!" The crowd roared and cheered as the referee raised his arm toward the Institute's people, who bowed as one to the crowd.

Then the referee's face turned sour. "On the other side, we have the Guild of Adventurers." He stared at the guildmaster. "I must ask you to show that you have the resources placed on this match."

One stepped forward and flicked something shiny toward the referee.

The referee grunted and took a half-step backward to catch the object.

Mendes's eyes thinned. "Make note of that one. We'll make an example of them after this is concluded." His voice was quiet, but it carried through the booth.

The elders nodded, their expressions cold.

"Assaulting the referee will lead to a loss," the referee said in a cold voice.

"Sorry, Guildmaster. I guess I should have used a twentieth of my Strength. A tenth was too much," the man lamented to the leader.

The guildmaster smirked and rolled his eyes. "Try not to break too much. The buildings around here are weak enough. Leaning on them might make them fall. Their foundations are corrupt."

Mendes felt an itch, an old, forgotten instinct that had regressed into the back of his mind. He ignored it.

"I would ask—your Institute has our resources, right?" the guildmaster asked the referee.

"You are too arrogant," the referee said. "Of course, our Institute has the required resources!"

With a flourish, the curtain on one side of the stage was withdrawn, revealing a mountain of resources.

"Good." The guildmaster sat back. "Shall we begin?"

"I must make sure of your own wager." The referee didn't even look in the ring and waved it, wanting to show the lack of wealth to the people in the arena.

Pill bottles, potions, ingredients, and mana stones dropped to the ground.

A wave of refined mana passed over the arena. The pile was a fifth of the size of the pile in the box.

A hush fell over the arena, as the expected face slapping was reversed.

"Why is it that I feel the items the guild brought are more powerful than the ones supplied by the Institute?" a spectator whispered to her neighbor.

"Quiet! Do you want to lose your head?"

"The items the Institute brought are many, but the guild brought refined potions, pills, and powders. They're much more effective and have a higher value."

"Those mana stones—are they from the Earth realm?"

"That can't be. You can only get those in the Fourth Realm and higher."

Mendes had seen Earth mana stones before. They were a resource he had used himself to increase his cultivation. Seeing the resources casually dropped on the ground, he wanted to hit the referee who had wanted to show off the difference between the groups. He had, but not in a way that he or anyone else had been expecting.

Mendes wanted those resources. Being from the Third Realm, he had a faint idea of the power of the different concoctions. *They must've brought their guild's wealth. If we can take this, we will have three times the resources that we would be usually given in a year.*

"Make sure that there are no issues," he said to one of his aides. "Have our elites ready in case we need to make a substitution. They might have hired others to fight for them."

"Yes, Grand Elder Mendes." They moved off to the side, passing the message on.

"Good enough?" The guildmaster seemed amused. There was a small smile on his face, making Mendes grip his fists together in anger.

"I think it will suffice." The referee moved the materials back into the storage ring with a swipe of his hand and then placed the storage ring on an altar next to the stage.

Mendes looked over to the people in black cloaks who were to represent the guild.

"We will start with the first fight!" The referee stood back on the stage.

"Isn't that the Storm Witch?" someone said as the first person from the Institute stepped up.

"She is one of the younger students but has already shown promise. Her temper is something to behold. If anyone challenges her or she thinks they are slighting her, she will go all out to destroy them."

One of the Adventurer's Guild members stepped up, still hooded.

"Maybe the guild has brought a hidden Expert?" The Spectators were eager, excited by the display of resources.

The two reached the top of the stage, staring at each other.

"You will need to remove your cloak," the referee said.

They pulled off their cloak and put it into their storage ring, revealing a man wearing a sword on his hip.

"A knight. Their fate is too bad. The Storm Witch has high Agility and can double cast spells. They won't be able to get close to her."

"Why do I feel like they are a beast in human form? I think that I have seen them before."

"Yeah, that is one of the guild's group leaders. They take on a lot of trader protection details."

"Being a caravan guard, he'll have good fighting experience, but his cultivation will be nothing compared to the Storm Witch's."

"All right, let the fight begin!" the referee said.

There was a shift of air on the stage. The Storm Witch gathered her power. There was a crunching noise and a scream before something hit a solid object.

The arena fell quiet.

People's eyes adjusted to a new scene.

The guild member held his hand and looked meekly at the guildmaster. "I am sorry, Guildmaster." He bowed, and people's eyes moved to where the noise had ended.

The Storm Witch had been struck, flown off the stage, and collided with the wall.

A chill ran through Mendes. Was that a combat technique? No, it couldn't be! For someone at such a low level… Only geniuses understood those, and there was no way a guild would pass those things around to the lower ranks. They were trump cards for their strongest fighters. It had to be something they were using. Maybe they were using something to hide the appearance of the fighter?

"Make sure that is really a person from the guild," he hissed. There had already been too many surprises for the day.

"We need to confirm your identity," the referee said.

"My identity?" The man was already leaving the stage; it was clear who had won as alchemists fed the Storm Witch healing and Stamina potions.

"I am Lennaert Breukink, level twenty-six member of the Adventurer's Guild. I swear on the Ten Realms." Light descended around him, and nothing happened. He stared at the judge.

"That should be all," the referee said, looking haggard.

"They are an even lower level? How is this possible? Only someone who is a higher level should overwhelm the Storm Witch, right?"

"I thought they were the weaker group?"

"Did you hear what had happened at the gate? One of them bent the pauldrons of the gate guard's armor with just his Strength."

"How strong must they be? Do you think they have reached Body Like Iron?"

"There is no way. There are people in the Sixth Realm and Seventh who are unable to reach that level of Body Cultivation. The cost in resources is high, and it is many times more painful than it would be to increase your Mana Cultivation."

The second fight started. It was an archer on the side of the Institute and a sword user on the guild's side.

The archer got off one arrow that the swordsman cut down with their blade, showing incredible Agility.

They hit the archer with the flat of their blade, but the referee didn't call out the loss. The archer got distance and prepared to fire again.

The swordsman glowed green; their attack made the air shift around their blade. They hit the archer with the side of their blade and pushed them back. The archer's hair was thrown to the side with the breeze, and they yelled as a crunch sounded from their arm.

Their arrow dropped to the ground, and the swordsman peeked at the referee.

He didn't step forward, an awkward look on his face.

The swordsman frowned and ran toward the pale archer, who switched out her bow for a blade. The swordsman stepped past her, punching the archer in the back with a free hand.

The referee still didn't call it.

Then, like a machine, the swordsman dodged around the woman and started hitting her from all sides. There was a cruel look on the swordsman's face.

He hit her kneecap, dropping her before a vicious kick to the head, sending the archer sprawling on the ground.

"What are you doing!" the referee said in alarm.

"I thought you were telling me they could take more hits." The swordsman put his sword away. "Should've just fought with my legs. Might've killed something so weak with my sword."

"Excessive use of force!" the referee said. "You're disqualified!"

"Disqualified? He was the clear winner! What is this, a contest or a fraud?" people complained in the stands.

The third fight ended in just three moves, with the Institute's member laying on the ground with a broken nose.

The fourth fight went the same way, before there was a change along the sidelines of the arena's floor.

A group of five people stepped out of the tunnel, and five of the Institute's fighters left.

"What is happening?" the guildmaster's voice boomed through the arena.

"Those people were placeholders. The real combatants were preparing," the referee said.

"The Willful Institute—a bunch of con artists and fools."

"Watch your tone!" an elder warned.

The guildmaster chuckled and didn't even look at the elder, completely relaxed as the group around him bristled.

The fifth fight was the same as the first four.

"That is the Young Mistress Blue. It is rumored that she will soon reach the Fourth Realm!"

The woman stepped onto the stage from the Institute's side. She wore a blue set of armor and held a spear.

Her opponent was an assassin.

"Are they that confident? They haven't even changed their fighters or their lineup," one of the elders said.

"Silence," Grand Elder Mendes said. To get the resources on the altar, he had thrown away a part of his face that would be hard to recover. People would bring it up for years to come. If others in the Institute learned about it, it could severely affect his standing. Though all of that would be forgotten with the powerful members he could raise out of the resources earned.

The two combatants took their positions.

Mistress Blue drew on her power, making the air stir around her. A faint blue glow covered her body and spear.

"She is really going all out, using one of her half-learned combat techniques to start. They don't stand a chance!"

The referee started the round with a wave of his hand.

Mistress Blue charged forward. Her spear shot out like a snake.

The assassin shed their cloak and threw it. Mistress Blue's spear hit the cloak and punched through it; it blocked her sight. The assassin turned their body along Mistress Blue's spear shaft.

As Mistress Blue caught sight of them, they were within arm's reach.

She tried to jump away, but the assassin's hand clamped onto her arm and flowed with her, circling around to her back. Mistress Blue stilled as the assassin's left blade pressed against her neck, his right blade against her ribs.

Mendes grit his teeth. The enemy had played him. Mistress Blue had been raised without any issues and had been raised within the Institute. The assassin, judging from their use of environment, was no orchid in a greenhouse; they had been through life-and-death battles. They were a veteran fighter.

Skill and power had been on the side of the Willful Institute, but suddenly, their opponents had increased in power. With their power on the same level, it was clear that the Adventurer's Guild's skill wasn't lacking.

They had to win the next fight and the next four after to at least get a tie. If not, they would not only lose their face, they would lose the resources needed to raise their students.

"You have pushed me this far, so don't blame me for being ruthless." A cold light shone in Mendes's eye as he called over his aide, passing some quiet words to them.

Their expression turned colder with each word.

Once Mendes was finished, the aide bowed and left the box to carry out his orders.

Blaze watched the fights. He nodded to the different fighters as they stepped down from the stage.

He didn't care about the position of their seats. He didn't care whether people looked down on him. He had been looked down on before. He silently smiled and looked around, wondering what expressions people would show if they knew the truth.

He coughed to hide his amusement. He had great confidence in Alva. Erik and Rugrat had shown again that one should play the pig or dog—to have others underestimate them. Then, at the time of their choosing, when the odds were in their favor, that…that was when they struck.

Mistress Blue had murder in her eyes as she peeked at the back of the assassin, turning and strutting away.

Blaze's expression was remorseful. Arrogance was the greatest weapon they could use against their enemy. *Thinking that we should just roll over and open our necks for them. Are we not people as well?*

"Seems our hosts are anxious," Derrick said in a low voice, using his communication device so others couldn't hear them.

"Are they moving?" Blaze tried to not look up at the booth of Willful Institute elders.

"They are," Derrick said.

Blaze watched a swordsman step up from the Willful Institute. The man had a proud and arrogant air. Even with all the defeats before, he looked down on the Adventurer's Guild.

Sok Young-Min stepped up on the side of the guild. There were faint streamers of white behind him. He reached the stage and took off his cloak. He wore the complete Ice Knight set. A chilling air surrounded it; cold, white wisps of air flowed around his body.

His opponent stared at him.

The referee stepped forward.

The two swordsmen drew their weapons and prepared for the coming fight.

Sok Young-Min lowered himself, his eyes locked on the other swordsman.

"Begin!"

The Willful Institute's swordsman threw his hand forward. A purple-and-pink powder shot out in a stream, hitting Sok Young-Min.

"Poison," Derrick hissed.

In competitions, poison would only be used in life-and-death duels. It was rare to be seen in smaller competitions.

"Using poison right away? I have heard that Young Master Ilwu is highly competent with poisons, but isn't this too much?"

"Truly, the Willful Institute doesn't care about their face. Shameless to the extreme!"

"They have the power. The Adventurer's Guild might have some powerful people, but how can a small guild compare to the entire Willful Institute? See how they haven't raised any objections? If they did, it would allow the Willful Institute to strike out at them."

"I have seen the truth. The Willful Institute is a group of black-hearted cheats. Even the referee is on their side. See how he isn't covering his face? They must've given him the antidote ahead of time."

Sok Young-Min didn't turn away from the poison. Instead, he ran forward, deflecting his prey's slash.

Ice patterned the blade. Ilwu lashed out, his blade attacking Sok Young-Min's openings.

Sok Young Min fought desperately, defending against the oncoming attacks.

Blaze watched, seeing the patterning of ice travelling up Ilwu's blade with each strike.

Sok Young-Min cried out as Ilwu's blade cut through his leg armor.

Blaze's lips pinched together at seeing the skin blacken.

Sok Young-Min fought on. Ilwu's reaction time slowed, and he fought harder to try, confusion on his face.

Ilwu left an opening, and Sok Young-Min kicked his knee out, grabbing his sword arm and punching Ilwu in the face.

Ilwu used an Air spell, pushing him away from Sok Young-Min.

The ice patterning wasn't fading anymore; it was coloring Ilwu's armor.

Sok Young-Min ran at Ilwu, who jumped to his feet and dodged Sok Young-Min's attack.

Ilwu's reaction speed and Agility had dropped, but Sok Young-Min was showing signs of poisoning across his body.

Sok Young-Min used his armor to protect his life, attacking Ilwu's openings and un-armored body. While Ilwu grew up within a sect, Sok Young-Min had grown up in the wilds of the Ten Realms.

It turned into a brawl as Sok Young-Min used his fists and sword pommel instead of trying to slash, getting in close so his opponent couldn't use his weapon. Ilwu looked punch drunk as Sok Young-Min hit him with a cross, breaking his jaw and sending him spinning to the ground.

Sok Young-Min staggered and coughed. Blood appeared around his helmet as he stared at the referee.

He stared at Sok Young-Min with vicious eyes.

Ilwu's feet slipped on the ground as he tried to push himself up. Sok Young-Min kicked out his arm, coughing and staggering back. He glared at the referee, who watched the fight emotionlessly.

"Is he going to wait until Sok Young-Min dies to announce the winner?" Derrick hissed.

"A poison for a poison." Blaze's voice cut through the arena, which had grown quiet through the fights, everyone having given up on the farce.

"A poison for a poison." Sok Young-Min glanced over to the referee. "This is upon you."

He took out a pouch and threw it, sending a blade of Air at it. The pouch exploded in reds and blues, covering Ilwu.

Ilwu was still on the ground and had nowhere to go.

Sok Young-Min stepped backward, coughing blood through his helmet as he staggered over to his corner of the arena.

Ilwu coughed as the poison cloud settled over him.

"You!" the referee cried out as Ilwu's face distorted and changed colors. Blood ran from his nose. He dropped his sword and grabbed at his neck as he writhed on the ground.

Ilwu stilled. A tombstone appeared above him.

Sok Young-Min showed a dazed smile as he coughed.

"Drink the potion, you idiot," Derrick growled.

Sok Young-Min's eyes cleared as he pulled out a potion, poured it down his throat, and followed it up with a second quickly afterward.

The referee looked up at the elder box and then at Ilwu.

Deathly silence fell over the arena. People's eyes flickered from the dead Ilwu to the elders, who all bore terrifying expressions.

"A battle of arms turned into one of poisons. It looks like this is over with six wins." Blaze sighed and stood. It was not his desired outcome, but what the Institute had started, they finished.

"This has been an *eye-opening* experience on the ways of the Willful Institute." Blaze's dry voice made some in the audience wince and pull their necks back as they felt the killing intent wash out from the elder box.

"It seems my students are in need of some further training, and that if we were wasteful and gave them high-level gear, then we might have another match," Elder Mendes said.

Seems that they did notice the gear our people were using.

"We will take our leave now. Derrick, gather our winnings. Joan, check on our fighters. Don't want any lasting injuries."

Derrick jumped over the wall and went to where the prizes were kept. He took back the storage ring and waved a hand, gathering the materials the Willful Institute had put out. Even if they had vicious looks on their faces, the Willful Institute dealt with it in silence.

Like that, the competition came to an unsatisfying end.

Blaze got a message request. He opened it without anyone seeing.

"Looks like you guys really messed up their day," Niemm said.

"You in position?" Blaze asked.

"Of course. A little birdy told me that things might get interesting today. Are you good on your side?"

"We'll just have to see if they take the bait," Blaze said. His hood hid the ruthless look on his face as he gripped his sword tight underneath his cloak.

"Once this kicks off, there's no stopping it," Niemm said.

"The guild is ready, the army is ready, and we have ears within every nook of the Institute. We've been preparing for this for months."

"All right. Well, you lead them out, and we'll stab them right where it hurts," Niemm said.

Mendes left the box with a flick of his sleeves. His cheeks burned from what had happened in the arena.

The elders grouped around him as his aide approached.

"Are our forces ready?"

"Yes, Grand Elder," his aide said.

"Good! All of you, prepare your weapons and armor. If we let them get away with those resources, we won't be able to raise even one Expert, and the other branches will start looking into our matters. If they find out we were schemed against by the small Adventurer's Guild, we will lose our funding and possibly our positions. We cannot let that happen!" He glared at the elders. They all bristled with anger. Where they went, people would show them respect every step. The Adventurer's Guild had gone too far, crossing their bottom line again and again.

"Yes, Grand Elder!" their voices rang out in unity.

They headed out of the arena, going their separate ways. They gathered their weapons and closest supporters and then headed out of the city.

Mendes commanded everything.

"The Adventurer's Guild took their time wandering the city, showing off to other people. They didn't take the totem," Mendes's aide said.

Mendes breathed a sigh of relief. If they had taken the totem, they could have gone to another city. In that case, Mendes would not have an opportunity to strike.

The heavens might have forsaken us before, but the arrogance of the guild will become their downfall!

It wasn't long until the guild and their people appeared. Some were riding mounts while others walked, talking to one another. All of them wore their cloaks still.

Mendes waited as they became enveloped in the fighting formation of his Willful Institute. "Now!"

Archers and mages hiding in the trees along the road attacked; the archers' arrows shot out as spell formations materialized.

A mana barrier snapped over the Adventurer's Guild, covering them. The arrows struck and the spells hit; their force exploded against the barrier, throwing up dust and shaking the trees around them.

"You dare!" The guildmaster's voice came from near the front of the formation.

"Did you think you would get away with stealing the Institute's resources? Kill them!" Mendes yelled.

From around the guild, dozens of fighters ran out with a yell.

The elders were right behind them, wearing their strongest gear.

"Defensive formation!" the guildmaster yelled.

The guild shifted their people as they tore off their cloaks and drew out their weapons. There were eager expressions on their faces as Mendes's people ran through the barrier.

Yells filled the air as the two groups clashed. The guild held their ground as they viciously defended.

Mendes's eyes thinned as his people were dropped to the ground. The guild's weapons tore their lives from them, not giving them a chance to withdraw.

The bloodlust of the guild seemed to ignite like a wild animal.

"Send the mages and archers forward!" he ordered, as more of his people's bodies were broken under the guild's weapons.

One of the guild members was struck in the arm, cutting down to the bone. She yelled out in pain, and a golden glow covered her.

Mendes's eyes snapped to the man behind her who had healed her, using a shield to defend.

The healed woman glowed with power. Her blade turned white, and it moved like a fish in water, slicing out at the attacker her comrade had defended against.

The attacker screamed as the blade tore through armor and drew blood.

"Advance! Don't let the ranged get inside the barrier," the guildmaster said. He and the two with him hadn't taken off their cloaks as they remained in the middle of the formation.

Four assassins appeared around the guildmaster; their blades aimed at his blind spots.

He shot forward, kicking one. They were tossed to the side, their chest with an unnatural dent in it as his shield took one hit and his sword cut off another's hand.

An arrow crossed his shoulders, hitting the handless assassin and a second unharmed assassin. The blocked attacker didn't feel the blade that had stabbed through his back, into his chest, and was withdrawn before he dropped dead.

"Healers, watch your mana. Remember to use your potions." The guildmaster spoke as if nothing had happened; his breathing hadn't even increased.

"Send in the elders," Mendes said, seeing that the students were unable to compete with the guild, who was getting in a rhythm and pushing the Institute backward. A dozen bodies lay on the ground.

The elders rushed forward, clashing with the guild members. The battle seemed to tilt in their favor. Two elders struck a guild member down before they were blocked.

The fighting was fast and savage. The clash of steel and the rush of spells filled the forest.

Mendes got a sound transmission but ignored it, watching the fight. The ranged fighters hit the barrier uselessly.

"Have the rangers and archers with close combat abilities join the fight." Mendes wasn't panicked. The fight was nearly even; with time, he would wear them down into nothing. But he didn't want to spend more time. There was a possibility that others could find out about the fighting and spread word.

More sound transmissions came in, but he continued to ignore them.

The guild's ranged fighters created elevated positions with gear from their storage rings. They shot over their allies' heads and attacked those at the edge of the fight.

People from the Institute ducked their heads from the attacks, and some fell under the deadly rain.

They had the numbers on our side, but the enemy was stronger than he thought. Without knowing it, Mendes's greed had overcome any cold calculations toward losses.

"Grand Elder, we're under attack!" One of the older elders who wouldn't have been useful in the fighting had remained behind to watch over the Institute and used a sound transmission that Mendes couldn't block.

"What do you mean?" Mendes's stomach dropped.

"A group of people rushed through our defenses. We don't know who they are. They were able to get through everything, as if they were students and elders of the Institute itself. They cut their way to the warehousing district!"

"The warehouse district? Why? The resources! They dare to steal from us! The Adventurer's Guild is bolder than I thought!"

"I don't think they're from the guild. They are fighting as a group, and their equipment is all the same. They aren't different like the guild, and they are much more powerful. Their power is greater than people from the Fifth Realm!"

Mendes gritted his teeth so hard they hurt down to the root. He had brought most of the combat strength with him to take down the Adventurer's Guild, leaving his Institute open to robbers and bandits. He felt that the Adventurer's Guild had something to do with this, but there were no signs that they and the other group were connected, and the other group's power was much higher!

"We are using our formations and Experts to try to slow their advance, but they are breaking into all of our warehouses!" The elder's panicked words drew Mendes out of his thoughts.

"If we lose the warehouses, we lose all paths to advance! I will be there soon!" Mendes cut the sound transmission.

"Break off the attack and get back to the Institute!" Mendes yelled.

"Pull back!" Roska yelled as she kicked a wall. It shattered, transforming into blades under her spell. They stabbed into the Willful Institute fighters behind her.

Tully roared as her spear cut one fighter down, and she kicked another; they slammed into a wooden stall.

Yang Zan threw daggers, taking out three ranged fighters on the roofs.

The group rushed through the maze. Imani was waiting for them with the rest of the special team. They had six new members, rounding out to a total of ten.

Two mages used Earth spells to throw up walls as another member called down multiple spells; fog and smoke spread across the area.

Roska used a special spell. Her world turned purple, but she could see through the smoke. The group ran away from their position, perpendicular to where they had been heading.

Imani led the way. Her arrows cut down any of the Willful Institute members chasing them.

"Seems we really pissed them off," Yang Zan said.

"Might it be because we just cleared out their treasury?" Tully laughed.

They reached a side street as the first group spread out, covering the area.

The rest pulled out gray beasts that looked like a mix of bears and rhinos.

Roska jumped onto her mount as those already on mounts covered the first group.

"Contact!" Imani called out, standing in her stirrups. Five arrows shot out from her bow. It was as if they had eyes of their own as they killed two and wounded another two.

One arrow missed as the axe-wielding attacker slid on the stone, saving his life.

Ras Mangath, one of the newer members of the team, yelled. He turned into a blur, leaving smoke trails behind him. He took a hit on his shoulder armor. He didn't even slow as his left blade tore through the first opponent's leg and his second blade stabbed into their neck.

Roska didn't have a clear line of fire.

Ras pushed the man he'd stabbed to the side as Yang Zan's dagger forced the next attacker to defend.

Ras hit with his sword, blowing the weapon to the side. His blade shone white, creating an arc in the air.

His opponent had been cut in two and was bleeding. Ras tried to push them away and to the side to reach the last attacker, the second axe wielder.

They turned and started to run as Tully raised her spear.

Roska held up her arm.

Tully glanced over to her in question.

"We need some witnesses to say it was the Grey Peak sect," Roska said.

Tully lowered her spear.

Ras threw out some pieces of metal that looked inconspicuous but could be linked back to the Grey Peak's sect if one studied them.

"Get on your mounts!" Roska yelled to the few who had been half-mounted. She snapped her reins, and they moved forward. They were big beasts but soon picked up speed.

People yelled as they appeared out of the smoke and mist. The games had only just ended when the attack was carried out. People were only now coming to find out what the noises and commotions were in their city.

"Gate," Imani said.

"Don't worry. I have a key." Roska grinned as she circulated her mana.

She saw the gate ahead of her. A few sect guards on duty looked at the approaching group, years of boredom making them slow moving to their positions.. They wouldn't make it in time.

Roska raised her arm, and several spell formations appeared in front of her hand. Mana from the surroundings dropped in seconds, and her spell glowed brighter.

A drill made of spells and mana shot out from the formation. It lit up the ground, blowing wind in every direction as it passed.

The guards turned pale. None of them dared to face incoming drill head-on. They jumped out of the way.

The drill struck the stone gatehouse and drilled in deep.

Yellows, reds, and blues appeared inside the gatehouse.

The world took a breath and then returned in thunder and light.

One of the new members cast a mana shield over them all; it shimmered with the rocks and parts of the gate, gatehouse, and wall that had been blown apart.

The nine-foot-deep walls spread out across the road.

Roska led her people forward, making it through the rain of rubble. They exited the city and rushed down the road, past surprised traders and people who had been waiting on the other side of the wall.

They had been far back as the gates were closed. Roska felt relief upon seeing that the stone had rained down to the side instead of directly on the road.

Roska pulled out her map and checked it quickly. The location of the elders, the guards, and the Adventurer's Guild were all highlighted. She used spells on the beasts to enhance their speed as she activated her sound transmission. "Eagle One, this is Special Team Two. We'll be at the rendezvous in four minutes."

"Special Team Two, this is Eagle One. Understood. Be ready for pickup," Kanoa replied.

Roska and the team made it to a rest spot along the road. The area had been cleared out by traders needing some place to sleep on the side of the road.

"Tully, get those pickups ready! Everyone, harnesses on!" Roska ordered. Her beast had barely come to a stop when she jumped off her mount, taking the impact in stride as she checked her map and sent another message.

"Eagle One, we are in position."

"Special Team Two, understood. We're ready and on station. You have a group five minutes from your location."

"Understood." Roska pulled out a harness, stepped into it, and pulled it over her shoulders.

Yang Zan pulled on her straps without her needing to ask.

He checked them and then she turned, returning the gesture as Tully pulled out a box with a length of rope. Some of the team members with their harnesses on hooked up to loops on the rope.

Roska finished with Yang Zan and took the last place on the rope. "All secure?" she yelled.

"One secure!" Tully called from the front, holding her hands up to be visible.

"Two secure!"

"Three secure!"

They went all the way back to Roska.

"Fire up the balloon!" Roska said. "Eagle One, balloon going up."

"Special Team Two, understood!"

The metal box formations activated and shot into the sky, pulling on the rope slightly.

There was a sound of rushing air as two birds dove and banked around the area; the mages on them were ready for anything.

The kestrel flapped his powerful wings. On his stomach, a formation activated. It stuck to the metal box; the harness-attached metal and the box fused into one, and there was a pull on the line. Then the kestrel was rising higher and forward with greater speed.

Tully was off in the air, then the next person, and so it went, people being rapidly pulled up, attached to the line.

Roska used a spell to clear the ground of their footprints and cause the mana to settle. It would be hard to track anything that had happened.

She was pulled up and forward. Her harness held her as they dangled below the bird, picking up speed.

"Last man off the ground!" Roska yelled into her sound transmission device.

The two sparrows moved beside them, ready for anything.

Ten minutes later, they dropped back down toward the ground.

Roska dropped first and ran forward. The others did the same, so they wouldn't land on top of one another.

There were two kestrels waiting for them.

They split into two groups and ran up the ramps that ran down the kestrel's tail feathers. The cabin was inclined. Roska looked around, checking everyone was loaded. The first kestrel had landed, detaching the metal box. The box and rope were hauled into the cabin.

Roska ran up the ramp, the last person off the ground, and smacked the crew chief on the back. He talked into his own helmet as Roska sat on the bench along the wall of the wood cabin.

The crew chief pressed a formation, and a tree limb moved to the middle of the ramp. The crew chief looked out of the ramp; he was using the new belt-fed machine gun—a modified automatic rifle that accepted belts of ammunition and could be split apart easily to clear.

The pilot was up front, manning spell formations as he commanded the kestrel, who waved her wings, pushing them all into their seats.

Two secondary gunners were on each door, wearing their aerial sharpshooter badges and medical patches.

Roska looked through the portholes in the wood cabin.

The kestrel took off, and in moments, they were above the trees and climbing. The three kestrels and two sparrows rose higher. Roska looked out past the crew chief. In the distance, she could see the Willful Institute's city.

Roska sighed. The tension faded from her body as the city became smaller each second.

"All right, how is everyone looking?" Roska asked on her command chat with the rest of her team.

"All good here, boss," Tully reported as her second-in-command.

"Okay. Everyone, check your equipment. We'll be replacing our mounts and heading to the Grey Peak sect to stir up trouble and plant traces there."

"Looks like we'll be busy." Imani laughed.

"Time to earn our pay."

Blaze watched as the enemy weakened and pulled back. Finally, they turned and ran; the guild started to give chase.

"Not today. We've landed the opening blows. If we chase them, we might be going into a trap. Quickly, gather up our people and head to the rally point!" Blaze yelled.

They finished off the wounded Institute members and used healing concoctions and spells on their wounded. Unfortunately, three of their people had gone too far and nothing could be done for them.

The group mounted and rushed away from the city.

It wasn't long until a group of panthers jumped out onto the road. Atop them was Niemm with his special team members, including some new faces.

"How did you do?" Blaze asked as he sped up.

"Well, they'll be feeling that for some time." Niemm laughed and tossed over a storage ring to Blaze.

Blaze caught it. It was filled with piles of ingredients and concoctions. Being a city in the Third Realm, Meokar had nearly forty thousand students, all of whom needed resources to cultivate with. Now all those goods and the items the sect had been holding onto for years or even decades were turned over to Blaze.

"The council approved the mission. We have enough resources. Use this to bolster the ranks of the guild. This was just the opening attack; the campaign is sure to be a long one." Niemm grinned.

Blaze nodded. Alva had reached the point where even these resources, although interesting, weren't enough for them to fight over. With their different outposts and the vast amount of high-quality resources they were able to acquire every day, they had more materials than they had crafters to process them.

They were still working through the resources they had gotten from Vuzgal.

"So, what's the next move?" Niemm asked.

"We have their lifelines in our hands. Now we squeeze and see what happens." Blaze took out a sound transmission device. "Send a message to Elan. It is time to begin."

The message traversed the distance back to the city.

A simple-looking trader sat in a bar, talking to the bartender. "Ah, 'scuse me, looks like there is work for me to do!" He slapped down his money on the bar.

"Come back anytime, Old Sawai!"

He waved to the bartender and pushed through the door. He made sure there were no eyes on him as he stretched.

"Move!"

He shifted quickly as guards rushed past toward the walls.

Old Sawai accessed his sound transmission device and listened to the message.

His eyes turned solemn and then he smiled as he headed to the totem in the middle of the city. Three totems later, making sure no one was following him, he made it to the grand city of Vuzgal. Through a bar and downstairs through a fake cask and the hidden tunnel beyond. A quick trip through the undercity, and he rode a hidden elevator up.

The doors opened for him, and the old man's lackadaisical smile was replaced with a serious expression as he walked out into a kitchen. A man waved him forward, taking him through the Sky Reaching Restaurants backrooms, into the quiet corridors before reaching a room with two guards outside it.

Elan Silaz looked up from his papers as Old Sawai entered the room.

Old Sawai felt the pressure of Elan's gaze on his body. There was no trace of Elan's level or his cultivation, though there was power in his eyes of a man who could see through people's lies and secrets. He was the intelligence department's director and one of the few people who directly answered to the council and to Erik and Rugrat.

"I hear you have a message for me?" Elan asked.

"The Adventurer's Guild won their fight. The Willful Institute took the bait as we predicted. The special teams were able to sneak into the city, empty the warehouses, and escape unharmed. I was sent a message by Blaze to move forward with the next part of the plan."

"Very well." Elan nodded.

Sawai bowed and left the room.

He saw a flash of a sound transmission, not knowing the commotion it would create.

28 Calm Surface, Raging Depths

In a teahouse in the Fourth Realm, four men sat in a corner, having a quiet conversation.

"Did you hear that the Ghost Wolves sect and the Thunderous Mountain Consortium announced a trade agreement the other day?"

"Weren't they in an agreement with the Willful Institute?"

"I heard that they had found out the Willful Institute was attacking their own caravans to drive up the cost of protection and goods. They broke the contract and chose to work together!"

"That is audacious! To rip off such sects! What kind of tricks are they using against us smaller traders?"

"You best watch out if you say you are from the Willful Institute these days. The Earth Dragon and Great Mysterious sect have put their differences aside after it was revealed that the Willful Institute was the real force behind their animosity. Seems they forced the two groups into a battle to try to suppress them both. They have contacted the Ghost Wolves and Thunderous Mountain consortiums, offering their protection. If these four sects can unite against the Willful Institute, who knows what might happen?"

"I think you are right. It might be a good idea to take our families and assets and trade in calmer waters than these."

Erik sipped tea as he looked out over the snow-covered city. It seemed calm on the surface, people going about their daily lives. But in the back of teahouse and behind closed doors, everyone was talking about the latest developments surrounding the Willful Institute.

The once-powerful leg they had clung to for protection seemed to have daggers pointing in every direction.

He glanced over to his drinking companion. "Seems that things are not going so well for the Institute, Mister Niemm."

"Not at all. While everything is calm on the surface, the different branches and roots are trembling. We've paid special attention to them all. The Trader's Guild and the intelligence department are more effective weapons than me or my team could be." Niemm shook his head.

"It is all about finding your enemy's weakness and their enemies' tipping points. If they don't have enemies, then you can create them—a betrayal, the right information in the wrong places. Even the wrong information in the right places. Sometimes people just need a reason." Erik drank his tea again.

"I somehow feel that it is more brutal than a straight-up fight."

"It is, but wars and battles are waged in the shadows and gray areas well before a true confrontation." Erik's eyes were deep, cold, and rough. "At least this way, the people who are not affiliated with the Institute will distance themselves. We cannot take it all down with our own power, so we borrow the power of others to do so."

Niemm looked out over the city. He was silent for some time. "Should we head back?"

"Yes. There is a lot to be done still." Erik stood.

The Adventurer's Guild headquarters in Vuzgal was a hive of activity. Messengers entered and left with grave expressions.

In the center of it all was Jasper and Blaze.

Around them, there were mounds of dust as they went through information reports. While the messengers brought in official messages, their assistants slipped them information that Elan had gathered.

"So far, other than our little fight, there have been no disturbances between the Adventurer's Guild and the Willful Institute. The attacks seemed to have materialized out of nowhere, and the people who were on the fence about attacking or going against the Institute are all looking to gain from their misfortune," Jasper said.

"What about Meokar itself?"

"Mendes has all of his people on alert. They are licking their wounds, but from our reports, they are readying their forces to attack Grey Peak Sect. They are talking to the leaders of the cities we have bases in to influence them and isolate us," Jasper said.

"While the traders and the intelligence agents are the blades in the dark, the other groups are preparing to stab the Willful Institute in the back as they are fighting us. They don't expect to defeat the Institute, only decrease their power. We have some teams in the field. See if they can't turn the minor conflict between the two groups into an unstoppable grudge," Blaze said.

"Thinking about it, doesn't the Silver Moon sect have an issue with the sects on the fifth continent of the Third Realm?"

"Yes, there were rumors that the Willful Institute's students were stealing from the Silver Moon sect's fields, taking their ingredients." Jasper nodded.

"We've worked with them in the past, no?"

"Yes, they are a harvesting sect, only based in the Third Realm. It is a relatively peaceful realm, and they have been able to become a power, paying off the surrounding groups with their ingredients and raising powerful alchemists who have entered the Alchemist Association," Jasper said.

"All crafters have the ability to draw in massive amounts of support. Talk to the traders; see who in the Third and Fourth Realm might be interested in the ingredients of the Silver Moon sect. In the meantime, why don't we send a representative to talk to them? It would not be bad if we can become closer; we are two sides of the same coin. They grow and trade while we protect and take on missions requiring our fighting abilities. If we can introduce them to more people in the higher realms, then they have more routes to sell their products. If nothing else, their newfound alliances will turn them into a strong wall that the Willful Institute needs to watch out for," Blaze said.

"That makes sense, but what if they don't want to work closer with us?"

"That is fine. The more people we have to split the Willful Institute's power and people who are calm and could work with us in the future, the better. We need to plan for what will happen in the power vacuum of the Willful Institute losing their branches. If they collapse, then fighting over their corpse, more people could die than actually fighting them," Blaze said in a bleak voice.

"Greed knows no bounds," Jasper agreed.

Kanoa saluted as Delilah and Erik walked close. Erik saluted him back.

"Looks like you've settled in well and you've been raiding our stables." Erik glanced past him at the rows of men and women standing next to their mounts.

"I had no idea what the hell I was getting myself into when I agreed to try out Alva," Kanoa muttered.

"Hey, that's part of keeping it all secret. Hard to find out about."

"My feet are starting to hurt just standing here. At least I'm not standing at attention," Delilah interrupted.

"I remember when you used to be meek and quiet."

"Yes, and then I was corrupted, having a teacher like you. So, Captain Kanoa, can you talk us through your new units? I'm excited to meet your people."

Kanoa stifled a laugh with a cough.

Erik looked at Delilah in shock.

Kanoa waved them to review the units.

Afterward, they retired to Kanoa's office. The barracks were on the Wood floor; it hadn't been heavily developed and maintained a balanced temperature and atmosphere compared to the cold Metal and Water floors and the boiling Fire floor.

Combat companies were training alongside the new air force.

"Not what I was really expecting." Kanoa stared at the two groups training together. "I was expecting us to have to train people into airborne units, air assault squads. You've gone more of the way of the Brits. We control the skies; army controls the ground."

"Our military is much smaller. We don't have the numbers of the United States military. We pack all of our training into the people we have, give them all the tools possible," Erik said.

"How is training going?" Delilah asked from where she sat in front of the desk.

The two men turned and made their way over to their seats.

"It has gone well. The learning curve with the mounts is much shorter than it would be with helicopters. We got the carpenters and farmers to create the tree hulls. They're lightweight but strong. The birds get used to them quickly."

"I thought you were going to have three types of birds: the gliders, sparrows, and kestrels?" Delilah asked.

"That was the thought. But the gliders were redundant. I was thinking in Earth terms, not Ten Realms. The glider was supposed to be a bomber, but if you have the pilot of the sparrow underneath in a tree hull instead of on top, they have a better vantage point, and they can drop bombs out of their storage rings. There's two machine guns mounted into the tree hull and a formation plate to increase the power of the pilot's spells. They can strafe, bomb, and spell the shit out of whoever pisses them off."

"How about cross-training with the kestrels?" Erik asked.

"They're damn strong. Scary strong and pretty damn fast. I've modeled their loadout and operation on a Chinook." He glanced to Erik. "They have a back-mounted tree hull; the kestrel leans forward to allow loading. It can take forty people, though we've just been saying two squads, so thirty-four people. Three gunners: one at the ramp, one at each side. Two pilots linked to the kestrel; they're also casters. Provide magical support, spell scrolls, buff the kestrel, coordinate with the other units in the air."

"Sounds powerful," Delilah said.

"Weapon-wise, sure, though their biggest strength is mobility. We can use them to get combat companies inserted behind enemy lines, even into their cities if they're big enough."

"You've run some missions with the special teams, but what about with the regular army units?" Erik asked.

"Doing that totem and teleportation pad training helped. Just adapting it. Instead of pushing out around the totem, they push into a semi-circle at the rear of the kestrel then follow what they've been trained before. Same thing to mount up, defensive fire; they rush people on, and off we fuck," Kanoa said.

"What about the air mobile medics?" Delilah said.

"They'll be on kestrels as well, loaded with the supplies they need. Idea is to stabilize, get the wounded into the field hospital as fast as possible. We pulled copies of Stamina and healing buff plates, like what's in the hospital here."

"Why the tree hulls? Why not use the beast cages?" Erik asked.

"Beast cages can store more people, but they're fragile. They can take a round or two, but then the whole thing collapses with everyone inside it. Two, with the tree hulls, we have more guns and more protection. Three, morale. You can't see outside of the damn cage. Knowing it can just break and you all die in an instant? It was messing with the troops. Tree hulls cost less, can repair themselves, acts like armor for the bird, can have formations added to buff the kestrel's abilities. Even has a 'crash mode.'

"Say the bird is going down. It goes all Groot—sprouts more limbs, branches, and leaves; creates a protective ball around everyone; straps them in. Sure, it won't be a fun experience, but it's no helicopter crash."

"Well, I don't have anything else. I'm completely positive you're the right man for the job and you've thought through all the angles," Delilah said.

"Thank you, Council Leader. Might I say, even though I have only been here a short time, I think you do one hell of a job too."

"Thank you." Delilah smiled and pushed out of her chair. The others rose with her. "Talking about jobs, I need to get back. Got an oh-so-exciting meeting with the farmers and then a tax review meeting for afternoon napping."

"I'll keep to my birds, thank you." Kanoa smiled.

"Keep up the good work." Delilah reached out a hand.

"Yes, miss." Kanoa shook her hand and Erik's.

The duo left his office.

Kanoa looked out at the training area again. "I never thought I would work with real-life, actual birds as transport and fighter craft. Guess anything is possible in these here realms!" He glanced at his desk and the papers on it. "Seems that paperwork is an unfortunate disease, no matter the country or realm."

29 Fall of a City

Storbon walked through the Fourth Realm, Willful Institute-controlled city with his team. They were attached with a group of traders, dressed up as their guards.

"Well, those guards weren't very nice," Tian Cui said out the side of her mouth.

"Do you feel that?" Storbon asked.

"What?" Tian Cui asked.

"The tension, the fear, the bloodthirstiness?" Yao Meng asked.

Storbon grunted as they led the traders to a warehouse at the edge of the city.

The traders pulled their mounts and carriages into the warehouse and started to unload.

"Cover us," Storbon said. The others nodded as Storbon and Yuli headed deeper into the warehouse.

They reached a large wooden crate. Storbon circulated his mana and braced the crate. He grunted as his muscles contracted and his veins expanded. He dug his feet into the ground, and the crates shifted. He powered through, and a trapdoor was revealed underneath.

Yuli opened the door and cast a spell on her eyes. She pulled out a silenced rifle and headed down the stairs underneath. Her head was covered by her helmet.

Storbon dismissed his cloak, pulled on his helmet, and grabbed his rifle in practiced moves.

He followed Yuli down. A Night Vision spell allowed him to see through the darkness easily. Yuli reached another door; she slid it to the side, and Storbon pushed inside. He swept the right, spotting the podium in the middle and the blank stone walls.

Yuli swept the left side.

"Clear!" Storbon called.

"Clear!" Yuli replied.

They relaxed, and Storbon lowered his rifle.

"Looks like the cover remains intact." He pulled a dungeon core from his storage ring.

"Yeah. Though would you think that we would be using dungeon cores to sabotage a sect's city from the inside? Niemm's one devious bastard."

Storbon placed the dungeon core on the carved podium. The lines along the podium lit up with power as mana was drawn in toward the dungeon core and transmitted to the podium.

> You have come into contact with a dungeon core. With your title, *Dungeon Hunter*, new options are revealed.
>
> **Do you wish to:**
>
> Take command of the Dungeon
>
> Remodel Dungeon
>
> Destroy the Dungeon

"Take command. Show me a map of the dungeon and surrounding area," Storbon said.

The screen disappeared, and a map appeared above the dungeon cover. There was a faint image of what was above the dungeon. It became fainter and fuzzier the farther up it went.

"Okay, looks like we're ready here. Once we destroy the dungeon, we will leave no traces of it. The pillars supporting the main wall will collapse, and it will fall apart." Storbon checked his timepiece.

"They should be ready out there, right?" Yuli said.

"I'm surprised the other sects have been able to keep it to themselves."

"Don't trust them to keep a secret?"

"I wouldn't trust them to piss in the right direction. Of course, I don't trust them to keep a secret."

Yuli snorted as she put her helmet on.

"Check with the aerial forces. Let's make sure they're ready to extract us," Storbon said.

"Yes, boss." Yuli pulled out her sound transmission device as Storbon used his own.

"Yao Meng, tell our 'traders' to be ready to move. They can mingle, but in four hours, I want them back here. If they're late, I'm not staying around."

"Got it, boss."

The hours slipped by as the traders went off to different taverns and acted as they would normally. They secured their mounts and took down their carriages, placing supplies in the warehouse to sell later.

The special team spread out over the warehouse. Monitoring the alarm formations, they pulled their cloaks over their armor and weapons as they sat around.

Storbon and Yao Meng were playing dominos and spitting out seeds as they watched the area.

"You're going to lose." Yao Meng organized his pieces.

"So you say." Storbon checked the crate they were playing on as Yao

Meng looked over his shoulder and around the area.

Storbon put down a domino and then looked around. "What do you think about that." Storbon chuckled as he saw Yao Meng's sour expression out the corner of his eye.

"I think you have too many damn blanks," Yao Meng grumbled as he picked up a piece from the pile.

Storbon put down another with a grin. "What do you think of the additions?"

"Jurumba, Foster, Sang So-Hyon, Rajkovic, and Jamie?" Yao Meng put down a domino, his expression turning serious.

"They're well-trained, better trained than we were when we became special team members. Stronger, too. While they were waiting for us, they've been exploiting the potential in their bodies—high levels, Mana and Body Cultivation—meeting our own. Though that is just training. They've been on combat operations before, and they have fought in the Ten Realms in their own ways, but only a few as soldiers under Alva. Jamie is quiet but focused, switched on. Rajkovic has a damn scowl on his face all the time. Only time he smiles is when he is doing something insane or he's in a fight. He'd charge into anything with that damn stupid grin. Not too much pre-planning, man of action—he'll get shit done. Sang So-Hyon has a chip on her shoulder; something must have happened there—sealed her lips tight. When she is fighting, it's like she's getting something out of her system." Yao Meng glanced over to Storbon in question as he put down a domino.

"Family ran a farm, bandits came in, cut down her family and the people in the village, plundered them. There was a group of our traders in the area. They went to their aid and killed the bandits, but there were few people left in the village…broken people."

"Shit. She's a wild card. Not sure if she'll handle it well or hold it in until it all falls apart." Yao Meng sighed and picked up another domino.

"Foster and Jurumba?" Storbon put down a domino and tapped his remaining domino.

"Jurumba is solid. He's laying quiet right now, same as Foster. We're evaluating them; they're evaluating us. He's got a great understanding of artillery, guiding fire in from distance. He knows how to control the battlefield and work with different resources at the same time. Mean bastard in a fight. He uses two damn hammers, and he's pushing to be the most body-tempered bastard out there. Catching up to Erik. Foster is a tech nut and loves his guns, his formations, and machines. Through and through engineer, loves taking things apart and putting them back together. Great for demolitions, traps, decent shot." Yao put down a domino, and Storbon hissed, picking up a new one as Yao Meng followed up with another domino down.

"Can you stop making me pick up damn pieces," Storbon muttered as he got another.

"Just repaying the favor." Yao Meng put down another domino piece gently.

Storbon kept the expression on his face as he felt someone calling him.

He tapped twice on the crate and pointed his thumb at his head. Yao Meng nodded and glanced around. The color in his eyes changed several times as he used different sensing spells before making eye contact again.

"Go," Storbon said.

"They're in position ahead of time. We need to move up the schedule," the agent on the other side of the sound transmission said.

Storbon circled his finger and raised his eyebrows to Yao Meng, who mouthed, "*Now*?"

Storbon nodded.

Yao Meng grimaced. "Ah, I think you won." He sighed and shifted the dominos. "I've got to take a piss. Another game later?"

"Sure," Storbon said.

He headed into the warehouse and raised his hand, circling it in the air.

"What are your positions?" Storbon asked the agent as he pulled out a map and put it on a shelf.

"Grid square one two eight, by four three seven."

"Okay, I'll need another twenty minutes to make a clean exfil," Storbon said.

"They're all hyped up here. A lot of unstable factors in one. I don't know how long I'll be able to hold them back from taking action," the agent replied.

"Do your best and be ready with those spells on my mark."

"Understood."

Storbon cut the channel and glanced over to Jamie, one of the new members of his special team. "Contact the traders. Things have been moved up."

"Understood." Jamie activated his sound transmission device as Storbon opened his team channel and relayed everything to them. Everyone got the alert, and Yuli went on a walk with another new member to patrol the area. Yao Meng and Tian Cui wandered off to meet with the different traders, using some excuses to pull them back to the warehouse with minimal problems.

We need to get a move on. Storbon pulled out his rifle and checked the grenade launcher to make sure it was loaded. He tightened the silencer and the screws on the sight. He reached to the Conqueror's Armor and the screw formation that he would need to twist to activate it.

This is going to fucking suck. I hate waiting.

Storbon found a ladder and climbed it, getting into the walkways above the warehouse. There were small windows to watch the surrounding warehouses, and they could see part of the outer wall.

He took a knee, shifting his cloak out of the way so he could see the street leading up to the warehouse. People were moving supplies to and from carriages, to head out of the city or to take them to the markets.

It was quiet. Most of the traders had already left, possibly sensing that something was going to happen.

The minutes crawled by. People returned to the warehouse in twos and threes. Some were in high spirits; others seemed grumpy to return to work after a few free hours.

Storbon sat on a crate and shifted the armor that was pressing in on him.

They were all real traders and intelligence agents, but they'd had no hesitation in carrying out their plan. Even laborers could be a great weapon. *One should never look down on the small people.*

Thirteen minutes passed before Storbon got a message.

"We've been spotted!"

"Shit. All right, send up your loudest and flashiest spell attack!" Storbon smacked his foot on the catwalk.

Everyone looked up at him, and he switched to the general channel.

"The attacking force has been made. Everyone, get your asses back to the warehouse as soon as the attack spells go off!"

Moments later, spell scrolls were activated around the wall. The city's mana barrier snapped into existence, and a notification appeared in front of everyone's eyes.

Event

The city of Swadu is under attack! Pick a side!

Defend Swadu

Attack Swadu

The mana barrier lit up under the barrage of attacks as the once-hidden force emerged and started their attack.

"Move it—now!"

The gates sealed shut as the guards from the Willful Institute manned their defensive weapons.

Storbon switched to a private channel. "Meng, talk to me!"

"We have less than half of our people back. I am rounding up the last few. Should be there in a few minutes."

Storbon got off the crate and took a knee, moving to make sure he was free to engage. A group of Willful Institute members ran through the warehouse district.

"Ready! Incoming Institute!" Storbon barked.

Everyone in the team shifted. The dull, bored look and hunched backs disappeared as they straightened and grabbed onto their cloaks and handles tighter, ready to pull their cloak to the side and raise their rifle at a moment's notice.

The group didn't pause as they ran toward the walls.

"Stand down, just running through. Jamie, Yuli, Foster, take north, south, and east. Get the secondaries down into the tunnels now. Lucinda, you're my eyes and ears."

They acknowledged their roles and got to work.

More people streamed into the warehouse and pushed down into the secret underground chamber, where they got changed into their new gear.

Attacks continued to shake the mana barrier. The light of impacts flashed overhead in the late-afternoon light.

Storbon scanned his sector, keeping an eye on the wall. More soldiers ran through the warehouse district to the wall from across the city.

Mana cannons roared along the walls. The defenders poured in more power and reset the massive weapons to fire them again.

Willful Institute Mages stepped upon formations and unleashed their spells, working individually or as groups to bring out the greatest power. Spell formations colored the wall before unleashing their devastating power.

Storbon saw Yao Meng and Tian Cui rushing back as a group of guards ran for the wall.

"Get the hell out of the way!" the guard leader yelled.

The two swerved out of the guards' path, letting them past.

Storbon stretched his hand, relaxing as the adrenaline bled off.

Yao Meng and Tian Cui crossed the last hundred meters, making it to the warehouse.

"That's all of them," Yao Meng said in the team chat.

"All right. About time we were moving. All elements into the tunnel. Then outer security will move down!"

"Yes, boss!" the team replied as the remaining members moved down into the hidden entrance.

"Yao Meng, get in touch with our observer. Relay everything to them and keep them and me updated!"

"On it!" Yao Meng said before Storbon could finish.

"Outer security, pull back!" Lucinda yelled.

Storbon turned and ran. The outer security collapsed as they ran down the walkways. Storbon jumped over the railing; his cloak shifted, revealing his armor and his weapon at the ready. He slammed into the ground, taking the impact easily. He ran past Lucinda and Rajkovic, who were covering the entrance of the underground tunnels.

The others filed down into the room, which was packed with all their personnel.

Storbon reached out to the dungeon core. With a command, a section of wall opened, revealing a passage. "Get moving. Jamie, Sang So-Hyon—you're on point!"

Lucinda and Rajkovic moved down the stairs and, with Tian Cui and Yao Meng helping them, pulled the crate back over top.

People flowed through the tunnel. Everyone passed through until there was only Storbon and Yao Meng in the room. They'd both removed their cloaks and put on their helmets.

"Relay to our contact—time for them to pull out the big guns. We're ready to drop the wall," Storbon said.

Yao Meng added him into the channel.

"We're ready on our end," Yao Meng said.

"Understood. Activating the spell scrolls now." The message was distorted with the spells and mana that were being tossed around by the two groups in conflict.

Storbon and Yao Meng waited, tense and blind. The ground shook and dirt fell from the ceiling.

"Spell f-formations are a-ac-tive!"

Yao Meng glanced at Storbon, who was studying the dungeon menu.

You have come into contact with a dungeon core. With your title, *Dungeon Hunter*, new options are revealed. **Do you wish to:** *Take command of the Dungeon* *Remodel Dungeon* *Destroy the Dungeon*

He grabbed the dungeon core, remodeling the dungeon to take out key supports of hardened dirt and stone. The ceiling started to crumble, and the pedestal disappeared with the runes along the walls.

He and Yao Meng sprinted out of the dirt tunnels. They smelled the sewers before they saw them. Storbon didn't have time to shiver in disgust as they left the dirt tunnels and exited a broken stone wall. They were inside the city's sewers. They ran to meet up with the rest of the group. Everyone wore fully covering suits, so not even the smell could get into their noses.

They ran through the tunnels. Tian Cui guided them as Lucinda's beasts made sure there was no one else in their way. They ran under the city, passing through grates and metal bars with a few slashes of mana blades.

Along the way, special team members tossed formation plates into the sewers or stuck them to walls and ceilings.

Finally, they pushed through a large door, revealing a larger room ahead.

"Jump!" Tian Cui yelled. She jumped into a large water pool that was thirty meters wide and with unknown depths.

"Woohoo!" Rajkovic stored his rifle and jumped, Foster a half-step behind him. The traders and agents gritted their teeth and followed afterward.

Storbon jumped into the water. His spear appeared in his hand as he hit the water and started to sink. His clothes fused together, keeping the water out and his air in.

He used Dark Vision to see through the murky depths as his boots touched the bottom.

Tian Cui pulled out a light and turned it on. "Follow my light."

Everyone marched across the bottom of the pool. Tian Cui slashed through a grate, and they dropped to their knees, crawling for several meters.

The tunnel opened, and they could stand again. The special team members pulled out formation plates and put them down.

"Ready to board!" Tian Cui said as she finished checking her formation plate. Each plate was big enough to fit five people.

"Plate is good to go, boss," Yuli said. There were only members of the special team on her formation plate.

"Let's go up then." Storbon stepped onto the formation plate. He and the others took a knee and secured their harnesses. They put their melee weapons away and pulled out their rifles.

Yuli activated the formation plate by turning a metal dial in the middle. The runes activated, and the plate started to rise slowly.

They readied their mana and bodies to fight as they kept their barrels pointed low.

Storbon used a Detect Life scroll.

Green light only visible to him and the rest of the special team spread out, highlighting fish and other animals in the area. No large signatures or humans appeared in their vision.

They broke the surface of the water with barely a splash, finding themselves in a large well with several grates that light shone through. They came out of the water, tilting their rifles to drain them before they scanned the area.

The formation plate accelerated its ascent now that it didn't have to deal with the water pressure.

"Rise up," Storbon called to the rest of the team.

Yuli threw out grapples to the ceiling. She and Jurumba used them to pull the formation plate over and under one of the holes in the ceiling. The other platforms appeared from the depths of the water, one by one, as they ascended the tunnel. Yuli shot out mana blades, cutting the grate apart, and put the parts into her storage ring. The formation plate squeezed by the opening, and they were inside an icy cave.

Jurumba threw out a grapple and pulled them to the side as the others scanned.

"Dropping!" Yuli deactivated the formation plate.

They braced and dropped to the ground. Hitting the quick release on their harnesses, Storbon, Foster, and Rajkovic moved off the formation plate, pushing out to establish an all-around defense.

One by one, the rest of the formation plates appeared in the cave.

"All here," Yao Meng reported.

"Okay, let's find our rides." Storbon opened a new channel. "Eagles, looking for pick up at the rally point."

"Understood. We are holding ready. Moving to the rally point. It appears to be clear."

"All right. Be there in a moment." Storbon paused the channel. "Yuli, Tian Cui! Clear out the alarm formations. Our ride is nearly here."

Tian Cui and Yuli pulled out their own formations, using them to break the Willful Institute's alarms and traps, leading the way out of the cave.

As they got to the entrance, Storbon pulled out a formation that resembled an Earth clacker. He pulled the trigger three times. The ground rumbled, and water shot out of the holes.

Lucinda pulled out a formation block and rotated it into place, activating it.

Storbon got a message.

"We see your beacon. Ready to land. Confirm LZ is clear?"

"LZ is clear. You're free to land," Storbon replied.

"Our ride is coming in. Stay alert." Storbon looked over the icy world. The water droplets on their clothes started to form into ice.

"All right, you fifteen—you follow Yao Meng." Storbon slapped fifteen people on the shoulders, and Yao Meng came over to them, organizing them to board the craft.

"You seventeen are with me." Storbon pulled them out, creating a line.

"When we board, continue all the way inside. Don't sit down at the entrance! Just as we practiced! First person will take a seat to the right, the second a seat to the left, third to the right, and fourth left. I'll number you out—odd numbers right, even numbers left!" Storbon got them organized as the rest of the special team covered him and Yao Meng as they organized them.

Storbon heard a cry from above. Two kestrels flapped their wings, sending snow outward as they landed.

The wooden backpack cabins rolled down their tail, creating a ramp. The twin gunners on either side covered the landing area as two sparrows flew around, scanning for threats.

"Move it!" Storbon yelled, grabbing the first person in his line.

The crew chief was at the base of the ramp, ready for them.

Storbon pushed them up the ramp and to the left or right slightly and used a Clean spell on them, removing the water and gunk from their suits. One gunner was there, making sure they got in the right seat and rough handling them into it if they fucked up.

"Collapse in!" Storbon yelled through the channel to the rest of the team. They rushed toward the bird. Storbon checked the area before running up the ramp after the last team member.

He took a seat midway up the bench, grabbing onto a handhold and storing his rifle in his storage ring.

The crew chief tapped buttons on the branches—his weapon system—and the ramp closed and fused into a new position. He glanced over to the other bird and held out a thumb.

Their kestrel shifted and unlimbered its wings; the cabin moved out and cinched tightly around her body.

Storbon peered through the portholes as a spell flashed over the ground, removing all signs of them being there.

The kestrels rose into the sky with the cover of the sparrows, heading away from their rendezvous location.

The half-open rear showed the mountains and the forests before revealing the Willful Institute's city.

The mana barrier had failed, and a large section of the wall had collapsed. Smoke came from inside the city. Spells were being hurled back and forth, hitting the empty land around the city where varied groups were working together to attack the city. The long-range catapults and mana cannons were silent; mounted forces were fighting the defenders while foot soldiers clambered over the remains of the walls.

Storbon used Eagle Sight, looking into the city with greater clarity. He could see where lines cut through the city. Some buildings were tilted into the broken sewers, and chaos reigned.

The city became distant as they flew away, toward another city. There, they could store their aerial beasts and teleport back to Alva for their next mission.

Nearly an hour earlier, Wang Xi had gritted his teeth in anger. After months of work, he and his fellow intelligence agents had pulled together several smaller sects that had grudges with the Willful Institute or those who were immoral and greedy.

It seems we gave them too much damn room to breathe.

The sects, not wanting to lose out to one another, moved into their positions for the attack.

He pulled out his sound transmission device to talk to his contacts inside the city.

"Go," Storbon said.

"They're in position ahead of time. We need to move up the schedule," Wang Xi said.

There was a pause.

"What are your positions?"

Wang Xi checked his map. "Grid square one two eight, by four three seven."

"Okay, I'll need another twenty minutes to make a clean exfil," Storbon said.

"They're hyped up here. A lot of unstable factors in one. I don't know how long I'll be able to hold them back from taking action," Wang Xi replied.

"Do your best and be ready with those spells on my mark."

"Understood."

Wang Xi sent messages to other agents among the ranks of the various sects and empires. He squatted in the snow. A scarf covered everything below his nose as he surveyed the line, wearing the garb of an Apprentice fighter. No one cared about a simple Apprentice fighter.

Under the scarf, his throat moved but no noise came out. All Alva sound transmission devices had built-in sound cancelation formations so others couldn't hear them. The special teams took it to another level, talking through their throat microphones and sound transmission devices instead of talking openly, lest someone read their lips or overhear them.

These same practices had been passed down and drilled into the intelligence department's agents.

Wang Xi kept listening to the sound transmissions from his subordinates.

"I don't know what happened, but we just got hit with a scan! The forces on the wall are reorganizing and sounding the alarm," one of the agents called out, their voice strained as they used their throat mic.

"Ready!" Wang Xi told his agents as he opened the channel back up to Storbon. He heard it click; the channel connected.

"We've been spotted!"

"Shit. All right. Send up your loudest and flashiest spell attack!"

"Ready covering attack spell scrolls!" Wang Xi ordered his people. *Our people are our priority.* No matter what, they needed to get out of the city safely!

The sects, seeing they had been discovered before the scheduled time of the attack, started to panic and fall into disarray.

"Ready with spell scrolls!" the last person reported in just moments later.

"Activate them!"

Dozens of attack spell scrolls were activated. They hurled out different kinds of magics that slammed into the barriers that had appeared around the city. Ripples appeared on the surface.

With the attacks, the sects started to pull themselves together and some moved forward.

"Push the sects to attack now. Keep up the attack scrolls and be ready with the covering scrolls!" Wang Xi ordered, waiting for communication to be restored with the team inside the city.

The seconds ticked by. His agents exerted their skills, pulling the sects together, convincing their leaders to approach the city with their weapons at the ready. Ranged cannons and trebuchet were pulled out from storage rings. Mana barriers appeared, and attack spell scrolls were deployed.

Several groups worked by themselves. The tree line they had been hiding in became a hive of activity deep within the forest. Formation-covered rocks shot out, and pillars of light tore through trees to hit the city's mana barrier.

More people showed up on the defenses with every passing minute, reinforcing the besieged forces.

Wang Xi had spent months working on these different forces. It had taken incredible patience, guile, and cunning to bring them all together. He had infiltrated half a dozen various sects across the Fourth Realm, created alliances and laid plans. Now it was coming to a head, and his patience was wearing thin as he waited, nearly rocking on his feet for something, anything from the team inside. All kinds of scenarios popped into his mind. He shook his head to clear them, listening to the reports coming in from the agents planted among the sects, unknowingly guiding them without them knowing any better.

They were the control and command, and none of the sects realized it.

Units' orders were changed as they left the commander's mouth, shifting units to support one another without them knowing. They weren't a unified army, but with discreet changes, they were no longer a rabble of various sects fighting for their own actions.

Once they were inside the walls, there would be a wave of deaths, and they could start to pull out their people before they entered the city, removing any traces.

The fighting heated up. The sects had their mounted forces preparing on the wings and the foot soldiers were moving forward, using protective measures to close with the wall. If they could take out the mana barrier, the mounted forces could rush into the heart of the city.

"Black Snake, this is Special Team Four. Ready your covering scrolls!" The voice was crackled and distorted, but Wang Xi was able to make it out.

"Understood!" He switched to his people's channel. "Ready on cover scrolls! Prepare to launch on my command!"

"We're ready on our end," Yao Meng said.

"Understood. Activating the spell scrolls now." Wang Xi pulled out his own covering spell and sent messages to his people as he activated it. A blue-and-white spell formation covered the frontage of the city. Dozens of others appeared, and smoke spread out from the spell formations, covering the city and obscuring the wall. Rotating drills that seemed to be formed from water appeared in the sky and then launched through the air, disappearing into the smoke.

"Spell formations are active!" Wang Xi yelled to the special team.

Nothing was visible in the sea of fog that covered the walls.

He heard a rumbling sound, followed by crashing. The city's mana barrier flickered and then died as its formation cracked.

Wang Xi activated another spell formation. The smoke started to dissipate, revealing a very different view from before. Mana cannons and trebuchets fired into the city. There was no mana barrier to protect the buildings below; the wall had collapsed into piles of rubble. The defenders were either wounded or killed in the collapse.

"Sound the advance!"

The mounted forces heard drums and trumpets and watched the different flares and spells going off. They lurched forward like hungry wolves seeing a wounded beast. Hundreds and then thousands of riders crossed the snowy plains, rushing toward the opening in the walls.

The various sects ordered their foot soldiers forward. Ranged attacks slowed to a halt as they didn't want to hit their own people.

The Willful Institute guards were in disarray. Their wall had collapsed and their mana barrier weakened as sections of the city collapsed.

The attackers' mounted forces stabbed fiercely, carving a path through the Willful Institute's forces. Lines of beasts pivoted under command, breaking up the field of battle into a slaughter.

Wang Xi watched as different agents "died" on the battlefield. Corpse collectors dragged them back and out of the way, clearing the path for others. Then the corpse collector numbers would grow as the agent changed clothes and headed out, gathering more of their comrades.

Explosions went off within the city; buildings collapsed, adding to the chaos.

Willful Institute students marched out in groups from their headquarters to create stability. Their guards and the first wave of reinforcements engaged in a gory and bloody street-by-street battle inside the city.

The fighting grew in intensity as elites, Experts, and leaders on both sides were drawn into the battle. It was turning into a true war! Smoke came from dozens of fires, small and big. Different fights involved dozens of people. In other locations, one or two leaders tore up the inside of the city.

It is easier to destroy than construct. Wang Xi had a cold sneer on his face, watching the sects tearing off chunks of the Willful Institute. Various sects or people with grudges used the chaos. The war was a backdrop to some unfortunate losses.

Wang Xi and his agents watched it unfold until word came to

withdraw. There was not one Alvan inside the city anymore, though plenty of secrets were covered over and hidden in the midst of battle.

The eyes and ears of the intelligence department captured it all.

Elise sipped from her cup, staring at the trader sitting across from her. She could practically see the conversions and calculations inside the trader's head.

He smiled and picked up his cup to take a drink. "Very well. Your offer is more than generous. The Ronhua traders will be happy to work with you!"

"I look forward to our partnership. I can expect delivery at the end of the week?"

"Yes, I will have the wood delivered to you promptly." He smiled.

They made small talk before Elise left the teahouse.

With the Ronhua traders no longer supplying wood to the Willful Institute cities in the Third Realm, there would be a decreased production of bows, staffs, and, most importantly, arrows. Swords, once made, required maintenance unless they were broken, at which point, they could be reforged into new weapons. Arrows, once they were used, were hard to recover. Without a steady supply of wood, the sects in the Third Realm that were the main crafting headquarters and supply centers of the Fourth Realm Willful Institute wouldn't be able to keep up with an increased demand. Thanks to Elan's people, the people in the higher realms would think those below were holding back materials. The ones in the lower realms would think those from the higher realms were being unfair and trying to get more out of them when they didn't have much left.

"Let's head to Doran. We have a deal to make," Elise said to her security detail. She got into the carriage and pulled out her sound transmission device.

"Hello, Trader's Guild, Third Realm," a voice said on the other end of the line.

"It is Elise. I want a sell order, a weekly supply of one thousand red-veined trees. See if there are some crafters who are willing to create arrows. We can sell them to those fighting against the Willful Institute at a discounted price. Make sure they have the supplies they require."

"I will put down the information. What if not all of the wood is sold?"

"Sell it to the highest bidder—tax reduction for those who are making arrows. They will count as weapon exports, so only people who have a contract with us or those who are whitelisted will be eligible. Anyone found selling to non-whitelisted groups will have their trading license removed."

"Yes, Guildmaster."

Elise cut the channel and watched the world moving by outside as her carriage headed toward the city totem.

With the Alvans-turned-bandits, rules had to become stricter. Losing a license would be a death sentence to most traders. They would not be able to buy or sell to Alvans. Anyone who was part of the deal would be fined, and they would have to do hard labor. All their materials would be seized as well.

Elise had always thought wars were fought with swords and shields. She never thought of how traders could affect the balance of a war with the right information.

She rode in silence, thinking on plans to gut the supply chain of the Willful Institute piece by piece.

Most traders cared about profits and security. Seeing a large leg for them to hold on to, they would tell the Willful Institute they were blood brothers, while behind their backs, they would make deals to protect their future. Money was their master. Some were loyal to the Willful Institute and required some more work to break that trust before they could be drawn away too. The Institute had their hands full; their people were getting killed, and there was inner strife. *How do they have the time to worry about small suppliers? In peacetime, they might not need any of these items. In times of war?*

Different materials are needed.

The carriage reached the totem, and Elise disappeared in a flash of light. She reappeared with her security in the city Doran.

Time to buy out the Willful Institute's stock of healing ingredients. Who told them to be so reliant on autumn weed? Thankfully, they had Erik to test their healing concoctions and tell them the most used and crucial ingredients. The cheaper and more inconspicuous, the better!

30 From Afar

Elan stood in Alva's command center in the barracks. The room was surrounded by ten other rooms and was the Alvan nerve center of the Ten Realms. Intelligence agents and people from the Adventurer's Guild, Trader's Guild, and Alvan armed forces—they were all there. Information would come in hourly, and the globe taking up half the room would have markers changed. Boards of information were shifted as well. Reports passed between the command rooms.

"The Trader's Guild has bought up to three-quarters of the supply of autumn weed. Competitions have started between four more Willful Institute locations and other sects in their area. There have been eight small-scale skirmishes. Three Institute locations are preparing for an all-out fight and are calling on their allies and supporters from above," a military aide said.

"How many locations are fighting currently?" Elan asked. People rushed around; his eyes flicked to the boards of information.

"There are thirteen locations fighting openly."

"How many are fighting our forces and other forces?"

"One is fighting our Adventurer's Guild. The others are fighting foreign forces."

"Have any of them looked for support outside of their internal factions?"

"Not at this time," the military aide said.

Glosil walked into the room, and the military members snapped to attention. He saluted back to them and walked over to Elan.

"Commander." Elan nodded to Glosil.

"Special Team One and Four have returned and are readying for their next mission. Special Team Two is watching over the commanders, and Three is prepped for deployment. The air force is on standby for insertions and evacuations. Domonos and his Dragon Regiment are biting at the bit, ready to put boots on the ground," Glosil said.

"Once their cities start to fall, the Willful Institute will gather together and assert their full strength," Elan said.

"Sirs! The city that Special Team Four hit broke their silence. They're sending out messages to the higher sections of command," an aide said.

"Contact the lords," Glosil said.

Rugrat was covered in grit, dirt, and grease. Weapon parts and formations lay in front of him. Unlike his appearance, everything was lined up with almost clinical precision. He looked tired, but his eyes were filled with calculations and plans.

He sat in a Mana Cultivation room where mana materialized as a mist. With every breath, the room shook as mana shot into his body through his mana gates.

The air around him turned turbulent and chaotic.

His veins were traced out by mana as it burned through his body. His eyes stopped flickering from weapon part to weapon part as he raised his sound transmission device, listening to the message.

"I'll be there."

Rugrat rose from his chair. Power seemed to flow around his body in invisible currents. He quickly transformed into a warrior with sharp eyes.

He used a Clean spell on himself and checked the gear on his belt, eyeing his boots as he walked out of the training room. "We're heading to the command center."

The special team members flanked him as he strode forward. The glow of his mana channels and his eyes faded. The special teams were able to withstand the pressure coming off Rugrat.

People moved to the side.

Rugrat's easygoing attitude was gone. He was a man at war.

Erik's body was like broken charcoal; mercury, like blood, flowed from hundreds of wounds as it cracked.

He hissed in pain.

There were several metal strips on his body, needles that he had inserted to make sure that his cultivation would continue to increase and not find a setback.

Erik grunted as he pushed against the ground. Veins stuck out of his arms and his forehead, breaking his skin and covering him in blood. He didn't blink as he stared ahead, waging an internal battle.

His body trembled. Giving up would be so sweet. But surrendering was a poison of the mind and would eventually tear him apart.

Erik stared at his elbow. *Come on, you motherfucker—all the way!*

He started his push-ups again, finding strength as he reached the top. He held it; his blood poured from him, staining the ground as he dug in again.

Erik fucking West doesn't give up! One more—come on, you have it in you!

He lowered himself, not seeing the testers watching him. They were barely holding themselves from rushing forward. The drawn, dark faces of Roska and her half-team.

Anyone who had seen some shit or pushed their bodies to the limit would understand the respect in their eyes at seeing another pushing himself past his absolute limits to reach a new high.

Erik dipped down, flexing his back and stomach harder, trying to push his chest forward while everything else wanted to sag and collapse.

"One more," he muttered. He struggled upward; he seemed to reach his limit, holding and then pushing again. Inch by inch, he got himself up.

Erik hissed as he reached his last push-up. He moved his knee forward, leaning backward as he rested on his knees, fighting for air.

His entire upper body shook as he drew in powerful breaths. The wounds on his body were slowly starting to heal, but there were so many.

His sound transmission device went off. Erik raised the wristlet and tapped a command.

"I'll be there right away." Erik grunted and pushed himself to his feet. He used a Clean spell, removing the blood. He took out another needle; he put it on his side and secured it. He put another on the opposite side. With a yell, he hit the backs of the needles, driving them into his sides. Black and silver shot out from where the needle pierced his body. He quickly pulled on a shirt before it got covered in blood and walked out of the room.

"Command center," he said to Roska.

Glosil looked up when Erik and Rugrat entered the command center.

It had been nearly two years—or was it closer to three—since he had seen them in a battle. Out of all their forces, they trained harder than anyone and were always out fighting. With how relaxed they could be with handling things within the different areas of Alva, he forgot just how powerful they were.

Glosil stood a little straighter as he saluted. His eyes were dark, but in the depths, they were shining with pride at being their subordinate.

He led them to a conference room and debriefed the two men.

Storbon finished his report of everything that had happened in the city, and Elan followed up with Wang Xi's viewpoint and everything he had seen.

"Options?" Erik adjusted his collar to cover his burnt-looking neck. There was a bulge under his shirt where he was squeezing an IV bag of what must've been healing concoctions.

"We move up the schedule, hit them everywhere. Where we can't use the special teams, use the CPD squads from the Dragon Regiment. Have the Dragon Regiment in support and call general mobilization," Glosil said.

"I agree," Elan said.

"Why?" Rugrat asked.

"We have a small window to weaken the Willful Institute in as many directions as possible. Once the higher-ups realize they are fighting on different fronts, they can rally people together. They can move more forces and resources around. They can go on the offensive and worse, they can retreat," Glosil said.

"Why is retreating bad?" Erik asked.

"If they retreat, they will pool their strength. They lose a city that they would have lost already, but now they have one city with a strengthened core and the resources of two cities instead of one."

"Do it. We've started it now. We can't back out, even if we wanted to."

Keeping Up Appearances

"I got back from my task just some days ago, but your mind is elsewhere," Mira said. Her pouting face softened.

"There is a lot going on." Chonglu sighed.

"You are the head of the Battle Arena and are being groomed to be the leader of Vuzgal. Neither of those are small tasks. With the competition coming up, it will be a big deal."

She didn't know the half of the things that were happening. When he thought of Alva, he used to think of it as a wide network. He had never thought that it reached quite this far or had so much power. Vuzgal was just the tip of the iceberg.

"Yeah, the upcoming fighter's competition has me on edge," Chonglu lied. He couldn't tell her anything about Alva and what was happening in the shadows.

"I heard from the Vuzgal Fighter's Association Branch Head Klaus that there are some hundred fighters coming just for the competition and the prizes. More are coming to check out the weapons and wares of the crafters.

Really, Vuzgal is impressive with how it can draw so many people to it."

"Vuzgal has spread its wings over the past year. All the old land across the city has been recovered. New buildings go up every day. House prices have increased by twenty times. Traders come from across the realm, and people with money and without crafts go to the academy. The Blue Lotus hosts a general auction every other week and a special auction every two months," Chonglu said.

"Seems that becoming a lord was your vocation." Mira smiled.

"I became a lord in the First Realm because we needed to settle down. I was not letting us raise our children between fighting."

"You were always the mature one." Mira curled up closer to him.

Chonglu couldn't help but smile and kiss her. "There is a lot happening."

"I wonder what will happen at this year's fighter's competition. Last year was exciting!" Mira grinned.

Chonglu bopped her on the head.

"What was that for?"

"You are not entering the competition!"

Mira pulled her neck back and pouted again.

Chonglu smiled, but there were worries in his heart. He would be happy if there were no unplanned incidents with the fighter's competition.

The Vuzgal totem was paused for the night. They said that they were updating their formations and the defenses—not abnormal in the Fourth Realm. They could block people from coming in and going out, so no one could teleport in and see their secrets. A stone wall inside the defenses around the totem shifted and shook, revealing a tunnel underneath. Men and women marched up the tunnel's ramp. They marched out of the defenses and circled the totem.

Guards on the walls were alert, watching outward.

The totem filled with power, and the guards disappeared in a flash.

The next group marched into position and disappeared.

Domonos watched over them as they disappeared. Things were moving faster than they had predicted. Once the fighter's competition was done, he would support Glosil being the commander in the field.

The glow of the totem faded.

A few minutes later, it ignited again. A group appeared around the totem from the Tiger Battalion. They marched down the secret tunnel that would take them to the barracks.

The totem lit up as another group appeared; it flashed a few more times. The last group to arrive was the newly minted air force.

The Eagle Company. They would cover for the missing soldiers in the coming fighter's competition, and they could train up even more people for the army and air force.

Seeing those men and women marching away from the totem, Domonos's heart beat in time with their feet.

32 Rear Echelon

Rugrat pressed the pins into place. Turning the rifle to the side, he pulled on the charging handle. It took a little effort to pull on. He needed to cultivate to Body Like Iron stage or have a high enough attribute from leveling up. Though with it, even if he were out of mana crystals, he could still fire the rifle at the lowest settings.

He pulled a magazine out of his vest and checked the rounds. They were mini sabot rounds with mana stones, where the propellant and primer would be in a regular round.

Rugrat was excited, but his hands moved with mechanical precision as he slapped the magazine into the rifle. He pulled on the charging handle, cycling a round up and into the chamber, priming the formation powering pin.

He peered down the sight. It looked like an ACOG sight, but it was one hundred percent Alvan made. Two rows of metal blocks rested along the barrel, pointing off at angles. A floating heat shroud was positioned between the two rows and under the barrel of the gun.

Rugrat had put a bipod there. He placed the gun into a mount and tightened down all the nuts that secured the weapon, making sure that while lined up with the iron plates at the other end of the range.

He laid out a cord and backed up behind the testing blast shields.

Everyone related to the project, and the military was there to see the display.

"Fire in the hole!" He checked around and tugged on the string.

Rugrat felt the mana rushing through the weapon. Two blocks on each rack popped up, formations activating to cool them down rapidly.

"Shit!" Tan Xue said, using spells to enhance her eyesight.

"Damn." Rugrat followed right afterward, staring at the hole through the test plates.

A screen blocked his vision, making him frown. He was about to swipe it away, but he had already scanned the content. "Hell fuckin' yeah! Oh right!" Rugrat laughed as Ten Realms Experience flooded his body. It felt like the weight that had been resting on his heart lifted and he laughed, his body absorbing the Experience wildly.

"Fucking expert at beer drinking, gun shooting, freedom loving and goddamned smithing. Take that, Miss Watson. Never amount to nothing, my hairy ass!"

He wondered if other groups who were working to create applications found that they gotten some Experience for creating their components and then more when they finished them. He would have to ask them later. *Didn't Erik get Experience after working with Old Hei on that pill? Damn.* Maybe the Ten Realms wasn't so bad. It was just that people weren't working together, which was why no one ever heard of five people breaking into a higher skill level together.

"Range is safe. Get those plates for me, will you?" Rugrat yelled to some helpers.

They ran off to get the plates, and Rugrat waited for the others to gather around him.

He pulled out four items, putting them on the table with the weapon.

Each were as long as his arm and as thick as his large thighs.

"This is the AR Eight, as in automatic railgun version eight. Instead of using gunpowder, this uses formations to accelerate the round out of the weapon. The rounds are fired at a much higher velocity and can impact with greater kinetic energy."

These words would have confused them before but were now understood.

"This weapon is prone to overheating. You have to watch how many rounds you are shooting and how fast, much like when you are firing our modified machine guns."

He tapped the rail of blocks. "These will disperse heat as quickly as possible but watch out for it. You could deform the firing mechanisms. As for effective range, we haven't tested out just how far we can shoot these. Think a kilometer for regular troops; say two to three kilometers for sharpshooters and above?"

It sounded insane compared to people on Earth dealing with hundreds of meters. Though with their reaction speed and their control over their bodies, it wasn't outside the realm of possibilities.

"That is just stupid. Our engagements are all within one hundred to two hundred meters thus far. Even based on the information from the higher realms, forces can effectively engage one another at one hundred meters. With us doubling that effective range, in battles with distance, we'll have an advantage. If fighting becomes up close and personal, dial down the acceleration and increase the rate of fire." He tapped a dial above the trigger and forward from the fire select.

"This will increase and decrease the velocity of the round. We are working on presets for close range, mid-range and long range. This here is a pressure valve." He tapped a dial at the front of the rifle under the barrel.

"You crank this to either side, and it will open and close the recoil valve. Meaning you get more or less air into the gas piston system; that will create more recoil, but your rate of fire will increase. All these items are not formation-linked, so we didn't have to waste formations on them and instead increased the energy directed to shooting. Rate of fire varies as well. We will be modifying as we go to create presets."

"How does it operate?" Erik asked.

"Similar to the firearms we have now, the round is fed into the chamber; a formation pin strikes the back. All the mana stone that is inside the cartridge surges through the gun. A repulsion formation sends it into the barrel, and more formations increase the speed of the round."

Rugrat touched a large round. It was similar to a regular round, but the bullet had a little spike on the top. He picked up a round from the weapon that was much smaller.

"This is the round as it goes into the rifle. This is it in the barrel. The formations on the cover make it so that it doesn't mess up the barrel. Once it leaves the barrel, it turns into this finned dart till it strikes the target. These darts have formations on them to increase their lethality."

"Production time?" Glosil asked.

"Each weapon right now is assembled in several parts and then pulled together," Taran said. "It will take a month before we can go into mass production, and then we can create ten rifles in a week."

"What about the ammunition?" Yui asked.

"Ammunition is slower to make and more expensive, but we can create five a minute with one assembly line. We're hoping to step up five such assembly lines," Taran answered.

"Also, this is just the regular service version. The sharpshooter version will have a longer barrel with more heat sinks, and it will have four rows, two up and two down. With the higher heat management capabilities, you can shoot rounds with Mortal mana stones powering them. You can shoot Earth and even Sky-grade rounds. The machine gun version will have that longer barrel and a modified box magazine storage system. We're aiming to combine the storage devices with magazines, but it is the early stages. Bipods will be standard with the sharpshooter and machine gun versions."

The helpers brought over the iron plates. People let out noises of interest and shock as they saw the glaring holes in the plates that got smaller with each pass through.

"This should bridge the gap that we saw in the Sixth Realm," Rugrat said.

"Those orcs would be a lot easier to deal with. Had to dump nearly half a magazine into them," Storbon agreed.

"The rail underneath will allow you to hook up any extras you want: foregrips, bipods, grenade launchers, and so on. For the rounds, although they will have a base formation, you can, of course, put your own spells on them to increase their lethality or base it on the situation that you are in." Rugrat looked over the weapon and shrugged. "That's about it. Any questions?"

"I hate this shit." Rugrat scowled at Erik. The two of them shared a room still. Rugrat sat back in his chair as Erik checked his rifle.

They were both taking a rare break from their cultivating. They had been pushing their bodies so hard that when they had undergone medical examinations, the medics didn't know whether they would be able to heal the hidden wounds if they continued. The two men, although determined, weren't suicidal, and they didn't want a repeat of what had happened to Rugrat. Now, if their bodies were to break, the power that would be unleashed would be no small thing.

"What?" Erik checked the metal he was cleaning and then scrubbed it harder with his brush.

"Sitting here and waiting while people are acting out in the Ten Realms. All the CPD teams of the Dragon Regiment are out there attacking the Willful Institute. There is just a month to go until the fighter's competition in Vuzgal. We're sitting back, having to be figureheads and shit, all rear echelon sitting on our damn hands," Rugrat said.

"This is our job." Erik put the brush down and started to assemble the weapon.

"I hate this job. Can I just be a soldier?"

"You, just a soldier? Even when we were in, you were never just a soldier. A loud-ass, smart-ass marine maybe?"

Rugrat threw a scrap of paper at Erik, but he felt better.

Erik snapped the weapon together and checked the action. "We have to get through the fighter's competition. Show up, scare the people who think that we're dead. Once that is over and done with, then we can hide in the darkness and maybe work with some of the special teams if they need our help."

"Still, this sitting here and waiting shit sucks."

"How do you think the soldiers in the camps feel? All of them want to join in the fight, but it might only be in the last fights that they come out to show some of our strength and scare others. Really, it is kind of like whack-a-mole. Someone shows up, we go over, scare them, and then they leave us alone. Then someone stronger comes over and we do it all over again. With the strength of Vuzgal and the Adventurer's Guild secured, things should be smoother, and we can focus on increasing everyone's Strength and returning to the Sixth Realm."

"You don't want to go to the Seventh Realm?"

"Most of the people who go to the Seventh Realm don't return. Hell, the only person I know who came down here from the Seventh Realm is that one from the Sha."

"Yeah, those people set me on edge. They have something like rudimentary gunpowder weapons. They usually kill off everyone who tries to imitate them, but instead of killing us, they sent us terms and want to meet us when we get stronger." Lines appeared on Rugrat's forehead.

"The Sixth Realm has plenty of dungeons for us to get stronger in. There is plenty to learn there. Once we have power to reach into the Seventh Realm, then we should check it out. I feel there are a lot of secrets about the

Seventh Realm and higher. We have vague descriptions of what is going on up there."

"First, we take out those Willful Institute dicks."

"First, the Institute dicks," Erik agreed. "Wait a minute…did you…? The mana?" Erik stared at Rugrat.

"I formed my Liquid Mana Core. I'm resting before I try to create my Solid Mana Core." Rugrat's voice was flat.

"Nice work. That's a big achievement!"

"I guess. I wish I were putting it to more work than just sitting here." Rugrat sighed.

Erik grunted. He agreed and started to oil up his weapon.

33 A United Front

Cai Bo's expression was neutral as she marched through the halls of the Willful Institute's headquarters.

A sound-cancelling field wrapped her and Elder Kostic in its embrace.

"Are the preparations in place?"

"Yes, High Elder, all the cities you command are ready and waiting. They have started to mobilize their fighting forces in secret. Are you sure that a war is coming?"

"All of the clans are under attack, and we're summoned by the sect head."

She left him to make his own conclusions.

In the chaos of war, change is inevitable.

Low Elder Kostic walked quickly behind her, followed by other elders of her faction.

She reached the doors to the conference room.

There were six other high elders; each of them had brought their own people with them. Their eyes clashed with one another. They had fought one another in the shadows and within this very room again and again.

None of them dared to speak as they glanced over to a middle-aged-looking man sitting at the head of the table. He waved his hand, commanding all the elders and their supporters.

Cai Bo quickly took her seat. *Head Foster must have figured out what is happening for him to come out of seclusion.*

A woman stepped next to the head. "Four weeks ago, a city in the Fourth Realm was attacked and defeated." The woman's voice was light and uninterested, as if it had nothing to do with her.

One of the high elders grit his teeth as people behind him fought to contain their anger. *How useless are they to lose a city?* Cai Bo sneered internally, showing nothing on her face.

"Recently, resources gathered in the lower realms and presented to us here in the Fifth have decreased. The head wants to know what is happening."

Foster looked around the room. The weight of his gaze made Cai Bo shiver. A cold sweat ran down her back.

The lady waved to one of the high elders.

He stood up with a grim look. "We have been seeing rising food prices in the Second Realm, and many of our sects there have had issues with their stored food. They had to purchase more, and it reduced the amount of money they could spend on cultivation resources. Bandits have grown in number and have been bold enough to attack our caravans of food. We have some trade disagreements in the Third Realm, though we are looking for new suppliers."

Another stood. "There have been some minor fights with other sects in the Third Realm and the Fourth Realm. It is strange to have fights in the Third Realm."

"There were some trade issues with iron ore. The amount they could supply us decreased."

"A guild of adventurers is making some noise in the Third Realm. They humiliated our people, and then a group from the Grey Peak sect used the cover of the competition to steal resources from us. We are gathering people to strike back."

"We had a decrease in contributions with the contract issues with traders. There were bad crops, and some mines have dried up. We have not lost money, but prices are escalating, so resources will be thinner for some time. Once the prices return to normal, everything will be fine," Cai Bo said.

"What the fuck have you idiots been doing while I was in seclusion?" Foster's words shook the high elders.

"One by one, these are small incidents. To each of you who only see one part of the whole, maybe you don't realize what is happening. Tell me this: How many of our locations haven't had a fight in the last three months?"

"Uh, just five haven't."

"Two."

"Eight."

"Nine."

"Four."

"Sixteen."

"Two," Cai Bo said.

"Over eighty percent of our locations have fought in one way or another. Now think of how many are supplying us with resources. Think of how many are having trade difficulties. What do you see?"

Silence fell as the high elders stared at one another. Instead of anger, they communicated with their eyes, and their faces turned pale.

"Do you understand what is happening now? Staring at everything in parts, it looks like small regional issues. The rest of the Institute is fine. When you look at it as a whole, you see that we are under attack."

"Under attack?" a high elder asked.

"Maybe it is a coincidence. Maybe it isn't. There are people from various trading groups and sects hitting our weaknesses. It doesn't matter.

We need to treat it like an attack to regain our strength and assert our power, or else the Institute will be pulled apart in chunks!"

The high elders' expressions changed.

Looks like you figured it out, finally.

Some of them were truly phenomenal actors.

"What are your orders, Head Foster?" Cai Bo asked.

"Settle down the Institute. Use our stockpiles and trade among the branches to relieve the resource issues. Send groups from the higher realms to the lower realms. We will secure our positions in the Second Realm, then the Third Realm, and so on. If we do not have the resources of these lower realms, it will be harder for us to fight. Investigate who is attacking us. Call on our allies to assist us where they can. On the outside, nothing must appear different. We will retain our position in Henghou city. If the other sects learn of what is happening in the lower realms, they will call out their Experts and drown us in fighting requests. Our students will come away with injuries and be unable to cultivate properly!"

"What about the fighter's competition in Vuzgal in two months?" a high elder asked.

"The fighter's competition exists for forces to show their power. We need to show others they shouldn't overlook the Willful Institute! Make sure that we place as high as possible in the rankings. Take down Expert students to increase our standing. No expense should be spared. High Elder Cai Bo, you will lead the group personally!"

"Yes, Head Foster." She stood and bowed, accepting the position.

Powerful figures from across the Fourth Realm would attend this year's competition, as well as people from the Fifth and Sixth Realm. This was the perfect opportunity to watch some fighting and represent the sect.

"If I hear that you are trying to gain rewards instead of fighting for the best interests of the Institute, I will deal with you myself!" Head Foster stood.

The high elders rushed to their feet, cupping their hands and bowing as the doors opened with a bang ahead of the head.

Cai Bo looked at the people in the room. Some stared back at her; others tilted their heads.

She would follow his lead for now, but this sect would be hers—one day.

"The Willful Institute suffered a loss and are telling their people that we attacked them?" the Grey Peak sect's Branch Leader Heidi Storgaard roared as the report was read out.

"It appears that way. They say that the people who robbed their treasury were ours."

"What would we want from the useless Willful Institute?" Storgaard slammed her fist into her chair, cracking the stone.

"What will we do now, Branch Head?" one of her captains asked.

"Send word to the other branches and the higher-ups; send them these reports. Tell them we are preparing for an attack and await their instructions. If the Willful Institute dare to attack, we will call on our people to reinforce us."

"We're just a Third Realm location. Do you think that they will help us?" another captain asked.

"You spend too much time training and not enough time fighting!" she bellowed. "On the battlefield, numbers count. But you know what is more powerful than numbers? Their armors, their weapons, the Stamina recovering concoctions that will enable us to fight beyond the enemy's endurance, and healing concoctions so we don't lose too many troops and we can recover quickly to win the battle. Losing just one city in the Third Realm, the alchemist's realm, will rapidly reduce our combat capabilities in the Fourth Realm!"

The captain clasped his fist and bowed his head. "I was ignorant, Branch Head Storgaard!"

"If a fight comes, you and your forces will be the vanguard to learn the truths of war! Think of this as a learning experience. If you do well, you could all head to the Fourth Realm. If they dare to come out of their city, do you think the Grey Peak sect will be scared? It is within our rights to attack them head-on if they raise arms against us."

"What about this Adventurer's Guild?" asked the man who had brought the report before the leaders of the city.

Storgaard held her chin, her deep-brown eyes deep in thought. "They disrupted Elder Mendes and his people to this extent; they could be useful. Send someone to contact them. If we can use their strength against Elder Mendes and his people, it saves us the effort. In fact, isn't the Red River sect in a minor dispute with the Willful Institute? If we ally with them, wouldn't that give them a reason to attack the Willful Institute?"

The members in the room nodded after some minutes of thinking.

"I am looking forward to the Institute testing out their abilities. It will be a way for us to test our own capabilities as well!" Storgaard laughed, but there was a malicious look in her eyes.

"The Grey Peak sect wants to talk to us?" Jasper glanced up at the messenger in surprise. Blaze was busy organizing everything for the competition in Vuzgal. They had to show their strength there to continue expanding. Everyone who was competing was training in the arena's training rooms and the guild headquarters.

"I didn't think they would approach us." He tapped his pencil on the reports in front of him, thinking. "Accept their invitation. I will head there personally. Send a message to command. Request some of the intelligence agents and military members to come with us."

A week after she had sent the message to various sects, mercenary groups, and the Adventurer's Guild, Branch Head Storgaard was busy checking her gear. She wore light armor, and her weapons were sharpened and cleaned. She was just missing her final layer of armor.

"The Adventurer's Guild representatives are here."

"Ah, I am interested to meet their guildmaster. He is bold to march into the Willful Institute and beat them in their own city!"

"Uh—" The messenger's face turned awkward. "Branch Head, they sent their vice guildmaster. From what I have learned, he is not much of a fighter. He cares for the administration of the guild. The guildmaster is training his people for a competition."

Storgaard frowned. He sent his subordinate? Was he looking down on her? She recalled hearing something about a competition in Vuzgal, but they were just a small guild in the Third Realm. There was no way they would qualify to enter. Still, as long as they agreed to bleed for her sect, it didn't matter.

She checked her attire gave off a war-ready vibe without being outwardly aggressive to her guests.

"Let's head down." She walked across the rough stone room. Beast hides were laid down on the floors while beast heads lined the walls.

Outside the windows, a lush jungle-covered mountain range sprawled into the distance. The city was built into the highest mountain range, protecting the valleys that were broken up into steps where people were growing and cultivating Alchemy ingredients.

Jasper walked with his people along the wall, looking over the area around Reynir

"Good vantage points. Heavy weaponry and spell formations. They've got the entire valley covered. It would be hard for them to deal with multiple smaller forces, but if one force came, they could hammer them with their large-scale weaponry," Niemm assessed as he sat beside Jasper.

Sound-canceling formations were active so that no one could hear what they were talking about or read their lips.

"They have a detection formation that allows them to see where anyone is in their area of operations. Although it might be harder for them to deal with multiple groups, they can send out forces in the different guard houses in the valleys to deal with them," Mister Yi added.

Even the intelligence agent in charge of the Third Realm was tagging along.

"This place is built like a war fortress. The information we have on the Grey Peak sect is accurate. They were a bunch of mercenary groups who banded together and rose through the realms. They have been able to get to this stage because they never operate on their own. They rotate people who have served in the Fourth Realm to the lower realms to prepare them for what is to come," Niemm said.

"Their progress and position in the Fourth Realm are impressive. They haven't entered into a fight they didn't win. They have been hired out by all kinds of forces to bolster other sects' power as well," Jasper said.

"Their population is smaller than the Willful Institute. They don't have many crafters and rely on external sources. But their fighters are strong, and many them have reached the Seventh Realm and higher."

"Not a good group to piss off," Mister Yi replied.

The various sects, clans, mercenaries, and others that had gathered talked and greeted one another.

"A lot of sects are friendly with one another in the Third Realm. The Alchemist Association controls the realm, and few people want to piss them off. So, they play nice. Politicizing is power here, not just one's military might. Look over there—a representative from the Alchemist Association is here as well. Before they do anything, it needs to be okayed by the Alchemist Association or else it will be hard for them to develop in this realm," Master Yi said.

The talking died down as a strong-looking woman with short-cropped brown hair walked into the room. She looked as if she were in her training clothes. She was missing her upper body armor and helmet.

"Well, she knows how to make an entrance." Niemm grinned.

"How strong?" Jasper asked.

Yi moved closer to hear as well.

"Powerful. Body Like Stone stage, possibly looking to break through to the Iron? Mana Cultivation is limited. She has a half-dozen mana gates open. Vapor mana stage? She hasn't condensed liquid to form her core yet."

"Half a dozen in the Ten Realms is a lot," Mister Yi said.

Niemm shrugged. In Alva, it wasn't all that rare. Before someone stepped on the path of Mana Cultivation, they opened all their mana gates. It was one of the first tests that children underwent to find out where their mana gates were and to come up with a treatment plan to open all their gates. The assessment was free, and the cost to open the gates was small, comparatively.

Storgaard greeted the leaders as she walked through the lobby.

"Your cultivation is stronger every time I meet you, Branch Head Storgaard."

"This humble Master was pleased to receive your invite."

"Progress in the Third Realm?" Jasper asked Yi.

"Mixed. We have been instigating things here. It is known that Old Hei passed to the Sixth Realm, and his direct disciple had an issue with the Willful Institute. He didn't come outright and admit there was an issue, but the Alchemist Association has been cold toward the Willful Institute. We inflated these rumors among other groups. It made them bolder, and they have made more applications to the Alchemist Association to deal with the Willful Institute. No matter the mood of the Alchemist Association, seeing so many people turning on the Willful Institute—they aren't stupid to stand in the way of the tide. The Association has lasted for centuries because they know when to step back. They've turned a blind eye to it all while holding out a hand behind their back. As long as they see a return, they will be fine with a change in the Willful Institute's position in the Third Realm."

Storgaard smiled as she walked through the groups, greeting people here and there. She made sure to meet with them all. When she looked at the last group, her eyes tightened. The leader was talking to one of his aides, not caring about where he was.

"Adventurer's Guild." Her aide's sound transmission sounded in her ear.

Storgaard's cheek twitched. The leader, the *vice* guildmaster, seemed to sense her presence as she walked up.

He cupped his fists and bowed his head. "Branch Head Storgaard, thank you for the invitation." The man's words were simple and straightforward. There was no groveling in his tone, no display of his obedience or subservience.

"I heard of your *guildmaster's* actions against Elder Mendes, and I couldn't help but want to meet him." She reached out her hand.

"I am sorry he is not here to meet you. I am Vice Guildmaster Jasper." The man smiled genially.

She squeezed his hand, trying to show her dominance. His smile didn't falter, but his eyebrow arched. It felt like gripping an iron bar; she increased her strength steadily, but Jasper looked confused.

"I heard that he is training some of your members." She focused her Mana Cultivation and shot her aura out—it covered Jasper and no one else—looking to suppress him. She didn't care to humiliate him; she wanted to test his limits.

Jasper scratched his neck. His breathing didn't even change. "I am sorry about that, but we only got a few places in the top ten rankings of the Vuzgal competition last year. With the greater competition this year, we're hoping we can hold on to those spots and get more people in the top one hundred."

Storgaard was so focused on suppressing him with her aura that her mind was slower and turned chaotic for a moment.

"Vuzgal?" she asked as her Mana Cultivation fell on the two men standing behind Jasper.

The man in a black cloak glanced up with a dangerous look in his eye. His finger touched his ring, and the people with him became alert.

She felt as if she stared at a pack of wolves, and she was nothing but an ordinary human. The other wearing simple clothes let out a controlled breath before showing Storgaard a look of displeasure.

She quickly dissipated her aura, and the pressure eased off. The cold, killing intent disappeared from the other members of the group as if it never existed; the simple-looking man faded into the background again.

"Yes, we were lucky enough to enter the competition last year, and we even got a guild house inside the city. Have you heard of it? I heard that the Grey Peak sect is looking to enter some of their warriors into the competition as well?" Jasper said, as if nothing had happened.

"I didn't know you were competing in the Vuzgal competition."

"We are hoping to use it to launch into the Fifth Realm. We are a neutral party unless someone attacks our people. There are many missions that people need to be completed across the realms. We'll take on any mission that will not anger another group."

"That seems hard," Storgaard said. With her background, she knew how difficult it was for independent forces to operate on their own.

"We work mainly with the associations, guarding traders from place to place, as well as crafters. There are also people who want to act in another area, but because of their position and who they are allied with, they can't always be seen to act. We can be that intermediary."

Why do I feel like there are more mysteries behind this association than one can see on the surface?

Her aide cleared his throat.

"Thank you for coming." She clasped her fist.

Maybe having the vice leader here is not such a small thing. They were already looking at getting into the Fifth Realm. To deal with such sensitive missions, their connections couldn't have been small.

She headed to the front of the room and saw the person leading the Alchemist Association cup their hands in greeting to the vice leader of the guild and bow his head deeply.

Vice Guildmaster Jasper cupped his hands, showing that his position was much higher.

The Alchemist Association representative looked pleased to get even this acknowledgment.

She cleared her throat to get everyone's attention. "We have all gotten information that the Willful Institute has not been calm in the last few weeks. They lost several competitions, and their treasury was emptied by an unknown force. They have been trying to pin this on my Grey Peak sect branch. Here, today, I will swear on the Ten Realms with my life that neither I nor my people stole from the Willful Institute!"

The golden light of the Ten Realms descended and then disappeared.

Storgaard stood there, unaffected, and people started to talk amongst themselves.

You all thought that we had stolen from the Willful Institute?

"If they can falsely accuse my branch, will they then accuse others in the area, using that as a reason to attack our branches? They are the ones who have said my branch attacked them. Could it not be that they created the attack themselves, using it as a ploy to attack others? Use it to show their weaknesses? In the last few days, people from the higher realms have been gathering and reinforcing Elder Mendes. The build-up is coordinated. Does it just seem like a simple ploy, or are they trying to expand their territory again?"

The murmurs and talk in the room increased before it settled down again.

"All of us are members of sects no less powerful than the Willful Institute. What I am proposing is that we create an alliance to work together and remove this branch location. It will be a fight restricted to the Third Realm. Few will care. The gains would be too much for my own Grey Peak sect branch to take, but I think that we can come to an agreement between us all under the instruction of the Alchemist Association." She cupped her fist to the Alchemist Association representative, who stood there passively and nodded.

Grand Elder Mendes and his fellow elders all had cold expressions.

"The Grey Peak sect is shameless! They used the cover of the Adventurer's Guild to stab us in the back and steal our treasures!" Elder Tsi slammed her fist on the table.

"How will we have the face to deal with the other factions? We are barely able to keep up our contributions." Elder Rei sighed.

"I have sent word to the people in our faction. This is not something we can hide. Their attack might be the start of something more." Grand Elder Mendes looked as though he had aged decades in just a few short weeks.

The door flew open, and a woman burst into the meeting room.

"You dare to interrupt!" Grand Elder Mendes' power gathered as the anger that rested close to the surface fought to be released.

"Elder Xiao has arrived!" the terrified-looking student said.

Grand Elder Mendes' mind ground to a stop. "He came here? So quickly?" Hui's mind started to turn over when there was a sound of rushing wind. The doors opened wider. A group of people wearing the robes of the Willful Institute walked into the room.

"Elder Xiao!" Grand Elder Mendes bowed to him. He and the people with him didn't suppress their cultivation. They were all in the late stages of the Vapor Mana Core to the early stages of the Mist Mana Core and in their late level forties.

Mendes scanned them. There were members from all the factions. They looked harmonious in their actions instead of the usual bickering between one another.

"Branch Head Mendes, branch elders," Elder Xiao said.

The doors slammed shut behind the group, and formations activated so no one would be able to listen in on their conversations.

"We have been sent with a group of members from the Fourth Realm branches to make an example of this Adventurer's Guild and Grey Peak Sect. Others are watching this battle closely. We cannot appear weak," Elder Xiao said.

Mendes and the other branch elders peeked at one another, surprise in their eyes; some panic but mostly anger.

"We are not the only branch under attack?"

"Just a few weeks ago, one of our branches in the Fourth Realm was attacked by several sects. In just a day and a half of fighting, the city was torn apart and the sects divided it up."

A chill ran through the room, and the elders hardened their expressions.

Seeing them all together, it makes sense. We cannot deal with this in just our factions.

"Elder Xiao, what about the Grey Peak sect?"

"They are a large power in the Ten Realms. If we show them how we deal with the Adventurer's Guild, then they might remember their previous actions and hand back what they took—with interest."

"Well, it looks like things will be harder in the future." Glosil's eyes flicked to the information coming into the command center. There were more operations going on around the clock now. People barely returned to Alva to rest before they were sent out again on a new mission.

"In some ways, yes. The Willful Institute is starting to work together. Their leader isn't in his position just because of his Strength, it looks like," Elan said.

"Kind of stupid to have someone as the leader just because they are stronger. People who are stronger in the Ten Realms are usually stubborn and hard-headed. They have a path to follow, and they'll follow it; they won't be flexible." Glosil shook his head.

"Which is perfect for the next part of our plan."

"When you smile like that, I almost feel sorry for them. What are you thinking?"

"The factions are working together on the surface; it will take time before to truly come together. We can exacerbate some issues, create rifts, and get the factions' cooperation to show faults—elders taking advantage, bribes, favoritism? Assassination or at least attempted?"

34 Progress

"Consortium Leader Quan," Lord Aditya greeted, waving him to his couches.

After all he had seen, the power backing them, he didn't know if he should be awed, terrified, or feel lucky to have picked the right side.

"You look stronger every day! How are things with the sect?" Aditya poured Alvan tea.

"I was able to get some Age Rejuvenation potions. I look and feel like I did back in my prime. With the help of our benefactors, I opened more mana gates and used the impurities in my mana to temper my body. I would not be where I am without their efforts and teachings, or your trust in me," Quan said.

Aditya dismissed his comments with a wave and passed Quan a cup of tea. "We are but two servants to the same master. We have both been lucky!"

Quan saw that there was nothing more to say and drank his tea.

"Things have progressed well with the sect."

Erik sat in the Metal floor. He picked up a piece of metal and tossed it. If this were back in his days on Earth, he would have been scared of cutting his hands. Now, metal shards were like pebbles. He picked up another piece and tossed it.

Gilly let out a low yowl, nudging him.

Erik smiled and scratched her neck as he sat back. "I know, I know. I'm half-broken, can't cultivate anymore while the Adventurer's Guild is out there fighting for us."

Gilly butted him with her head and glared at him.

"I know, Melissa is right. If I keep on pushing at this pace, I could tear my body apart. I wouldn't do it intentionally!"

She butted him again, her eyes narrowing.

"Yeah, I guess you are right. I'm turning that frustration and anxiousness onto myself, trying to distract myself and get as strong as possible, so when I am needed, I can do even more. Being a lord is a pain in the ass." Erik sighed, thoughts floating in his mind.

Maybe it was time for Alva to be officially governed by the council and be made the true power. Having so much authority over everyone was kinda scary.

He sat there, absently throwing rocks and petting Gilly.

"I can't even increase my Mana Cultivation. I've reached a bottleneck in forming my Liquid Mana Core, but my body, as feeble as it is right now, if I were to do it, I could kill myself."

Erik cursed and threw another stone. "Egbert, how is work going with the dungeon?"

"Slowly. The Water floor is huge. I am using the dungeon core here to redevelop the entire floor, remaking formations as I go. Also, with all the floors back under our command, issues I didn't notice before are appearing.

I have to keep going back to fix things on separate floors. Just takes time."

"How long until the dungeon is at one hundred percent?"

"Should be in a few weeks, like after the fighter's competition, I think?"

"That makes me feel secure," Erik muttered.

"You got something on your mind?"

"It's nothing, Egbert. Just training, training, and more training while people are out there fighting for their lives, for Alva."

"Sure doesn't sound like you have nothing on your mind," Egbert said grumpily. He made a noise and stopped talking.

"What is this place?" Ledell stared at the long line of people leading into a small shop.

"Is that Iron Wolf Killer Ledell?" someone in the line asked their friend as he walked up.

Ledell heard them talking and hunched over, looking more ogre than human. Scars and piercings covered his body. Studs stuck in his nose and along his ears.

"What is this place?" he asked one of the people standing in line.

"Momma Rodriguez's Restaurant," a bystander said before turning around; instantly, they backed up and their legs shook.

"Restaurant—is that like the Sky Reaching Restaurant?"

"I-I'm not sure." The person shook out of fear.

Ledell grunted as he glared at the line.

A group of people left, and a young, tanned girl appeared.

"Sorry for the wait. Your table is ready," the girl said to the people first in line and smiled.

This was the Fourth Realm. There weren't even any guards around. Restaurant? He had heard they could make food that would return Stamina over a longer period compared to the potions. *Must be my lucky day to find this place. All those mana stones and no one to guard them.*

Ledell pushed past the group about to go inside.

"Get the next one." He shot them a glare and walked in.

"Excuse me, you need to line up!" the girl said.

"If you know what is good for you, you'll find me a seat!" Ledell said.

"Lusia, is everything all right?" called a voice from the rear of the building. Fierce heat leaked through the swing door.

"He cut the line!" Lusia said.

The door opened, and Ledell looked over. If it were a powerful Master, he could apologize. If not, then he would do as he wanted. The Fourth Realm appreciated tough people. He needed to maintain his outward appearance.

A diminutive woman wearing an apron walked out. Her skin spoke of a lifetime of hard work, while her shoulders showed that she allowed nothing to break her down or bend her back. She held a wooden ladle in one hand casually. "Did your momma not teach you any manners!"

Ledell sneered. "What are you going to do about it?"

He didn't know when she moved, but he felt the smack before he heard it. He jumped up, grabbing his backside with a yell. Tears appeared in his eyes as memories from his childhood appeared.

"You make so much noise!" *Smack!* "Cut in line!" *Smack!* "Are you so much bigger and better than others?!" *Smack!* "You want to get away from Momma Rodriguez?!"

Ledell looked as if he were dancing, jumping up as she struck his backside and then ducking as she somehow reached up and cuffed his head.

How was this happening! *Please! Please, just stop.* "I just want to try your food!" he yelped.

The hits stopped coming.

He had fought wild beasts with his bare hands, even when heavily wounded, but he hadn't even seen this old woman move! No wonder there were no guards. He looked back at the people in line pitifully. They could have warned him!

"I am over here, boy," the lady said.

Ledell's head turned slowly, seeing her standing there with a smoking wooden spoon in her hand. What was that spoon made of? Just looking at it made his cheeks hurt! He had even tempered the foundations of his body.

"You will go out there, and you will apologize to those nice people in line. Then, you will say sorry to Lusia, and then you will wait until I am done with work. Don't make me come and find you." Her eyes narrowed, and Ledell trembled. All thoughts of fleeing were followed by a tanned wooden-spoon-wielding demon.

"Y-yes."

"Yes, Momma Rodriguez," she enunciated, with her spoon.

"Y-yes, Momma Rodriguez."

"Good." She lowered her spoon and turned toward her kitchen, as if nothing had happened.

Ledell apologized to the people in line and to Lusia before meekly walking to the back of the line to wait his turn.

When he sat down, he ordered crawfish boil. He forgot everything as he dug in. Once he finished, remembering what Momma Rodriguez said, he hung around. She gave him small jobs to do: help Lusia, seat people, and serve drinks.

People were nervous around him, but he did as he was asked. It wasn't like fighting, and he admired how relaxed it was, the organized chaos of it all.

As the shop closed, Ledell felt less embarrassed and more fulfilled than he had in a long time. Working with other people and doing simple jobs was nice compared to the everyday chaos of his life.

"Come and take a seat." Momma Rodriguez put down two iced teas. She was outside on a simple bench, staring at the simple road she lived on.

Ledell moved to the other side of the bench and took the iced tea with both hands.

"You might be a good person, but you can't go around bullying others. You will turn into a bad person with all that negativity," Momma Rodriguez said.

She looked tired in the moonlight—a woman who worked every day in her kitchen, preparing ingredients and turning them into fine meals, meeting and greeting people as they came by.

"What is troubling you?" she asked.

Ledell opened his mouth and then closed it. His lies were useless in front of her.

She raised an eyebrow. "I had one son. In our neighborhood, to make some extra money, I looked after the kids. I've seen it all and then some. I had many sons and daughters, nieces and nephews. My boy went to be a fighter, and all the people he met in the marines became my kids as well. Don't try to dodge the question."

"It is the Fourth Realm. If you show weakness, people step all over you. I have to show how strong I am to get dangerous jobs."

"You need to get some friends."

Ledell drank from his cup, feeling somehow worse.

"I don't mean that in a bad way. I just mean that if you are always doing things by yourself, it will be harder."

"How?" Ledell asked.

"First, stop acting like a damn ogre. What is it with all these piercings?" Momma Rodriguez asked.

"They make me look hard."

Ledell rubbed his head; he didn't know when the spoon had tapped him on the head.

"Lose those tattoos. Stand straight up. Stop hunching; it is bad for your posture! You want to stay like that for the rest of your life? Go and talk to one of the mercenary groups and see if you can sign up. Then go on a few simple jobs. Get to know them first."

"But people use one another in the Ten Realms."

"That they do. Watch your back in your line of work. Though I have heard the Adventurer's Guild and Fighter's Association are good groups."

"I have to be stronger to be in those groups." Ledell slumped. A spoon smacked him several times, and he found himself in proper posture.

"Have you tried?" Momma Rodriguez asked, taking a sedate sip from her drink.

Ledell was quiet.

"If you never try, then you won't know what will happen. Others call you a brute. Don't be defined by others. Define yourself."

Ledell was quiet as he sat there, unable to express what he felt. His mind started to turn over.

He felt a small hand on his shoulder. He glanced over to Momma Rodriguez at the end of it.

"And don't cut lines in my shop. If you want to have a meal, line up earlier."

The hairs on the back of his neck rose before Momma Rodriguez broke out into a smile.

"Tomorrow, go and apply to the Fighter's Association and Adventurer's Guild, then to the other mercenary groups. And come and tell me how it went. I'll give you a ten percent discount!"

Why do I feel that I am going to be spending all my money here? Though he couldn't complain. The food was really good.

35 Gearing Up

Rugrat looked through the store window. There were all kinds of drawings on display. Artistic designs, spell designs, formation designs. Some glowed with different mana-imbued colors; others were vibrant inks or simple, plain inks.

Rugrat glanced at his arm and then walked into the tattoo parlor.

There were different rooms where people were getting tattoos, talking to the artists.

"Looking to get some fresh ink?" Moto asked. She had designs running up her neck and down her arms. The lines were clear and powerful. She had piercings along one ear. She had shaved off her hair on half of her head; the other side was longer and half-covered her eye.

She pulled on the herbal-wrapped leaves as if they were a loose cigar. The burning incense helped to recover one's Stamina and keep them alert.

Moto looked to be in a perpetual half-asleep state.

"Same again?" She breathed out. Her eyes shone as she looked at Rugrat's arms.

"Keep staring at me, and I'll think you want nothing more than to pin my tattoos to the wall."

Moto laughed and waved Rugrat back. He followed her. The fragrant smoke smelled like rich cherry wood.

She patted a lounging seat and sat in her own chair.

"Names in the same places," Rugrat started.

"Of course, I have an outline for them."

"I was thinking of dragons and tigers fighting, running up my right arm, leading to my hand. In the web of my right hand, I want an American flag. Left arm, something tribal?"

"That could be fun. Any designs?"

"Surprise me."

"You always give me so many options!" Moto smiled and pulled out a book and passed it to Rugrat.

He opened it and saw spell formation designs. "What are these?"

"Formation tattoos. They're new. We combine tattooing, spell formations, formation creation, and spell scroll creation. We have tattoos to increase Stamina and mana regen, or even healing. We can't increase one's Stamina pool or mana pool, Agility, or Strength—takes too much toll on the body. With those new formation armors, not so useful—though healing and Stamina tattoos are useful for any fighter."

"That's pretty sweet," Rugrat said.

"Put it right on your chest, over your heart, keep you going."

"What about power. Does it pull from the body?"

"No, there is a power formation that can link to it so you're not drawing from your own internal power. You need to keep it within a few of you."

"Sign me up!" Rugrat pulled off his shirt and sat back down.

"Names first." Moto moved the tables around and took a deep puff of her rolled cigarette, putting it to the side.

She pulled out an outline and placed it on Rugrat's arm. Rugrat read the different names, turning solemn as memories appeared. He chuckled, patting his shoulder, imagining patting his friends on the back.

Moto finished up the names and drafted outlines for the rest of his tattoos.

"It's annoying that every time I temper my body or heal my skin, I remove the tattoos," Rugrat complained.

"As if? You can change what kind of tattoos you have. Pretty sweet. More return customers, for sure."

Rugrat laughed. "I guess that makes sense. Easier to change it if people have a new idea."

"You haven't visited me in a while. Not got anything to work on?"

"New weapons are done. I've tempered and cultivated the hell out of myself. If I keep going, I could do some real damage. Don't want to do that again! The fighter's competition in Vuzgal starts in a few days. Need to head up and show the face."

"Aren't you wearing masks?"

"Yeah, but just being there should be enough, right?"

"Weird way to run a city."

"Hiao Xen runs it. We just show up from time to time."

"Glad it's your job and not mine."

"With those new tattoos, I'm sure there will be more people from the army who want to get tattoos. Well, from all of the branches."

"Already, things are heating up. I heard there might be a large fight soon?"

"Maybe. We'll have to see. That is on a need-to-know basis," Rugrat said.

"Just making small talk. Plus, with my oaths, not like I can go telling someone." Moto smirked. "Part of a secret ultra-cool and ultra-secret city. I don't think I would believe myself if I said it out loud."

"The army's production has increased rapidly, going from just getting the extras off the crafting workshops to having seven purpose-built supply compounds, along with all the factories they need to supply the army," Rugrat said to Erik as they reached the gate into Supply Compound One.

"What is it, three in Alva, one in the Second and Third each, and then two in Vuzgal? Overkill much?"

"Just planning. If anything happens, our people can fall back to these positions and have supplies, weapons, and armor ready to go. The locations are known by a few select crafters, officers, and higher-ups."

The doors opened fully, and they walked inside. Gong Jin and the rest of Special Team Three trailed in behind then.

"I'm looking forward to getting new gear, though breaking it in is always a bitch," Erik said.

"Nothing sexier than new armor and weapons," Han Wu said.

"Or new explosives?" Gong Jin said.

"Oh, I like it when you talk dirty, Sarge."

Rugrat snorted.

"Like you can laugh. Are you any different? You and your gun porn," Erik added.

Rugrat's face turned dark as the special team members fought to keep their lips under control.

They passed through ID checks then through more locked doors before they entered the supply compound. Factories were working at full production speed. Recruits filed in, staring around with wide eyes as their training sergeants and corporals got them into order in front of boxes of kit filled with everything they would need from canteen to carrier, socks to helmet.

Airborne members were working with engineering crews to get their aerial mounts fitted with armor and weapons fresh off the assembly lines.

"Recruiting has accelerated with the opening of the sect—mercenaries from Vermire, recruits from the Adventurer's Guild ranks, and members of the Beast Mountain Range army. The recruits from Vuzgal are being trained by the forces based there. There are air and ground force trainers. Squads are training every day in the new dungeons, fighting endless waves and all kinds of creatures. Their leveling up speed is impressive, and it allows them to get real combat experience," Erik said.

"We're not just holding off a beast wave with twenty or so guards from Alva," Rugrat said.

Crates of ammunition were collected by carts to be taken to distinct armories and supply dumps. Rations, clothing, armor—all of it was collected and sent out.

"How is the re-armoring going?"

"The new formation-enhanced armor has been issued to the units deployed in combat operations. Four companies have made the switch—all army units. That should double in the next two weeks with the airborne getting the armor as well," Rugrat said.

Gong Jin and some of the team members walked ahead, opening the door into a building that looked like a bunker. They cleared the area.

Rugrat and Erik walked in and found Taran there.

"So, you got the good stuff for us?" Rugrat asked.

"Please tell me it doesn't follow Rugrat's naming scheme," Erik muttered.

"No butt-chaffing ass greaves around here." Taran smirked. He led them through some gates. They reached a room with racks of supplies on them. There was everything from socks and underwear to brand-new carriers and mag pouches.

"First, protection." Taran went down the racks and waved his storage ring, collecting items. He returned to the long table and looked at Gong Jin. "Since you're here, you get new gear too."

He waved his hand, and boxes appeared. "Formation-enhanced armor, extended range, level-three protection." Taran opened a box. Inside, there was a front and back plate and side armor plates.

Formation Armor Plate (Front/Rear) Extended Range Level III

Defense:	457
Weight:	7.2 kg
Charge:	10,000/10,000
Durability:	100/100
Slot:	Takes up Front/Rear Armor slot. Requires Carrier.

Innate Effect:

Increase defense by 5%

Socket One:

Empty

Socket Two:

Extended link—Link to more sets of armor (3km Range)

Requirements:

Agility 58

Strength 47

Formation Armor Plate (Side) Level III

Defense:	213
Weight:	5.3 kg
Charge:	1,000/1,000
Durability:	100/100
Slot:	Takes up side slot

Innate Effect:

Increase defense by 5%

Socket One:

Self-Heal—Increase natural healing by 3%

Socket Two:

Stamina Rejuvenation—Increase Stamina Recovery by 2%

Requirements:

Mana Pool 35

Strength 51

With the sound of tearing Alvan rip-tape, everyone took off their vests and opened them. They worked in twos, one holding the carrier's material and the other holding the plates inside as they fought to pull out the plates.

"I hate changing side plates," Rugrat said as they finished pulling out his and Erik's.

"The front and back plates are much easier." Erik pulled out the padding and the plate on the front and rear.

"I knew I was forgetting something. This is a new padding." Taran passed them thick blocks that fit behind the armor plates. "Should take more of the impact and a few more hits without changing your point of aim."

He started to take out long-sleeved shirts and pants that had armored knees. He checked them against the different people, changing out different sizes. "Good, firm support. Set of these and your Tropic Thunder Gloves—damn, you'd be a hit in any marine base."

"Dude, you're fucked." Erik finished replacing his plates and padding and grabbed a pair of pants.

"Heh, couldn't not!"

Combat pants (reinforced knees)

Defense:	81
Weight:	1.3 kg
Charge:	1,000/1,000
Durability:	100/100
Slot:	Takes up Pants slot

Innate Effect:

Increased tensile strength 5%

Camouflage clothing will make small alterations to blend into the environment.

Waterproof

Formation One:

Heat regulation—will maintain comfortable temperature in hot and cold climates.

Requirements:

Agility 31

Strength 27

Combat shirt

Defense:	65
Weight:	0.7 kg
Charge:	1,000/1,000
Durability:	100/100
Slot:	Takes up Shirt slot

Innate Effect:

Increased tensile strength 5%

Camouflage clothing will make small alterations to blend into the environment.

Waterproof

Formation One:

Heat regulation—will maintain comfortable temperature in hot and cold climates.

Requirements:

Agility 31

Strength 27

"Clothes, as you might know, can't handle that many formations, but they can have more innate effects. These pants and shirts try to blend with your surroundings and keep you dry and warm. Also, they're hard to tear. You lot are driving the tailors nuts with your rapid movements."

Taran threw out drop pouches and medical bags. "Eyes here! These drop pouches are selective storage devices!" He pulled out a magazine and put it into the drop pouch.

"Dump what you need in here. It will remain like this unless you close it." He closed the top of the drop pouch and opened it. There was no magazine. "Ta-da! The magazine is stored away. You can set it to accept everything or just when you close the drop pouch!"

He picked up the medical pouches and opened them. "These are new-issue medical pouches! Open yours as well!"

Erik looked inside.

"Erik, you were the one who designed these things?" Taran said.

"Inside, you have two IO devices. Apply these to the IO locations in the shoulders, under the knees, and above the ankles. They will automatically drill into the patient. There are also two IV needles. There is one potion pack, with three units of Stamina potions to one unit of healing potion. Medical scissors to get through clothes. Chest seal is pretty self-explanatory. Make sure you have them in a position to drain blood if you can. Gauze to plug that wound, bandages to hold it in place, a fourteen-gauge catheter if people get tension pneumothorax, duct tape to hold shit in place, a treated gauze with a clotting powder embedded into it, and a tourniquet. These basic kits should deal with most issues. You can do self-aid or buddy aid, even with a fucked-up hand, till a medic can get to you.

"Pack them up with the things you'll need first in an emergency last so you can grab it first. Tourniquet to start, scissors, then have chest seal, clotting gauze, normal gauze, bandage, IO and IV kits, catheter, duct tape at the end. Oh, also have a casualty tag. If you do not have a pen anywhere else, keep one here. Write on the patient's forehead and chest if you can. If you're working on yourself, use the casualty tag. The potion bag contains two hundred milliliters of the good stuff. Deal with the bleeds and get it into you as quick as possible. Healing and Stamina formations will help you out, but they're general. Plug the potion bag closest to the site of the wound. You won't have much time with the bag, but you should have extras in your storage rings. Remember to use your patient's equipment before you use yours. Unless you are the medic."

Erik saw them all digesting the information.

"On the topic of self-aid formations, some of the formation masters have created a new type of tattoo that you can place on your body. It will passively heal and link to a power device you can hold on your belt or vest," Rugrat said.

He pulled down his shirt, showing a formation tattooed on his chest, and held out a small pouch on his belt. He popped it open, revealing an Earth-grade mana stone and formations surrounding it. "The tattoo can be removed later."

"Great, looks like I need to get a tattoo now." Erik packed up his medical kit.

"If your body will let you. Need to make some new needles to get through your chest. Also, it might be destroyed with you tempering your body. I had to get my tattoos redone. Kind of sweet, being able to get a different set of tattoos."

"I wondered if they looked different."

They got extra sets of clothes, and Erik checked the rest of his gear. It had been repaired and maintained since returning from the Sixth Realm.

Tropic Thunder

Defense:	157
Weight:	1.8 kg
Charge:	1,000/1,000
Durability:	100/100
Slot:	Takes up Glove slot

Innate Effect:

Stores blood energy

Socket One:

Blood drinker—Consume blood from opponents to increase attacking power.

Socket Two:

Mana strength—Increase the power of mana spells/attacks.

Requirements:

Agility 41

Strength 51

Commander Helmet MK2

Defense:	387
Weight:	4.5 kg
Charge:	10,000/10,000
Durability:	100/100
Slot:	Takes up Helmet slot

Innate Effect:

Increase defense by 5%

Socket One:

Vision projection—See through helmet's armor.

Socket Two:

Clean air—Air is cleaned and temperature regulated

Requirements:

Agility 42

Strength 42

MK7 Semi-automatic Rifle (FAL)

Damage:	Unknown
Weight:	4.25 kg
Charge:	10,000/10,000
Durability:	100/100

Innate Effect:

Increase formation power by 12%

Socket One:

Punch Through—Penetration increased by 10%

Socket Two:

Lightning Round—Attacks numb and slow enemies by 3%

Range: Long range

Attachment: Underbarrel Grenade Launcher

Requires: 7.62 rounds, 40mm grenades

Requirements:

Agility 53

Strength 41

Healer's Hands

Weight: 0.3 kg

Health: 100/100

Charge: 100/100

Innate Effect:

Increase mana spell's effect by 5%

Enchantment:

Assisted Recovery—Patient's Stamina recovery increases by 5%

Requirements:

Mana 40

Mana Regeneration 50

He was waiting for a new rifle; there wasn't currently anything better than his helmet and gloves. Having both meant he could do more healing, and if he was really needed, he could put on the Tropic Thunder gloves.

"How long until I can get one of your rifles?"

"They are still going through testing with the army units. Once tactics are ironed down, more of the rifles will be available." Rugrat spoke like a senior to his junior.

"You got the rest of the team to work overtime to make your rifle."

"It's awesome, right?" Rugrat pulled out a large rifle. It had a meter-and-a half-long barrel; four cooling blocks ran down it. It had a bipod forward and a short cut-down foregrip behind.

"Gun porn."

Rugrat's face twitched as he heard Erik's "cough."

They got changed into their new gear; some replaced gear that had broken. The old armor plates were tossed into a bin to be passed to new recruits if they were in good enough condition or to be melted down and turned into the next gen plates.

"These are the new stealth sheets and formation-tapped rounds." Taran tossed out boxes of ammunition and then sheets.

They passed magazines around. They had color-coded stripes on the tip of the bullet for what type they were. Silenced rounds were the most popular.

"Silencers too."

Everyone checked the new silencers. They had just one formation on them to remove the sound. They would silence the weapons and the rounds.

Erik checked the magazines, taking explosive round-filled magazines, silenced rounds, non-lethal lightning rounds. He pulled out his rifle, sliding on the silencer and snapping it into place over the barrel.

Stealth Sheet

Defense:	10
Weight:	2.3 kg
Charge:	1,000/1,000
Durability:	100/100

Innate Effect:

Waterproof

Thermal insulation—Will not allow any heat or cold out of the sheet

High-grade camouflage—Will replicate the look of the ground underneath

Formation One:

Stealth—Will replicate the ground underneath the user.

Requirements:

None

"Those things are sweet. Real pain in the ass to track anyone down in," Gong Jin said.

"Short power life when the formation is active. Should last about three minutes off internal power."

"So, charge them before heading out and whenever you can," Rugrat said.

"Yeah, and a really cool feature"—Gong Jin pulled on tabs on the sheet—"these can attach to your carrier. You jump on the ground, pull the top of the sheet over your head, and you disappear. Can even crawl with this thing on you. There's another tab you can hook to your upper legs and helmet. Easy to pull it off if you need. Great for recon ops, even if you don't power up the formation."

"The newer versions will have a second formation that will allow you to power with a remote power device, like Rugrat's new tattoos," Taran said.

"Damn, this is some comfortable gear." Erik moved in his new clothes as they headed out of the compound.

"Zhou Heng and his people know how to make a nice pair of pants and shorts!"

"You can barely call those things shorts."

"Girls have miniskirts. I have short shorts."

Erik rolled his eyes as he pulled out a necklace and a mask.

Shadow Mask

Weight:	0.3 kg
Health:	100/100
Charge:	1,000/1,000

Innate Effect:

Stealth coating—Requires Master-level spells to see through mask

Enchantment:

Mana Aura concealment—Hides one's Mana Cultivation

False impression—Create a fake face under the mask

Requirements:

Mana 45

Mana Regeneration 64

Amulet of Conceal

Weight: 0.5 kg

Health: 100/100

Charge: 1,000/1,000

Innate Effect:

Increases formation effect by 7%

Enchantment:

Body concealment—Hides one's Body Cultivation.

Body of Shadows—Distorts one's body when perceived through spells

Requirements:

Mana 53

Mana Regeneration 71

Erik put on the mask and the amulet. Then he pulled out the emblem of the city lord and affixed it to his cloak.

Rugrat changed as well, while the special teams pulled on their armored helmets. The aura around them changed. People bowed their heads in greeting and moved to the side as the cloaked party passed.

Rugrat whistled as they neared the totem.

The sound of wings and feet could be heard. They paused before the totem defenses; the special team mounted up as George dove in from above, landing next to Rugrat. He wore all new armor; his eyes were clearer, and there was a sense of maturity.

Gilly came to a stop next to Erik. She wore her own armor as well.

"You're growing again, aren't you?" Erik patted her back and jumped up. Two lumps had started to form above her shoulders and ran down her sides. She leaned forward more now as her front limbs were growing out and thickening.

She turned her head to look at Erik.

"Let's head to Vuzgal."

Gong Jin and his team moved around Erik and Rugrat on their own mounts before they headed through the gates of the totem's defenses.

In a flash of light, Alva disappeared, and real sunlight shined down upon them. The totem was packed with people coming and going, orderly lines moving in each direction.

Quest Completed: City Leader 2

You have unlocked the City Leader Quest Line. Grow your territory and your population, and protect what you have.

Requirements:

Have a permanent population of at least 100,000 for 3 months

Rewards:

+10,000,000 EXP

Attackers stats decrease by 15%.

Able to create two (2) village cornerstones.

Can name Successor(s).

Quest Completed: City Leader 3

You have unlocked the City Leader Quest Line. Grow your territory and your population, and protect what you have.

Requirements:

Have a permanent population of at least 1,000,000 for 3 months

Rewards:

+100,000,000 EXP

Attackers stats decrease by 15%.

Defenders stats increased by 10%

Able to create five (5) village cornerstones.

You have reached Level 61

When you sleep next, you will be able to increase your attributes by: 5 points.

99,218,195/136,700,000 EXP till you reach Level 62

Quest: City Leader 4

You have unlocked the City Leader Quest Line. Grow your territory and your population, and protect what you have.

Requirements:

Have a permanent population of at least 10,000,000 for 3 months

Rewards:

+10,000,000,000 EXP

Upgrades to defensive formation.

Increase in city's Mana density.

Able to create (20) village cornerstones.

"We'll have to build another totem soon," Rugrat said, moving screens around.

Gong Jin led them toward the exit. People stared at them and their mounts. The special team members had all kinds of mounts now, one of the privileges of their position.

Erik and Rugrat quickly cleared the screens, waiting for somewhere more private.

The beast trainers had excelled with access to all kinds of different environments and training the beasts in the combat dungeons. Each beast was battle tested and true alphas of their race.

The mounts near the totem shied away from their powerful auras, bowing their heads. Some of the weaker mounts were shaking.

"Making a ruckus with their mounts—who do they think they are?" one merchant demanded as his leading beast was filled with fear and stopped moving forward.

"Friend, if you want to have your head cut off, please do it with other passengers," a noble-looking man sitting beside him said in a low whisper.

"What do you mean?" the trader asked indignantly.

The group headed toward the gates out of the totem. Members of the army and the police saluted and moved to the side, opening the gate and allowing the group past.

"Allowing them into the city without checking their information. They must be from the guilds or the associations," the trader said with a pale face.

"Even the Adventurer's Guild has to be checked before entering Vuzgal. I heard that the Fourth Realm Blue Lotus leader had to go through a brief inspection," the noble-looking man said.

"Then who are they?" the trader asked.

"Did you notice the masks and the emblems on those two men's chests?"

"It looked like the tower at the center of Vuzgal."

"I have seen that symbol once before, but it wasn't as grand. Hiao Xen wore it. Those two…I think they're the city lords."

"The city lords?" The trader shook, just as his beast had earlier.

A carriage waited for Erik and Rugrat. They quickly stepped inside.

Ten Realms Experience flooded their bodies.

Rugrat laughed. "Shit, I just leveled up and got some titles."

"Same here. Damn, they've been working hard." Erik pulled up his stat sheet.

Name: Erik West	
Level: 60 (+1)	Race: Human
Titles: *From the Grave II* *Blessed By Mana* *Dungeon Master IV* *Reverse Alchemist* *Poison Body* *Fire Body* *City Lord III* *Earth Soul*	

Mana Reborn *Wandering Hero*	
Strength: (Base 54) +51	1050
Agility: (Base 47) +72	654
Stamina: (Base 57) +25	1230
Mana: (Base 27) +79	1166
Mana Regeneration: (Base 30) +61	73.80/s
Stamina Regeneration: (Base 72) +59	27.20/s

Hiao Xen was in his office, looking over Vuzgal. There was a knock at the door.

"Come in." He turned back from the gardens and Vuzgal. The door opened, and Erik and Rugrat walked in.

They pulled off their masks as their security detail waited in the lobby.

"Hiao Xen." Erik smiled and shook his hand.

"Erik, Rugrat." He nodded in greeting, smiling as he shook Rugrat's hand and waved to the couches. "I heard you were back in contact some time ago. I wondered how long it would take before you appeared here."

Rugrat pulled out tea, waving Hiao Xen off as he made to pull out his own tea set.

Hiao Xen smiled awkwardly. Some things they copied from the Ten Realms, and other habits came from wherever they came from.

"We had some things to take care of. Once the competition is over, there is more work to be done," Erik said.

The two looked grim but Hiao Xen didn't press. There were many secrets he didn't know.

Rugrat passed out cups.

"Chonglu sends his apologies. He will be here shortly. He had some tasks to handle and was kept back."

Hiao Xen took a sip of tea. His whole body felt rejuvenated. "Good tea!"

"Thank you. Never was much of a tea drinker, but I've been getting into it more and more," Rugrat said.

They went through the reports on expansion, the academy, and the crafters.

"The crafter dungeon underwent a transformative change, nearly doubling in size and adding in many more Expert-level workshops. There are ten or so mid-Expert-level workshops. The combat dungeons also increased in size, and there are a few mutated types."

There was a knock at the door.

"Come in!" Hiao Xen said before it opened, revealing Chonglu.

"Sorry I am late." Chonglu cupped his fist and bowed.

"You are running one of the largest fighter's competitions seen in the Fourth Realm—being a little late is fine. We just finished going over everything happening in the city," Erik said.

"Which brings us to the next part of the meeting. Talking about the future." Rugrat waved Chonglu over.

"We can't go into it too much, but things might change here in the future. Hiao Xen, what do you think of Chonglu's ability to run the city?"

Hiao Xen's eyes widened before he sat back. "I think that he is ready to take over. It is a lot to do, but he has the staff and people here to support him. He has been grooming another to take over his position in the Battle Arena."

"He needs some more training. You met him before—retired Captain Quinn and his people. I hired them and trained them up to deal with any issues that might arise with the Battle Arena," Chonglu said.

"Good. And we want to be clear. We want to do this not because we do not appreciate your work. If we could, we would hire you away from the Blue Lotus, but it's your home," Erik said. "For now, we'll keep it quiet, but after the fighter's competition, Quinn will take over the operations of the Battle Arena. Chonglu will start to take over city-wide operations, and then we will release you from our contract to do as you want with the Blue Lotus. You have done so much for us that we can't possibly give you enough to express our thanks."

"I appreciate the gesture. Being in this position, although hectic, I have been learning every day. I have met new people and contacts who I would have never met in my previous position in the Blue Lotus. Being the acting city lord of Vuzgal has been an honor. With such an achievement, I'm sure that I will be able to help you in the higher realms once you come to visit." Hiao Xen smiled. "I'll miss Vuzgal. It was an honor to be trusted with the city. Though I am also excited to return to the Blue Lotus."

"You are always welcome back. Many people will miss you here," Chonglu said.

Hiao Xen was touched. He felt heavy and light at the same time. Moving on was as hard as it was exciting. He missed friends he had made over the last few years.

"I do have a small request," Hiao Xen said, feeling guilty.

"What?" Erik asked lightly.

"Dougie…I have worked with him closely for so long; he feels like an extension of myself. I have not asked him personally. I wanted to check with you first. As I return to the Blue Lotus, with your blessing, I would like to recruit him as my aide."

Erik and Rugrat glanced at each other and then at Chonglu.

"Although I would appreciate Dougie, I have people I can bring in as aides," Chonglu said.

Rugrat nodded to Erik.

"Very well. We will allow it."

Hiao Xen released a pent-up breath. "Thank you." He made to stand but found Rugrat's hand on top of his own, holding him in place.

"You're our friend. Please."

Hiao Xen was touched. They had gained incredible power but had never let it go to their heads. They had made him an acting city lord, someone from the Blue Lotus, and trusted in him.

He thought of how Erik spent his time helping his son, how he had saved the people from the Blue Lotus, was ready to wage a war over Dougie. *Friendship is truly the one thing that can't be bought or sold.*

"People wish to meet with you—the branch head of the associations, guildmasters, alliance leaders, powerful traders, and such," Hiao Xen said.

"Do we have to?" Rugrat winced.

"I slimmed it down to the people you should talk to. The traders were mostly dealt with by Elise. I spoke to the various sects and alliances, but there are some I think you might be interested in talking to. I discussed different agreements, trade routes mainly. Although the agreement is in place, the Ten Realms places a lot of emphasis on leaders meeting to talk and sign the agreement. You should meet with the branch head to show them face. All of them are looking to expand on your current cooperation. Some don't want to talk through someone from the Blue Lotus. Others just want to do it in person."

"Here I was thinking that we would only need to watch the fights," Rugrat muttered.

"You *are* the city lords." Hiao Xen smiled.

"I feel like wrangling these two into meetings will be harder than the rest of my job," Chonglu muttered.

Rugrat and Erik's expressions turned dark.

"If you show up, that is," Chonglu amended.

Hiao Xen cleared his throat as Erik and Rugrat's eyes twitched.

Too accurate, Chonglu. Good luck! Getting them here even a few days earlier was hell, but you can do it!

Erik and Rugrat were the first to look away.

"All right, we'll meet with the different branch heads." Erik slumped, defeated by the administration.

Blaze watched the various screens that showed his Adventurer's Guild training. Trainers from across the realms were with his people, assessing them and eking out every bit of potential.

The training technique Erik and Rugrat had created was powerful and came with a lot of information, taking into account one's nutrition, activities, and fighting style. When he was training, he was always focused on getting better weapons and learning stronger fighting techniques. He never thought about the role nutrition took in it all. The new weight training and resistance training allowed them to fully utilize their power. Blaze shook his head.

There was a knock from the door. He pressed a formation and opened it. "Emilia," he greeted.

"Hey, boss. I have the latest results." She walked into the office, her eyes turning to the screens that displayed the trainees.

"How do you think this batch is doing?" Blaze asked.

"They're as strong as we were last year. Though we took the competition because no one knew who we were and there weren't that many people competing. This year's competition is going to be much harder. There are so many powerful people competing."

"It will make things more interesting." Blaze took the reports and went through the information. "Good. Everyone's cultivation has increased faster than we predicted. This total body coaching has changed everything."

"I thought that it was useless when we started, then I spoke to some of the people from the army. When they go through their medical certification, they have lessons on training other people. It allows them to accelerate their growth and draw more power out of what they already have. Knowing how fast they can run or how much they can lift gives them new goals to overcome. Did you hear about the twenty percent loss?" Emilia asked animatedly.

"I was just thinking about that. People were actually using twenty percent less than their overall power, and only in life-and-death situations were they using their total power." Blaze nodded.

"With all the weight training, resistance training, and putting numbers to everything, we can push our bodies to the limit and draw out that power safely. Then learn to maintain that output and how to scale it up and down."

"How are you feeling about the competition?"

"I don't think we will place as well as we did last year, but I'm excited for it. Though will this change things about the attack?"

"The Grey Peak sect is organizing it. The Willful Institute is gathering their power and allies. These things take time. It should be another month before the fight starts."

"What if they move things up?" Emilia rested her hand on her sword.

"Well, there are more people in the guild than just us. Under the command of Domonos, they will lead the attack and then we will move to support as needed. Don't forget that this is a Third Realm city. They have reinforcements that have been fighting in the Fourth Realm, but they're in the low level fifties. They could've gone to the Sixth Realm but are here fighting instead."

"We have plenty of people in the level fifties, though they might not be as experienced."

"Correct. And I will be sending down ten adventuring parties to assist in the attack. The announcement has gone out that the guild will pay for the transport of anyone in the Third Realm to join the battle."

Emilia took in a cold breath. "Are you sure about that? There will be a lot of people willing to go."

"It will bring the guild closer together, show that they are united. It is rare for all the members to meet up. This will bind them together. While they show the Willful Institute what happens when they mess with us, we will have to do the same here."

"What do you mean?"

"I heard that the Willful Institute is sending down a high elder from their council to oversee the fighter's competition. They will be bringing some of their elites. I don't care about our placement in the overall competition, but I want to beat those bastards!"

Emilia grasped her sword. "If they dare to come, even if we have to break our bodies, we will take them down!"

"Don't be so drastic. This is the beginning of our fight," Blaze warned.

"Isn't that why we have powerful healers and concoctions?"

"There are things they can't help you recover from."

"Don't worry, Guildmaster. We will teach them a lesson. From the Fourth Realm to the Second Realm, we will tear them out by the roots."

A hot feeling buried deep in his bones started to emerge.

Your people came for ours, to rob and to murder them. You might have turned a blind eye to it all, but we do not. For our fellow guildmates, for our fellow Alvans. For your attempt on our dungeon lords.

Blaze shook with rage. These people had saved him and his. They had protected him or been under his protection. His rage had reached a point where it could no longer be held back.

The Willful Institute will be our steppingstone, our example to others. Do not test Alva or those under its protection.

36

Vuzgal's Second Annual Fighter's Competition

Erik and Rugrat stood at the top of Vuzgal. The grand tower that supported the massive mana barrier array had been returned to its previous glory. Formations ran down the interior of the tower, modified by the dungeon core hidden underneath.

In the morning light, the carved and filled runes along the tower shone blue and silver in contrast to the white stone.

Erik pulled up his character sheet. He'd taken a power nap with the aid of sleeping powders and input the five attribute points he'd got from leveling up.

Name: Erik West	
Level: 61	Race: Human
Titles:	
From the Grave II	
Blessed By Mana	
Dungeon Master IV	

Reverse Alchemist *Poison Body* *Fire Body* *City Lord III* *Earth Soul* *Mana Reborn* *Wandering Hero*	
Strength: (Base 54) +51	1050
Agility: (Base 47) +72	654
Stamina: (Base 57) +35	1380
Mana: (Base 27) +79	1166
Mana Regeneration: (Base 30) +61	73.80/s
Stamina Regeneration: (Base 72) +59	27.20/s

He had placed all five points into Stamina. His Strength and Agility were high in stat points alone, and his Stamina was lagging behind.

Erik waved the character sheet away and looked over Vuzgal, taking in a deep breath of the crisp early morning air coming off the surrounding mountains.

Smoke rose from workshops that never ceased work. Traders were already heading through the totem and out of the five gates that connected to the Eastern and Western Roads.

Erik used the Eagle Sight spell. He looked at the secondary mana towers that ringed the inner city. Undead beasts and skeletons were powered down, waiting to be called on. Members of the Alva military patrolled the towers, scanning the city below. Erik's vision blurred as he looked down to the base of the tower and the wall below, taking in the patrolling guards, gates, and checkpoints.

Erik pulled out his standard rifle, which he had mounted with his four times magnification scope. He cancelled his Eagle Eyes and used the short wall as a brace to aim at the outer wall. Nicknamed Bunker Way.

Erik looked at the barracks and command towers that dotted throughout the city. The city's planning was first focused on defense and movement second, and it showed.

All the command centers could cover one another. The barracks were set up to quickly deploy reserve forces and have artillery platoons manning them constantly. They were set back from the exterior wall, so even if the wall was taken, they could continue to fire. Erik thought they would do away with the wall, but it made it easier to manage people visiting the city.

The wall was broken into three sections; the left and the right flank were on a forty-five-degree angle to the central wall. It was five meters tall with roving patrols. Roads led to ten different entrances. Beyond the wall was Bunker Way.

Tall four-story bunkers stood near the wall, standing above the one-story and two-story bunkers that proceeded them. The bunkers were a self-contained system so one would never see people moving around or know where they would appear. They could be empty or filled with soldiers.

Each of them was buried deep. Breakaway formations and explosives turned them into a death maze if they were breached. They were all built to be moved, so as the city grew, the defenses could be pushed out and upgraded.

Tamed beasts wandered around in front of the bunkers, eating the shrubs and grass, meandering through the barbed wire.

"Looks like this year's competition is going to be even bigger," Erik said, scanning the Battle Arena. Bars and restaurants were already opening while crowds gathered around the Battle Arena. Some were entering the venue to get their seats.

"If there's a fight to be had, the people of the Ten Realms are more than happy to watch." Rugrat turned away, making his voice muffled.

Erik lowered the rifle and turned. Rugrat was studying a big pedestal in the middle of the tower.

"That has to be the biggest formation socket I have ever seen." Erik admired the pedestal covered in dense runes mana, like smoke blanketed it in a haze.

The pedestal was two meters wide and covered with a massive formation. It was a blue-and-silver circle, filled with runes and forgotten script. Triangles and squares were hidden within internal circular formations. The formation was alive with mana, flaring and then dimming, spreading and receding.

"It's a beast. In a half-second, it and all the primary mana formations can activate, covering the entirety of the city in a mana barrier," Rugrat marveled. "Though it is just the fake primary."

"Huh?"

"The towers are a little obvious, right? We have formations to protect them, but they're big damn targets. The really powerful mana barrier formations are located there and there." He pointed to the cliffs that lay to the southwest and northwest of the city and framed the valley the Alchemist Association commanded and the dungeons within.

"Inside the cliffs are four separate formations that, when activated, will create a mana barrier. They're supported by formations built into the Sky Reaching Restaurant towers and the bunker systems. It is much uglier, but it is hidden and much more powerful, with four layers of backups. Even if one formation burns out, the second one can cover for it while another formation comes online."

"Are they all socket based?"

"Yeah, so with some minor repairs, we drop the old formation and toss in a new one. Hmm, that could work with the rail cannons. If we were to put formations on the shells inside the cannon, they're much bigger than the rifle rounds, so we can get more detail and larger formations. I always get the good ideas up here. Well, part of them."

Erik walked to the edge of the tower, looking over to the Battle Arena. Even up here, one could hear the faint noises of the city.

"It gets bigger every damn time."

"The fighter's competition had to be broken down by age group and level this year, just to make it easier. There will be six competitions, between level forty and forty-five, then forty-five and fifty. For each five-level bracket, only people between twenty and forty are allowed to compete. These people are still young, but they have grown enough to be mature in their fighting style."

Erik frowned before he shook his head, getting a questioning stare from Rugrat. "Sorry, I forgot that people in the Ten Realms can live for hundreds of years. Do you wonder what it would be like to live a few hundred years?"

"No clue. I didn't think that I would make it this far, to be honest."

They leaned on the railing, staring at the city below: crafter's district, fighter's district, the new crafter's stadium that was being built. The Battle Arena had expanded dramatically, turning into a wide and large tower to host different fights. The trading districts, crafting districts warehouses, industrial centers. Restaurants, housing, and parks. The Association Circle, where each of the associations had changed their previously humble dwellings into grand buildings that were rarely seen in the Fourth Realm.

The barracks with their arrays to keep prying eyes away. The castle district, the heart of Vuzgal and home to Vuzgal Academy. Today, it was quiet, but the campus still had people wandering across its paths, heading to the libraries or to classes and workshops. Bunkers and hidden defenses were nestled into the cliffs around the valley that Vuzgal stood guard at the mouth of, extending down and around the city.

"If you could, would you go back?" Rugrat looked wistful, but his voice was serious.

Back to Earth? To a place without magic, without Alchemy, Alva? Missing limbs, having to carve out work in a business no one wanted to do and everyone wanting to kill you while you were doing it? To a life without mercenary work, without fighting?

Erik frowned. He would be lying to himself if he said he didn't enjoy fighting. *The rush, feeling alive as if everything led up to that moment.*

"I don't know. Would you?"

Rugrat continued to stare off as the sun rose slowly. "Warriors aren't vital commodities on Earth anymore. There was a time when someone who was good with a weapon was worth their weight in gold. Now, we're a liability and a life insurance payout."

"So, would you?"

"Well, if I learned one thing from the recruiter who had signed me up, it's to read the fine print. I'd only go if I could come back. If not, well, this feels more like home."

Erik clapped Rugrat on the shoulder. "Anywhere you go, brother, I'll be right beside you."

Rugrat snorted. "Alrighty, you mopey shit, we shouldn't be late to this competition."

Erik pulled his hand back and pushed off the railings. "Look at you, being all professional and on time."

"I am for the important things! Cheeseburgers, for instance."

They reached the stairs to the tower, and Rugrat stopped. "Thank you, brother."

Erik simply nodded before Rugrat turned back to the stairs and walked down. "We need a fucking elevator in here!"

"Right, shit! Actually, do we have any of those skeleton mages on birds left?"

"Uh, one sec. Yeah, I can see some in my interface."

"Call them up, or else I'll have stitches all day from these stupid stairs. Why did you want to do them?"

"I was told I was too sedentary, that I should do stairs more often," Rugrat complained as they went back to the banister.

"You, sedentary? Aren't you bashing the shit out of steel all day?"

"Iron, not steel!"

"Whatever—metal, you ass."

"Well, I've been cultivating my mana, you see. Just sitting there all day, bringing in the mana, compressing it! Accept the mana into your core!" Rugrat gave his best impression of a noble sage teaching the world's mysteries. "It's fricking boring, and my ass goes numb from sitting that long! Now I'm getting told that I should move more often! No fricking pleasing some people!"

"You think that's bad? I had some trader offering me damn skincare treatments!" Erik said darkly.

"Okay, well, you do look like a half-charred piece of meat with mercury coming out of you."

Erik's face twitched as they heard an eerie call from beside the banister.

Two undead birds landed in the room.

"What the hell do we hang on to?" Rugrat asked.

"The vertebrae? The mages make this look easy."

"They're cheating with their magic spells. One sec." Rugrat jumped up and cast a spell on himself to chain himself to his mount.

"Did you just use your immobilization chains?"

"Yeah, one magical aerial seat belt. Want one?"

"Sure." Erik shrugged. Spell formations appeared on the creature, and chains wrapped around Erik, securing him to the bony creature.

"Need to add in some damn seats. This is as uncomfortable as hell," Rugrat muttered. "Nowhere near as comfortable as George."

"Was that meant as a compliment?"

"What? He's way more comfortable."

"I guess that's a compliment in some weird way." Erik shrugged and tapped his legs on the side of the undead creature.

With a screech, it jumped off the banister and opened its wings. Faint shadowy wings appeared to catch the air as they banked and circled down the tower.

High Elder Cai Bo looked out of her carriage as it entered Vuzgal. Ahead of her, there was a procession of Willful Institute soldiers marching with their flags raised high. People moved to the side as they were checked and passed by the Vuzgal soldiers.

Cai Bo's carriage was checked briefly by an officer before continuing on.

"The security here is very high," Low Elder Kostic said.

"With so many powerful sects and fighters in one place, this much is expected. Even the head of the Fourth Realm Blue Lotus was checked."

"They can do that?" Mercy Luo, Low Elder Kostic's grandniece, asked before she closed her mouth and bowed her head in shame.

Cai Bo smiled slightly. Mercy was prideful and arrogant, though she had the right to be, becoming powerful and gaining her own loyal followers. Some might think her brutal ways were a flaw, but if used correctly, they could be a warning to others to keep them from crossing her. For someone so young, Cai Bo could see a bit of herself in Mercy.

Low Elder Kostic shot his grandniece a reproving look while Cai Bo looked away, as if it had nothing to do with her.

"There are many powerful forces gathered here. Vuzgal emerged as a power just over two years ago. Already, they host a massive amount of trade in the Fourth Realm and are the base of many crafters, fighters, and traders. They have alliances with different guilds, trading houses, and large sects with their innovative weapons, armors, and supporting formations and gear. Few people want to anger the Vuzgal leadership. With so many interests, if one person were to aggravate Vuzgal's operations, it would cause everyone associated with them to rush in and assist. The Fighter's Association is one of the few groups that are willing to host fighter's competitions. That speaks to how powerful or connected one needs to be to hold a competition like this." Cai Bo studied the people on the street. Weapons and armor were on sale everywhere: Alchemy concoctions, powerful consumable spell scrolls, defensive and offensive spell scrolls.

"Are those mana cannons?" Low Elder Kostic pointed to a nearby store.

Cai Bo's eyes narrowed as she cast an identification spell. "They are, but there are bands of formations around the barrel. I think those adjust the power of the cannon's attack and how fast it shoots. Few people are willing to sell strategic weapons. Sects make them and hold on to them internally. Vuzgal must be fearless to sell these to outsiders. There might be a flaw in them. I would suggest buying a defensive amulet. The seller has to prove their effectiveness. You can find a lot of powerful defensive gear here that one can hide on their person."

The convoy continued toward the Battle Arena. More people filled the streets. Restaurants and taverns were full of people talking about the groups and fighters who would be making an appearance.

Cai Bo's convoy reached the Battle Arena. With quick commands, groups of fighters of varying levels separated from the convoy and headed to register for the competition.

They had brought elites from the fortieth to the sixtieth level, intending to show the other forces that if they wished to attack the Willful Institute, they would pay a heavy price. The Willful Institute nurtured members accepted into academies in the Seventh and Eighth Realm!

Cai Bo's carriage came to a stop before a side entrance. The door opened for her, and she stepped down. Other carriages opened. Elders filed behind her as they walked up to the side entrance.

The soldiers there had an odd expression, but they quickly covered it up. A few checked their tickets and others stood by as backup.

Interesting. They must be wearing powerful formations to hide their levels and cultivation.

Cai Bo and her party strolled into the Battle Arena. With a few directions, they were guided to elevators that took them up through the Battle Arena, close to the peak.

Domonos and Chonglu were in the operations center of the Battle Arena. From here, they could coordinate everything happening in the city and in the arenas. It allowed them to communicate with the higher-ups and be close at hand if they needed to make decisions.

"I'll have to thank your soldiers and medics for once again refereeing the matches," Chonglu said.

"After the last fighter's competition, we got a lot of good recruits and turned them into soldiers. My people use your training facilities all the time. Aren't we both from the same place?" Domonos smiled.

"I guess you are right! I was overthinking. How is the security in the city?"

"We are operating the same way we did last year, but now, we have more police officers. It takes the burden off my sergeants. My soldiers are good at fighting. But they are not police officers. Thankfully, there were no issues last year. I feel better having more cops and just backing them up with my soldiers."

"Any major issues?"

"Some local fights and brawls, nothing much. Just a few warnings so far. Things will probably heat up as people win and lose. With the associations being so close and the high-profile sects and figures here, most people are calmer than last year. Don't want to piss off someone who could turn their life into shit."

"Nice way of putting it," Chonglu said. "I remember you being such a nice young boy."

"You remember me being a training fanatic who was way too arrogant because of his father's position."

"Well, not anymore."

"Yes, that Young Master Domonos doesn't have a place in this new world. Although I hate the Willful Institute, it is because of them I learned the realities of the world and understood what Alva was offering me. If I hadn't lost it all, I would have looked down on Alva."

"The Willful Institute pricks are here," Dominik Zukal said.

"Such a professional, Lieutenant Colonel," Domonos said dryly.

"Not going to compliment the enemy. I'll understand them, respect them, but ain't gonna compliment them."

"He even thinks like me—it's weird."

Zukal rolled his eyes and went back to reviewing what was happening across Vuzgal.

Domonos activated his sound transmission device, listening to the message. "Erik and Rugrat are on their way. I'll go and organize things on the ground and receive them."

"I'll see you in the box." Chonglu checked the screens that showed all the fighters who had qualified to participate in the competition. "Thankfully, we have extra arenas. Why are there so many fighting fanatics out there?"

"The Willful Institute is reinforcing Elder Mendes's Meokar city. They have brought forces from the Fourth Realm. I sent word out to the rest of the guild, and they are mobilizing. Command units from Dragon Regiment have reached us and are organizing at different rally points. I hope you have some savings. We have people from across the realms coming to participate."

Jasper's sound transmission ended, and Blaze lowered his arm, glancing at the group behind him.

The branch heads and the competitors from the guild were there.

There was Kim Cheol and his heavy-armored juniors: Joan with her bow and light armor, Stephan, and the mages. Lin Lei and her assassins were talking lazily and tossing their weapons around. Emilia and her paladins were next to Kim Cheol and his people, checking one another's armor. Derrick was drinking tea, though it wouldn't have been strange if he were drinking alcohol, given the lazy expression on his face.

Blaze pulled out reports and studied them, jotting down notes on a different pad of paper. They had all matured since last year. Instead of worrying about their own strength, they took on others and taught them what they knew. Instead of just being the strongest members of the guild, they were real leaders. Even Derrick paid attention to the operations of his guild branches. This fighting had brought everyone together.

"All right, let's head to the competition." Blaze's voice carried through the courtyard.

Everyone did their last checks and pulled out their mounts. They had no set mounts; they had all kinds of beasts. Most came from Alva. As time went on, more people went for "advanced training" with Alva.

Their gear was among the best one could get. They had adventured across the Fourth and Fifth Realms, carrying out missions and gathering wealth. Fighters were well paid, and the Adventurer's Guild had more quests than they had guild members to carry them out.

There were tons of fighters between the levels of thirty and forty. Some were trying to get money together to head to the higher realms and the academies; others had settled into life in the Fourth Realm.

The new guild members allowed the Adventurer's Guild to enter the Fifth Realm and carry out jobs.

Blaze waved his hand, opening his beast storage crate.

A massive beast as big as a carriage appeared. Her tail stretched out behind her covered in rocky spikes. Her skin was dull black armor plates covered with natural magical runes that sparkled with white light. She looked around lazily, letting out a baying cry.

"You've been sleeping for the last three days, Bassilla!" Blaze pulled out a Metal monster core.

Her eyes, which were filled with complaint, turned to excitement, and she shook her tail. Her entire body quivered, and her tongue hung out of her mouth, drool falling down her chin.

What am I going to do with you? "Sit."

The ground trembled as she sat down. Her tail left scratches on the stone as it moved back and forth. She was taller than Blaze now, but she still had those puppy eyes.

Blaze reached forward and she leaned up. "Sit!"

She planted her butt back on the ground, looking offended.

Blaze held the treat for a few more seconds and tossed the monster core.

She reached out her neck and crunched on the monster core. It only lasted a couple seconds before she swallowed, staring at Blaze for more.

"Come on, we have work to do."

She rested on all her limbs and shook herself. Just being around her, one could feel the power stored in her body.

Blaze jumped on her back. The rest of his group mounted up. Kim Cheol grabbed the flag of the Adventurer's Guild and raised it high.

"Let's go!"

The gates to the guild opened. Kim Cheol was in the lead, and the rest of the guild followed. They made a grand sight on their beasts. They all wore the Adventurer's Guild emblem on their chest, and people moved to the sides of the road.

Other guilds opened their gates and marched out. Blaze nodded to some of the leaders.

They made a powerful procession through Vuzgal, their destination the Battle Arena.

I wonder what this year will bring.

Olivia listened to her sound transmission device.

"They're here," she said to Nadia Shriver, the temporary branch head who had turned into the true branch head in the last few months with the support of Elder Lu.

"It has been a long time since I last saw them," Elder Lu said beside Nadia. He held the hand of his wife, adoration in his eyes.

She patted his hand and smiled back.

It wasn't long till the helmeted bodyguards appeared, preceding Erik and Rugrat.

Olivia stared at them. They never showed up in public without masks and hid their cultivation deep. Was it really them? They could have been switched out.

The two men didn't move to their seats and instead spread out to talk to different people.

"Elder Lu, this must be Lady Lu! I have heard a lot about you," the shorter masked man said.

"Erik, I believe?" She reached out her hand.

"The one and only." He shook her hand. "I see that the pill worked. If you have some time, please come and see me after all of this. I would like to assess you personally. It might not be anything more than what other healers have said, but I'd like to give it a shot, if possible?"

She glanced over to Elder Lu and then Erik. "I don't want to waste your time. But I know it would put my husband's mind at ease."

"I took an oath to help others. If I didn't try, I would be going back on my values."

"Thank you, Erik," Elder Lu said.

"You have done so much for us, and the Blue Lotus has always been kind. We've had some issues in the past, but that was the past."

Olivia tightened, remembering the withdrawal from Tareng to Vuzgal.

"Miss Shriver, I hear that congratulations are in order! You have become the official head of the Vuzgal branch! Your auctions are legendary across the Fourth Realm!"

"Vuzgal has become a truly diverse city, one of the pillars of the Fourth Realm. It would be foolish not to develop in step with you! We might get left in the dust otherwise!"

They laughed, and Erik glanced over to Olivia.

"Commander Gray, you have become stronger since I last saw you. It is good to see you healthy and well. I hope we can put the past behind us." He held out his hand again.

Olivia had wanted to hear those words for so long. Now that she did, she was thrown off. She had seen this moment in her mind so many times.

"Thank you, Lord West." She clasped his hand and bowed her head.

"You were trying to do your best in a shitty situation. I should have explained things instead of keeping it secret. The Ten Realms makes it hard to trust others. Thankfully, I have come to trust the Blue Lotus deeply."

"While the Blue Lotus is a neutral association, with business, we will return trust with trust," Elder Lu said.

What he said was true, but if another power came to fight Vuzgal and didn't threaten the Blue Lotus and its operations, then by their code, there was nothing to be done.

"I understand and thank you for everything." Erik's words lingered before he cleared his throat. "I hope we can talk later, but I have rounds to make. It has been some time since I saw a lot of the people here."

Cai Bo watched the city lords as they arrived.

"Those are the leaders of the associations. Lord West is close to the Alchemist Association, Lord Rodriguez is close to the Crafter's Association, and they are both patrons of the Fighter's Association and Blue Lotus. It's said that they got personal lessons from Klaus, the branch head of the Fighter's Association," Elder Kostic said as Lord Rodriguez and Klaus bear-hugged each other, chuckling and patting each other's backs. Klaus introduced his people cheerfully.

"They are both fighters and reported crafters. Rodriguez is a smith, and West is an alchemist, a direct disciple of Zen Hei, one of the former pillheads of the Third Realm. Zen Hei has since reached Master level in Alchemy and has ascended to the Sixth Realm to teach the younger generation. It is suspected that he will rise to the Seventh Realm soon with his teaching abilities. West has an Alchemy student who has never been seen in Vuzgal. She is supposedly at the Expert level." Low Elder Kostic stealthily pinched his grandniece's side, making her pay attention as well.

Two men walked in, wearing distinct armors and emblems.

"Those two are from the Silver Dragon adventure group and Adventurer's Guild. They had tensions last year at the fighter's competition, but many say they are now brother guilds. They share contracts with each other and have become a powerful force in Vuzgal. Smaller guilds are allied with them to get their protection and connections. They carry out normal mercenary tasks."

Adventurer's Guild? That sounds familiar.

A few moments later, another man and his wife appeared.

"That is Acting City Lord Hiao Xen. In a rare display of gratitude, the Blue Lotus and the lords of Vuzgal reached an agreement, lending him to Vuzgal. Through him, Vuzgal has become what it is now. Those three ladies—that is Tan Xue, the head of Vuzgal Academy, an Expert-level smith; Qin, the department head of the formation masters; and her friend Julilah. They are both supposed to be formation masters of the Expert level. Behind them are the other department heads and some of the Experts from the academy. Based on what I have learned, there are close to one hundred Experts in different crafts in Vuzgal Academy, either learning or teaching."

"Interesting. How were they able to attract them?"

"We are not sure where most of them came from, the Ten Realms being as large as it is. Some were hired, others were groomed. Vuzgal has the highest density of Expert crafters in the Fourth Realm. One Expert crafter from the Blue Lotus tried to use her position to gain power on her side and force the lords into submission. I hear she is now a teacher and that the Blue Lotus reprimanded her.

"Seeing that while a fair place and that Expert-level crafters wouldn't be able to play their games here, other crafters started to come. Most are unaffiliated and just looking for a place to carry out their experiments. Vuzgal has workshops, materials, entertainment, and a platform to discuss with others in their field."

Well developed—the neutrality has made it a haven for many.

"Those two men are the core power of Vuzgal." Low Elder Kostic pointed to two men talking to each other at the side. "Chonglu is the current head of the Battle Arena and is possibly being groomed to be the next acting city lord. His wife is a high-up member of the Fighter's Association. The younger-looking man is Domonos." Kostic pinched Mercy again, making her pout slightly, but she hid it.

"Colonel Domonos Silaz commands the Dragon Regiment, supposedly seven thousand strong. The soldiers we see in this very city."

Mercy shifted and narrowed her eyes, memorizing the faces.

"This Domonos, he must be quite the genius to achieve a high level of cultivation at his age," Cai Bo said. He must have made several breakthroughs as a teenager into his young adult life to remain looking so young. He must have been two or three times as old as he looked to be the head of Vuzgal's forces.

"Elder Cai, we believe that he is less than thirty years old," Low Elder Kostic said awkwardly.

"Julilah and Qin?"

"Younger still. Expert Qin Silaz is Domonos Silaz's younger sister."

"The Silaz family must have a high standing in Vuzgal."

Low Elder Kostic coughed. "Expert Silaz spends her days teaching or locked in her workshop. Colonel Silaz spends all his time training his soldiers. They do not have a family backing them. Few people who are part of Vuzgal have clans. They are frowned upon."

"Why? Clans can create greater competition, and the strongest stand at the top." Cai Bo gave Kostic a sharp look.

"They believe that it only leads to internal strength. They have a philosophy: 'Best person for the job.' Regardless of one's strength or position, whoever is the best person for the job will get it. No clans or forces have been able to bend or break this rule. Some who tried to use their familial connections were found out, and all who were linked to them were fired from their positions, never to be hired by Vuzgal again."

"Not based on strength or connections? How were they able to get this high? Everything in the Ten Realms relies on strength."

"Their ability to negotiate and pull people into alliances is powerful. They have such a small army and train them well. They call themselves soldiers. They have none of the individuality of warriors. They work in groups to achieve results instead of fighting on their own and unleashing their own power. Military contribution points for killing the enemy—they have no such thing!"

"How do they motivate them to fight if they will not get rewards for killing the most powerful creatures?"

"They don't. The army was only engaged in battle once. With close to a hundred people, they killed thousands of warriors from the Blood Demon sect. They were supposedly using projectile weapons like the Sha clans."

"Are they linked?"

"Not that we were able to find in our research."

Cai Bo watched Lord West clap the Adventurer's Guild leader on the shoulder. Blaze smiled and laughed, introducing his friend from the Silver Dragons.

After a quick talk, Lord West and the Adventurer's Guild leader walked to the rear of the box. Lord West signaled Colonel Silaz over, and the three of them walked out of the booth.

A sound-cancelling spell covered Kostic and Cai Bo

"What's the news from the sect?" she asked without turning.

"The Elders are forced to work together. They are trying their usual tricks, diverting resources to their clans and supporters first."

"You have been recording it all?"

"Every transaction we learn about, my Kostic Clan and the Tolentino Clan are having friction but are forced to work together. The other high elders are working to reduce your power while you're away."

"What does the head think? Is he paying attention?"

"He has been in his chambers, but his messengers and people have been moving around. It is reasonable to think he knows most of what is going on."

"Right now, he needs allies, people he can trust to carry out his wishes," Cai Bo muttered.

"Continue to show that the various clans under our control are unhappy working together. We will need to make it appear that I have little support."

"What about the other high elders? Will they not call for your dismissal?"

"If they do, all the better. Foster needs someone he can control. If he thinks that I am clinging to him for protection, then I should do everything to make sure my one remaining support doesn't leave me. It is interesting how people in power always think they can use people who appear weak."

Erik pulled off his mask as he got in the elevator. "Good to see you both again."

"Having fun with the meet and greet?" Blaze asked.

"Rather be out there instead of being stuck here," Erik grumbled as the doors opened to the command center. Vuzgal guards checked them and let them past.

"How are things on your end, Domonos?" Erik asked.

"I got word of the deployment of the Willful Institute just before I came down to see you."

"Seems they are finally getting their shit together. Too bad for us."

"What are your orders?" Blaze asked as they walked into the actual command center.

"Domonos, send out a leader to take command of the battlefield. Use CPD forces from the units in Alva. If we move too much from here, it could be difficult. The close protection squads will be your command and control, and the members of the Adventurer's Guild will be your sword and shield. When the battle comes, Domonos, I want you leading it. Things can change rapidly down there."

"I'll send word to Commander Glosil to request more support. Dominik!"

Dominik, who was checking something with one of the aides, heard his yell and jogged over. "Sirs!" He came to attention and saluted.

"Dominik, you will head to the Third Realm and work with Jasper and the units. I am sending you to create command and control. Hide units within the Adventurer's Guild to support them in the coming fight in Meokar."

"Yes, sir. I'll get things ready for you and head out right away." He saluted again and jogged off.

"How many people can we expect from the guild?" Erik asked.

"The guild has grown to eight hundred thousand strong. I wouldn't be surprised if we get two hundred thousand volunteers, possibly more."

"Meokar is reinforced with a hundred Fifth Realm elders, three thousand warriors from the Fourth Realm, and twenty thousand of the Institute's guards with power comparable to the peak of the Third Realm," Domonos said.

"What about the Grey Peak sect and others?"

"They haven't called anyone down from the Fourth Realm. They could win with swarming."

"Though they're more likely to back out instead," Erik surmised.

Domonos nodded.

"Good thing we'll have those CPD squads. Target the elders and people from the higher realms. The Willful Institute operates with the strongest being their leaders. If we take them out, we can tear out their command and control."

"Yes, sir," Domonos said.

"You were going to do that already, weren't you?" Erik grinned.

"Yes, sir." Domonos smiled.

"Okay, show us what you're thinking. With Blaze here, we can get a preliminary plan sorted out."

Rugrat glanced at Erik as he sat next to him. Around them, people cheered and yelled as people walked out to the hundreds of stages across the Battle Arena complex.

Rugrat used a sound-canceling formation. "Blaze, Domonos?"

"Organizing operations. Things moved faster than we thought in the Third Realm."

"First preliminary matches are about to begin."

Chonglu stood and went to the front of the box. "Thank you all for gracing my Battle Arena with your presence once again! Today marks the beginning of Vuzgal's Second Annual Fighter's Competition!"

All of Vuzgal clapped, excited to watch the matches.

"Let the games begin!"

The yells and applause grew as the fighters on their different stages raised their weapons to the crowd before going to meet their opponents and referees.

As the fighters returned to their corners to start the fight, Rugrat saw one turn and throw a dagger.

The referee who had calmly backed up moved in a blur, appearing in front of the fighter who had thrown the dagger. Holding the hilt of the blade, the referee passed it back to the pale-faced fighter.

With a smile, the referee's foot snapped out, and the fighter was sent flying out of the arena.

"Looks like there are a few people who don't know how to follow the rules." Rugrat rested his chin on his fist.

"Gives the refs something to do!"

Rugrat snorted. Some fights didn't even last a move. Fighters who were waiting at the side were called onto empty stages. Hundreds of fights progressed in a similar manner across the stages.

"The fighters this year are much stronger," Rugrat said.

"Well, we had to announce the prizes before the competition started. There were a lot of people who wanted to know beforehand," Chonglu said as he sat beside Rugrat.

"I wish I could enter the competition."

"You already have the best gear," Erik said.

"Yeah, but private training suites, membership upgrades, custom weapons and armor, as well as concoctions to cleanse the body and reach Body Like Iron? Give that to some motivated troops and see what they do."

"Why do you think we have them as referees?" Erik checked the sound-canceling field around them. "They fight in dungeons after they complete their basic training. They get access to the Battle Arena training rooms, crafter workshops, and more. They're training maniacs. There is a reason why they quickly progress their specializations. When they start, they might not be geniuses, but hard work and competitive spirit are instilled in their bones. Glosil raised one hell of a military."

Rugrat sat taller with a small smile hidden under his mask. "We lucked out with people."

"I've never heard of two people getting all reminiscent and thoughtful while watching a fighter's competition," Chonglu said dryly.

"Do you remember the days he was calling us lord and bowing all over the damn place?" Rugrat asked Erik, pointing to Chonglu with his thumb.

"Yeah, he's changed."

"I got to know you two!"

"Really changed," Rugrat agreed.

"Tea?" Erik asked.

"Tea? Chonglu's right. This is a fighting competition! It ain't no NASCAR, but hell if I am having tea! I brought some beer back from the Sixth Realm." Rugrat pulled out a clay jug and cups, pouring it out.

"Shit. Good to get a day off. Do you have seeds?"

"Hell, yeah!" Rugrat pulled out a sack of seasoned seeds.

"Aw shit, you're prepared."

"Hell yeah, man! Shit, we should get a tailgate party going."

"Don't have trucks."

"Well, nah—a carriage-gate party sounds dumb."

Erik and Chonglu accepted the beer from Rugrat. Chonglu looked more perplexed than Erik, who simply accepted what was happening.

"Cheers!" Rugrat raised his cup, and they smacked them together before Erik and Rugrat tapped them on their armrests and then awkwardly moved their masks to the side to have a swig.

"Need a straw or something. These masks suck," Rugrat complained.

"Shit. That is strong, but good," Chonglu said.

"Reminds me of moonshine. Yeah, it needs to be strong. Stupid fricking body tempering. Hey, Erik, your leaking metal."

"Fucking body tempering." Erik used a Clean spell.

"You two are strange, even by Ten Realms's standards."

Erik and Rugrat glanced at each other and shrugged before getting handfuls of seeds.

"Nice. Spicy dill?"

"Yeah, my own blend," Rugrat said as they drank and spat the shells into a second cup.

Elise appeared at the entrance to the box to see the three people at the center of attention, drinking beer and chewing on seeds.

Erik grabbed some extra cups and passed them out to people, changing the serious atmosphere and making it easier for people to mingle.

Elise walked down, and Rugrat passed her a drink.

"Good to see you," Rugrat said with feeling, putting his arm around her shoulders.

Elise sighed as he squeezed her in a sideways hug. "It's been a hectic couple of weeks, but everything is in place."

"I've been paying attention to the reports. The traders have been the backbone of our operations."

"It was made clear that we can only trade and do as we want because we have your protection. This is a way for them to give back. I don't think you understand the support behind you. If someone doesn't contribute toward the fight, other businesses and people shy away from working with them."

"I didn't think people would back this." Rugrat sounded troubled.

"Strength is power in the Ten Realms. Our enemy is a sect that cares little about others. They attacked our leaders, attacked Domonos. They hunted down and killed a party from the Adventurer's Guild and tried to bully them into accepting it. If we let this go, it will tarnish our reputation. How can we say that we stand for everyone if we don't fight?"

"You sound passionate about it."

"I have had a lot of time to think on it, and I have been putting in the hours to shift the scales in our favor. I wouldn't have if I didn't believe in it."

Rugrat patted her on the back and drank from his cup.

"If another man saw your arm around his girlfriend, he'd be scared," Blaze said from behind.

"Everything sorted?" Rugrat asked Blaze and glanced over to Domonos.

"We should be," Blaze said. His faint smile turned grim.

Domonos nodded.

"All right, have a beer. Today, we relax. Tomorrow, we'll deal with what comes."

Mistress Mercy kept glancing at the box. Her eyes fell on Domonos. *Why does he look so familiar?*

"Has something caught your eye?" her granduncle asked.

"I-I think that I have seen him before," Mercy said.

"Who, Lord Rodriguez or Blaze?"

"No, Colonel Silaz."

Low Elder Kostic lifted his brow. "We don't have any information on where he came from or his family."

"I'm sorry. I might be mistaking things."

"No, with your cultivation, it would be rare that you think you know someone from the past and be wrong," Cai Bo said, having overheard their conversation. "There is a hole in our information on Vuzgal. There has to be a power behind it, something working in the shadows. If not, how would they get so many crafters? How would they create a trading network so quickly? They had to have contacts and people they already knew. Look at Lord Rodriguez. He is conversing with Elise, the head of the Trader's Guild, which manages things for the traders who come to Vuzgal. Also Blaze, the leader of the Adventurer's Guild. These two guilds, while they might be separate from Vuzgal in name, based on how they interact, Lord Rodriguez is their leader, and they are part of Vuzgal's power."

"You mean—"

"Vuzgal is not as simple as we first thought. Where did half of their forces go? Where are these Experts, traders, and fighters coming from? Look into both guilds and see just how deep their roots are."

Mercy looked from Cai Bo to her granduncle.

Even if they did have deeper roots, they were still weaker than the

Willful Institute. She looked around the box the Willful Institute had booked for them. It was a half-step lower than the main box at the peak, where the leaders of associations were talking with trading magnates and sect leaders.

"Mercy, see if you can find out more information on Domonos through your own memories or looking through the records we have on him."

"Yes, High Elder Cai Bo." Mercy stood and bowed deeply to her.

Cai Bo nodded slightly. Her eyes had never left the stages where fighters were going all out, trying to make it through the preliminaries.

Never hurts to know more about possible future allies or enemies.

37 Qualifiers

"After three days of fighting, we have our top one hundred competitors for each category! Now it's time to start the real matches!" Chonglu's words gathered cheers across the arenas, across Vuzgal. "Let's begin today's matches!"

A gong sounded out and fighters walked out to the stages.

Chonglu took a seat next to Erik and Rugrat. People cheered for the fighters they had come to support or who they were associated with—by sect, by business, or by other means.

"So, competitors have to be between twenty and forty years old, use weapons that are of the mid-Apprentice-level, and they have to be within five levels of their opponent?" Erik asked.

"Yes, at reaching twenty, they have been learning to fight for a few years; their fighting methods have matured. By the time one is thirty, one could call them a veteran fighter; at forty, most people who have survived that long are powerful fighters. There are exceptions, but most fighters belong in these ages. Also, they usually don't have that many resources because they have been training so heavily. Older than this, and they probably have some savings or skills to earn resources and have established their methods of fighting. Duels are a way to train for them instead of a source of entertainment. Keeping them inside five-level brackets means that they can't use their levels to overwhelm others with too much power. Cultivating one's mana or body will give them a greater advantage, though these things are gained with effort and are much harder to get than levels."

"Huh, you've really thought this through."

"We have a lot more people at different levels and skills compared to last year. I just stole the information from Klaus." Chonglu shrugged.

"Work smarter, not harder." Rugrat pulled out a seed shell and winced. "Oh, that one had *a lot* of seasoning."

"Look—Stephan is going up," Erik said.

Rugrat took a few gulps of water before he cleared his throat. "Tanya was surprised with how quickly he picked up pure magic. He still needs more education on the basics, but he has a solid foundation and has started to create his own spells."

"How is your own spellcasting going?"

"With Tanya's help, I can cast spells faster and four of them at the same time now."

"Nice. Well, looks like Stephan is up against a bard."

"A bard? Aren't those like singers and music players who get into all kinds of shit? I heard about one who accidentally wooed an orc."

Chonglu spat out his wine and sputtered as he stared at Rugrat. *Dude! Come on, just what kind of mental images are you trying to put in other people's heads?*

"Bards back home are more romanticized than here. Yes, bards can use instruments and sing. Some of the best out there, but they are verbal spellcasters. Their instruments and voices allow them to create spells that are stronger than regular mages."

"Stephan doesn't look much like a scholar anymore," Rugrat said.

"After his last fights and a few training lessons, he realized that training and not actually fighting was holding him back. He ran around the realms, completing all kinds of missions to get real-world experience," Blaze said. "He tightened up his casting, picked out effective spells over flashy ones. Sure, robes make you look cool when you are casting a spell, coming up and moving around with the mana movements. Armor is king, so he got armor and plenty of slots on it so he could have Mana Regeneration potions on hand."

"He has a short sword as well," Erik noticed.

"Well, if someone takes you for a swordsman and you're really a mage, it can be advantageous to you. In his own words, 'There is no written agreement that people are going to fight me from a distance.' He's not a great swordsman by any stretch, but he's being trained and he has a bunch of buffing spells he can pile up to overwhelm his opponents with power."

Stephan and the bard walked up to the referee, who explained the rules to them and then sent them back to their own corners.

Stephan pulled out his sword and gathered the surrounding mana. The bard did the same.

"Look at that bow. It has an extra set of strings in front," Rugrat said.

"Smart. Those strings, if I'm not wrong, are a kind of instrument as well. He can use his bow as a weapon and an instrument." Erik nodded in approval.

The referee dropped his hand, and the match started.

Stephan's body glowed as he applied a buff. The air around Stephan's blade shimmered as he cut out twice, and wind blades shot out at the bard as he started to sing. The bard's fingers plucked the strings at the front of his bow; he shifted to the side, loosing an arrow covered in lines of magical power.

The Wind blades cut past the bard after he sidestepped, but several others were still coming for him. A mana barrier appeared in front of Stephan, though it broke under the force of the arrow. Another barrier behind it shattered as well, but the third mana barrier that appeared stopped the arrow. Wind blades attacked the bard while arrows slammed into mana barriers.

"Why doesn't he use his blade to deal with the arrows?" Erik asked.

"He's fucking up the bard's spellcasting."

"You know, you're this close to sounding like a sage and this close to a redneck."

"Thank you." Rugrat winked behind his mask. "The bard, he makes songs or music to create spells, right?"

"Yeah."

"So, what is the medium for sound?"

"Air!" Erik had an epiphany.

"Right. So, if the air is distorted, it's going to mess up the spellcasting. If he were to use his air blades against the arrows, the bard could use stronger spells. Look at Stephan—he doesn't look stressed. He's excited. He's holding back to enjoy the fight." Rugrat's eyes glowed as he pierced through the realm's mana with his eyes.

"It is rare to find a bard to fight. This is a fight over mana pool and regeneration."

"He's unaffiliated. I'll see if we can recruit him," Blaze said.

"You are worse than the Marine Corps recruiters."

"Except the deal isn't as shit, and we're not forcing them to sign," Erik countered.

"What is your hatred toward recruiters? Didn't you enjoy your time in the marines?" Chonglu asked.

"Yes, but recruiters are...recruiters. It's hard to explain. They're sneaky shits who somehow get you into the marines and then, when you're in, you find out they screwed you over."

"You did the thirty-day temporary recruiting duty, didn't you?" Erik asked.

Rugrat ignored the comment, just muttered darkly about recruiters and Temporary Additional Duty as he chewed his seeds into oblivion and watched the match.

Stephan was wearing down the bard. With his attacks messing up the bard's spellcasting, the bard was looking pale as he was forced to use more mana to compensate.

The bard jumped backward and pulled out a guitar, letting out a couple of fast rifts; electricity appeared around him and shot out like snakes. Stephan frowned and defended with his sword.

"Oh arrow, my arrow, fly for meee," the bard sang. As he played his guitar, arrows from his quiver jumped up and shot out toward Stephan. His playing became sharper and the notes closer together, like the rising tides of war.

Arrows shot out from behind the bard.

Stephan grinned. The glow around his body increased as he applied more buffs. He used one hand on his sword; the other created spells.

Stone from the ground turned into darts; air turned to blades; mana barriers were his shields and his steppingstones as he was forced on the defensive, unable to close with the bard.

"For my blood and my warrior spirit! Change for me!" The bard left on a high note, and the arrows turned into javelins. "With my power, with my words, enliven the elements, and bring down your righteous wrath!"

One's heart couldn't help but speed up. All eyes were on the soul-stirring musician and the battle.

Stephan yelled as tentacles of elements appeared around him, and his attacks sped up again. In a semi-sphere in front of him, his sword flashed; nothing passed his defenses as the ground around him was torn apart.

The arrows-turned-javelins showed elemental properties: lightning, ice, twisting wooden vines. Metal and stone spears rained down in so many numbers and at such speed it was hard to follow.

"My heart goes to the forest and protects me from my worries!"

The ground underneath Stephan cracked as a tree grew around him.

A frost stretched out from Stephan, freezing the air. Stephan cracked the tree trying to bind him with a simple movement. He reached out to his side; lightning extended from his hand into a whip. He snapped it out.

Lightning drained from his hand and ran down the length of the whip, letting out a snapping noise. The lightning gathered at the tip into an orb and exploded outward, tearing through the javelins and arrows, raining down on the ground. The bard was forced to retreat.

The stone he stepped on was as soft as water. He yelled; it was strengthened, and the counterforce against the ground sent him backward out of the spell's range.

A ball of power appeared next to the bard and exploded in light. The bard had a mana barrier up, but his eyes were wide open.

Stephan waved his sword in a circle, stirring up the Wind and gathering the frost. Water was injected into the air, creating snow. The lightning field gathered into the spinning vortex of snow.

Stephan stood there, a god of the elements, watching the bard as he blinked rapidly to recover his vision.

"Do you wish to continue?" Stephan asked, casually spinning his sword, controlling the lightning-frost vortex.

The bard regained his vision; his clothes were ruffled, and his hair was in disarray. Seeing the storm waiting for him, the bard lowered his guitar. "I admit defeat," the bard said bitterly.

Stephan waved his sword, and threads of energy returned to his body as the spell fell apart.

"Spell Reversal?" Rugrat sat forward.

"Huh?" Erik asked.

"When you cast a spell, you pretty much accept that you are losing that power. People believe that if you are holding onto a spell, you can reverse it and draw the power back into your body so you don't lose it and don't have to regenerate it. Most of the people who have tried to do it have been met with disaster. The power turns on them, hurting them instead. Stephan canceled the spell and drew the power back into himself without any wounds."

"This is the first stage of spell reversal. Stephan has been working with two new techniques called Spell Alteration and Spell Combination. When he combined the lightning field and the frost spell effect, that was him utilizing Spell Combination. The three techniques, if combined, will allow someone massive flexibility on the battlefield. He could be halfway through casting one spell, something changes, and instead of dismissing the spell and wasting the power, he can change it into a new spell through combination, and alteration, or he can take that power back and recast it in a new way," Blaze added.

"I always thought that spells, once cast, had to be used. I didn't think they could be changed," Erik said.

The referee announced Stephan as the winner, and the two fighters walked off their stage. Although it had been an eye-catching fight, there were plenty of other soul-stirring fights happening across the battle arenas.

"Looks like Junior Kaya is going up," Low Elder Kostic said to High Elder Cai Bo.

"Yes," she said distractedly, turning her head from Stephan and the bard's fight. Her gaze reached the Vuzgal city lords, who were talking to the Adventurer's Guild leader. As the fight finished, they got up and walked around to talk to others.

An aide walked up to Low Elder Kostic, and Cai Bo's attention turned to Junior Kaya.

Her opponent was a tall man who stood as straight as the fine spear in his hands.

Kaya walked to the middle of the stage, and the referee talked to her as she moved the shield on her left arm, her right hand hooked on the hilt of her sword.

"Are you sure?" Low Elder Kostic asked in a grave voice.

What has him so aggravated?

The aide continued to talk in Kostic's ear.

He had a dark expression as he dismissed the aide with a wave and turned to Cai Bo. "In the Second Realm, nearly a year and a half ago, a group of Willful Institute disciples ambushed a group of mercenaries. They had some valuable items on them. They killed nearly all the mercenaries, but some escaped to their guild. The guild sent messages to the Willful Institute branch, looking for the attackers to be disciplined.

"The elders dismissed the group. They were just a minor power, and the group who had killed the mercenaries had already used the resources they had stolen and were strong enough to go to the Fourth Realm. The elders disregarded the words of the guild. The Adventurer's Guild have been harassing our branch through various means, including taking missions from the branch. It came to a head, and the branch challenged the guild directly to showcase their strength and weaken their enemy by taking their resources."

"The incident in the Third Realm that the Grey Peak sect took advantage of?"

"Yes, High Elder. The same guild that has reportedly allied with the Grey Peak sect branch. That guild is called the Adventurer's Guild, a simple and widely used name."

Cai Bo's eyes moved to Kostic. "Are you saying—? Those idiots."

Kostic nodded gravely. "That *simple* guild is the Adventurer's Guild that calls Vuzgal its headquarters."

Cai Bo balled her hand into a fist under her sleeves.

What a bunch of incompetent fools! She replayed the fight between Stephan and the bard, and the other qualifier matches she had seen with the Adventurer's Guild. Her eyes moved to the highest box, and she stared at the Adventurer's Guild leader, who was talking with several other fighting guild leaders, Chonglu, the leader of the Battle Arena, and powerful trading leaders.

"How could they miss something so important?" Cai Bo hissed.

Her eyes fell on Kaya, but her mind was working overtime.

Kaya and her opponent reached their corners, and the referee waved her hand, starting the match.

The two fighters charged out. Their bodies glowed as they gathered the surrounding mana, using combat techniques right away. The spear user thrust out; his spear turned into a slippery eel, lashing out. It moved so quickly it seemed to create several copies, layered over one another.

Kaya's shield was an iron wall, deflecting and shifting the spear attacks away. Her eyes shone as she looked for her opening.

The two figures were hard to watch from the sparks made by each impact. Wind blew over the ground as the spear wielder's attacks left lines on the floor, even as they connected in the air.

Having a powerful enemy in the Fourth Realm with access to Vuzgal…it remains to be seen whether they want to go all out against the Willful Institute or whether we can reach an agreement.

"Find out just how strong this Adventurer's Guild is and if the rest of the Institute knows. If we can present this information to the head first and make it appear that other clans are hiding the information, it could be our opening."

"Yes, Elder Cai Bo."

In a flash, Kaya moved to the side with a yell, igniting the power of her mana-enhanced muscles.

The spear user's feet moved in a complicated manner, shifting to his new target. Kaya charged as he shifted; using brute force, she rammed her shield into the man's spear. He grimaced as the force transmitted through his spear and threw off his attacks, changing the momentum and pace of the fight. He was on his back foot.

Kaya's shield appeared to grow to twice the size, and lightning covered it. It sounded like a bell from the underworld when the spear struck it.

Lightning danced down the spear shaft, stunning the spear wielder for a half second. Kaya dodged to the side and back in. Her shield seemed to grow heavy as she brought it down on his spear, slamming it into the ground. She jabbed forward with her sword, aiming at the man's neck.

There was a flash in front of her sword, diverting it to the side.

The referee was right there, and a mana barrier spell separated them both.

Kaya was announced the winner. She showed an arrogant sneer and walked off the stage, not sparing the spear wielder a second glance.

Cai Bo didn't feel a sense of victory; she felt a thrill. *It feels suddenly as if I know nothing about what is happening around me.* There were too many shadows and mysteries. She had been playing political battles within the sect, controlling her own useless clan and several others to reach the position of high elder.

"The forces at Meokar are heading out tonight to attack the Grey Peak sect as a warning to the surrounding sects," Kostic said. "Should we say anything?"

"Will it help? We must learn more and see if there is anything we can do. Although they are a small power in Vuzgal, it remains to be seen how powerful they are in the lower realms. If we can make it clear they will lose more than they will gain, they might back off with less effort on our side."

38 Cooperation? Aren't We Cooperating Already?

Grand Elder Mendes's fine robes had been replaced with armor as he watched the Willful Institute's disciples marching past on their mounts.

On the fringes, guards and the disciplinary elders watched for scouts and sentries. They were nearly at the Grey Peak sect's territory. Once they entered, with their dense alarm formations, they wouldn't be able to hide their presence anymore.

"Elder Mendes," said a voice that came from behind.

"Elder Xiao."

Mendes's guards moved to the side as Xiao and his guards approached.

"Once we enter the Grey Peak sect's territory, it will take us several hours to attack their main city," Mendes said.

"You are wondering if in that time they will get reinforcements from the higher realms?"

Mendes nodded.

"We have only leaked that we got reinforcements. It makes sense after the attack. They wouldn't imagine that we would attack them first. Even if they did, their higher ranks will think this is something for the lower realms to deal with. If it were not for the recent issues we ran into, we wouldn't be here. If they are willing to sign a nonaggression contract and give us back our resources—with interest—then we can end this all. If they don't..." Xiao's eyes turned deep and cold as he seemed to look through the dark forest and at the Grey Peak sect's city.

The silence stretched before Elder Xiao patted Elder Mendes on the shoulder.

"They can only call on a few allies in the surrounding area. They have their own interests as well. If we can show our power here, those other powers will retreat. No one wants to fight a tiger, but they will pick over the corpse of a weak deer."

Heidi Storgaard didn't need much sleep with her advanced levels. She had been tempering her body in the heart of her Grey Peak sect branch when she was interrupted.

"So, the Willful Institute dares to cross our borders. They are bolder than I thought," she said as she entered the war room.

Konal Gudriksson snapped to attention. He was a large man with a braided beard and an armored vest that revealed his large arms. He looked as solid as the war bear he rode on.

"They have come in force. They must have had more reinforcements than we thought. They are making good time, but they aren't hiding their presence. It is a clear provocation."

"Well, we'll just have to answer them. Send out word to our allies and ask them to reinforce us. We will break the Willful Institute's attack and chase them back to Meokar."

Lieutenant Colonel Zukal entered the room of four people.

"They will reach the Grey Peak sect in a few hours," Mister Yi said to a tired-looking Jasper and the fierce Zukal.

Jasper took a breath and pulled out a small Stamina potion. He took a swig and wiped his face with the back of his hand.

"They're really going to kick things off? This isn't a ploy?" Zukal asked.

"They are hoping to warn the Grey Peak and surrounding sects that they are not to be messed with. If the Grey Peak has the numbers and the power on their side, they now have a clear provocation. We can tilt things in favor of pushing back the Institute."

Energy filled Jasper's body, and he half turned his head toward his aide. "Send word to the guild. Those who wish to participate in the battle should get ready."

The aide bowed her head and left the room.

"Well, let's see what happens. How are things on your side, Lieutenant Colonel?"

"All of the Adventurer's Guild members have trained for large operations. We've integrated smoothly. No issues on our side. We'll be ready."

"Good. Then I'll leave command in your capable hands." Jasper patted him on the shoulder.

There was a knock at the door.

"Come in," Jasper said.

The door opened. Niemm walked in and closed the door behind him. He passed Jasper a scroll with a seal on it. "We checked it. No traps. From the Grey Peak sect."

Jasper opened the scroll. "The Grey Peak sect is officially requesting our support." He passed the scroll to Mister Yi.

"I have received word from my five special team operatives. With the help of Mister Yi's operatives, they were able to gain access to the city. Once we lead the attack on the city, they will be able to act. The whole place is locked down right now, and there is little they can do. Communication is hard, so they will be waiting for your signals."

"It used to be that battles were just people fighting one another," Jasper said.

"This is still a battle. We're just stacking the odds in our favor," Zukal said.

"What is the meaning of this?" Branch Head Storgaard hissed as she looked through a formation screen. Groups of fighters walked out of the totem.

"Seems like token forces. Now the Willful Institute has moved, the other sects want to see what will happen and are holding back their strength," Gudriksson said.

"They want us to weaken one another and take the benefits afterward." Storgaard gritted her teeth in anger.

"The Institute is strong and brutal. Crossing them is not something to do lightly. I don't agree with the other sects' actions, but I can understand it. At least they sent some people. The smaller forces that came to your meeting haven't even showed their faces. That Adventurer's Guild said that they would send some support, but it has been a couple of hours already."

Storgaard hit her fist on the banister, displacing snow as the totem lit up.

Through the formation screen, she heard feet moving before the light dimmed. As it did, fifty people were revealed, marching away from the totem. In the fore, they held a flag that snapped against the cold, bitter wind.

They stood in ranks. Their gear was various, but they wore heavy armors, large weapons, and shields. Each wore an Adventurer's Guild emblem on their chest. They were spread out because they didn't know how to march well, but they all listened to the commands of a woman in the lead.

"Seems I was wrong about the Adventurer's Guild. It looks like they scraped together some fighters." Gudriksson snorted as the totem lit up again.

Another force, as big as the first, marched out. This one had fighters with bows.

Storgaard frowned. They wore the same emblems as the force before. Already the number of people that the guild had sent was more than some of the major sects she had talked to.

Another group walked out; the third group had Jasper among their ranks. He wore light armor and sported a spear.

Units kept coming out. They were roughly put together, but they worked well in their individual units.

How many people did they bring?

"What do you think now, Gudriksson?"

"Either they have brought their entire guild, or the Willful Institute pissed off someone who shouldn't be pissed off. Look at their gear; look at the way they move. They're mercenaries through and through. But their gear is some of the best to be found in the Fourth Realm. The way they work together. They are individuals, but it is clear they have trained together and have a deep connection to their guild. They're loyal and angry."

Coming up from the lowest rungs of society, Gudriksson wasn't as blind or arrogant as many of the older sects had become. It was the reason she took him to be the head of her armed forces. He was too blunt to care about plans in the background but smart enough to understand them.

"We should greet them. I think things just changed."

Blaze returned to his office in the Fourth Realm.

"You're still working? I haven't seen you in weeks." Elise pouted.

"There is always more to be done, especially in these times."

"The fighting has you worried."

"We sent ten thousand people over to the Grey Peak sect. In the next few hours, our guild will, officially, be at war with the Willful Institute."

"We have been for a while, though," Elise said.

"Yes, though it was in secret. Now, we will become one of their targets. Even if they never learn of everything else we've done."

"We can't regret what is going to happen now. We can just deal with the results." Elise rubbed his shoulders.

He patted her hands and she leaned forward, draping her arms over him and hugging him from behind.

There was a knock at the door.

Elise stood up and moved to the side.

"Come in," Blaze said.

The door opened, revealing Emilia.

"There is someone here from the Grey Peak sect who wants to talk to you about cooperation."

"Looks like they figured it out already," Blaze said.

"I have a meeting over at the academy. I'll see you later," Elise said.

Blaze stood and kissed her. "All right, see you for dinner. Emilia, bring the representative up to see me." Blaze sat and read some of the reports, trying to get some extra work done.

Three information books later, he was nursing a headache and there was a knock at the door.

"Come in." Blaze stood, showing no signs of fatigue.

A man with a braided beard with metal rings in it stood at the door. He wore a heavy-armored vest, and braided hair hung down his back.

"Guildmaster Blaze, thank you for meeting with me!" The man laughed and walked over to Blaze and shook his hand. "My name is Ragnar Haddsson. I wanted to talk to you about cooperating together."

"Ah, so you are here about the Third Realm?" Blaze said.

"Third Realm?" Ragnar frowned.

"Your Grey Peak sect and my Adventurer's Guild are working together in the Third Realm. My guild is sending people to help your branch deal with the Willful Institute and Meokar city."

"Ah, news travels slowly through the realms," Haddsson said with an awkward laugh.

Seems I was wrong. They didn't connect the dots. Oh well, they will now. Be hard not to.

"Forgive my ignorance," Haddsson said. "And let me thank you on behalf of the Grey Peak sect for assisting us."

"It is a small matter. We have an issue with the Willful Institute. Staring at the other sects in the area, I believe it would be best if the Grey Peak sect took over the control of Meokar."

"You have no interest in the city?"

"No. We will take some treasures, but they killed some of our people. We will be happy when there is no Willful Institute presence remaining in the city."

"The Willful Institute is arrogant in their ways, killing grand elites of the Adventurer's Guild!"

"They weren't elites. They were regular adventurers, but if you attack one of our members, you attack us all. I am glad that we were able to find an ally like the Grey Peak sect."

"Thank you, Guildmaster Blaze."

"Did you have some other matters to discuss?"

"My Grey Peak sect has run into an issue with a mine in the Fourth Realm. We found a new vein in one of our territories, but it is far from our cities. Traders and workers need to travel far before reaching the mining town. We are expanding the mine rapidly and need to position more people there, which gives us fewer forces to protect the convoys. Bandits have appeared in the area. We could deal with it, but it would pull strength away from our cities. We are not sure if the attacks are truly bandits or other forces. We would like to contract out the protection of the convoys to the Adventurer's Guild."

"I think we will be able to assist with this and get information on the bandits so you can decide what you want done with them," Blaze said. "We might need to bring in some people from other allied guilds to meet your needs. Would that work?"

"If they have your recommendation, we would be only too happy to hire them."

"Very well. I will need some more information, but I look forward to our continued cooperation." Blaze reached out his hand.

"To our continued cooperation!" Haddsson smiled and shook Blaze's hand.

Jasper and Niemm walked into the war room with two other special team members. Mister Yi and Zukal should be setting up their own command center shortly.

"Vice Guildmaster Jasper." Branch Head Storgaard excused herself from the conversation to greeted him personally.

The other group leaders had awkward expressions on their faces. They sneered and showed disdain toward the guildmaster. He had shown them up, bringing his entire guild to fight.

"Your support is as welcome as coal in a snowstorm." Storgaard's attitude had changed since she had first met Jasper.

"We made promises, and the Adventurer's Guild places our entire reputation on those promises." Jasper's smile widened.

The other leaders' faces darkened.

"Well said." Storgaard laughed lightly. "I'd like to discuss tactics with you, if possible. There are still people coming through the totem. It seems you have endless warriors at your command." She guided him over to the large planning table, where a large formation connected to the alarm arrays. The Willful Institute's moves were clearly outlined on the table.

"We asked the guild members who wanted to participate in the attack to gather in the Third Realm. We were surprised by the number of volunteers. We had to limit it to just ten thousand."

If they hadn't held those idiots back, they would have had ten times that number. *Do they want the guild to go broke from paying their transportation fees?!*

"*Just* ten thousand." Storgaard coughed and blinked.

"More than that, and it is harder to maintain command and control. We brought the strongest members to make sure younger members who overestimate their strength don't make a deadly decision."

"That makes sense. With your forces and that of the Grey Peak sect, we'll be able to beat the Willful Institute back easily."

"You only want to beat them back?" Jasper asked.

"Once we do that, we can regroup our forces." Storgaard shot a look at the different elders in the room. "And we can lead an attack on the Institute and make them listen to our demands."

"Oh, well, we're here to eliminate the Willful Institute from Meokar completely."

"That won't be a simple task. They have close to thirty thousand people in their vanguard and another five thousand guarding their city."

"We know. How about this? We will work together to defend your city and bleed the Willful Institute. Then, if you wish to join us or not, we will attack Meokar."

A bearded man flicked his sleeves. "You think too much of yourselves! You are just a guild from the Third Realm! You want to take down a sect city! Impossible!"

"Who said our headquarters are in the Third Realm?"

"You don't even have a headquarters here!" another elder added in a huff. "You made a lot of noise about bringing ten thousand people over. Will we find your branches empty when we knock on their doors?"

Did you get annoyed with a "smaller" power showing off in front of you? Why were these sects always thinking of how great they were? Jasper shook his head and sighed.

"Can you even face our great sects, a simple guild like yours?" the bearded elder said. The other elders showed the same looks of disdain.

"You—" Storgaard made to step forward, but Jasper reached out and stopped her.

"I guess I should re-introduce my guild." Jasper's voice tapped into the power of his body and his mana. His aura was deep and heavy while formations made it impossible for one to understand his power. They could all feel as if the scholar-like man had turned into some powerful demon in front of them.

"The Adventurer's Guild has branches from the First Realm to the Fourth Realm, with over seven hundred thousand members. We are headquartered in Vuzgal, in the Fourth Realm. We are part of the Seven Shields and Two Swords Fighter's Alliance. We are a subsidiary guild of the Fighter's Association. In the army I brought, a third could enter the Sixth Realm, another third the Fifth Realm, and the remaining members are from the Fourth Realm."

"Vuzgal? That is the holy land of fighters and crafters!"

"What is the Seven Shields and Two Sword Alliance?"

"It's an alliance between fighter guilds that are subordinates of the Fighter's Association. They came to an agreement to support one another, so that their people wouldn't join the Fighter's Association with anger in their hearts. Some people call them the roots of the Fighter's Association."

"So many Experts! I thought they were from the Third Realm. Even for a group from the Fourth Realm, isn't that excessive?"

"Never mind a city in the Third Realm—couldn't they attack a city in the Fourth Realm?"

"I wondered why their guildmaster isn't here! The Vuzgal fighter's competition is going on!"

"What are you talking about? Do you think their guildmaster would come down to the Third Realm to deal with something like this? Having the vice guildmaster here shows their determination."

Jasper's aura withdrew, and he appeared like a simple scholarly man once again as he turned to Storgaard.

"Elder, why do I feel like they are stronger than our own sect?"

"It seems like that might be true. We are just a medium power in the Third Realm."

"Didn't you say that no powerful forces would want to be involved and that we should only bring a small force so when the real battle comes, we can increase our rewards?"

"Silence! Do you think that I could predict such a power would appear?"

"So, Branch Head Storgaard. What is your plan?"

39 A Small Force?

"Lieutenant Colonel, everyone is ready," an Alvan soldier in adventurer's gear said.

"Good. How are things on the side of the sects?"

"They are waiting to see how things turn out. The Grey Peak sect should be in the fight. We might need to push them further if we want their help to take the city," Mister Yi said.

Zukal turned from the tower he had claimed as his command post and looked out across the snowy mountains. "Whether they join us or not is up to them. With our force, if we are not able to take the city, then I will resign in dishonor."

"You're that confident?"

"Mister Yi, I would leave nothing to chance." Zukal's face spread into a frigid sneer. "And Colonel Domonos is coming down with a full combat company as reserve. With all we know about Meokar, they have few secrets that they can keep. We have built counters for most of their main attacks and to bypass their defenses."

Mister Yi fell silent.

"The Dragon Battalion and the Adventurer's Guild have not been able to show their true strength before. We will hold back our firearms, but everything else is allowed."

Mister Yi nodded, not as confident as Zukal.

They had been training for so long that people had forgotten how less than a hundred Alvan soldiers were able to hold back and bleed an army of thousands.

In the forests in the Grey Peak sect's territory, one could hear the sounds of marching and metal as the armored members of the Willful Institute marched to the heart of the Grey Peak sect's territory.

Grand Elder Mendes looked up from his mount. The low-lying fog curled around the Grey Peak sect's branch city.

It was set in a mountain range. The tallest mountain had been turned into their city. Flat areas had been turned into vast gardens to cultivate rare ingredients. Walls ringed the outside of these plateaus. The mountain sprouted out of the middle of a plateau and stretched to meet other mountains that led down into valleys that fell under the Grey Peak sect's control.

"Our lead elements have made it out of the forest. Half of the force is heading to the southern entrance. We should reach the eastern entrance in less than an hour," Elder Tsi said beside Mendes.

"That will only leave the northern entrance into the plains open. The fools built into a mountain. With such a design, it saves building time, but their formations will require much more power. Once we break through their gates, we will flood through their gardens, spiraling up to the city at the peak. With the plateau two-thirds up the mountain, our ascent will be hard but not impossible."

"Do you think they will last longer than our initial attack, Grand Elder?"

Mendes tightened his grip on his reins and kicked his mount forward. "I hope they do. That way we can make a true display of our power, so that no one else challenges us for several decades. With a new sect under our control, we can wipe away our previous losses."

"Should I mention this to the vanguard units? If they accidentally don't listen to orders or can't let the dishonorable Grey Peak sect branch survive?" Elder Tsi lowered his voice, his eyes checking to make sure no one was listening to their conversation.

"It is hard to contain the younger generation. They are prone to bouts of anger that clouds their judgment and leads to mistakes."

The two elders looked at each other.

"Anyway, I must check with the vanguard and their progress, Grand Elder."

"Elder."

They separated, and Mendes glanced over to the trails that led to the plateau.

A sudden flash went off, and the mounts shifted uneasily.

Magical traps. Seeing the attacks light up, he raised his voice. "Push the Grey Peak villagers out in front."

Storgaard stood there, a statue in the snow and wind as she watched the two black snakes reaching toward her branch city. Her face was as cold as the rock around her.

Behind her stood her command team, strong men and women with war paint on their faces and braided beards and hair.

Magical traps went off in the entrances to the plateau.

There was an unwritten rule in the realms. If one sect took over the city, then all the connected region fell under their control. It was a rule that had been passed down by all the associations. It saved the normal people and stopped wars from spreading too far. They didn't have the time to draw in more people. Holding up in the castle was the best move as they could pit their defenses against their unsupported attackers.

The Willful Institute stopped their advance.

"Looks like a few spells have scared them," one of the women behind her said.

Storgaard narrowed her eyes. The Viewing spell allowed her to zoom in on the advancing army. "Fucking savages," she hissed through gritted teeth as her knuckles popped from holding them so tight.

"Vicious." Gudriksson stood beside her as they watched the Willful Institute driving forward shivering bodies.

"Calculating, using our villagers and farmers as a shield to activate our traps." Storgaard's eyes were dull, reflecting the cold, merciless light of the blind magical traps that activated as the shivering serfs were shoved ahead of the Willful Institute's soldiers.

"Even if they fail, we will have issues with our people. They will be angry that we allowed this to happen. If they win, they will take on the issues. With showing their merciless side, the voices will be quiet, scared of being the next victim. It can also serve as a warning to the other sects. Even if they lose, they will gut our sect's serf population," Gudriksson evaluated coldly.

"Is there any—"

Gudriksson shook his head. "Unless we want to use our trump cards, there is nothing we can do."

Storgaard unclenched her jaw and rested her hand on her sword, returning to the unfeeling Valkyrie. "Tell the Adventurer's Guild if we can beat back the Willful Institute, then our Bear Legion will support their attack on Meokar, and we will give them all the support we can. I will give them an oath if they desire it."

"What about the higher-ups?" Gudriksson asked.

"To pull over an ally like the Adventurer's Guild—do you think that they'll deny this?"

"Permission to join the vanguard?"

Storgaard stared at Gudriksson. "They are just serfs."

"Yes, but they're *our* serfs. And the Willful Institute is stepping all over our honor."

Storgaard turned her head back toward the battle. "If you don't bring me back at least two elders' heads or that worm Mendes's corpse, I'll have you and the Bear Legion clearing forest for three months!"

"My axe is meant to bite into armor and bone, not trees." Gudriksson's deep voice rolled over the stony ground.

"Show me."

Those two words ignited the fighting spirit in the Grey Peak sect fighters.

Domonos finished talking to Blaze and passed command of Vuzgal to one of his junior lieutenant colonels.

"Are you sure a combat company will be enough?" Erik asked.

"If it isn't, then I didn't train them well enough," Domonos said.

Rugrat reached out a hand.

Domonos took it and was pulled into a bear hug.

"Bring them back safe."

"Yes, sir."

Erik reached out his hand and hugged Domonos. "Tear them apart, but make sure the rage doesn't cloud your judgment."

"I serve the army first, my soldiers second, and myself last."

Erik patted him on the shoulder, his expression worth more than a hundred words.

Domonos felt as if he had taken in an extra breath but couldn't breathe anymore or let it back out.

Gong Jin cleared his throat.

"I'll let you get back to it. When I see you next, Meokar will be under new management," Domonos promised. He snapped off a salute.

Erik and Rugrat pulled themselves up and saluted back at Domonos.

He about-faced and marched out of the command center. His guards fell in around him, guiding him through the Battle Arena and toward their mounts.

Domonos pulled out a map of the situation reported by Lieutenant Colonel Zukal.

The group marched through the halls, and people moved out of the way.

There was a startled yell as they turned a corner and nearly ran over a young woman who was walking by.

"Sorry, miss," one of the soldiers said.

Domonos glanced up. His eyes locked with Mistress Mercy's. He clenched his jaw, and hot rage ran through his body.

"Colonel Silaz, what a surprise."

"I am sorry, Mistress Mercy. I have things to do." Domonos said civilly, stopping himself from spitting the words out. He felt that darkness was always a half-step away from calling to him. "I hope we can meet up later."

He shot a look to his guards, and they kept moving.

Next time, I will take your head from your neck. In his mind, the image of her whipping him and enjoying it overlaid the pure-looking woman before him. He heard the screams of others who had drawn her ire and felt the burning pain on his back and limbs. He unconsciously shifted his armor, feeling as if his back was itchy where the old, healed wounds had once been.

Domonos looked at the map and reviewed the information from Zukal again.

The Willful Institute entered the plateaus, spreading out and laying out their weapons of war.

"I heard they sent a messenger to the branch head," Mister Yi said to Jasper.

"What was the result?"

"It looks like they were willing to turn back if the Grey Peak sect agreed to pay back the resources they took, plus interest. Storgaard didn't take too kindly to their demands."

"What if it was not the Grey Peak sect but another sect that got the message?"

"Depends. Though in this area, most of them would have given in. They don't want a war; they want to hold on to their lands, send up resources to the Fourth Realm, and get support in the Third. This is the start of negotiations. If they could return the supplies or a little less than what they took, the other sects would give in."

"Without your information, we might have allied with one of the other sects. Feel bad that we dragged them into this."

"They will get a new city out of it, and we can see what they're made of. You said the sects in the higher realm want to cooperate with us as well now."

"Still."

"Yes, we are tricking them in one way, but are we not taking on the risks with them?"

Jasper sighed. *When did it all become so complicated?*

The totem flashed with light, and a group of adventurers walked out. Their marching fell in step. They wore distinct armor but still looked like a single entity.

The groups marched past Jasper and Mister Yi. Their officers nodded to them as they passed.

With the third group, Domonos came out. He walked over to Jasper and Mister Yi.

"Good to see you, Domonos. Zukal gave me this for you." Jasper held out an information book.

Domonos opened it; the pages flipped and burnt out as light drifted through his eyes. "Looks like he has everything in hand. Shall we head to the wall? I want to see it myself."

Jasper's guards led the way.

Domonos stood at the top of the wall. Guards and people were in the different towers and heating huts, ready to rush up to the wall at a moment's notice.

The walls were good and thick, though they were all over the place, creating their own small bastions on the mountain instead of one continuous wall around the area.

"With the height advantage, our range is going to increase, but that cross-wind doesn't make me happy. What do we have for ranged weapons?"

"Trebuchets, catapults, javelin throwers, spell scrolls, formation spellcaster platforms—Ten Realms standard, not our own brand—and some mana cannons. The Grey Peak sect has to have some powerful tools they're holding on to," Jasper said.

"Have the mages work with the catapult and trebuchet teams. Spell up the ammunition. They're going to hit like a mother with our extra height. Explosive Shot with remote ignition will turn one stone ball into raining shrapnel. Is the Willful Institute still using the lightning-attenuating mana barriers?"

"Current information points to it," Mister Yi replied.

"Good. We have plenty of Fire-based spell scrolls. With it being a Metal element array, the Fire element suppresses it and does greater damage." Domonos pulled out his map. It automatically updated through formations in the command center that Zukal was operating.

He checked the unit type deployment again. "Everything looks like it is in place. We will need to draw in the Willful Institute. During the attack, we will slowly leach fighters to gather at the northern passes. When we break the Institute's lines and they start to pull back, we'll rush their lines, creating disorder. Mister Yi, will you be able to get us the elder targets?"

"Once they attack us, I will be able to find where the different elders are. I have researched them all; I would be able to do it with a telescope."

"Good." Domonos looked at the snow-slush on the walls. "Send out orders to clear the walls and to lay down powder and make sure the water doesn't turn to ice. One misplaced foot, and people are going to slip and fall."

An aide braced and then started to transmit the information via his sound transmission device.

"Are the medic stations set up?"

"Yes, and we are serving warm Apprentice-level food to give the soldiers minor boosts and calm their nerves."

"Good. We don't know how long the battle will be or how long it will be before we can get another warm meal." Domonos looked at the walls, seeing the different banners from the other sects. "How are they?"

"I would only rely on the Grey Peak sect until we have the enemy on the run," Mister Yi said.

Domonos nodded. *I never put much faith in them.*

He rested his hands on the rocks, feeling them cooling his hands. He stared at the dark snake spreading out over the plateau, setting up their long-range weapons. They wouldn't put out tents or supplies for more than a short battle. It seemed they were confident about winning. If it were just the Grey Peak sect and the other sects' token forces, they might be able to take the city. Their confidence came from their reinforcements.

"Information leaks?"

"A few people have tried, but we have restrictive formations, and the Grey Peak sect is not letting anyone leave."

"And those who sent messages?"

"They were dealt with," Niemm said, walking up to the group. "Just handled another leak. Good to see you, Domonos."

"Niemm." Domonos tilted his head to Niemm, who stretched out his hand.

"You feel it yet?"

"Feel what?"

"The thrill?"

"My gut's turning over right now. Don't have time for the thrill."

"Wait. When it starts, no one will feel more alive than when their life is on the line," Niemm said as they released each other's hands.

"How are things in Meokar?"

"Everything went to plan. The agents and teams went radio silent a few hours ago to avoid detection. We won't know what's happening until we reach the city."

"So many pieces moving at once," Jasper said.

"Today we start putting them to use." Domonos felt a power staring at the men and women on the wall.

Meokar will fall, slow and steady. Who will die to do so?

A cold hand reached into his body and clamped onto his organs. This was what he had trained for. There were too many people relying on him. He couldn't fuck up.

He pulled out his map, reviewing it once again, and pulled out his sound transmission device to check in with Lieutenant Colonel Zukal.

He hadn't understood when Erik and Rugrat had said that the worst thing about commanding was being left with your thoughts. *I hate this waiting shit.*

Elder Xiao stared at the messenger as a reply came back from the Grey Peak sect.

The messenger coughed and cleared their throat, looking angry. "They disagree with the terms set forward."

"Is there any more?" Elder Xiao asked.

"They called us dishonorable dogs, using weak excuses to try to bully them. They were not scared of flea-covered dogs before, and they are not now. They suggest that they will chase us back to Meokar and out of the region."

Elder Xiao was calm while others in the tent pressed their lips together, swallowing their words.

"Who the real dogs are is still to be seen. The Grey Peak sect is as dull as the bears they ride on. Ready our people. In an hour, we will give them a response with our blades! Whoever kills a member of the Grey Peak sect or the Adventurer's Guild will get an extra five contribution points!"

The elders and aides let out excited yells.

Let's see how many of you survive with a bounty of five contribution points on your heads.

"Here they come," Gudriksson said as extra mana barriers flared to life over the Willful Institute's army.

The lead forces marched forward. A screen for the ranged siege weapons rolled behind them.

"What do you think of the proposed battle plan?" Storgaard wore her complete armor, checking the strap holding the shield to her arm.

"Playing the pig to eat the tiger? It will weaken our defenses, and we will need to lose some bastions, though if we can draw out the Institute and are really able to pin them in with the Adventurer's Guild, we can tear out their throat, leaving only dregs to flee."

"What about Jasper's stipulation to not let the other sects communicate with others?"

"We'll take some flack, but with the forces the sects brought, it is clear they are token forces, wanting to see how things play out."

"They shouldn't blame us for being cold." Gudriksson lifted his battle axe and rested it on his shoulder.

"Send word to Jasper. I agree with his plan," she said to an aide.

Time went slowly as the Willful Institute rolled across the plains. Their troops marched on ingredient-growing beds, and their wheels left divots in the ground, crushing anything that had once been there.

"They are in the range of the outer walls," Gudriksson reported.

"Hold steady. I want the middle walls to get in range first."

"The commanders of the middle walls are in range."

"Send the command."

"Fire all weapons!" Gudriksson yelled into his sound transmission device.

The walls rumbled as the heavy siege weapons fired.

They hurled magical payloads from the walls. Enchanted stones and mana cannons left trails of light before they crashed into the mana barriers. The interconnected lightning arcs took the impact of the attacks that went off like grenades, exploding and creating shockwaves that bounced off the flashing barriers.

The younger members of the Willful Institute paused as the attacks landed just tens of meters above them. Massive boulders the size of a man turned to dust. The Willful Institute trudged forward under the shadows of the attacks.

"Inner walls are in range," Gudriksson said. A catapult near them was released, with the sound of wood shooting back and slamming into a stop and the whir of the arm flipping forward; the catapult's payload released, arcing over the middle and inner walls.

The walls were all over the place, but with them at different heights going out, they could fire three times the amount of weapons compared to having a regular defensive castle.

Another catapult fired down the line, and then the next, jumping as the arms reached their full extension. Teams of beasts were hooked up to the catapults and trebuchets, pulling them back into place while mages cast spells on the payloads.

"Mages are in range," Gudriksson said.

Casting formations under the mages lit up, multiplying the spell's effects.. Area of attack spells: lightning, ice, and rain descended from the heavens. Meteors leaving burning trails through the low-lying cloud cover.

Plant, earth, and stone golems rose from the ground and charged the Willful Institute.

Some of them were cut down by friendly fire. Storgaard was unmoved as the golems closed in on the mana barriers. Willful Institute members unleashed their attacks, cutting the golems down with ranged weapons such as bows, arrows, spells, and spell scrolls.

As expected of a force that had been able to reach into the Fifth Realm, they worked well together and weren't moved by the attacks falling upon them.

Storgaard frowned. "We heard they were getting reinforcements from other groups in the Third Realm, right?"

"Yes, Branch Head."

"Where did that information come from? Because those soldiers look too steady for a group from the Third Realm. They look more like a veteran troop from the Fourth Realm."

Hidden behind Reynir's city walls, the Adventurer's Guild's siege weaponry remained silent, covered in protective tarps, waiting and ready. Most of the guild waited beneath the walls so the defenders looked sparse across the city.

It'll be one hell of a shock when they join in. Domonos looked out at the defenders, attacking, recovering and preparing, aiming and attacking again.

Crews worked together seamlessly, cranking back catapults and trebuchets, loading massive boulders enhanced with quick spells and formations. Mana cannons were recharged and rolled forward before being fired again, sending out lances of destructive power.

Trebuchets and catapults creaked and groaned, releasing their massive payloads into the heavens, passing over Reynir and dropping on the Willful Institute's mana barriers, creating ripples like a god smashing their fist into a calm pond. Those that missed hit the ground, throwing up great waves of dirt as they exploded and released their destructive magic.

With the height advantage, they could hit them earlier. It wouldn't be long until they were in range. *I wonder what they'll do,* Domonos thought.

"So, what are we waiting for?" Jasper looked at the silent reserves of people and weapons behind the walls.

"We're waiting for them to commit," Domonos said. "If we keep our numbers and ranged abilities hidden, they will assume that what has hit them already is all we have. They're probing right now and looking for openings. Once they are comfortable and commit to an attack to enter the city, we can show our hand. Use it to shock them. They're using their veteran units in the vanguard to show the younger and less experienced members how it is done. They'll have more confidence, and even if they're scared shitless, because others did it, they'll push themselves to do it as well. We want their morale to be high and bring it crashing down."

"What if we hit them now?" Jasper asked out of curiosity.

"Then they can pull back in an orderly retreat, say there are too many people here, and get reinforcements. Or they pull back to Meokar, securing their rear as they do so."

"How long will it take?"

"However long it needs. Looks like they're in range of the gates."

The Institute stopped their advance. Their soldiers deployed siege weapons, securing them to the ground, manipulating it to create hardened surfaces. Walls grew from the ground to create an ad-hoc camp.

Formations deployed to cover the camp. Mages set up amplification formations.

A mana barrier failed, and debris tore apart a newly formed wall and the people working on it. A new mana barrier was thrown out, and soldiers kept working.

A massive mana barrier covered the area, much brighter than the others. Impacts slammed against its solid, golden surface.

"They're well-trained, which will make this harder. They are building four support camps and two forward camps. With that, they can retreat from their forward camps, having a clean line of retreat. We'll have to take care of those."

"How?"

"Kinetic penetrators. Three spell scrolls overlaying one another."

"That sounds a little terrifying."

"Yeah, it's said to be a peak sixth-tier spell, touching on a seventh-tier spell formation."

Jasper nodded, accepting it. "How long might it be before they commit?"

"Could be hours, could be days, with their actions. They're not fools. They'll take some hours to set up their camp. From there, they'll start truly fighting."

The Willful Institute's siege weaponry attacked.

Jasper half-jumped while Domonos surveyed the different weapons.

Their pillars of mana from their spells, and mana cannons left burning lines of light across the watcher's eyes and the gray mana barriers with red and yellow lines running through them.

Event
The city of Reynir is under attack! Pick a side!
Defend Reynir
Attack Reynir

Defend

"They're using Fire-based siege weapons, mainly mana cannons and spell scrolls. Standard tactics," Domonos said to the side, ignoring Jasper's reaction. *He'll get used to the sound of incoming fire all too quickly.*

"Looks like they are serious. We must have rattled their cage. Those must be their dark birds." Domonos pointed at some new siege weapons as they were pulled from storage rings. They rested on five wheels, two at the front and three at the rear; tubes were stacked one upon another in a square. Formations were carved along the weapon barrels, and there were ferocious bird heads on the end of the cannon's mouths.

"They look rather dominating," Jasper said dryly.

"What? Not impressed by their craftsmanship?"

"Why does it matter if they have eagle heads on them and fancy formations?"

"Traditionalist crafters instead of our more utilitarian ones." Domonos patted his simple-looking armor. "Though they are pretty powerful. They use a Fire spell medium that looks like a bird and shoot it out of the tubes. Their damage is lower, but they're more accurate and can shoot multiple attacks in a row. If you hit mana barriers in the same place again and again, then it can create a spotting effect, opening it up as the power needs to reach that area. If they punch a hole with their dark birds, they can flood through the barrier, and the dark bird projectiles can change their point of aim, raking targets inside the barrier. They might use different gear, but we would be fools to think of them as weak opponents."

"I understand. I guess it is just part of being an Alvan."

Heavy siege weapons of both sides hammered on the other's mana barriers; projectiles were turned to dust with their impacts, and beam weapons left traces on one another. The heavens and the ground were transformed as golems turned into the main ground forces, looking to attack the other's stronghold.

Where projectiles missed, they slammed into the mountain. Rock exploded, leading to landslides. The ground was turned into craters, and precious ingredients were ruined. Unlucky golems disappeared under the attacks, turning into spreading shrapnel that rained down on the ground, only to be re-summoned into other golems.

Domonos saw it all, but his eyes were focused on the mana stones being absorbed into the tube squares.

A mage activated the weapon. They were set four tubes across and four down. The top row of tubes ignited from the right side, ripple-firing across all eight tubes to the other side. The wheels rolled back, and a stream of red lights impacted the mana barrier, exploding with fiery results.

The upper tubes were recharged and were allowed to cool as the second row ignited, letting off an ear-splitting ripple-shot. A dozen of the dark birds fired, spitting out projectiles that looked like fiery phoenixes crashing into the Grey Peak sect's mana barrier.

"Interesting. Looks like they've been drinking their own medicine," Domonos muttered to himself.

"What do you mean?" Jasper asked. With all the fierce attacks around him, he was walking along the edge of fear and complacency.

If the attacks were to hit them head-on, like those golems, they would be torn apart and turned into rubble. The massive mana barriers of Reynir were keeping them at bay. The dark birds were terrifying weapons, capable of firing faster than the regular mana cannons repeatedly. Like a group of mortars strapped together.

"The weakness of most of the Institute's mana barriers is Fire spells, right? Their siege weapons all tend toward the idea that they would be going up against lightning-based mana barriers. The crafters used Fire-based attacks to look better to the purchasers."

"So, you're saying that these attacks are good against Metal attribute mana barriers but not as strong against other barriers?"

"Exactly."

"What is our process for attacking barriers?"

"Fire a volley with each type of element and figure out what the composition of the enemy barrier is. We can alter the formations in the artillery shells and the spells our mages use so they cause the most damage."

"What about the kinetic penetrators?"

"Well, when that tactic takes too long, we overwhelm them with power."

"Why does it sound simple when you say it but terrifying when you explain it?" Jasper wiped away the sweat, blinking, trying to understand what he was seeing.

"Best to take a walk. Don't know how long this will take. The troops will feel better seeing familiar faces. I'll rotate them on and off the wall; that way they can get used to the sights and sounds," Domonos said.

Jasper nodded, breathing heavily. "I'm glad to have you here. I put my adventurers in your care."

"I'll treat them as I would my own soldiers."

Jasper clapped Domonos's shoulder again and walked down the wall.

"Is something wrong, grandniece?" Low Elder Kostic asked Mercy as they reached the Wayside Inn where they were staying.

"I ran into the colonel."

"Did you remember where you know him from?"

"I-I think I might, but it doesn't make sense."

He waved for her to continue.

"When I talked to him, he knew my name—my nickname. He called me Mistress Mercy without blinking. Not like he had to recall the name; he *knew* it. He made me think about this nobody I had seen in the Third

Realm. He had a powerful piece of gear that he used to get there. I trained him with my whip and turned him into one of my attendants."

His eyes narrowed. "Colonel Silaz is one of the strongest people in Vuzgal. Few people have seen how powerful he is, but through our sources, the soldiers say that he is like a demon in human skin. The referees on the stages—they are apparently three places weaker than him, and the places are supposed to be large gaps."

"I know, which is why I am not sure. I beat that man halfway to death. I broke his body, and I wasted him. I sent him to the darker side of the city, though he never made it to the slaver. He was rescued by two people. That was why I remembered him. Knowing that there was one person who got away…he could be a possible threat. He wasn't that strong. Even if he escaped, there wasn't much he could do. What if…?"

"That is a dangerous thought." Low Elder Kostic held his chin. "If he is that person, we have waded into deep waters."

"What do you mean, granduncle?"

"Make sure that you cover your tracks. Is that slaver you sold him to still alive?"

"I am not sure." She cowed under his gaze.

"This one time your *inability* to clean up loose ends might help. Ensure that he and others who know about that man are silenced. Remove any possible link to him. Research just who that man is, his name, and where he came from. If it matches up, then I can take it to Elder Cai Bo. If used right, you might get a reward from the sect."

"Do you think that is possible?"

"I do not know anything until you find more information. Next time, make sure there are no witnesses or people with loose lips," he growled, staring at Mercy.

"Yes, granduncle. I was too short-sighted."

"In these turbulent times, if you can prove yourself, everything can change—for the faction, for our own clan."

"I won't let you down, granduncle."

40

Breaking into the Top 100

Ledell looked around Vuzgal. After meeting Momma Rodriguez, he'd lost most of his piercings, and instead of hunching over, he stood straighter. He'd applied to different mercenary groups, and on his third application to the Adventurer's Guild, either out of pity or something else, he had been accepted.

Since then, he'd made several friends within the guild.

"You want to get food?" a mage asked as Ledell led the party through Vuzgal.

"The fights are still going on. We can just have Stamina potions!" another said.

"Trust me, I got a recommendation!" Ledell waved his hands, dismissing their comments. He reached the entrance to the Sky Reaching Restaurant and looked up at the tall building.

"Really, Vuzgal is crazy! Those skyscrapers and towers that reach up into the sky are made of stone, filled with houses, rooms, stores, and several that are just restaurants." One of his group clicked her tongue in disbelief, shifting her sword.

"We know!" the others said in unison.

Since going to Momma Rodriguez's, Ledell had turned into something of a foodie. Every place he went, if there were restaurants, he would try them out. Few were able to beat Momma Rodriguez's menu.

They waited in line, interested more by the building and mollified with the powerful people entering ahead of them and in the queue behind them.

"Party of five, please come with me." The man led them through the restaurant. On the lower floor, people sat around a large bar; people made drinks, and the customers watched the events in the fighter's competition. People talked about their different crafts and mercenary companies to spread their presence.

They went in through a doorway to a platform. The host pressed a button, and they rose slowly and then quickly.

"What is this, a floating platform?"

"It is called a lift. There are multiple safety formations put in place. Please hold on to the railings," the host said.

Ledell did so as the tube around the lift disappeared and they were in a glass tube.

"Ahh!"

A few of his party members freaked out as they looked out at the city tens of meters below them and separated by a few pieces of glass.

The host continued to smile.

The lift stopped, the doors opened, and they all quickly left.

Ledell took them to a booth and they sat down, enjoying the panoramic view. Several towers were dotted around the city. The towers weren't crowded together, giving them an unobstructed view.

The fights continued on the screens. In the distance, they saw the famed Battle Arena where everything was happening.

The waiters came and went, and soon they arrived with food.

"I'm starving! Good call, brother Ledell!"

"I said I wouldn't take you somewhere bad!"

"What did you get, big brother Ledell?" a younger-looking woman asked.

"Deep fried chicken!" Ledell grabbed the chicken and took a bite. He closed his eyes. The crunch, the perfectly cooked and flavored chicken. The spice set his mouth on fire. "So crunchy!"

"Ah, it's the cornflakes."

It is so damn good. It could almost compete with Momma Rodriguez's chicken! Wait, did he say cornflakes?

Ledell turned, but the waiter had already left.

Shrugging, he left the talking to others as he dove into his meal.

Erik and Rugrat watched the matches, distracted by the reports they were getting. Domonos had left Vuzgal two days ago, while Elan and Glosil continued to work in the dark to affect the Willful Institute across the Ten Realms.

Thankfully, they were kind enough to send one of their elders over to Vuzgal. With the answering statue, they had been picking up parts of different reports and getting up-to-date and accurate information—without needing to put an agent's life in danger.

The fight at Reynir and Meokar would be their opening blow. If it went well, it would show that their military was on the right path. It would raise their morale. With the Adventurer's Guild and the people from the Dragon Battalion remaining hidden, people were starting to get anxious, including Erik and Rugrat.

"Looks like Kim Cheol is heading up on stage. After his soul-stirring fight last year, I was determined to bring him to the Fighter's Association. You know, he turned me down? I guess that only makes sense for someone who would go to extremes to win a simple competition." Klaus, the leader of the Vuzgal Fighter's Association, sounded more excited than upset.

"He is a powerful fighter," Erik agreed.

"If he wants to make it into the top one hundred, it won't be easy. He is up against Tilly, the trainer. She's a ranger, and she has three trained Iron wolves under her command. It is said they reached a level of compatibility that allows them to work together seamlessly. She can buff them and support them with her own attacks."

A young-looking lady wearing gray-and-white armor stepped onto the stage with three wolves that reached her chest height. The four of them moved together as if a single entity.

Kim Cheol walked up to the stage with his massive shield and a large hammer that rested on his hip. His boar helmet showed scars, and one horn was broken, no longer as clean and perfect as it had been last year.

They marched across the stage and reached the referee. The wolves snarled at Cheol as he reached out his hand. Tilly shook it, and they returned to their sides of the stage.

Cheol dropped the visor of his helmet and pulled the hammer from his side while Tilly pulled the bow from her shoulder.

The referee started the match.

Tilly fired arrows as she cast spells.

"She's dual-casting buffing spells on herself and on her beasts," Rugrat said.

Cheol moved out of the corner and along the side of the rectangular stage. His shield rang out with impacts, his eyes focused on Tilly.

"He's using the side of the stage to protect himself; he's outnumbered," Klaus said.

Tilly had him on the defensive, holding him back. She sent out her wolves, glowing with buffing spells. They advanced and spread out. Cheol slipped on the ground, and the wolves charged at Cheol's open side. Tilly anticipated where he would land and fired. The arrow looked as if it would strike his helmet, but went right past.

He faked the fall!

Cheol used the fall to gain momentum. He jumped up and ran to meet the wolves. They came from his right, left, and straight on.

He made to bash the first wolf and fell, sliding. The wolf jumped above Cheol. He used a Wind spell. It was badly placed, but it pushed the wolf high enough so that it came down outside of the fighting stage. Cheol dug in his foot, coming to his feet at a run as he shot out a blast of air at the woman. She took the hit head-on and released an arrow. Cheol knocked it to the side with a yell. The half-pause was what the wolves needed; they jumped up and clamped on his arms, dragging his shield down. Tilly held an arrow ready, aimed directly at Cheol's head.

"I lose!" Cheol declared.

The referee came out, and Tilly lowered her bow and her wolves released Kim Cheol's arms. He opened his visor, a smile on his face. He bowed his head to Tilly, who returned the gesture, and they walked off the stage.

"That is a shame. Even Kim Cheol wasn't able to make it into the top one hundred." Klaus sighed.

"Are you jinxing my guild, Mister Klaus?" Blaze complained.

"Jinxing you? You have sixteen people in the top one hundred. I have four!" Gu Chen, one of the Silver Dragon managers said.

"With that, the top one hundred are decided. Come on, you should be able to have some people reach the top fifty, right?" Blaze joked.

"Don't start jinxing me too!"

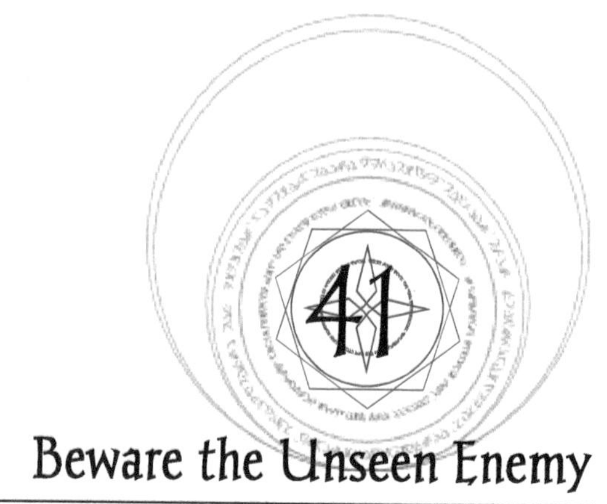

41 Beware the Unseen Enemy

Darkness fell over the city. A group of men walked through an alleyway, stumbling slightly from drink.

"The elders are working together now, using us to protect these cities. We should be in the higher realms, cultivating and getting stronger. So what if we lose some lower branches!"

"Right! The other factions are losing more than us. They are just bad at managing their cities!"

Roska stood on a roof, watching them, unmoving. She tilted her head toward another shadow. It moved and rose slightly. Other shadows shifted unseen behind the group.

"In position." Imani's voice was a soft whisper in her ear.

"Nothing in the surrounding area. You're clear," Tully followed up.

Roska dropped to the ground. Her cloak covered all but the bottom of her face. She walked out of an alleyway, turning in the middle of the street. "Disciplinary Elders Oskar, Alan, and Ren Yu?"

The men looked up at her in surprise.

"Ah, perfect. You brought some friends."

"Who are you?" Elder Oskar squinted and put his hand on his blade.

"And you're wearing your armor. That will make things easier." Roska didn't stop her steps and whistled.

"I asked who you are!" Oskar demanded.

"I'm your killer."

Roska was just some feet away as Oskar and Alan opened their mouths to cry out in pain, but they were struck by a Silence spell attached to the arrows that had pierced their backs.

Stun spells hit others as sword users who had been hiding in the shadows appeared. Their blades stabbed the remaining Willful Institute members.

Before they fell to the ground, Roska waved a storage ring.

Not even a drop of blood hit the ground, leaving several shadows to resolve themselves into the members of Special Team Two.

Each of them held weapons forged by the Willful Institute. They quickly split up and headed in different directions.

They had less than twenty-four hours to carry out the next part.

It was mid-morning in Vuzgal. High Elder Cai Bo had finished her reports and sent them back to Sect Head Foster. She included her speculations that Vuzgal and the Adventurer's Guild were in close association, possibly even an alliance.

The fact that the Adventurer's Guild was the same one that the Meokar branch had offended indicated some bond.

She looked out of her room at the grand buildings of Vuzgal.

The Ten Realms was not a merciful place. To get to her position, she had needed to silence and deal with others without a trace. She had always felt in control. There were guilds and sects from across the Ten Realms that had been suppressed to keep their position. They were not that strong apart, but working together, they could take a chunk out of the Willful Institute. If they were weakened, wouldn't other large sects think about taking more? She would connect with some other sects in secret to bring her followers over if necessary. She did not intend to fall with the Willful Institute.

There was a knock at her door.

"Come in."

"High Elder Cai Bo," Low Elder Kostic said.

"Has your grandniece Mercy remembered anything more about Domonos?"

"I do not have great hope for it, but she is looking into her past and searching for information. I hope she can find something of use for us."

"If we can find out anything about Vuzgal, we will have an advantage over the others. For a place with so many mysteries, those secrets will be their weakness."

"As you say, High Elder."

"Do you have the reports from Meokar?"

"Yes. The battle started three days ago. The Adventurer's Guild is there. Supposedly, their vice guildmaster is leading them, a man by the name of Jasper. Based on the scouts' observations, it looks like the guild and the other sects took a token force."

"Good. If they aren't devoted to the cause, there is room for negotiation. If they are, then it will be nearly impossible to deal with them."

"Why is that, High Elder?"

Cai Bo's brows pinched together. "There are two groups of people who survive in the Ten Realms. Those who are so strong that others don't want to compete with them because it will cause more losses than gains. The second are mad dogs. Groups who, if they are slighted, will go all in to get retribution. They rarely last long. But the ones who do last become massive powers. No one wants to fight them. After a point, there is no going back because they will devote everything to protect and get retribution for their people."

The third are people who can use those stronger and more stupid to their will, making them think it was their idea in the first place.

"What kind of sects could possibly live like that? Even we have lost people here and there from some kind of challenge. Sometimes we must give slight concessions to advance later."

Cai Bo's eyes shifted to a grand circle of buildings. "The associations are mad dogs. That is the true reason no one would want to deal with them. Think of what happened to the powers that were involved with the Tareng and Vuzgal battles. The Blood Demon sect fell apart and was absorbed by other sects that had close ties to the associations. Other sects were given concessions, but they didn't try to fight. Why? Because the associations were behind everything."

"I have heard of associations backing down in the past, though," Low Elder Kostic said.

"It is rare, nearly never seen in the lower realms. In the Seventh and higher realms, the associations tend to be neutral. There are powers that can make even them think twice about taking action. Although the associations might back down from some things, if you attack one of them, they will do everything in their power to grind you down. If you attack a city they are in and make sure to not harm their people, then everything is fine. Do you understand?"

"They're mad dogs if you attack them directly, but others, even friendly sects, it is rare for them to step out and protect. Even they have limits," Low Elder Kostic said.

"Correct. Now, with so few people at Reynir, the Adventurer's Guild doesn't rate Meokar that highly. It must be a minor incident, but they have to show at least a token force to appease their people and their interests. Taking the resources from Meokar is about the limit of what they can do, unless they want to declare war on the entire Institute." Cai Bo's words hung in the air before she turned around.

"It has been too long since I last left the Willful Institute. So many new powers have risen. Our Institute has only got seven places in the top one hundred of this competition."

"We will take the top ten spots," Low Elder Kostic said.

"Yes, our people have finer heritages and combat skills. Though what was a small guild last year, dominating the top one hundred, becoming a famous black sheep—this year, still has sixteen members who are in the top one hundred."

"They aren't as strong as our people on a one-on-one basis."

"In a fight, is it ever one-on-one?" Cai Bo's eyes shone as she gazed into space, seeing something only known to her. "Guilds fight as groups, protecting merchants and carrying out different missions. Fighting by themselves is disadvantageous to them. In our Institute, one has to rely on their own power to advance. How else could we make a large group of Experts? Those who can't be the best take spots in the guards or fighting forces. There they can hone their fighting skills and Strength, gaining contribution points to make a comeback and get greater backing of the Institute."

"We have raised many fine warriors, even powerhouses in the Seventh Realm. Our power in the Fourth Realm continues to grow."

"I agree that our system is much better, but we can't be blind to each other's systems and methods."

"High Elder is wise. Our system is the best, but we should not discount others for their own strengths." Low Elder Kostic seemed to have been caught by an inspiration and cupped his hands, bowing.

"What about the relationships I had you look into?"

"Blaze, the leader of the Adventurer's Guild, is in a relationship with Elise, the leader of the Trader's Guild, which acts as the manager of all traders in Vuzgal. Although she is stated as independent and is neutral in all matters, she is from Vuzgal. Weapons and armor for the Adventurer's Guild is purchased from Vuzgal Academy. So are their potions and their clothes. They have healers trained by the Vuzgal-controlled healing houses. Other than the relationship with the trade guild leader, these things may be coincidental. They are, after all, headquartered in Vuzgal. Playing nice with the landlord makes sense. Though, with everything…" Low Elder Kostic held back his words.

"What do you think?"

"What if the Adventurer's Guild and Vuzgal are connected on a deeper level?"

"Then Vuzgal as we see it might only be the tip of the iceberg. It brings everything into question. Best case is that Vuzgal was settled by a group of mercenaries that switched to be the Vuzgal guards to look good for the associations. They had the connections to stabilize Vuzgal and invited other guilds they knew to help them out in creating a sect. Otherwise, I have no idea what it might be. If they have a backer, how strong must they be to do all of this and keep their hand hidden this long?"

The Tolentinos were seen as hot heads. She could get them to take action and test the waters.

Roska put the fruit down, not listening to the vendor as she turned, trailing behind a passing carriage.

Guards wearing the clothes of the Willful Institute flanked the carriage on their mounts watching the crowd with the bored derision born from repetition and numbers.

He never leaves with less than a hundred guards. Seems he has a high opinion of himself. I guess he should, being a high elder of the Willful Institute.

She heard two clear clicking noises through her sound transmission device.

Spells appeared around the carriage. Green smoke spread out from the spell formations, covering the people in the convoy and making them and their mounts cough.

Guards yelled out and civilians ran away.

"Ambush!" a guard yelled as special team members appeared on roofs, shooting arrows at the convoy, killing some and wounding others.

Defensive formations covered the carriage, protecting it.

A team member on the roof's activated a spell scroll.

A spear of Fire evaporated the water on the street as people ran in every direction, screaming. Other spears shot down from the roof, making a whooshing noise as the first flaming spear seemed to suck in the air around the carriage, turning it into scathing heat. Noise, like a wall rolled away. The smoke had been a flammable gas, not a distraction.

Mounts and guards had been thrown clear, killing some, injuring others.

The mana barriers flared to life, and the impact tilted the carriage onto its side.

"Kill them!" The remaining guards jumped off mounts and into the fray.

Roska pulled out a spell scroll and tore it.

A spell formation appeared above the carriage mixing greens, browns, and pure white. A pillar shot down like doomsday. Instead of piercing the carriage, it turned into threads of power that raced out to the surrounding area, entering the beasts.

Their muscles bulged, and their eyes turned red as they roared. Their primordial, brutal bloodlines ignited as they charged at one another, not caring about their riders anymore. The team pulling the carriage broke free of their harnesses and turned on the driver, who was trapped under the carriage. They attacked the carriage and one another, turning into pandemonium. The guards had to kill their own mounts as they created a protective barrier around the carriage. The dead and dying were strewn across the ground as the carriage lay broken on its side. Fire bolts shot through the air again, killing more guards and striking the carriage; smoke and flames spread.

Up—he sees me. Come on down!

An arrow shot past Roska; she turned and ran.

"Catch her!" the guards yelled.

Roska ran. Arrows shot out at her, hitting random items in the narrow alleyway.

"Arrow incoming," Imani said.

Roska braced herself, ducking behind some crates at an intersection in the alleyway.

An arrow shot out from behind the group of guards pursuing her. None of them would have noticed where it came from, thinking it was one of their own that had hit the attacker in the back.

Roska went down with a blood-curdling scream. Hidden by the crates, she waved her storage ring. A body from the night before appeared with an arrow in the back. Fresh blood flowed from the wound.

She stared at the rat sniffing the ground near her feet. She touched the beast crate on its back and disappeared in a flash.

The rat scampered away, entering a sewer grate with its payload safe.

Moments later, armed guards turned the corner, staring at their "victim." With a boot, they flipped over the dead attacker.

"Put the body in your storage ring. We'll figure out who they are later. There are more attackers we need to capture!"

Glosil walked into the command center. Elan had become a permanent feature there, while Yui and Kanoa seemed to rotate in and out.

Kanoa stood off to the side, coordinating an air lift for several ongoing missions. Yui was checking incoming information.

Roska was there too. She was wearing her combat fatigues and war belt and looked almost peaceful compared to her complete body armor and weapons.

Yui and Elan looked up from what they were doing.

Glosil waved to the conference room.

They all entered and took their seats, staring at Roska, who was sitting down rubbing her face tiredly. She'd bypassed taking a shower to get debriefed.

"All right, let's go through it," Glosil said.

"We infiltrated the target city Leeto three days ago. We met up with the local intelligence agents. They gave us the itinerary of the target High Elder Dastan. We watched him the first day on his route through the city that he takes every two days. We used the information and planning from the intelligence agents to modify the plan. With such a short time window, we had to move quickly. I would have preferred more time to set up the attack—a week or two."

"I understand. We have been rushing things to hit the Willful Institute as hard as possible," Glosil said.

Roska nodded. "The night of the second day, we found a group of people from an opposing faction of High Elder Dastan. We set up the ambush in a short period of time. Honestly, the intelligence agents have been nothing but the best to work with. If not for them, this would have fallen apart. We've got a deep trust with them now." Roska glanced over to Elan, who bowed his head in thanks.

"We attacked the scapegoats, killing them from behind. This way, their wounds would match with Dastan's guards killing their attackers in the chase. We used weapons we received from a consignment of arms stolen by the Adventurer's Guild. There shouldn't be any flaws. Elan's people had letters, plans, and information that we inserted into their storage rings. We matched people with the bodies and kept them stored, so their blood was still fresh and their bodies warm." Roska coughed.

"Water?" Yui asked.

"Please."

Yui grabbed a glass and filled it with water as Roska kept talking.

"Once that was done, we had three ambush locations set up across the city to hit the convoy. They bypassed route Alpha, and we moved to Bravo. Thanks."

Yui passed her water, and she drank it quickly.

She quickly debriefed them on the operation, finishing it off with some large gulps of water.

"Based on what my people are hearing, Dastan knows who his attackers are. He's in a rage, and he is going to the Willful Institute's head to seek an explanation. It should stir things up in their command and control," Elan said.

"It was a complex mission, and your team thought outside of the box and used all the resources at your disposal to carry it out flawlessly." Glosil pressed his finger into the table. "You and your team should get some rest."

"Sir, I wanted to ask about what is happening in the other operations?"

"Sorry. It has been a little crazy." Glosil cleared his throat and organized his thoughts. "Operations in the Second Realm have hampered the Willful Institute to such a high degree that it is a matter of time until the locations there start to fall. The Willful Institute is consolidating its power in the Third and Fourth Realms. The Third Realm is on a tipping point, even if the Willful Institute doesn't know it yet. The other sects that are against the Willful Institute are watching Reynir and Meokar closely. If we can pull off a win there, it will have a domino effect and the other sects will pile in and work against the Willful Institute. Things in the Fourth Realm are trickier. The sects are all holding back. If the Willful Institute is cut off from traders and from the lower realms, they will die a slow death. Moving items in the higher realms costs more money; people are more expensive to hire and are more turbulent.

"Our aim is to win at Meokar and send the Willful Institute reeling. Once they are on their back foot, we'll continue to put pressure on them in the Fourth Realm. They did lose a city in the Fourth Realm, but that is not unheard of. It is even recoverable, and some groups come back stronger. The other sects are waiting for a vicious counterattack or to see the Institute's decline. Then we have two options: have Vuzgal lead other sects to take down the Willful Institute cities, thus inciting others to attack before the Willful Institute's cities are all taken, or we commence operations in the Fifth Realm to remove any possibility of the Institute progressing, holding them down and pushing the other groups to destroy them from below," Glosil said.

"Your mission adds to the instability of the faint alliance the different factions within the Willful Institute are forming. It will force Head Foster to divert his attention to rooting out those who want to use this to gain a higher position, focusing on internal threats instead of external ones, allowing us greater breathing room," Elan added.

"What is our next move?" Roska asked.

"Defeat them at Meokar. With that and using the guise of the Adventurer's Guild, we will support the taking down of the Willful Institute and recruit more people to the guild and to the Alva military. Then we will be ready to fight the Institute in the Fourth Realm as the Vuzgal Defense Force," Glosil said. "You and your team have done well. Get some rest. The special teams are the tip of the spear. We'll need you honed and sharp for the next mission."

"Yes, Commander." Roska stood and saluted. The others stood as well and saluted, other than Elan, who bowed his head.

"The Willful Institute's days are numbered," Yui said.

"Anyone who attacks Alvans can only count down the days they have left," Roska said.

Glosil felt his jaw lock together, and he nodded.

42 Committed

Erik sat in his chair. Without moving his head, he glanced over to the side, watching the Willful Institute's box. He returned his attention to the stages as Lin Lei, one of the three remaining branch heads in Vuzgal's fighter's competition, stepped up.

The fighting had been intense. The Adventurer's Guild had their people steadily knocked out of the running. In the top twenty, there were three of them left, though Blaze didn't look affected.

Erik stood and walked over to Chonglu.

Chonglu said goodbye to the few people he was talking to and joined Erik in a corner, watching as Lin Lei's opponent—an armored knight with heavy armor and a single two-handed bastard sword—stepped up opposite.

Erik used a sound-canceling formation, silencing the crowds around them and stopping anything from leaking out. "Stiff competition this year. The Adventurer's Guild isn't doing so well."

"Sixteen spots in the top one hundred, fourteen in the top fifty. Their rankings aren't as high as last year, but there are more competitors out there.

Also, most people might not have noticed, but the Adventurer's Guild took one-third of the top five hundred spots. The branch heads are all wearing devices to hold their Mana and Body Cultivation in check. They're fighting at two-thirds of their overall power."

"Seems that Alvans are always keeping some secrets," Erik muttered.

"You taught us well." Chonglu laughed.

Lin Lei and the bastard sword fighter started their fight. Lin Lei had two daggers in her hand, making her look pitiful in front of the sword fighter.

He moved forward, neither too slow nor too fast. Lin Lei moved from side to side like a cat cornered, slipping out and away from him when one thought that she was pinned in.

She cast a spell. Smoke rose around her, and two Lin Lei's appeared.

One of them moved the smoke when they left; that has to be her.

The man swung his sword at the fake Lin Lei as it closed on him with the real. He used the momentum of his swing to turn around, slicing at the real Lin Lei. The Wind shifted and turned into a Wind blade as it cut through Lin Lei.

Erik straightened, feeling the cut across his own body. Lin Lei's body dissipated into grinning smoke. A foot kicked out, hitting the bastard sword user in the back of the knee. He dropped down, and the smoke turned to ice shackles, freezing his knee to the ground. Lin Lei jumped up, her attack pausing just a few centimeters from the bastard sword fighter's neck, creating interference with the mana barrier medallion he was holding.

Erik's heartbeat was just starting to come back to normal under the thrill of the fight and the fear of Lin Lei being killed with the bastard sword user's reversing attack.

"Damn, she would have tricked me as well if I didn't use my mana domain," Erik muttered.

"Few things are how they appear on the surface."

For several days, the forces of the Willful Institute had been attacking the Grey Peak sect's city of Reynir. The once-orderly rows of ingredients had been turned into a wasteland filled with craters and turbulent magical energies. Siege weaponry on both sides had fired day and night, keeping members of both forces awake at all hours.

High Elder Mendes cursed as he stepped off the mage-maintained path and into the mud. "Damn, what are those mages doing?" Mendes hissed. Sleeping in a tent for several days was not what he had envisioned as his fate as the leader of Meokar.

The camps had grown out of the mud and storage rings. Solid stone walls surrounded the orderly tents. The main roads between the gates and around the solid buildings where the elders and leaders of the sect made their plans were maintained by mages—simple, broken stone shavings and sand mixed with the mud to stop one's feet from sinking into the calf-high mud.

The plateau had been farmer's lands for unknown years, being tilled constantly and watered. Now, with a few thousand Willful Institute guards and disciples walking on it, it had turned into a swill perfect for one to lose their shoe in.

People huddled around fires, covered up against the chillier climate. A few let out wet coughs. The cold, the lack of sleep, and the damp were getting to their lungs.

Mendes and his guards continued to the large command building. They had erected six camps in the same layout. Two supporting camps lay near the plateau's entrances, and although they couldn't reach one another in the large openings, anything that wanted to enter or leave would have to fight them.

The forward attacking camps were smaller than the supporting camps, with larger walls and stronger mana barriers. Providing a location, the Willful Institute could launch ranged siege attacks against Reynir.

Even now, attacks raged across the two forward camps and across Reynir's barriers.

Mendes peered into the late-night darkness, seeing the flickering of Fire and the display of destructive forces.

A guard opened the door for him, and he walked into the warm headquarters. Others made room for him as he walked up to the command center.

Elder Xiao was there, staring at the map and talking to a scarred lady, who pointed to sections of wall surrounding Reynir.

"Elder Xiao," Mendes announced his entrance.

Xiao looked up without moving his head before saying something to the woman beside him. She bowed and strode out of the room.

"Elder Mendes," Xiao greeted and waved him forward. With their relative positions, he dropped the grand part of Mendes's title.

"We found our leverage. The Grey Peak sect is digging their heels in. We heard that people from the Fourth Realm have come to support the battle. Unless we want to pay a massive fee, we need to apply more pressure and gain a better negotiating position. With our seemingly random attacks and golems, we have found our opening."

Elder Xiao pointed to several positions. "Blind spots in Reynir's defenses. They don't have a good way to watch these areas and don't have any weapons they can bring to bear on them. Now, these locations here… and here are right next to the defenses. If we can get in close enough, we can push through their lower defenses, taking some pressure off us."

"This is great news, Elder Xiao." Mendes studied the map. "I am just an administrator. Your words have opened my eyes to the realities of war."

"My people are out, waking up different elders and officers to get their people ready. The forward camps will push forward, open the breaches, and hold them. Once they are secure, we will rush reinforcements forward. But we must wait until we have those openings, or our people will get stuck outside and be unable to push into the defenses. Then, we can send new demands to the leaders of Reynir, throwing them off their game and bringing them back down to reality."

"Your words have opened up the truth to me," Mendes praised. *Anything to get out of these damn mountains and show those Grey Peak bastards what happens when they attack my city!*

"Good. You will head to the other plateau entrance to stabilize things there and carry out the attack."

"I understand, Elder Xiao." *Damn, you are just some guard leader, and you are ordering me, a sect leader, around? I will let it slide until you deal with these ants!* "I will set off immediately."

Gudriksson and Storgaard walked along the walls, showing their faces. The wall was sparse, but there was little room in any of Reynir's buildings and storehouses as they were packed with men and women of the Grey Peak sect and the Adventurer's Guild.

Storgaard was silent, digesting all that Gudriksson had told her. "What do you think?"

"I think we should never piss off the Adventurer's Guild."

Storgaard was surprised by how serious he sounded.

"I think we should follow their plan. If it fails, they are the ones leading the attack, so they will take the most losses. It's clear they don't want it messed up. They have a blood grudge with the Willful Institute."

"Over a single group of guild members from the Third Realm?"

"Yeah, they might be a little crazy, especially taking on a power like Meokar and Mendes. Though they're well organized, no discipline issues. They organized themselves, so they haven't had any health issues. Brought all the essentials with them. Rotating their people in and out all the time to get them used to the large-scale battle. I have reports of the leaders talking to the lowest members, teaching them about the enemy, their positions, what their aim is, and numerous plans."

"Those are closely guarded secrets!"

"Not in this guild. If anything happens, even the most basic soldier knows where to rally, who to follow in the fight. Also, they're going to respect their leaders more if they take time to talk to them."

"All right, we'll follow their plan. Just be ready with the Ice Domain spell scrolls in case we need to push the Willful Institute out of Reynir."

"Of course, Branch Head."

"They agreed," Jasper said to Domonos and Mister Yi. Domonos and Zukal were never in the same spot; in case something happened to one, the other was there to keep up command.

"Well, it looks like we're committed." Domonos glanced over to Mister Yi.

"The orders went out. They're preparing to make a dawn assault. Mendes will be in the eastern support camp Charlie, while Xiao is commanding from the southern camp Bravo," Yi said.

"The beast mounts are still located in the eastern camp Delta?"

From the southwest to the northeastern camp, they had named the support camps Alpha to Delta; the forward camps were called Sierra for the one to the south and Echo to the east.

"Correct," Yi said.

"Delta will be our first target, followed by Bravo."

"Why?" Jasper asked, curious.

"In the Third Realm, sound transmission devices, although not rare, are too expensive for most people. Mounted forces relay messages to most units. If we have the enemy running, the beasts will give them greater mobility, and they can shift their defense or attacks while pulling back. We remove that capability. Take Bravo, and it will take out Xiao and his closest associates. He is the only person with more power than Mendes. Command and control can fall apart. Nothing is for sure in war."

"Here they come," Bai Ping said.

Several mounted Willful Institute groups rushed out from Camp Sierra.

The attacks redoubled, making it hard to see through the mana barrier, which had turned into an opaque wall with the attacks.

Bai Ping was happy to not be attacking innocents.

He had been rescued at the gates of Vuzgal and accepted into the Vuzgal Defense Force. His family thrived in Vuzgal as he learned of the monster behind the city. He trained in Alva and had tested out the new formation armor. After testing was complete, the close protection details were deployed across the Ten Realms, taking up the slack from the special teams, supporting intelligence agents, and leading attacks against the Willful Institute.

Bai Ping and his squad were one of the first to transfer over to Meokar.

They integrated themselves into the guild units. Having worked in various units and done different jobs in the army, they fit in well. There were Alvans among the adventurers who made things easier. All the CPD members had the same experience as veteran sergeants, allowing them to work well even when broken up.

"Remember the orders?" Bai Ping asked the men and women around him.

"Hold the enemy. Kill them if we can. Retreat to the broken shed if the wall is breached. Fall back unit by unit to the mid-wall," the nineteen others repeated as one.

"Good. Now, let's see if we can't send some Willful bastards down to greet Robertson and his party." Bai Ping's voice was met with cheers and yells. "Load!"

Everyone grabbed their arrows and placed them on their bows.

He eyed the oncoming enemy. Feeling the wet cold of the mountains, he was unaffected.

"Draw!" The order came, and everyone pulled back on their bows and cast their spells upon their bow and arrows.

"Fire!" Across the wall, archers released their arrows. They dropped in the early morning light and people rang alarm bells, alerting Reynir that the enemy was sending an attack forward.

The noise had become all too familiar in the last few days.

"Load!" Bai Ping called again.

The first arrows peppered their target, meeting a mana barrier, and releasing their attacks.

An errant trebuchet boulder passed through a spotting in a Willful Institute barrier. It struck the ground, crushing soldiers, and skipped over the broken landscape, crashing through the golems that called this unnatural place filled with destructive magics their home.

Powerful Institute mages threw lances of power as they found trap spells that had been cast in the depths of the night. They soaked up the losses and trudged on.

They might be bastards, but they are a strong enemy.

Mana barriers came down, and the mounted force broke apart, fleeing back to Camp Sierra and its promised safety. Many didn't make it.

The majority pushed forward; a third got within two hundred meters. At this range, the density of spell traps rose, and the defenders attacked with ease, though the attackers were so close that the siege weapons on the mid and inner walls couldn't hit them anymore. The possibility of striking their own walls and people was just too high.

Bai Ping didn't know how many times he had called out corrections, altering the crew's aim, but now the enemy was too close to reload the siege weapons anymore.

"Ready weapons!" he barked. The mounted beasts would close the few hundred meters quickly.

Everyone grabbed their melee weapons, ready to repel attackers.

"They're heading for the wall!" a spotter called out.

"Drop rocks!" someone yelled. People kicked rocks down the slits in the wall, dropping them onto the enemy below, creating ripples on their different mana barriers.

Inside the mana barriers, the Willful Institute riders attacked the defenses, tearing into the walls.

Formations carved into the stone came to life, making it harder for the enemy to break through.

Bai Ping saw several people place formations on the wall that drew massive amounts of Water and Wind energy, creating a sideways whirlpool.

"Get off the wall!" Bai Ping's words were drowned out as the whirlpools condensed, slamming into the wall, one after another. They were like elemental drills, with the force of Wind and Water. Those on the wall couldn't hold their footing anymore and were tossed backward as stone exploded outward.

Bai Ping hit the ground heavily and rolled.

Mana barrier!

The spell snapped into existence, covering him as he tasted dirt and blood in his mouth. Boulders smashed against his mana barrier, bouncing off.

Other sections of the wall were taken down by different attack formations and spell scrolls. Even the mounted raiders were breaking through, using their beasts and combat techniques.

Bai Ping canceled his mana barrier, getting covered in stones. He pushed himself up and pulled out his sword.

"Rally to me!" he yelled. "Adventurer's Guild, up and at 'em! Check on your buddies! Pull the wounded back to the mid-wall!" The walls were like broken teeth. Some people had managed to keep their footing; others had been tossed free. He saw legs sticking out from underneath a pile of rubble.

He spat the dust and blood in his mouth as a beast roared. A man was just picking himself up off the ground as a spear sprouted through his chest. Through the dust and smoke, a mounted warrior appeared; he shifted his spear, shaking the dying man free.

Bai Ping ran forward; his speed increased, and he jumped onto a rock, then to another pile of rubble.

More mounted members of the Willful Institute came out of the breach behind the man with the bloodied spear. With the close-in walls and the uneven terrain, they didn't have the protection of their mana barriers anymore.

The spear user turned toward Bai Ping, only to feel a cool breeze on his neck. Bai Ping jumped onto another section of wall, pulling three throwing blades. Power flooded through his body, lighting up his arm and the daggers.

"Fly true!" he yelled. Spells settled on the throwing blades, and he followed their trajectory. The blades seemed to have eyes as they shifted their point of aim before sinking into the necks of three more mounted attackers.

Bai Ping's sword deflected a spear thrust. A mana spike shot out from his left hand. He stabbed out with the spike, using it like a lance to drive it into the attacker's chest.

He heard yells and felt the rush of air of a passing spell. His squad had gathered themselves together and attacked. One grabbed a mounted man's spear, dragging them off their mount in a display of Strength and Agility.

Another stabbed the spear user as they landed on the ground.

A spell crossed over their backs, slamming into a rider, leaning over to slash at them with a sword. The spell sent the riders flying into a pile of rubble. The rider started to get up another squad member's war hammer slammed into their back, embedding them in the ground and releasing them from life's hold.

The war hammer user raised his hammer as a lance of mana struck him, exploding and tossing him away.

"Wounded to the rear! Pull back to the shed!" Bai Ping yelled as he checked the area with a quick scan.

The Willful Institute wasn't charging in anymore; they tossed out spells that covered the area in smoke.

Bai Ping grabbed a wheezing woman who was on her knees. In one motion, he picked her up and put her over his shoulders. Using a mild healing spell on her, he helped her back toward the rear.

He saw his squad coming back. He counted his people.

"Where are Ahkmet and Gwen?"

"Gwen was in the path of one of those tornados," the war hammer user said with a dark look and shook his head as he hauled his bloody war hammer.

"Ahkmet got hit with rubble," the girl holding onto Bai Ping forced out.

Bai Ping gritted his teeth. "All right, keep pushing back."

There were only four people who were combat capable. The rest were wounded or fucked up. He didn't remember how they got to the shed.

They reached the simple defenses, weaving between wooden furniture that had been fused with stone and earth.

"Fire!" Several mana cannons let loose, shooting at the openings in the wall and firing blindly into the smoke. Mages were using Air spells to clear the smoke, but it was a losing battle.

Bai Ping passed off the woman he had carried to a healer. They had set up a casualty collection point, assessing the wounded rapidly before sending them on the back of modified carts to medical stations.

Bai Ping gathered his people and moved to the defensive wall. He saw a familiar face from the CPD and walked over. "How are things looking, John?"

"Walls are fucked in several places, just as we planned. We took some wounded but nothing serious. You?"

"Two down, thirteen wounded."

John grimaced. "Shit. Sorry, man."

Bai Ping grunted.

"We're holding here. There are some stragglers still coming in. We just need to hold for five more minutes."

"All right. Where do you want me?"

"Take the defenses on the right side."

"All right." Bai Ping waved to his people and pushed to the right side. The wall was circular, running from the right to the left. Now it was broken with multiple holes in it. Their ad-hoc defensive line was back a hundred meters from the walls, creating an uneven semi-circle behind the main wall.

Bai Ping jogged with his people to the right. The ground had been hardened, so they weren't stuck in the mud. They passed other groups who were getting organized. Wounded poured through and were sent to the casualty points. Bai Ping checked behind from the second wall; a third wall was coming together on the road that angled up with switchbacks that led up to the mid-wall.

Bai Ping got his people in place. "Check your gear and re-stock." He looked around. Mana cannons fired out at the walls.

They got to their positions, and Bai Ping was spreading them out when beasts charged out of the smoke.

The defenders fired on them.

"Hold your fire, hold your fire! Watch for riders!" Bai Ping yelled. He checked on his people and scanned the area in front of the defenses.

The defenders couldn't be held back and kept attacking the poor beasts.

The riders charged out, throwing down mana barriers and creating forward fighting positions. They tossed out formations, creating a series of positions.

"Hit the people to the rear!" Bai Ping yelled. He drew and released his arrow, hitting a rider and dropping them.

Others with ranged attacks changed their focus.

More beasts ran out of the smoke from different locations.

"Riders on the beasts!" Bai Ping yelled, feeling frustrated. They were being pressed from every side, keeping them off-balance.

His arrow was smacked out of the air by a rider, smashing it into rocks on the ground. He drew another arrow, aiming at the beasts and sending piercing spell-enhanced arrows through the creatures and into the rider on top of them or killing the beast and sending the rider tumbling.

Some riders tossed out barrier formations, creating new positions for those behind to advance. Others were formed up and charging the half-wall.

Bai Ping saw a group of riders jump over the spike-covered half-wall on their beasts.

Some fell to the spikes or to spells and arrows. Most of the Willful Institute riders landed and charged after the Reynir defenders who were retreating.

A yell came from behind as a group of Grey Peak sect riders appeared on their armored bears. They crashed into the Willful Institute riders who were fighting the ground forces.

Bai Ping turned back to his fight, sending arrow after arrow into the enemy. Defenders started to get into a rhythm, and they held on against the Institute's attack.

Newly wounded were pulled back as bear-mounted Grey Peak members charged any Institute riders who made it over, overwhelming them with numbers and home-ground advantage.

Their defenses were stabilizing.

"Mages!" someone yelled.

Bai Ping looked over to see a stream of lightning shooting across the barrier. Errant arcs tore up the ground and barriers before striking several fighters, causing them to stiffen and drop to the ground.

Rocks and debris rose from the ground around a mage, protected by a mana barrier, before she cast her hand out. The debris turned into projectiles and hammered the defenses, hitting some defenders and forcing others to get cover.

A Grey Peak sect mage covered in spells chanted. His first spell was overlaid by a second and then a third that rotated into place before they stuck together, stopping suddenly like seized gears. The wind whistled as Air darts, small in size but great in number, shot out. They shredded the ground, leaving numerous holes. Several soldiers collapsed under a spray of dirt.

A group of Institute warriors charging forward under the cover of mana barriers that had been tossed out by the wave of riders.

Their yells rose as they charged.

"Hold the wall! Hold the wall!" Bai Ping yelled, storing his bow as he threw out a formation plate.

There was no thinking; there was just doing. He had trained as a sharpshooter of bows and rifles of every kind. He had trained with mortars and on the principles of artillery, learned the ways of magic, how to break and heal one's body, and the technical aspects of engineering. It had not been easy, but he had made it.

Now, all that training backed him up.

He stood on the formation. Power surged through his body. His eyes lit up as the world seemed to become his domain. "Burning Sand!" he yelled out, using the words to increase his control over the spell as he threw his hand forward. The power of the formation increased the power of his simple spell many times over as rocks the size of a man's fist appeared in the sky above. They glowed red-hot, just barely cool enough to not turn into glass.

They hit the ground like bombs, exploding on impact and sending burning shards in every direction. Impacts lit up the mobile mana barriers.

Bai Ping changed his point of aim.

He threw out his other hand, casting the spell again. Institute warriors who were charging the defenses yelled. The charge broke apart as they tried to get away from the attack from above. Others sped up or raised their shields.

"Stand with me! Stand, you motherfuckers!" another CPD leader yelled as he shook his spear. Power rushed through his body, igniting the air around him as his muscles bulged.

The adventurers got to their feet.

"Buffing spells! Ready on the heals!"

"Titan's Roar!" Bai Ping sent over the mid-level buffing spell, enhancing their reaction speed and Strength while increasing their body's toughness.

Buffs fell on the adventurers, and the enemy had to jump over the wall.

The adventurers, feeling their allies at their backs, roared. The Willful Institute warriors were coming back down to earth when three were hit with arrows, and another one was tossed back into the sky with a blast of Wind. The CPD leader's spear jabbed out, and the ground rose with him; several Earth spears shot out, as if he were the lord of the Earth. His spear killed one, and the Earth spears wounded two others.

The Institute's people landed and were met with the blades and shields of the Adventurer's Guild, cutting them down in moments.

"For the guild!" one person yelled out.

"For our guild members!" others yelled back. The fighting spirit along the line rose.

"Burning Sand!" Bai Ping harassed the enemy with one hand.

"Titan's Roar!" His buffing spell spread out to the allies around him. They didn't take time to wipe off the blood and sweat as they raised their bodies, feeling clear-headed and energetic.

"The wounded have been pulled back. The Institute is sending reinforcements. Set out magical traps. We're going to pull back!" The order came from the local commander.

"Those of you without ranged weapons, start using those trap spell scrolls!"

His people rushed to obey.

"Mana barrier-protected routes will activate upon the pullback. Remember to not bunch up and to follow the barriers," the commander spoke in the CPD leader's ears.

"Mana barrier-protected routes will activate upon the pullback. Remember to not bunch up and to follow the barriers," Bai Ping repeated. "We are not leaving anyone behind!"

His words were washed out by a tinkling noise that made his spine shiver.

Shit—ice!

Darts of ice shot out at Bai Ping. He pulled out a spell scroll and tore it.

A weird noise that rose and dropped like a wave came from the spell scroll as it blasted over the battlefield. Ice shattered and crumbled, turning into dust as it covered the sky.

"Covering fire!" a Grey Peak sect leader yelled.

Mages waved their hands on the mid-walls. Ice and Earth were combined and rose in the sky like a guillotine before shooting forward, one after another like cannon balls.

They struck the ground ahead of the defenses, tearing apart mana barriers. They struck, killing or wounding those unfortunate enough to be hiding underneath. Many more hit the open ground, causing explosions and leaving a massive crater.

The mages staggered from the attacks, but the Willful Institute took minimal losses. Emboldened by narrowly missing fate and not wanting to be caught by more attacks, they charged forward.

From the smoke between the broken walls, new yells were heard.

Mounted riders from the Willful Institute charged across the open ground.

Bai Ping raised a whip of ice and lashed out, hitting two Institute fighters.

His warriors looked up from what they were doing.

"Keep putting the traps down!" Bai Ping barked.

The enemy rushed across the ground like an unstoppable tide.

Graa-kerr!

A strange noise came from the ground, as if the earth were

complaining. A few heard it before the ground a few meters ahead of the craters exploded.

Hands of dirt with ice veins smacked beasts and grabbed riders as the ground shifted. Heads appeared out of the ground.

"Golems!" a Willful Institute warrior cried out as a golem smashed its arms into the ground, sending out a ripple that exploded within the charging riders.

Beasts and fighters were thrown in the air. Beasts broke their ankles and stumbled on ground that rippled like the surface on a lake.

Bai Ping looked up to the mages standing on the walls. They were pale-faced but moved their bodies as if they were in the fight.

It is not just golem creation; this is golem control.

A golem pushed out of the ground and dragged out a sword. It slashed back and down. The ground was torn apart, a snake of earth and ice that rose up under the feet of a Willful Institute commander.

Guards rushed forward to defend, using combat techniques. Red shields appeared in front of them. Mages cast Fire spells, striking the golems. It tore away chunks of their bodies and left them smoking as they tried to weather the attacks and advance.

The golems were being worn down, collapsing back into dirt.

"Attack the spells and the mages!" Bai Ping ordered. A spell formation as big as his chest appeared in front of him as he showed deep concentration. He worked for several moments before he released it.

The spell formations grew to be several meters large, and the formation under his feet enhanced it.

A pill shot out of the spell formation and toward the enemy. The light coming from it shifted, mixing blacks with greens, golds and yellows, brilliant red sparks and silver threads.

The Chaotic Blast entered deep into the Willful Institute area and ignited. Lightning surged out, then swapped to Wind, then Ice blades and Fire spears. Enchanted metals warped, and the mana in the area was distorted, tossed into chaos before it was sucked in and then exploded into a rain of burning flames.

"Pull back, first echelon!" a Grey Peak sect commander of the area yelled.

People turned and jogged through the mana barriers to the rear.

Bai Ping shot out spears of ice at the mages. The mana had been churned up with the mana blast, and other CPD members were using the same spell, forcing the mages to use their internal mana, making their spells much weaker, as they couldn't influence the mana around them as much as they had before.

Golems broke free of their chains and prisons and rushed to meet the riders and warriors on the ground.

"Second echelon!" the local commander yelled.

Bai Ping checked on his people with a glance and used the buff Clear-minded. Their spellcasting became easier, and they focused on their trap-laying, not worrying about the battle around them as much.

They tore spell scrolls apart as if they were confetti, dropping spell traps all over the place.

"We're next. Get ready!" Bai Ping saw the holes along the wall. The golems were doing good work, but the Willful Institute was recovering quickly, and their mages were pulling out mana stones to increase the mana density around them and enhance their spells.

The supporting attacks from the rear increased as the first and second echelon provided covering fire.

"Third echelon, pull back!"

"We're moving!" Bai Ping grabbed his spell-casting formation. "Move it, Melinda!" he barked, seeing she was still casting spells.

She dismissed it and started to run with the others.

"Spell traps!" Bai Ping yelled as he pulled out spell scrolls. He barely peeked at where they would go before ripping them apart and followed the steps of those ahead of him.

The Willful Institute, seeing them running, charged around the remaining golems toward the wall. They threw out mana barriers wildly to cover their advance and push forward.

The first groups started to make it over the wall when spell traps were activated.

Others were close behind them. They didn't have time to learn from their mistakes as mana pooled together into attack spells and targeted the poor bastards who had activated them.

Bai Ping and his people followed mana barrier after mana barrier.

At the rear of it all, Bai Ping waved his hand and collected the barriers or threw out attack spells to break them so that the enemy couldn't use them.

The others did the same.

Attacks rained down on the retreating groups.

Soldiers from the Grey Peak sect, Adventurer's Guild, and their allied groups were cut down, dropping bonelessly to the ground, leaving a sparse field of tombstones.

There was no option but to keep running.

Medics used their beast-storing crates to grab the wounded.

Bai Ping felt energy building behind him. He cast a protective spell just before a spear crashed into his back. It launched him forward into the ground.

"Team leader!" one of his people called out.

"Keep going!" Bai Ping yelled. He pushed himself up, gritting his teeth against the pain. If he hadn't been wearing his armor, it would have done more than break his damn shoulder.

Bai Ping felt more energy gathering. He turned and raised one hand, the other limp by his side. The snow around him turned into a shield as dirt rose, creating pillars to support the shield.

A fist as big as a human formed from the sky and shot forward, leaving streaks of white in the sky. It smashed into the shield, cracking through it and the pillars he had thrown up.

Bai Ping yelled as he drew power from his body and from his mana, igniting the power in his body, creating massive momentum and force. If Erik were there, he could have seen the similarities of Bai Ping's modified combat technique: One Finger Beats Fist.

The power around Bai Ping condensed in his finger as he shook from the power focused within his body, compressing, tightening.

The ground under his feet and around him deepened, showing the impression of a fist, and Bai Ping's cry grew deeper. He was forced back half a step before he surged forward, his finger reaching out to touch the immense fist.

Wind shot outward so fierce that it created a white wall that no one could see through. Dust, debris, and the ground Bai Ping stood on exploded outward. A rumbling noise was met with a powerful cracking noise. A tiny line pierced up to the heavens.

A second blast went off as the mage caster, a veteran over the level sixty, coughed blood and collapsed.

A wave of force exploded outward into the sky, throwing the falling snow away.

Bai Ping ran out of the dust and debris, his eyes filled with energy. "Who told you to stop moving?" His voice was thunder in the ears of his team. They turned and ran as if a demon were on their heels.

Bai Ping had a gloomy expression on his face as he released some of the suppression on his body. His arm healed at a visible speed as he held his arm up and used Bone Fuse before opening and closing his hand.

Shit, we're not supposed to show our actual power. We don't want to scare them off.

He kept throwing down traps and picking up the mana-barrier formations, running up the main road that led to another gatehouse. Weapons fired over the wall and into the enemy.

"You're the last one," a CPD member wearing the gear of a medic had to yell to be heard as Bai Ping passed the gate before the CPD member reached out a hand.

A team from the Grey Peak sect stepped forward, grunting as they closed the gate before slotting a massive bar across it.

Bai Ping tilted his head to the side as a healer pressed her fingers to his pulse, making him pause.

Other healers were checking pulses and using spells, while alchemists passed out concoctions freely.

"Healing well." She pulled out a small spell scroll and tore it. Bai Ping felt refreshed as the aches and pains fell away.

Mages used spells on the stone underneath the gate and the walls; they spread over the wooden gate, turning it into another fused section of the wall.

"Stamina and natural healing booster." She clapped him on the shoulder.

"True. Thanks." Bai Ping nodded. He wished he could have saved more people. Even if he had his full Strength unlocked, he wouldn't have been able to reach the people caught by the wall breaches.

"The outer wall and the outer defenses have all fallen. Most people are pulling back to the mid-wall locations now."

"What about the second part?"

"The Institute have their third group of defenders coming out still." She paused talking as a nearby siege weapon fired down at the Institute.

She grabbed onto his back so she could keep his ear close to her mouth to hear her. "They've established a supply line from Sierra and Echo. They're building up their forces. Command thinks with the next group of reinforcements they'll keep attacking to keep pushing us."

"Can we hold the mid-walls?"

"Don't know. Might lose some of them. Command moved out army squads to the weaker sections of the wall and have more ready as a quick reaction force with the Grey Peak sect."

Bai Ping shot a glance at the mana barrier covering the inner wall as it lit up with power, showing where a spell had impacted.

"Thanks for the update. I've got to check on my team."

"No worries. I'll be here if you need patching up." She hurried off toward the medical station while he jogged over to where the rest of his team was waiting for him.

They all had contrasting looks on their faces.

Bai Ping ignored them all and pulled out a sound-canceling device. The world turned quiet, even as siege weapons just tens of meters away fired, their crews rushing around to bring the weapons back to readiness.

"Everyone good?" He looked around to see a nodding of heads. "All right, we will be assisting the mid-wall here with defense. Wait here. I need to talk to the local commander and find out where they need us."

Noise returned, and Bai Ping jogged through the war camp behind the wall, checking his map to see where the local commander was set up.

He reached a covered tent. The sides were open; sound-canceling formations cut off the outside world. Bai Ping went over to a master sergeant.

"Sitrep?"

"Thirteen people left including me, just back from the outer wall."

"All right, you're Fighting Group Bravo. You move up to the wall in thirty minutes. You'll be under the command of Captain Choi. You are squad fifteen."

Bai Ping pulled out a pad and pencil. "Squad fifteen, command Captain Choi, Fighting Group Bravo, prep to move thirty minutes."

"Good!"

Bai Ping moved to the side and then out of the tent, checking the notes and putting away the pad and pencil. He headed for where he had left his team.

"Send the mounted reinforcements forward. The breaches have been secured!" Elder Xiao's orders rang in Mendes's ears. "Now we push into Reynir!" Those in his command center rushed about to carry out his orders.

"Thanks to the covering fire of the attack camps, our people were able to get to the wall with half their number and breach several outer walls. We have the momentum. It is a matter of time until we push them to the mid-wall. We need to push everyone up to capitalize. Hold nothing back."

"Yes, Elder Xiao," Mendes said. His anger was dying down, giving way to a deep sense of anticipation at the thrill of winning this battle and pushing everything at Reynir.

At the rear camps, several gates opened, and mounted forces and troops rushed out, heading for the forward camps. They were like a black stream as the forward camps sent out reinforcements across the churned-up ground to support the vanguard that had pierced into Reynir.

Now they had a foothold inside the walls, they could use the full strength of the higher realm fighters and take Reynir.

Jasper was in the command center as he watched the Willful Institute's attacks hit several outer walls and then breach them.

"The retreat is going as planned," Storgaard said. "We have to pull out units located at the lower walls, so they won't be hit in the rear. We'll lose the outer defenses unless we take some drastic measures."

"Are you not confident in our plan?"

"I wouldn't have listened to it if I didn't get a message from the higher realms saying to not piss you off. Though looking at things, it is shaping up nicely. The Institute is sending their reinforcements. The first group was hesitant, but they're piling in now. The anticipation is killing me."

"Once the fourth group of reinforcements are sent forward, we'll strike."

"I thought you were an administrator?"

"I am."

"You are handling this whole war-fighting business rather well."

"It is not the first time I have been in a fight, and luckily I have a lot of good support and allies."

"Sir, are you sure about this?" Lieutenant Colonel Zukal broke the rules as he walked over to Domonos, who was checking the riding gear on his mount, a grizzled-looking panther wearing full armor that had been roughly painted over, making it look unlike the armor and panthers of the Alvan army.

"You will remain here and coordinate supplies and support. I need to be up there to lead our forces."

"I knew you would say that, but I have one amendment." Zukal waved two people forward.

"Two more babysitters?"

"Ah, come on. Still sour about me beating you that one time?" Niemm laughed.

Domonos rolled his eyes and glanced at Zukal. "Happy now?"

"Just doing my job, boss."

"We won't let him out of our sight," Niemm promised. "Trust us, we trained with Erik and Rugrat."

Domonos chuckled and checked his map. "They committed their ground troops finally."

"Our people have just pulled back to the mid-wall," Zukal said, half-turning.

"I won't keep you. When I see you next, we'll be taking Meokar!"

"Yes, sir!" Zukal turned and ran off toward their own command center with his guards in tow.

Domonos looked over the northern area of the city. He saw people peering out from within their homes and other buildings. They'd come here to escape the fighting and the attacks smashing against the mana barrier day and night.

Hidden in the squares, men and women of the Alva military and the Adventurer's Guild waited, checking their gear, their mounts. All of them were elites from the Fourth Realm.

Domonos checked his map again, like a fortune-teller trying to read the mysteries of the world and a telepath trying to interpret just what his opponent was thinking.

At the same time, he was listening to the sound transmission channels, keeping him in the loop.

"We have pulled back all of our people to the mid-wall in sector South Five!"

"Looks like they're going all in now," Niemm said.

Domonos checked on the walls. The Institute worked quickly to secure their breach and pressure the mid-wall so they wouldn't get any surprises.

Minutes crawled by as the fighting on the walls continued, and the Institute's troops continued their onward march.

Domonos opened a sound transmission channel. "Mount up!" He jumped onto his mount, observing the courtyard he was in. Men and women with all kinds of mounts finished their preparations and got onto their beasts.

"Looks like a damn fine army," Niemm said as they moved forward and out into the market square filled with members of the Alva army. In every road, every open space, grim-faced men and women with the Adventurer's Guild emblem sat upon their mounts.

"Nine thousand battle-hardened adventurers who came to right a wrong and a thousand supporting members of the Alva military. The Willful Institute won't know what hit them."

The Institute's troops were quickly closing the distance to the outer wall. They passed through the breaching units and moved to the front. They operated in groups, hurling out mana-barrier formations to protect their advance.

"It's time we moved." Domonos assessed it all. He wouldn't get better timing. "Lieutenant Acosta, clear out those eyes for me."

"Yes, sir."

He used his command channel. "Zukal, we're heading out. Be ready with support as we need it."

"Yes, sir."

Domonos changed channels to the mounted force. "Move out!"

Elder Xiao stood at the peak of his command center, using a spyglass to watch the advance into Reynir. The siege fire spewed out from Reynir, tearing apart the plateau and striking the Willful Institute's barriers.

"With their walls all over the place, it makes it easier to see the battle," an elder snorted nearby.

"It makes for a good show." Xiao watched the black snake that pushed into the outer walls, passing through the breaches and spreading out again, reinforcing those at the front.

He could see the faces of the people on the middle walls. They activated their weapons, cast their spells, and shot their arrows, draining the power of the mana barriers ahead of them.

They had strong defensive equipment. But once their power was used up, they would collapse. In the fighting, watching the power levels of so many formations were nearly impossible. Once the locations were set up inside their defenses, they could coordinate their mana barriers for better protection.

"Anything from the spies to the north?"

"There hasn't been any movement."

"Good. What about from the leadership?" Xiao watched advancing groups move forward across the ground. Trap spells went off, killing and wounding Willful Institute warriors as they advanced. Mana barriers that had used up all their power collapsed, and attacks were focused on the unguarded members hiding underneath.

"Alter our targets, aim for the inner walls. I want to see how many mana stones they're willing to burn!"

Lieutenant Acosta let the body drop as she stood up, the stealth sheet attached to her armor, and she pulled up her silenced rifle.

The rocks around her moved as other people stood up with their sheets.

"Fr—" The scout went silent as she put two rounds into the man. The Silence spell on the rounds made sure his body didn't make a noise as it hit the ground.

She switched targets, climbing over the rocks and boulders to fire again.

Flashes appeared around her, but there was no sound, from the weapons or from their targets.

Acosta half-lowered her rifle, forcing her breath out as she checked the surroundings. She saw a member of her team take a knee and shoot one scout who tried to run for it.

"Observation post one is cleared."

"Observation post three is cleared."

"Observation post two is cleared."

"Understood. Good work," Domonos replied.

Acosta took a knee and raised her scope, using it to look at the northern gate.

The guards on the walls moved, opening the three gates.

Mounted beasts appeared in the streets, coming out of courtyards and market squares that were hidden from the outside.

They filled the streets, rushing out of the gate in groups. They spread out and lined up. Commanders took charge to create two lines that extended out from the gate. As dozens turned into hundreds and then thousands, the lines got thicker. There were bumps in them: one close to the wall, one farthest away from the gate, and a smaller bump in the middle.

In a handful of minutes, they were all lined up.

The lines started moved at a slow canter for those close to the wall and a quick gallop for those on the outside edge.

The two lines separated, headed in opposite directions.

Heidi Storgaard watched from the command center at the peak of Reynir.

Drums started to play across Reynir, sounding out low, rolling beats.

Guards along the walls moved crates and pulled tarps from hidden siege weapons behind the walls. Crew leaders yelled out orders as weapons were pulled back and loaded. Cannons were rolled forward into position. Reynir was filled with activity as the Adventurer's Guild and Grey Peak sect members who had remained under the walls now rushed to carry out their duties.

"Prepare to fire!" Her order passed through all of Reynir. It bristled with weaponry and pent-up action.

"Fire!"

Reynir seemed to erupt as catapults and trebuchets creaked and groaned, releasing their payloads. Mana cannons roared, releasing pillars of mana that cut across Reynir and slammed into the forward camps.

All of Reynir was in motion now as they reloaded, rearmed, and fired as fast as they could. The fresh crews were nearly twice protected from the wind that those at the top of the wall suffered from.

"I wonder what they'll think of that," Storgaard spat, staring out at the Institute's camps. She sneered as the latter ranks of Meokar troops marching to her outer walls stumbled as a mana barrier broke. Destruction rained down on the road, and siege weaponry payloads went off like artillery rounds, killing dozens.

Golems ambled out of the ground in renewed force, changing the golem balance on the battlefield.

Spells spotted the forward camps' Echo and Sierra's barriers. Dust and dirt filled the air, creating a screen around the camps. Lightning storms were summoned. The skies lit up with elemental energies; spells of Ice and Wind cut down at the Willful Institute. Burning boulders that resembled meteors smashed upon the ground, a scene of sudden and epic destruction.

The early morning sun was eclipsed by the sudden attacks. Reynir showed its true strength.

"Prepare the spell scrolls! I want mages attacking with all they have. Those siege weapons are not to fall silent! Keep their attention on us!" Storgaard barked.

Her eyes turned to the east and west. Mages stepped forward from the Adventurer's Guild. They stood on top of enhancing spell formations, each of them holding spell scrolls.

Tremendous streams of mana were pulled into the spell scrolls and rebounded through the spell formation. The mages chanted; the scrolls in their hands lit up with power that had been buried deep inside. The scrolls were not made from normal materials, but rare metals and skins.

One group of mages finished. Their spell scrolls were consumed, and their formations released a rush of power.

Storgaard felt a disturbance in the air. She couldn't see through the low-lying clouds of lightning storms and frost rains attacking the Willful Institute.

She felt fear, down through her mana system.

The drums, the weapon fire—it seemed to dim as she looked at the origin of where she felt a monumental amount of mana being channeled. Then there was a second location and a third.

A pillar of air shot through the clouds, dispersing them. Silently, a massive shard of ice as pure as the finest diamond hurtled toward the ground, gaining speed.

There was no sound, not even a whistle, as the tip of the ice crystal touched the leading edge of Camp Delta.

She could no longer see what happened as light filled the plateau, making her cover her eyes. A rumbling explosion rolled across the plateaus, chased by clouds of smoke, dust, and powdered stone that shot up into the sky.

The mana barrier of Reynir shuddered at the impact from the waves of dust and fallout. Wind howled through the mountain region as the two other mage groups finished their casting.

The smoke was shoved to the side as two new pillars appeared in the battlefield. Like the gods' own, two ice spears shone in the early-morning sun.

Their impacts were no less grand than the first.

Two brilliant lights illuminated the battlefield.

Storgaard grimaced. She had seen many sights in her life, but this was the largest display of attack magic she had ever seen.

She pulled out a telescope and glanced over to the east, focusing on a strange line moving across the ground. "They're charging into it still?"

The spell scrolls had activated great winds, forming a wall in front of the Adventure's Guild's mounted forces, creating a clear area around them.

Many pulled out strange crossbow-looking weapons and attached them to the backs of their mounts.

Spells appeared ahead of the force. Rain fell, pushing the dust down.

"Fuck me." Storgaard's telescope settled on what had been Camps Delta, Bravo, and Echo. The camps were nothing more than smoking craters.

"Keep up fire on Sierra! Prepare our people to retake the outer walls!" Gudriksson barked behind her. His orders broke her out of her thoughts as she swallowed and looked at the mounted charge rushing toward the Institute on both sides.

Elder Mendes stared at the smoking craters that was all that remained of their forward camp and two rear camps. He'd felt the power of the attack as it raged against his own mana barrier.

Elder Xiao, all the elites, other than the ones here and at Reynir—they're gone! He stumbled slightly, his body numb and weak with shock.

His hearing had dulled with the explosion, but he thought he heard noises nearby. People were walking around, opening their mouths, but he couldn't hear anything they said. His soldiers from Meokar were shaking. Some had dropped their weapons or just stood there, watching, as if they couldn't understand what was happening.

He felt someone smack him on the shoulder, returning him to reality. They turned him around and passed him a health potion.

Seeing his guard captain there, Mendes came back to himself and drank the potion.

In a moment, the world came back. It was filled with noise, and people yelling at one another, unable to hear. Rocks under massive heat exploded while Reynir's attacks continued and rain started to pour down.

"Grand Elder, you're in command now!" his guard captain yelled. "What are your orders?"

Mendes took a step backward, shuddering. "Elder Xiao?"

"The camp is gone, Elder!" The captain of his personal guard ground out.

"Pull them back! We'll regroup!" Mendes said, starting to come to himself.

"What is that?" an elder in Mendes's partly pointed through the smoke and dust that pervaded most of the battlefield.

Shapes appeared through the smoke.

"What are those?" someone asked.

"Flags?" Mendes said, squinting

"There's a force in the smoke!" the captain said.

"We can't hold. We lost our elites. We have a quarter of the army left, and they're all infantry." The elder who had first spotted the movement began backing up.

"Those aren't the legions of the Grey Peak sect," Mendes said, trying to bolster their spirits.

"No, that's the Adventurer's Guild." Elder Tsi pointed from the group they were watching and toward the wall.

Fear gripped Mendes as the guild charged toward their remaining camps. There was the sudden finality of losing half their camps in just one second. Then seeing the enemy pushing out right afterward, pinning in their advanced forces and splitting the camps apart.

Where did they get so many people? They didn't look weak. They were coordinated with tactics that could work against massive armies.

Mendes pulled his guard captain to him. "Send the order. Pull back to Meokar."

"Sir?"

"We will ride ahead. I need to communicate with the rest of the Institute to ready reinforcements."

The guard captain's face closed up as he nodded. "Yes, Grand Elder. I'll prepare our mounts right away."

Thunder filled Domonos's ears. He felt his mount's muscles moving underneath him, his people riding beside him.

The Alvan army members kept their people lined up and in order. Mages used weather magic to clear the area ahead of them.

"Mounted unit one heading to the breaches!"

"Unit two moving to Sierra!"

"Looks like we're heading into hell." Domonos turned to Niemm, who grinned like a madman. His other special team guard was the same.

Domonos's lips spread into a grin. "To hell we go!"

Siege weapons continued to bombard the camps.

"Shifting siege weapon fire!" Zukal reported.

The attacks rolled back across the enemy. Spells shot out at the Adventurer's mounted force. Mana barriers were revealed, rippling with hits.

"Looks like they've noticed us."

"Not soon enough to save their people in the breaches." Domonos opened his channel to those hitting the support camps.

"Use those spell scrolls, if you have them!"

Light appeared among the riders. Spell formations snapped into existence, spewing fireballs, lava spears, burning meteors, fiery rain.

Blue and red flames ignited the air around the mounted force. Like a rocket barrage, they struck out at the rear camps.

"The rear gates are opening!" a commander reported.

Domonos checked the map, watching markers fleeing the camp.

"Their mounted forces are leaving."

"Are they turning to fight?" Domonos demanded.

"The smoke makes it hard to see. No—no, they're not turning. They're running for the woods!" the commander yelled.

Domonos opened a channel to everyone. "Did you hear that? They're running! The Willful Institute is running scared! Listen to your leaders' orders! For the fallen!"

"For the fallen!" people yelled back.

The forces under his command moved to reinforce the walls and cut off the retreat for the Institute members who had breached Reynir. There were designated units to attack the remaining camps and another force to hunt down those retreating.

The Willful Institute didn't have many mounted members left. *I'd bet they'd race back to the safety of Meokar without caring for the allies they leave behind.* The smoke cleared enough for him to see farther.

"Get into formation! Speed buffs!"

Adventurer's tore spell scrolls, the buff's light wrapping around fighters and their beasts.

Their speed increased. Beasts jumped over craters on the ground; other craters were too big, and people moved into formations while they traversed these miniature valleys.

Units separated into their own formations.

Breaching units gained more buffs. In groups of four, they surged ahead, weaving around golems that were still fighting one another. As units closed with them, spells and arrows shattered their cores and broke their animating spells.

"Unit one has reached the breaches!"

Domonos spared a glance. The mounted forces were a spear through the Institute's heart. Disorganized and recovering from the blasts, they didn't stand a chance. The main force charged through the lines. Sub-units split off, heading through the breaches and closing off any chance of retreat.

"Mid-wall forces heading out!"

Bear legions from the Grey Peak sect and mounted forces from the supporting sects charged out from the middle wall gates.

Mana barriers stop magic, but not people.

"Storgaard is asking if we will accept surrender," Jasper asked on the channel between Mister Yi, Domonos, and Zukal.

"Yes, we will. Zukal, make sure that you broadcast through everyone to take surrenders. Jasper, might do good to come from you and Storgaard."

"Yes."

"Understood."

"We're closing, sir," Niemm yelled.

Domonos checked the map of the camp.

Several breacher units made up of the Adventurers were out front. Larger units followed in their wake.

The camp was coming back to itself, firing everything they had at the guild.

The ground exploded ahead of the Adventurer units. Mounted beasts went down in cries of pain, their ankles broken from the sudden change of ground.

Domonos's mount shifted to the side, and the formation shifted.

Secondary formations with beast tamers, mages, healers, and engineers moved to assist.

"Breaching units are getting in range!"

"Cover them!" Domonos yelled.

They held onto their mounted repeaters and fired at the wall of the camps.

It looked like a tropical storm coming down over a lake. It was impossible to see through the barrier with so many impacts striking it.

The breaching teams used the covering fire to get in close to Camp Bravo. They tossed out formation plates that stuck to the walls and rushed away.

"Into the breaches!"

Frost appeared underneath the formations and spread across the walls, rushing out tens of meters a second. They seemed to reach their limit after ten seconds.

Domonos thought he heard a noise like breaking ice. Cracks appeared under the formation, creating a web that ran across the wall.

The stone walls shattered, collapsing into rubble no larger than a man's fist.

Alpha and Bravo Company spread out, shooting their repeaters, keeping the defenders blind.

Mages at the lead of Charlie and Delta Company used Stone Fuse spell scrolls. The rubble from the breaches turned into a ramp, inviting the mounted forces into the heart of the camp.

Company commanders took over.

Squads acted as support, firing their repeaters into the camp. Others leapt off their mounts. In the camp, there were many obstacles the beasts couldn't get through.

Squads of shield warriors stepped up, creating an Iron wall for the long-range fighters. Melee units were ready to support either group as needed.

Spell scrolls were deployed in the heart of the camp. The ground lurched up and down, tossing people up into the air, destabilizing the camp, and breaking up the Institute's units that had pulled themselves together.

Mages cast group magic on formations. Spears of magical power struck out at the camp's mana barrier. A secondary barrier lit up with the attacks.

The shield units, under the flanking cover of the repeaters, pushed forward. Melee units and ranged followed them.

"Alpha Company, collapse into the camp! I want a casualty collection point on the stone watchtower foundations next to the breach."

The repeater squads fired out into the camp, using spell scrolls on anything that moved and wasn't friendly.

Friendly forces pushed through the breaches and pushed out to either side, linking up to the other units, clearing out the siege weapons and soldiers along the walls.

"Collapse all outside units," Domonos ordered. A line formed, pushing through the camp. Shield warriors were in the lead, followed by lighter armored melee types, archers, and mages.

Members of the Willful Institute couldn't take the swift changes. With their leaders rushing toward Meokar, the camp was leaking people.

They started breaking, Willful Institute fighters turned and ran from the battlefield, trying to escape. Others dropped their weapons to surrender.

Battle lines were quickly formed and started to advance.

They weren't a trained military, but they made their living fighting. They'd had some basic formation training. They were crude, but much stronger than if they were to operate in just their parties.

Domonos looked up at the mana barrier. There was not one ripple in it. Reynir's attacks had stopped, fearing to hit their allies.

"Colonel, the groups that breached Reynir are surrendering, one after another. We have breached all the camps."

"The Institute leadership?"

"Retreating toward Meokar."

"Some of the guild members have disobeyed orders and are hunting them down."

Domonos's mount shifted uneasily.

"Get them back into formation *now*!"

"Sir, they're not listening."

Domonos looked along the muddy path that led to the plains and forests beyond.

"The gates are opening!" another aide said.

"Which ones?" Domonos demanded.

"Reynir's sir. Jasper reports that the sects mounted forces are heading out!"

"Idiots. Call back our people if you can. Don't send any after to try and pull them back. Their deaths are on their own heads."

Leandra and her group of mounted guildmates had been separated from their unit. They had taken to cutting down the fleeing Willful fighters.

"Again, I order you to regroup on the captured camps!" Jasper's voice rang out in their ears.

Leandra didn't pay attention as her groups ran through a group of Willful Institute fighters.

She stabbed out with her spear, her momentum and speed slamming it through her opponent's armor and into their collarbone, bowling them over.

She let her spear trail behind, tearing free as she reset her spear position again.

"They're going into the forest. Should we turn back?" one of her guildmates called out.

"We're adventurers, not part of a sect. Kill the bastards!" Leandra yelled back. The others cheered, not yet satiated as they raised their weapons and continued the charge, cutting down those wounded and on foot.

"Mounted up ahead!" Leandra yelled. "Group on me!"

Others moved to her and saw the fleeing Institute members. They looked haggard, their horses slow as they were caught up with the foot soldiers.

Easy prey! We'll make our names with this, and their gear will be ours.

Leandra increased her pace; the other riders sped up with her, the ground disappearing under the thunder of their charge.

She aimed her mount down the left rear of her opponent, their blindside opposite their sword arm.

She braced her spear, ready for the impact; she could anticipate it already.

The fleeing mounted soldiers put their spear over their left shoulders. Their mounts turned underneath them as one to the left, facing right into the Adventurers' charge.

Leandra shifted her spear to meet the one coming at her left side, but it was too fast for her.

The mounted soldier's spear stabbed into her neck and stomach, her momentum working against her as she collapsed backwards, her stirrups holding her in place as she covered her neck, feeling the blood welling out.

The world turned upside down and backwards as the mounted Institute soldiers used their training to tear through her band of guild members.

They were waiting for us. It was a trap.

Darkness filled her vision.

43 Turbulence for the Willful Institute

"Well, it looks like none of our people made it into the top ten this year," Blaze complained to Gu Chen.

"Ah, well, we were up against sects this year. They have plenty of resources and connections we don't have. Next year, with Vuzgal's training facilities, I'm sure we'll do better!"

"That is true. And your Silver Dragons got ten spots in the top one hundred!"

"Not close to your sixteen!"

"With our two guilds together, we took a quarter of the top one hundred spots. That's not bad!" Blaze laughed.

Erik and Rugrat got up from where they were sitting and headed out of the box.

"I have to go deal with a few issues that arose while the competition was ongoing." Blaze excused himself

"I understand. I hope you resolve your issues. Let me know if the Silver Dragons can assist you."

"Thank you, Brother Gu." Blaze cupped his hands to Gu Chen.

Blaze left the box as the competition ended and the rewards were passed out. Blaze didn't look back.

This year, the competition was the last thing on all our minds.

Cai Bo looked over as Low Elder Kostic walked back to his seat.

"Two people in the top ten. That won't look good. How is the situation in the Institute now with the elders?"

"They want to put your dismissal to a vote and are gathering support. A group of Institute members attacked a high elder two days ago. We got a report from Meokar. The army there has been gutted. Less than four thousand remain. The head has requested us to return immediately."

Which was the perfect opportunity for her to get close to the sect head.

"Will we hold Meokar?"

"Doubtful. The enemy is organized. They can fight in formations. I was informed that a group of mounted Grey Peak sect and Adventurer's Guild members departed Reynir."

"What about our own mounted forces?"

"They were the first target, then Elder Xiao and one of the forward camps. They combined spell scrolls and formations to make a peak seventh-tier spell."

"Spell?"

"Yes, High Elder. It took one combined spell for each of the camps."

"What will happen to Meokar?"

"It seems that the high elders want to fight, but the head has passed an order. We will retreat from Meokar, taking everything that we can."

"And the Adventurer's Guild?" Cai Bo peeked at the main box to see Blaze leaving with his guards.

"The head believes this is an act of war. He has offered bounties on the Adventurer's Guild members."

Storgaard fought to keep her face neutral as Reynir's totem flashed and another unit marched out. They followed the other units out of Reynir and toward Meokar.

Now that the Willful Institute had taken a heavy loss, the other sects, seeing a weak opponent, were more than happy to send their units over to get greater rewards from Meokar's carcass.

The totem flashed again, this time revealing a small group wearing cloaks. Jasper walked out to greet them, Storgaard a half-step behind.

"Blaze, I hope we placed well."

Blaze, a large man, pulled back his hood, revealing some of his armor underneath. "Got some spots. How are things here?"

"The guild and Grey Peak sect are advancing through the forest between us and Meokar. We've rounded up five thousand prisoners from the breaches, and three thousand were caught on the run."

"How long until we reach Meokar?"

"By tonight. We're moving slowly to make sure there are no traps."

"Understandable." Blaze nodded. "Sorry for my rudeness. You must be Branch Head Storgaard." Blaze reached out his hand.

"Guildmaster Blaze." She shook his hand and bowed.

Some small guild, my ass.

"I'm sorry to trouble you like this. I wanted to see how things are progressing personally."

"I am thankful I got to meet with the Adventurer's Guild and fight beside you."

"We might yet have some more chances. Seems that people are eager to grow into the Willful Institute's land."

Grand Elder Mendes looked haggard. All around him, the people of Meokar rushed about with storage crates. Formations were being pulled from the ground and ingredients harvested early. Workshops were dismantled and books were packed away.

Meokar's totem didn't stop working night and day as people evacuated and the remaining wealth of the Institute was shipped off to other locations.

Anything of worth was ripped out of the city. The once-orderly streets were barren. Random objects were tossed out. Those who were too poor to use the totem fled into the surrounding countryside. Meokar's fields had been set ablaze, and smoke covered the city with the setting of the sun.

The swamp forests were dark already.

"No more members of the army have appeared in several hours," Mendes's guard captain said.

"Secure the gates and make sure the mana barrier is active." Mendes said. Streams of people were still coming and going, panic on their faces.

Horns called out.

"The enemy has been spotted!" Elder Tsi ran in. A bandage covered her side and part of her face.

"I don't want to leave anything that can aid them."

"Yes, Grand Elder."

Mendes put a hand on her shoulder and squeezed it. He sighed, filled with regret, and headed for the elder's chambers.

The room was in disarray.

Elders wore their weapons and armor. They hadn't washed since the battle and still had mud and blood on their clothes.

Mendes looked at the grand table in the center of the room where he had controlled Meokar from for decades. He sat where he had decided the fate of hundreds of thousands of people. Where he had passed judgment on the group of adventurers who some of his disciples had murdered and stolen from. Turning the other eye as they would bolster the power of the Fourth Realm and reflect well on his branch.

It all seems so useless now. How had the Adventurer's Guild got such powerful weapons and Experts?

Maps lay across the table. Communication devices lay ready with spell scrolls prepared.

The room grew silent. The other elders looked at him with hope, for leadership.

"We will evacuate all that we can. We will hold back the guards and those with a lower aptitude. We will fight alongside them. If we can survive, the Institute might look past our previous crimes. If we flee, then not only us, but our clans and the very faction, will be hurt. We cannot run."

The room grew still as they all processed his words.

We gave so much, worked so hard to get our positions. They should have had many years ahead of them, but with one stumble, they were here. It was the truth of the Ten Realms. What they did now would reflect on everyone they knew.

"The enemy is moving in the forest. They are having a hard time since we destroyed the road behind us," Elder Dean said.

"We have repositioned the mana cannons and siege weaponry we brought back along the walls. Please take a look," Elder Rei said.

Several faces were missing, killed in the first counterattack or chased down in the route back to Meokar.

Mendes moved to the map, studying the different positions.

44 Level Heads

Blaze's party raised a plume of dirt behind them as they reached the forward guild elements. Domonos stood waiting. The rest of the guild had been resting in position but perked up as he came to a stop. Joan and Kim Cheol were with him.

Blaze tore off his helmet, his face lined in anger.

"Good work, lad. Just need a quick talk with your people."

He stepped past Domonos.

"Listen up!" His voice cut through the forest and low-level conversations, scaring war beasts. He needed no formations to enhance his voice. "When you took this contract, did I not tell you to listen to the guild officers? Or are you a bunch of idiot-damned children that don't know how to do anything?" Blaze stomped over to rows of blanket-covered lumps.

He pulled the blanket off a corpse that was already being reclaimed by the Ten Realms.

"This is what happens when you don't fucking listen! This is not a party-level mission. There are thousands of guild members here! Look at them, dammit—look!" Blaze yelled, pointing at the body, his eyes boring into anyone's turned skull.

"You don't want to listen, then go back to the goddamn guild hall! This is a fight against the Willful Institute. That's a sect. They have more resources, more people; they control entire cities. We will fall apart if we are running all over the place! *This*"—Blaze waved his hand at the dead bodies—"*this* happens when you run off trying to get glory. You end up dead. You want to be part of a sect, go and join them!" Blaze waved into the woods around them. "There are plenty of those idiots out there in the forests. The *Adventurer's Guild* tore through those camps. The *Adventurer's Guild* broke the Willful Institute on the walls. It was also the Adventurer's Guild who lost their damn heads, didn't listen to others, and ran after the enemy, only to be lured into ambushes into a forest they didn't know! Did you think that the Institute is a bunch of idiots?" Blaze grunted and turned to the dead.

He bowed from the waist to them all.

The hardness in his face dimmed, showing the sadness that fueled his rage.

"Rest easy." Blaze carefully put the blanket on the dead guild member.

His face hardened again, and he turned to his guildmates.

"The Adventurer's Guild repays their debts and does the job they're contracted to do. We can only do that if we're alive."

Even the toughest guild member didn't dare to meet Blaze's eyes.

Domonos's eyes fell on those who looked ahead and stood straighter. Taking note.

"You're new to this, I know. Trust in one another; trust in your guild officers. It took most of the day to get you together and spread all over the fucking place. Now all the sects have reached the fields outside Meokar. If you're here for the loot, then you're here for the wrong reasons. We have a job to do and a debt that Meokar will pay for in full. We're here to wipe Meokar off the map. All loot will be collected, sold, and split amongst everyone based on contribution. Contributing means doing your task and not running off to get more loot. That's what sect members do."

Blaze looked over them all again and walked back to Domonos.

"They're yours to command. I'll ride with you to Meokar." Blaze put his hand on Domonos's shoulder.

"You did good."

Thirty minutes later, and the Guild was ready to move. There were five thousand guild members, forty-five hundred mounted warriors, and five hundred who acted as their support and would handle their mana cannons.

Domonos rode next to Niemm and Blaze. Mounted beasts strolled through the forest. They were calm as scouts spread out in front of them. Nothing was getting past them.

"How is the situation in Meokar?" Blaze asked.

"They're pulling everything out. Most of the Institute is gone," Niemm said.

"Are they just going to let us take Meokar?"

"They put in some nasty surprises. The actual compound of the Institute is a maze of traps. Better to blow it apart than step in it. They plan to destroy the totem as well. It'll take a week or two to repair. Mister Yi got information from higher."

"What about the people inside the city?"

"They're scared. Most have fled, but a few haven't been able to."

Blaze turned to Domonos.

"We told the guild members they're not to attack one civilian in Meokar," Domonos said.

"They transported out a lot of items, but they've got plenty of siege weaponry and soldiers. If they were to retreat, they and their clans would lose all standing. There's no retreat for them." Niemm shifted in his saddle.

"An enemy without any way out is a dangerous foe," Blaze said.

Domonos merely nodded.

"I thought they would try to hold on to Meokar more," Niemm said.

"Meokar is a small pawn for them. They have trouble across the realms, bad enough to make the head came out of seclusion and pull the elders together. If he didn't, they would be fighting us tooth and nail for Meokar."

"To survive, you have to be willing to cut off the limb to save the body," Niemm said.

"Exactly. This serves our purpose too."

Niemm shifted in his seat. "How?"

"In the last loss in the Fourth Realm, the Institute had few survivors. While it is surprising, it makes things distant. The people from Meokar? There are people from the Third Realm to the Fifth Realm. They all saw the Institute get defeated. Their stories will spread," Blaze said.

"It isn't enough to break them."

"No, it isn't, but you have to apply Ten Realms sect logic to the situation. Strength is everything. Alliances can shift and change, inside sects and outside. The sects in the Ten Realms control the land. They are always looking to expand and strengthen their people. One of the fastest ways is through war. They train their people, weed out those weaker, and get the spoils," Domonos said.

"Taking repeated losses can undermine the faith of others," Niemm said in a moment of realization.

"Correct."

"Well, this is why you're a guild leader and colonel, and I am a glorified sergeant." Niemm chuckled.

"You and your people cling to low ranks, but your people could command an entire battalion," Domonos said.

"We like it down here more. Small-unit tactics, a few people tilting the balance. Better in small groups instead of organizing all the moving pieces,"

There was a noise off to the east, and a mounted force charged forward.

"Stay steady—report!" Domonos called out through his sound transmission device.

"Captain Fontes here. Looks like the sects are charging ahead."

"Tighten up our lines. Be prepared for anything," Domonos said.

"What do you think it is?" Niemm asked.

"Sects being sects. The Grey Peak sect is a big exception. The other sects, now there is less danger, want to show off their power and get the best rewards. Looting is the primary purpose of wars and an incentive to get people to participate. They had a lot of people showing up when I arrived. With that, it's time I headed back. I hate this rear echelon shit. Send me a message if you need me."

Blaze held up a hand in goodbye and moved away with his people.

"So, what's the plan?"

"We go slow and steady. We have nothing to prove."

Rugrat looked out at Vuzgal, his thoughts in a haze.

"Something on your mind?" Erik was wearing light clothes as he sat down opposite Rugrat.

"I'm thinking about retiring."

"Well, I'm not sure about the state of our pension plans anymore. Don't think you can redeem them here."

"No, I mean as the city lord, dungeon lord—all that."

Erik sat there, waiting for him to speak as he organized his thoughts.

"Sitting there at the arena, watching the fighter's competition—I didn't care for the fights. The fake smiles, the mixing and talking to everyone. I wanted to be down in the Third Realm. I'm a damn grunt; I'm no lord. We created the council and picked out the leaders to lead all of this. I'm saying we let them do their jobs, and we do what we're best at."

"You've been thinking on this a while," Erik said.

Rugrat leaned forward in his chair. "We have a responsibility to the people who follow us. We used to be the only sources of information from Earth. We've recorded nearly everything we know. We have Tanya, Matt, Kanoa, and all the people he brought with him. We led the people in crafting, highest level Journeyman crafters. There are hundreds of Expert crafters in Alva, and we weren't even the first ones. Glosil has excelled at leading the military. We're figureheads right now." Rugrat slapped his leg.

"So, what are you saying? We should get away from this all?"

"No, nothing like that. I just mean, Erik, what we're best at is fighting. We've been doing it all our lives. As Major Kimber once said, 'Every job needs the right tool, and, son, you sure as hell look like a tool to me!'"

Erik chuckled, and Rugrat grinned.

"Fuck, all right! You've got me. Though how are we going to be useful?"

"That ain't my job. That's Elan and Glosil's problem." Rugrat sat back in his chair with a smile.

"You're totally pushing it all onto them?"

"Yup!"

"Basically, just turn into advanced scouts. Leave all the managing crap to the people who need it. We show up from time to time but fade into the background. Get to do what we want to do." Erik paused. "You know that they're going to put guards on us, right?"

"Probably. It's like having the president as a sergeant in the army."

"This is nothing like it! You as a president? Hell, man."

"I bet I could win it in my shorts."

"Your poster campaign would be the thing of nightmares."

"Or some ladies' beautiful dreams!"

Erik shook his head, sighing. "All right, just like with Glosil, we need to trust the people who are in place. If we are always over their shoulder, we will never be able to leave, and they won't be able to do anything without our approval. Shit, I'm looking forward to getting out there. Feels like we're only scratching the surface in all this. What is the Ten Realms? Why the hell did we get sent here? All of that!"

Quest: Purpose

There are many secrets and half-truths about the Ten Realms. Why does it exist? What is it for? Separate the myths and legends from lies and truth.

Requirements:

Reach the Eighth Realm

Join the Ten Realms Mission Hall

Become at least a one-star level hero.

"You asked, and the Ten Realms delivered," Erik said dryly.

"Fuck, more ascending!" Rugrat threw his hands up.

"It's not like we were just going to stop at the Sixth Realm."

45 Meokar

"How is everyone settling in?" Domonos said as Zukal, his second in command, entered the command tent. A map dominated one wall, nailed to a piece of wood that was staked into the magic-packed ground. Communication aides were setting up their positions. It was dark, warm, and dimly lit, unlike the opulent pavilion tents the sects had created.

"Got them learning the basics of large-camp hygiene. Had a few go to the bathroom in the wrong place. They should have the tents up soon. Cafeteria is getting pulled together, have something warm for them soon." Zukal moved to stand next to him.

"A few of the sects tried to charge the walls, thought that they were still fleeing. The Institute let them get in close and wiped out nearly four hundred before they fled. Did find out something useful, though. Magical traps underground. Can't see them before we activate them."

Domonos looked at the pentagon-shaped city.

A guard opened the flap and moved toward Domonos.

"Sir, there is messenger looking for you from the Grey Peak sect. Says that Commander Gudriksson sent him."

"Okay." Domonos headed out of the tent. "Get Niemm and his people. I'll brief them before we start."

Konal Gudriksson looked up from the massive table map. The twenty-meter-wide command center was bathed in a warm, yellow glow by light formations. Stone pillars reached out of the ground to support the building. A table of refreshments lay against one wall, and the various sect leaders stood around it talking to one another. Their engraved armor was untarnished and highly polished, and each wore a fine-looking sword at their side.

Already congratulating one another on the impending victory.

Gudriksson sneered, looking away from the pompous fools, surveying the markers that denotated the different camps.

An aide walked up to Gudriksson, pitching his voice low. "The guild's commander is here."

Gudriksson glanced at the entrance. A young man entered, wearing padded armor and greaves, only his sword and boots glanced over to be more than the cheapest item he could find.

The sect leaders glanced over with a sneer and continued to mutter among themselves.

The man's cold eyes passed over them and locked on Gudriksson. He walked over, unwavering and uncaring about anything else.

Gudriksson inwardly nodded in approval as the man approached.

"Commander?" Gudriksson asked as he approached.

"Daniel Stuart. You requested my presence, Commander Gudriksson?"

"As the largest contributor to breaking the siege, I wanted to get your opinion on some things." Gudriksson invited Commander Stuart to study the map with him.

Stuart's eyes flicked across vital points, tilting and half-turning his head to Gudriksson.

Gudriksson didn't miss the other sect commanders moving closer, having heard his previous words.

"Right now, we have nine thousand mounted fighters and seventeen thousand fighters on foot, all ranging from levels twenty-four to thirty-five. Our plan is for those on foot to push up and rush the defenses, breaking open the walls, and allowing our mounted forces to flood in."

"Did you bring any ranged siege weapons?" Daniel asked.

"We can bring some up. Now that we have them on the back foot, we can rush them before they establish their defense," Gudriksson said.

"If we wait, we will lose the initiative, like some forces did in the chase," a bald sect commander muttered, looking down his nose at Daniel.

Gudriksson cleared his throat. "You were asking about siege weapons?"

"Yes. The Willful Institute has dominated this area for decades. With that sort of time, they will have added more defenses, not less. They might have an empty city, but Meokar has hidden fangs. We need to clear those magical traps; otherwise, we will lose our foot soldiers."

"Their force is cut off. There is nowhere for them to retreat to. They are ours! We can starve them out!" A sect leader with a green sash raised his glass of wine.

"A coward's path!" another said, tugging on his thick handlebar mustache.

"The city is empty. There are no mouths to feed except the defenders, so they'll have plenty of food and water for months," Daniel said.

"By then, the Institute could recover and attack our own cities," Gudriksson said.

"So, attack!" the bald sect commander demanded. "The Adventurer's Guild has shown their ability to charge the enemy. They should take the vanguard position of honor!" The bald man's smug smile was filled with viciousness.

Other sect commanders made noises of agreement, like wolves watching their wounded prey.

The guild's contributions are too high, so they are targeting him.

"Very well," Daniel said. "We will attack in four days."

"Four days!" The handlebar-mustached sect leader's voice rose in anger.

"Are the Adventurer's Guild such cowards?" The bald man shook his head, apparently saddened by the turn of events.

"We have a job to do, and we will complete it." Daniel's eyes rose from the table with cold indifference.

Gudriksson felt as if a blade were pressed against his neck. He backed up slightly from the commander's aura.

Daniel's eyes slid to Gudriksson as he bowed his head. "The Adventurer's Guild would be pleased to lead the attack on nightfall of the fourth day."

"I will place my siege weaponry under your command. Please use it as you see fit. Once you have a plan, visit me again. I know your people must need you."

"Thank you, Commander Gudriksson." Daniel dipped his head lower and headed out of the command center.

Gudriksson turned to face the sect commanders.

"Mister Gudriksson, we are all from sects here. We cannot lose the momentum! We must not stall!" The bald man clicked his tongue, staring at the back of Commander Stuart as he walked away.

"And your Green Swan sect contributed so heavily in the defense of Reynir?" Gudriksson's voice came out in a growl. "Interesting how a few hundred scraps can turn into some thousand with one battle."

The sect commanders hid their snarls behind their drinks.

Niemm was waiting for Domonos when he returned.

"Had enough of the fine food and drink?"

"I could hardly get away." Domonos grinned.

Zukal stood from this field chair, joining them.

"We secure?"

"Yeah, no one is gonna hear what we say."

"Good. Preparations for the siege weaponry?"

"Trebuchets are being built and mana cannons checked."

"Have sound-cancelling formations on them, so they don't keep our people awake. For the next three days, I want to bombard the hell out of that barrier. Keep the Institute members awake and tired. Also, use the trebuchets to create paths through to the wall. Tear up the ground and destroy the magical traps. On the night of the third day, our mounted forces will rush the walls. We'll only use trebuchets to cover them until the last bit to the wall. They'll have mana barriers for cover. They're to breach the wall in as many places as possible. The mounted forces will charge into the city. No decisive engagements; just set fire to everything they can and avoid the center of the city. Rush out to the flanks and breakout of the city."

Domonos traced a line from where the guild was camped at the wall. Two lines split along the wall, while a third larger force entered the city and split into groups spreading to the right and left flank, hitting the left and right walls before exiting.

It looked like one Y stacked upon another.

"That will hurt them," Zukal said.

"Why do I feel that I'm not going to be part of the mounted force?" Niemm asked.

"Do you have a dungeon core?"

Niemm's face turned into a slow smile. "Yeah."

"Standard kit among special team leaders: one Lesser Mortal dungeon core," Zukal said, recalling from somewhere.

"Spells would get tracked if used under the city, though dungeon cores won't because they are part of the Ten Realms."

"Unless you use a special formation," Niemm corrected.

"A formation I doubt Meokar has. Niemm, your special team will decapitate the Meokar's leadership."

"Head off unseen, use the dungeon core to create a tunnel under Meokar, and kill the elders. Easy enough."

"Thankfully, Roska was able to get you a rather detailed map of the inside of the treasury and the inner compound. The treasury shouldn't have too many guards around it now."

"Damn, were you planning that far ahead?" Niemm asked.

"Things just came together." Domonos shrugged.

"If we offer them terms of surrender, it could weaken their resolve. They have nowhere to run. Some of them have clans and others with the Institute, but the low-level soldiers might just be sect students without backing," Zukal suggested.

"Do it," Domonos said.

"Do you think the other sects will honor it?" Niemm asked

"Well, Blaze is here." Domonos's lips cracked, showing teeth underneath. "And all the Ten Realms should feel scared if a council member gets angry."

It was two days after the fighter's competition had come to a close.

Commander Glosil, Director Elan, Lieutenant Colonel Yui, and Kanoa were in Alva's command center.

"Colonel Domonos has reached Meokar. He's been bombarding the city for two days. Tomorrow night, he will carry out his decapitation mission.

"Blaze and Jasper have been contacted by other groups that are attacking or making plans to attack Willful Institute locations.

"The manufacturing facilities of the military will operate at one hundred percent to create weapons, armor, and equipment to support the Adventurer's Guild. We will support from the shadows while Domonos will assist in leading. Yui, Kanoa—I require members from your close protection detail to assist the Adventurer's Guild and continue to support their chain of command."

"Yes sir!" Kanoa and Yui replied as one.

"That leaves our three targets." Glosil looked at Elan. "The Willful Institute spreads across the realms. There are three key locations they hold that few other sects would willingly attack. Two are located in the Fifth Realm, and one is in the Sixth Realm. The two in the Fifth Realm are Ashbourne and Saenora. Ashbourne is a training facility for warriors looking to pass the entrance examinations and enter the academies. Saenora is also a training facility, but for crafters. Both locations are heavily defended. With the ongoing attacks, this is only going to increase. These locations have trained members who have been picked by sects in the Seventh Realm."

"You said there was a third?" Kanoa asked.

"Henghou city, the seat of power of the Willful Institute. Well, to be more accurate, the dungeon outpost they control. It is a cornerstone of their entire sect. The resources they gather from that location are massive. Just in fees alone that they collect from adventurers using their outpost, they can support themselves and the training facilities in the Fifth Realm. While it is a target for us, it is secondary. Although things seem more civilized in the higher realms, they are much colder. As the Willful Institute's power declines, the powers that be in the Sixth Realm might be interested in taking the Willful Institute's outpost from them. There is also the opportunity for us to use it as a bargaining chip with other powers."

Glosil opened his mouth to speak. A massive wave of mana shot through the room like a wave, shaking it.

"What the hell was that?" Yui asked.

"Full readiness! Split up!" Glosil barked.

They ran out of the conference room. Elan was escorted away by his guards. Yui and Kanoa used the tunnels to head to different command centers.

"The work just finished on the Water floor formation. Mana went down instead of up!"

"What?"

"The power surge was too much. We're leaking mana!"

"Keep it contained! Focus all the mana inside Alva. I want every mana-gathering formation operating at one hundred percent. Check the area. See how many people noticed it!"

46 Change in Plans

Grand Elder Mendes stood at the window of the council chamber. The light from the cannons and ripples of the trebuchets stone payloads striking the city's mana barrier lit up his face.

"Grand Elder?" Elder Rei said from the entrance of the darkened room. The lights from the attacks brought any change in the room.

"Do you think I was wrong?" Mendes asked.

"Grand Elder, I-I don't know what you mean!" Elder Rei said stubbornly, holding onto something that allowed him to fight Mendes's words.

Mendes looked from the window, the deadly light illuminating his tired face.

"Rei."

Elder Rei breathed out slowly. It seemed to sap his energy, leaving an old, reminiscent man.

"If we were to give into the demands that everyone placed upon us, the Institute would surely collapse. Everything is a balance—with the other sects, with even a guild. Somewhere, the scales tipped out of our favor. Was it with the killing of the Adventurer's Guild members? Was it when we sent bandits to attack trading convoys of competing sects and sold their goods as our own?" He shrugged limply.

"What's done is done. What of our fighters?"

"They're rejects who didn't ascend to the Fourth Realm or they don't have the connections to get out of here. They were supposed to attain glory and position with the attack on Reynir. Their friends were killed at Reynir, and they were chased all the way here. They've been left behind. The enemy constantly asks for them to surrender, telling them they'll be treated well."

"At the same time, they attack day and night with trebuchet and mana cannons, making it nearly impossible to sleep unless you have sound-cancelling formations."

"They're using siege weaponry they recovered from us at Reynir and are moving the weaponry they had on their walls."

"Sorry I forgot those, Grand Elder."

Mendes chuckled to himself and turned back to the mana barrier and the attacks landing on it.

"Get some rest, Elder Rei. Our sources say that they'll attack tomorrow night."

"Yes, Grand Elder."

Mendes stood in silence. Blooms of light flashes burned into his eyes.

"So, is there a reason we're getting geared up without the other sects knowing?" Zukal asked as Domonos buttoned the top of his vest while walking down a camp road toward the forward observation towers facing Meokar.

Guild members were between their tents, checking their weapons and gear, nursing hot tea that the cafeteria had prepared for them.

"I don't trust them. That's why. I also told them that we would be attacking tomorrow."

Zukal snorted as they reached the wooden tower, climbing the stairs to the top.

Domonos looked at Meokar's mana barrier. "Looks good. The mana cannons moved to the flanks yesterday, so they should be used to it. The flashes will make the barrier hard to see through. And it gives us a clear corridor to advance our people through."

"The first two groups are ready to go," Zukal said.

"Send them up," Domonos said. "Make sure the trebuchets shift their fire."

"Yes, sir."

Domonos glanced over to the left of the tower. Behind a dirt berm hidden from everyone, a group of mounted guild members waited.

The group leader tore a spell scroll. An illusion fell over them, making them blur with the background.

They curled around the berm. Domonos used Mana Sight to track them as they headed across the dead ground, a sword aimed at Meokar.

Domonos glanced over to the right side of the tower, just able to make out signs of the group as they disappeared into the night.

A new group moved into position. Behind them, guild members got their mounts out from the stables.

"I was a little confused with the design at first. Why would the camp be a rectangle and have the short side facing the enemy? The entire camp is designed to move the guild members forward into the stables, ready their mounts, mount up, and head toward Meokar," Zukal said.

"Pre-planning. Try to get everything ready ahead of time, so it's harder to get fucked up. I hate this part."

"What part?"

"Waiting to see if all the pre-planning will work."

Gudriksson was studying the numerous plans the sect commanders had submitted to him. For all their talk, they were more than happy to wait out the attacks.

"Sir! Commander! The guild is attacking!" A guard ran into the command center.

"What?" Gudriksson dropped the plans, stroking his storage ring, ready to draw his weapon.

"They told the siege weapons to stop firing. Sent people to make sure they weren't attacking."

Gudriksson heard a sound *very* different from siege weapons hitting a mana barrier. He ran out of the command center. A hole had appeared in the Meokar wall.

Another explosion went off as another section of wall cracked and collapsed inward.

"Message from Commander Stuart," a man wearing the Adventurer's Guild emblem yelled, holding out a scroll.

The man seemed relaxed and at ease. Dew had formed on his armor.

Gudriksson took the scroll. "How long have you been waiting there?"

"Last three hours, sir. Was told to give you the scroll when the wall collapsed."

Gudriksson read the scroll that outlined Commander Stuart's plan.

"Prepare our people to attack right away. Mobilize everyone. Send my orders to the other sects."

The wall exploded in more locations. The Institute was waking up; siege weapons attacked where the breaches were, hitting mana barriers that dissipated the illusion spells that had covered the Adventurer's Guild's mounted forces.

"Spread it out, and remember, if you get lost, just follow the rest of your guild members!" Bai Ping yelled as he led his squad through a breach.

He rolled with his mount as they jumped down the hill of broken stone.

Beasts and guild members lay here and there, but the Institute's guards littered the ground. They'd been caught unaware until the last minute.

Bai Ping pushed down the road. He checked on his squad. They were all around him, with other squads mingling in.

"We're heading to the left!" Bai Ping yelled.

Bai Ping grabbed the Fire wand he'd tied to his saddle.

Arrows rained down from a rooftop, catching several mounted guild members.

Bai Ping activated the wand. The red formations along the metal bar activated the red gem at its point. It projected flame into the thatched building.

Archers screamed as the burning thatch collapsed on them.

"Healers!" Bai yelled out.

They rushed out from where they were hiding behind another building to help the wounded.

"Come on!" Bai's mount moved forward, leading the group, moving to catch up with the forward elements.

"One, two, three, four," Bai counted the roads to his left side.

"This is our road! Start lighting it up, buildings farthest away from the road!"

Bai used his wand, leaving a trail of flame across the buildings, adding to the fire spreading across Meokar.

"Were they lying to us, or are they just idiots!" Elder Dean grabbed at his hair.

The council chambers had changed completely from a few hours ago. Most of the elders and their aides were there, and messengers were running to and fro. Light illusions banished the darkness.

Flames danced outside the windows as fire spread through the city, assisted by the attackers.

Dull thumps told of more sections of wall being torn apart.

"It looks like the Adventurer's Guild is taking part in the attack," Elder Tsi said, sitting down, fatigued from the healing she'd undergone over the last few days.

"We need to stem the tide," Elder Rei said.

"Do we try and hold the outer wall or pull back to the inner wall?" Elder Dean asked.

All eyes turned to Mendes.

"If we pull back from the wall now, we will have lost all momentum. The fires are a distraction. We don't have to worry about them. Let the city burn. Reinforce the walls at once! We can trap the Adventurer's Guild here and take a chunk out of their flesh! Send out the mounted fighters; they'll meet the sects as they try to gain entry! We'll use the Area of Effect spells. If we can get the sects bunched together, it will be a perfect target," Mendes said.

Hope filled the other elders' eyes.

"Send the messages!" Mendes yelled at the aides, who had fallen quiet.

The room returned to movement, determined and driven once again.

Mendes heard a wet noise, and something dropped.

He stared at the entrance to the council chamber. A masked man threw a formation plate that tore mana out of the surrounding area.

Mendes opened his mouth as the doors to the room shut. The elders' and aides' eyes went wide as they stared at the formation plate.

Niemm drank from his canteen, wiping his mouth with the back of his hand.

Yawen, Deni, and Setsuko were holding bows at the ready.

"Let's go." Niemm pulled his mask down and used the dungeon core to destroy the supporting pillars it had created.

The ceiling fell, the pillars shrinking underneath it like an elevator.

Yawen and Setsuko jumped into the room, their bows scanning the area.

Light peeked into the underground tunnel.

"Clear!" Their voices came through sound transmission devices attached to the masks.

Niemm jumped up with Deni right behind.

The treasury was cleaned out; doors were open, and the shelves of the warehouse-like building were bare.

"Let's go." Niemm had his bow ready as they advanced down the shelves. They got to a side door. Niemm checked outside. Seeing no one, he pushed out.

There were no attacks on the mana barrier, and a red glow was rising from the outer city.

Attack is underway. Just need to do our part.

They creeped toward their target, slipping between shadows.

The treasury was in the inner compound, close to Meokar's headquarters.

"Target spotted." Niemm hid in the shadows. He prowled forward to get a better view of the entrance. There were people coming, talking to riders who rushed off on the side away from Niemm's approach. The whole building sat on a raised stone square with short half-walls between short half-staircases that led down. Where the riders and messengers were, the stairs fanned out.

Niemm traced a path to the building's nearest wall, jumping from planter to abandoned cart and stack of crates.

"Cover me," Niemm said.

Setsuko moved to a better spot and stood up.

"Got you covered."

"Moving." Niemm ran for the stack of crates.

"In position." He looked around the crates, ready to stand and draw.

"Moving!" Niemm ran for the cart. While slumped down, a wheel had broken.

"Moving," Yawen said, running for the crates.

"In position." Niemm watched for movement.

"In position," Yawen said.

"Moving." Niemm ran for the planter when he saw a man walk up to the short wall atop the stone platform, not three meters from the planter.

The man had spotted him. Niemm drew his arrow back, but he was too slow.

Setsuko's arrow took the man in the neck.

"Moving!" Niemm kept running. Using the planter as a half-step, he jumped over the half wall and onto the raised stone square around the headquarters.

Niemm scanned, but there was no one else.

Yawen was next over the wall with Setsuko and Deni afterward.

Deni grabbed the body and tossed it over the wall.

They moved toward the headquarters. Yawen reached the door first, and they stacked up on it. Yawen opened the door.

Niemm entered a kitchen with four people sitting at the long table that took up the middle of the room.

Niemm released his arrow as he cast Breathless.

The spell ripped away the air around the four men. One collapsed with an arrow in his neck. The others made to shout, grabbing their necks with the lack of oxygen, the temporary vacuum stealing their air and voice.

Setsuko came in behind him, killing a second.

Deni came in, releasing as one of the men dove for a door leading inside. Her arrow pierced his body, nailing him to the ground. The Silence spell on the arrow stopped him from making a sound. Setsuko reloaded faster than Niemm, killing the fourth man.

Yawen moved into the kitchen. Four new tombstones filled the room as Niemm released his spell.

"Setsuko, cover the main door. Yawen, cover the door to outside. Deni, help me find if they have maps."

A few minutes of searching later, Niemm had stored the bodies and used the dead men's maps to update his own.

"Deni, I think we'll head to this second stairwell and take it up to the same floor as the council chambers. If we take these corridors, that should get us to the offices next door. We hit the council chambers, toss in an exploding formation, then we take the same route back out, through the treasury."

Deni followed him, tracing through the map plans.

"Got it."

"Let's move. Deni, you're on point. Setsuko, second. I'm third. Yawen, you take the rear."

They got to the stairs. The headquarters was a massive building with multiple stairwells, offices, even kitchens and dining rooms.

The team reached the top of the stairs and moved into the administration corridors.

Deni crept down the corridor toward the offices that led to the council chambers.

"All of the council is here."

"What's left of it, you mean."

"Hey! Yo—" The guard's words cut off. Deni's arrow pierced through his armor. She moved to the side, clearing Setsuko's line of sight as she hit the second guard.

Niemm had his bow up as Setsuko moved to the side. He advanced past them, Yawen trailing.

He reached the two dead, storing them away.

"Good to go?" He looked around, pushing next to the office door they needed to go through.

"Good!" Setsuko and Deni replied.

Niemm opened the door, and Yawen flowed inside.

He heard the twang of bow strings being released, feeling mana gathering.

Niemm prepared his spell as Setsuko, the last person, went through the doorway. Someone screamed as Niemm cast Chains of Silence.

There were four people in the room. Two were captured with the chains; another was dead; the last had an arrow in his side, not long for the world.

Niemm shot one of the guards wrapped in the Chains of Silence. Yawen got the second.

"Go for it! Now!" Niemm stored his bow and drew his sword.

The door opened. Deni released her arrow, and the guard slumped and dropped to the side. Setsuko moved around Deni and toward the door. She released another arrow.

"Formation!" Setsuko yelled.

Niemm stored his sword and pulled out the formation. He ran out of the office. To his left, there was a big open doorway; golden light shone through it.

Yawen and Deni ran out. Niemm turned the formation, activating the mana blast formation.

Inside the office, there were people sitting around maps. He tossed out the formation. Yawen and Deni pushed on the doors, slamming them closed.

"Let's make like trees and fuck off!" Niemm yelled, turning and running toward Setsuko, she pushed out of the office door and covered them.

He ducked through the doorway as the formation went off. The doors were blown apart, windows shattered around the headquarters, and sections of walls collapsed.

Niemm and his team backtracked to the kitchen and sprinted to the short wall. They made it across the street in a blur. They drew melee weapons. People were yelling around the headquarters, with others rushing in from other locations.

They reached the treasury and jumped back into the hole they'd arrived through. Niemm took out his dungeon core. The pillars grew again and pushed into the opening above. Deni opened her storage ring, dumping out dirt.

They worked quickly, covering their tracks. Niemm compressed the dirt into supports and then returned them to dirt after the special team had passed.

"Can I do the honors?" Yawen asked as they paused, holding out a formation clacker.

"Do it."

She pulled on the clacker, and they felt a rumble in the distance.

"And then the city cornerstone was no more."

Gudriksson and his forces had made entry into Meokar. The fighting had been sporadic, but the Institute was pulling their people back together.

"Tell the other sects to keep up! Otherwise the Institute's fighters will get between us!"

There was an explosion from the headquarters building in the middle of Meokar.

"The hell was that?" No one had answers.

"Get me Commander Stuart!"

"Your leadership is dead. Your elders will not rescue you. You will die here without the Willful Institute ever caring about your great sacrifices. Surrender now so you might live tomorrow instead of with a sword in your gut today!" A woman's voice played through Meokar, repeating her message.

"Our people have secured the eastern command tower!" an aide reported.

"Good. Have the Rekichi clan's fighters move to support them and push into the city. I want to control the eastern wall!"

"I have Commander Stuart!" An aide handed Gudriksson a sound transmission device.

"What the hell is going on?" Gudriksson yelled.

"I'm winning the battle, Commander."

"Did you really take out their elders?"

"Yes."

Mana fluctuated through the area. Gudriksson felt as if his compressed body had been released, his Strength returning to him.

"And my people just took out the city's cornerstone. I would suggest holding back your people at the eastern command tower. They could lose the support of your western side. I have heard there's a group of Willful Institute mounted that are ambushing ground fighters around there."

Gudriksson choked on his words. He handed the sound transmission device to the aide numbly.

"Have the Rekichi clan hold their position, get the Thordsson clan's riders to reinforce them, and make sure that they don't get separated from the western flank."

Just who the hell is the real commander here?

Gudriksson stared at the headquarters that was now burning with the rest of the city.

47 Slight Problem

Egbert put his book away as he checked the formation for the Water floor. "All right. Well, that looks correct."

He waved his hand. A mana blade appeared, and he finished the last inscriptions off.

The different rings of the formation lit up. Water mana drifted toward the formation.

In the distance, secondary formations lit up with power. Light appeared on the ceiling, illuminating the ground below and revealing the rolling seas and islands of the Water floor.

Lines of mana power traced through the ice-covered mountain Egbert stood on, entering the outer rings of the massive master formation.

The dungeon core that rested above purified mana as it entered through the mana-gathering formation and powered the formation, altering the floor and linking it with the other floors and with the main dungeon core.

The mountain rumbled. Ice broke off in places, dropping into the cold sea below.

"Crap!" Egbert ran backward and then started to fly away from the center of the formation.

A pillar of mana shot up. The blue light from the Water-attribute mana colored the entire floor as it pierced through the heavens. Doorways opened ahead of it as it charged upward.

Egbert viewed the other floors. The Water mana reached the Wood floor. Blue and green mixed together as the Water mana was being utilized by the Wood formation. Plants opened their leaves, growing faster than before. The green-and-blue pillar disappeared, hitting the Fire floor. The dominating Fire mana had to bow to the Water and Wood as the pillar passed through, reaching the Metal floor. Black, red, green, and blue pierced upward; the Earth floor bloomed anew with the energies passing through. A kaleidoscope of colors filled the pillar, each time refined by the secondary dungeon cores at each level.

Then it hit the dungeon core on the living floor. The power was too much for the dungeon core to handle, and mana leaked all over the place. Formations activated, draining the different elemental mana out, pushing it to the crafting workshops and utilizing the training dungeon cores to purify the mana.

The ceiling glowed as the mana stones grew at a rate visible to the eye.

"Wait a second!" Egbert felt something was wrong. The formations on each floor turned and started to rotate, taking a new position.

Quest Complete: Restoring Beast Mountains Dungeon Part 1

Congratulations! You have taken control of the Beast Mountains Dungeon. Its condition isn't the best, and it will require work to repair. I hope you brought a hammer! Or crafters.

Requirements:

Repair the main Mana Gathering formation

Repair the secondary Mana Gathering formations (10/10)

Repair the Metal beast-controlling formations (3/3)
Repair the containment formation
Repair containment formation sub-arrays (0/12)
Repair the Metal floor's main control formation
Repair the Metal floor's secondary control formations (12/12)

Rewards:

Up to 200 ore per day
+100 Mana per day
+1,200,000 EXP

"What the hell is happening?"

The power seemed to reverse, and a beam of pure mana shot down through the different floors.

Quest Complete: Restoring Beast Mountains Dungeon Part 2

Congratulations! You have taken control of the Beast Mountains Dungeon. Its condition isn't the best, and it will require work to repair. I hope you brought a hammer! Or crafters.

Requirements:

Repair the main Mana Gathering formation
Repair the secondary Mana Gathering formations (10/10)
Repair the Earth beast-controlling formations (3/3)
Repair the containment formation
Repair containment formation sub-arrays (0/12)
Repair the Earth floor's main control formation
Repair the Earth floor's secondary control formations (12/12)

Rewards:

+1,200,000 EXP

Quest Complete: Restoring Beast Mountains Dungeon Part 3

Congratulations! You have taken control of the Beast Mountains Dungeon. Its condition isn't the best, and it will require work to repair. I hope you brought a hammer! Or crafters.

Requirements:

Repair the main Mana Gathering formation

Repair the secondary Mana Gathering formations (10/10)

Repair the Fire beast-controlling formations (3/3)

Repair the containment formation

Repair containment formation sub-arrays (0/12)

Repair the Fire floor's main control formation

Repair the Fire floor's secondary control formations (12/12)

Rewards:

+1,200,000 EXP

Quest Complete: Restoring Beast Mountains Dungeon Part 4

Congratulations! You have taken control of the Beast Mountains Dungeon. Its condition isn't the best, and it will require work to repair. I hope you brought a hammer! Or crafters.

Requirements:

Repair the main Mana Gathering formation

Repair the secondary Mana Gathering formations (10/10)

Repair the Wood beast-controlling formations (3/3)

Repair the containment formation

Repair containment formation sub-arrays (0/12)

Repair the Wood floor's main control formation

Repair the Wood floor's secondary control formations (12/12)

Rewards:

+1,200,000 EXP

Quest Complete: Restoring Beast Mountains Dungeon Part 5

Congratulations! You have taken control of the Beast Mountains Dungeon. Its condition isn't the best and it will require work to repair. I hope you brought a hammer! Or crafters.

Requirements:

Repair the main Mana Gathering formation

Repair the secondary Mana Gathering formations (10/10)

Repair the Water Beast controlling formations (3/3)

Repair the containment formation

Repair containment formation sub-arrays (0/12)

Repair the Water Floor's Main Control formation

Repair Water Floor's Secondary control formations (16/16)

Rewards:

+1,200,000 EXP

It descended like a god's hammer, passing through the center of the elemental pillars. While much smaller, but it's mana density was much higher.

Egbert watched it descend through the Water floor's main formation.

Quest Complete: Restoring Beast Mountains Dungeon Part 6

Congratulations! You have taken control of the Beast Mountains Dungeon. Its condition isn't the best, and it will require work to repair. I hope you brought a hammer! Or crafters.

Requirements:

Repair and Control the Metal floor

Repair and Control the Earth floor

Repair and Control the Fire floor

Repair and Control the Wood floor

Repair and Control the Water floor

Repair and Control the Living floor

Rewards:

+1,200,000 EXP

Quest Completed: Dungeon Master

Your Masters have returned your dungeon to its former glory. Advancement quests are unlocked. Grow your dungeon's power!

Requirements:

Increase your dungeon core's grade to Sky Grand

Rewards

60,000,000 EXP

Dungeon Master Title V

Nothing happened for a few seconds. Then the entire floor shook violently; ice cracked, and the seas shuddered.

"What?" Egbert yelled.

Quest: Upgrade the First Realm

Well, it looks like you took the hammer route! For the greatness of the Ten Realms, you are forging ahead! With your contributions, we will all become stronger!

Requirements:

Continue drilling into the depths of the First Realm.

Rewards:

Ten Realms Dukedom

Receive a Four-Star Hero Emblem; must be collected from the Tenth Imperium's Quartermaster

+400,000,000 EXP

"WHAT!"

"Egbert, what the hell is going on? I just got a quest!" Delilah yelled in her office.

Egbert was always looking for people calling him, so he picked up on it immediately.

"Shit."

Quest: Dungeon Master

Your Masters have returned your dungeon to its former glory. Advancement quests are unlocked. Grow your dungeon's power!

Requirements:

Increase your dungeon core's grade to Celestial Common Grade

Rewards

100,000,000 EXP

Dungeon Master Title VI

"No, no—it can't be true." Mistress Mercy stared at the name on the page. A shiver ran through her.

She read it out once again. "Domonos Silaz from the First Realm. Recruited by Elder Hui in Chonglu city at the Annual Beast Mountain trial. Reached the Third Realm. Found to be stealing from other Willful Institute students."

Mercy remembered the young man she had whipped after her competition with the Stone Spear sect. She had taken out all her anger on that young man. His face was always bruised or cut.

"It couldn't be."

She glared at the information.

"Could it?"

She placed the page on the table. Unknown and unseen, one of the three answering statues within Vuzgal's underground that recorded everything that touched any Vuzgal surface, with a priority on anything around the Willful Institute representatives, activated.

48 Across Realms, Across Worlds

"You miss him, don't you?" Fred sat down next to Racquel.

"I do," Racquel said. "Though I want to explore as well." Her vertical slit eyes reflected the turquoise sea.

Fred took a deep breath, watching the boats that entered the port city below.

The waters boiled over as a beast as large as a whale charged a ship getting close to the shore.

A formation activated. Wind cut through the ferocious beast, and its blood stained the water.

The ship passed without sparing a second glance.

Comparing it against the whale-sized beast, the ship was the size of twenty whales from tail-to-mouth long and five wide.

It wasn't a ship but a mobile city.

"Well, you have to pick one." Fred's hand turned into tree limbs, scratching the back of his head.

"There are so many wonders in the Eighth Realm. Even demi-humans from the Fourth Realm seem boring."

A part of the port city rose, glowing with runes. It floated up, and Wind mages activated their grand magic. The entire floating city picked up speed.

Smaller air ships weaved across the sky, landing at the port city or heading off to other locations.

"I wonder if we had seen all of this before we were locked inside the dungeon if we would have been able to last for so long." Fred waved his hand,s and it retracted into a human hand.

"I wonder how the Alvans, how Erik and Rugrat, have been."

"Do you think that Rugrat could win in a fight?"

"You have spent too much time inside the arenas. You're getting quite the reputation for yourself. Does it matter if he can win against you in a fight?"

Racquel's eyes moved side to side.

"You're looking for an excuse to go and see him. We owe them a great debt. While there are many grand things in the higher realms, one needs to warn them about the truth. About the empire, about how the Ten Realms was created, and about the dungeon lords." Fred's expression turned serious.

Ships as large as towers crossed the waters, and the skies and continued on their journeys.

Even this forest is a small park here.

Fred contemplated the city that spread in every direction. The distant mountains that had been taken over by the smiths. The rolling fields and layered growing houses that the alchemists worked in. The grand towers that reached into the sky, surrounded by flying devices as formation masters claimed this technological marvel.

A pyramid of three cities stacked upon one another created its own mountain.

Associations had sub-cities within the sprawling metropolis that covered the land, weaving between the mountains. Sects claimed entire ranges as their own. Islands created by the inhabitants dotted the sea, harvesting beasts or resources deep under the sea.

Fred's eyes fell on the simple towers that dotted the land. The buildings were ancient, standing for countless centuries. Around them, the land had been cleared away, with lines of people waiting to enter.

"I never imagined it like this," Racquel said.

"There are still many mysteries in the Ten Realms."

"Momma Rodriguez, did you hear about the fighter's competition?" A large man covered in scars and with large, bulging muscles said as he entered a simple restaurant.

"You just walked into my restaurant, and you are already yelling!" a woman's voice came from the kitchen in the back of the restaurant.

"Sorry, Momma Rodriguez!" The large man cowered slightly, as if he were about to get hit.

"Good that you are learning some manners. Haven't you had more girls talk to you now you don't have those piercings?"

The man's face turned red as his companions stared at him with raised eyebrows.

"I came with some guests!" he pleaded.

The door opened, and people might think that a dragon would walk out from the kitchen by the way the man reacted.

A smaller lady walked out with a wooden spoon.

"Ledell, why are you so scared?" one of the people in the group asked in a low voice.

Ledell stood taller, as if defending the woman he had been scared of just moments before. "Momma Rodriguez is a fierce lady. Don't cross her." He stared into all their eyes, and they were more confused than before.

"I hope you are all hungry! I have been working on tacos, though I'm not sure if you'll be able to handle my hot sauce!" She gave them a kind smile and patted Ledell's arm. She didn't even reach his shoulders, but, somehow, she was even more intimidating.

There was a sadness in her eyes that disappeared as soon as it had appeared.

"Come on, grab a seat. Lusia, five iced teas!" Momma Rodriguez headed into the back of the restaurant.

"Why didn't you join in on the Vuzgal fighter's competition?" one of Ledell's friends asked him.

"Join in? I think I would just be asking to be humiliated. They were the elites from the Fighter's Association and our Adventurer's Guild. I don't have even half the power of the branch heads and their enforcers."

"Did you get to see the mysterious lords?"

"I saw them through screens. They wore masks and cloaks, so it was hard to see what they looked like."

"I wonder what they're like," a lady in a blue robe said as Lusia served them iced tea.

"Five tacos, side of hot sauce," Ledell asked.

"Coming right up."

"I can take it," a woman wearing a purple shirt said.

"I'm sure you can. Just test it out first," Ledell said.

"No one sees them since they defended Vuzgal and the associations. There are rumors that say they are fighters and crafters. That they are stronger than anyone of their level." A man in a green shirt leaned forward, excited to share his gossip.

"What do you know?" Ledell snorted.

"I know that there are two leaders of the Vuzgal military, that one of the forces marched off somewhere and have not been heard of since. At the same time, people who are trained up by the Dragon Regiment disappeared through the totem."

"What are you saying?" Ledell frowned.

More people entered the restaurant and quickly took a seat. Lusia served them.

"Wow!" The woman wearing the blue dress looked at her iced tea in surprise, making those glance over. She gazed at her iced tea as if it were the nectar of life.

"Right?" Ledell grinned.

The others drank from their drinks, showing surprised and pleased expressions.

"Lusia, another round!" Ledell said.

"Coming right up!" she yelled back. More people were coming in for the evening rush. It was a modest restaurant, but there was always a line that ran down the street when dinner time came around.

"I'm saying that the whole of Vuzgal is mysterious. Half the army is who knows where, crafters popping out of nowhere, sworn to Vuzgal. People say they are a force from the association, that the whole attack was staged to showcase their power!"

"They wiped out three sects completely and auctioned off their cities." The lady in blue shivered.

"Vuzgal is interesting." Ledell thought of the strange buildings, of the crafters, and even the basic facilities. "I don't know of another place like it in the Fourth Realm."

The tacos arrived shortly. Everyone tried to pull the soft tacos together, but with their inexperience, they left food all over their plates. They didn't care for their appearances, and they kept eating.

"I thought there were a few places in the Fourth Realm that sold actual food. Doesn't Vuzgal have places that sell food?"

"Bah, the Sky Reaching Restaurants might sound impressive, but they are nothing compared to Momma Rodriguez's food!" Ledell said.

"You said their deep-fried chicken was to die for," the lady in purple said.

Ledell waved his arms, holding her mouth shut.

"Fried chicken?" A voice came from the door into the kitchen. Momma Rodriguez stood there, staring at the table.

"I spoke wrong—" Ledell started.

Momma Rodriguez walked over, but she didn't seem to hear him. She stood at the edge of the table. "They had fried chicken, deep-fried cornflake chicken?"

"Y-yes, though it was not as good as your homemade dishes!" Ledell looked as if he wanted to cry or hide in the folds of his seat.

"What is this Sky Reaching Restaurant?" Her eyes fell on the man in green.

"It showed up in the Third Realm first. They say they are associated with the city lords."

"These city lords. What are they like?" Momma Rodriguez asked.

"They don't show themselves. People say that they are crafters and fighters."

"What do they look like?"

"They wear masks, and they haven't been seen in public much. One is tall; the other is shorter. They both have a lot of muscle."

"What are their names?" Momma Rodriguez looked as though she wanted to climb over the table and shake the man in green. He was starting to sweat.

"They, uh, the first one, Erik? Uhh his last name was," He tapped his head.

"West? I think and the other was Rugrat?"

Everyone's faces turned pale as they felt Momma Rodriguez's aura run out of control and begin fluctuating.

They cowered as Momma Rodriguez shook, tears running down her face.

"Is something wrong?" Ledell asked, unafraid.

"This place. Where is it?"

"Vuzgal, the independent city?"

"Have you been there before?" she asked.

"I have."

"Take me there." Momma Rodriguez took off her apron and tossed it into her storage ring.

"Now? Why are we going to Vuzgal? You can't beat up the cooks for their fried chicken!" Ledell said, following her.

"I'm going to find my boys!" she yelled, marching out the door.

"Lusia, watch the shop!"

Author's Note

Thank you for your support and taking the time to read **The Sixth Realm, Part Two**.

The Ten Realms will continue in **The Seventh Realm**

As a self-published author I live for reviews! If you've enjoyed The Sixth Realm, please leave a **review**! (https://readerlinks.com/l/1445052)

Do you want to join a community of fans that love talking about Michael's books?

We've created this Facebook group for you to discuss the books, hear from Michael, participate in contests and enjoy the worlds that Michael has created. You can join using the QR code below.

Thank you for your continued support. You can check out my other books, what I'm working on, and upcoming releases with the QR code below.

Don't forget to leave a review if you enjoyed the book.

Thanks again for reading ☺